# Someone Has to Pay
## A Mike Devon Novel

# SOMEONE HAS TO PAY

Copyright © Joe McCoubrey 2012
ISBN: 97809579696501
Publisher: Inishfree Communications

# About the Author

Joe McCoubrey is a former journalist who reported first-hand the height of the Northern Ireland "Troubles" throughout the 1970's and 1980's, firstly as a local newspaper editor, and then as a partner in an agency supplying copy to national newspapers and broadcasters. He switched careers to help start a Local Enterprise Agency, providing advice and support to budding entrepreneurs in his native town, and became its full-time CEO. He retired to concentrate on his long-time ambition to be a full-time writer. His previous novels have all been published to critical acclaim.

He lives in Downpatrick, County Down, and is proud of its historic connections to Saint Patrick, Ireland's Patron Saint.

Also available by Joe McCoubrey:
**Quinn2 – No place to hide**
**Quinn – Thirst for Justice**
**Spent Force**
**Exposure to Truth**
**No Margin for Error**
**Absence of Rules**
**Absence of Mercy**
**Death by Licence**

## Dedication & Thanks

To the girls in my life – Teresa, Brenda, Lynda, and Lisa.

To the men in my life – my grandsons Alfie, Rory, Ellis, and Michael.

To the friends in my life, including my editing team of Brad Fleming, Martin Graham and Mick Keane.

To the readers in my life – thank you for your encouragement and support.

# Chapter 1
## Chicago – 1985

THE MAN STANDING IN the shadows of dilapidated buildings in an abandoned downtown warehouse estate in Chicago was not supposed to be there.

Fergal McSweeney didn't make a habit of sticking his nose into other people's business, but he had a bad feeling about what was about to go down. Something about the impending trade just didn't sit right with him.

McSweeney was following an innate sixth sense for trouble. He had learned to trust the instinct, knowing things usually never worked out as planned. That was why he was here, three hours before the appointed time, for what should be a straightforward handover. His side wanted the guns; the other side wanted the money.

If only things were that simple, he thought.

He spent the time checking the ground and buildings around the handover location. There was nothing, save for the odd scurrying sounds of a rat and the grating of flapping tin against the sides of the buildings.

He decided it was time to check out Warehouse 32, or what was left of it after the thieves and cowboy builders stripped it of any worthwhile fittings. The electrics were ripped out, along with plumbing, copper, and anything with resale value. Glass sky-lights had disappeared, together with the large up-and-over doors that gave the building the gap-toothed look of an old hag. Here and there, large chunks of corrugated sheeting had been removed from its skin.

McSweeney moved noiselessly across the pitted tarmac that separated the numerous buildings. It was the stride of a confident yet careful individual, his eyes constantly shifting in a one-eighty-sweep as he approached the target warehouse.

He picked his way through one of the many holes in the side of the sorry-looking structure and examined the interior. It was a vast open space, bathed in macabre colours by strips of moonlight pouring through its vents. Debris littered the floor and large steel girders stood silent sentry every twenty yards down the spine of the building.

He chose a girder in a heavily-shadowed section overlooking the entrance where he knew the trade would take place. Satisfied he couldn't be seen behind the pillar he dipped into a shoulder holster and withdrew a Sig Sauer P226 with a noise suppressor. He racked the pistol's slide mechanism to chamber a round, thumbed off the safety catch, and held the weapon in a loose grip by his side.

He leaned against the stanchion and settled in for a patient wait.

Fergal McSweeney was born to Irish Catholic parents at the height of the "troubles" in Northern Ireland and was on a mission that belied his boyish good looks. Shoulder-length fair hair framed a face etched in lines despite the tender twenty-two years of its owner. High cheekbones and a small, almost feminine, nose were strikingly handsome features most people mistook for Eastern European origins, but they were wrong.

At the age of fourteen, he had been noted as a

recruit of real promise, a cool, calculating individual who had seemed to radiate an aura of calmness, even among seasoned volunteers. Not for him the usual jobs of punishment shootings, target-spotting, or the disposal of weapons. McSweeney had been judged much more valuable by his handlers.

He was someone who could be groomed as one of only a select few, men who could handle the demands of being an all-round killing machine. They had to fly under the radar, with no arrests for minor offences, and no prison time at the notorious H-blocks compound at the Maze outside Lisburn, a thriving town less than ten miles from Belfast.

When McSweeney had left Northern Ireland just short of his fifteenth birthday, it was as if he had never existed. He underwent a gruelling three-year programme in various terrorist camps around the world, including an elongated stay in Libya after which a new identity had been constructed for him. His birth name had disappeared from records and he had become a born and bred Glaswegian, on the payroll of an IRA-fronted luxury car dealership specialising in the import and export of vehicles between Britain and the USA. For two years he had been based in Boston, followed by this latest stint in Chicago.


Ignoring the cold and cramp, McSweeney remained immobile behind the girder for twenty minutes until the sounds of approaching vehicles signalled the start of the trade.

Two vehicles - one an old high-sided Chevrolet all-purpose van, the other a white Transit half-tonner - drove almost simultaneously through the opening at the front of the warehouse and braked to a stop less than ten feet apart.

McSweeney watched as two men emerged from the Chevrolet, gripping Kalashnikov machine rifles. He noted the confident swagger as they pointed the weapons to the ground in a non-threatening gesture and motioned to the occupants of the Transit to join them in the gap between the two vehicles.

The Transit driver's door creaked open barely six inches and a hand appeared. It was holding a Magnum 44 revolver, held in a steady aim towards the man standing on the right.

McSweeney knew whom the gun belonged to. The voice that cut the silence merely confirmed the presence of Pat O'Driscoll. "Keep those weapons facing the way they are. We don't want any trouble. We've brought the money. Let's see what we're buying."

The two who had alighted from the Chevrolet were standing with their backs to McSweeney, but he could see the casual shrug of shoulders from one of them as he responded. "Sure thing, we also don't want trouble. Let us see the money then you can examine our merchandise."

The passenger door of the Transit opened, and a man stepped out holding a briefcase above his head. He was followed by another man, cradling a Steyr M1912 machine pistol across his left arm.

The driver's door was pushed fully open and McSweeney watched O'Driscoll step down and move to the front of the vehicle, where he was joined by his two friends.

"Okay, let's get this over with." As O'Driscoll spoke, he nodded at the man with the briefcase. After fumbling with the latches, the man opened the lid and displayed the contents. The men with the Kalashnikovs stepped forward to examine the briefcase, but in a blur of movement, brought their rifles up under the chins of O'Driscoll and the other armed man.

The gunman, who was standing to O'Driscoll's right, spoke in almost apologetic tones. "Throw down your weapons please. We don't want to kill you, but we will if we have to."

The guns clattered on the concrete floor and the assailants took two paces backwards, their rifles trained on the hapless group in front of them. One of them spoke again. "Put the briefcase on the ground and push it across to us with your foot."

McSweeney waited until everyone's attention was focussed on the sliding briefcase before he stepped silently out of the shadows and shot the nearest Kalashnikov-wielding intruder through the back of the head.

Without stopping to look at the fine mist spray of blood and bone fragments as the body crumpled to the floor, McSweeney continued to walk forward, watching the other gunman swing round to face him.

McSweeney got there a fraction of a second before the man completed his manoeuvre. He pushed the still-smoking suppressor tight against the man's forehead and told him: "We can do this the easy way or the real easy way. The easy way is that you drop your weapon and you get to live a little longer. The real easy way is that I give you exactly what your friend got. You've got one second to decide."

McSweeney watched the Arab's eyes widen in fear. The jaw hung open and the body seemed to stiffen as he ran through his options. In the end,

McSweeney knew he would take the sensible way out.

The man's gun clattered to the ground and his arms shot upwards, almost as if they had been yanked by an invisible puppet-master. "Please, please this was only meant to be a leetle joke. Keep the guns and the money. I think we make a big mistake, eh?"

"Oh, you certainly did, boyo," yelled O'Driscoll, as he picked up his Magnum and aimed it directly into the face of the frightened captive.

"Put that down and step away," McSweeney commanded in a tone that did not invite discussion. "I'll take it from here. You lot, load up the stuff and be on your way."

O'Driscoll was not one for backing down. He turned to McSweeney, his eyes full of challenge. "Listen Fergal, we're glad you popped in when you did, but we could have handled these assholes. You've had your fun. I reckon it's down to me and the lads to finish this off."

McSweeney imperceptibly shifted his weight to the balls of his feet, pirouetted through ninety degrees, and brought his left forearm down hard across O'Driscoll's face. The crunch of bone was unmistakeable as the nose collapsed under the force of the blow.

O'Driscoll stumbled backwards before his legs gave way and he crumpled to the floor. As he lay clutching his face with blood seeping through his fingers, he stared at his assailant in absolute shock.

"For fucksake! There was no call for that. We're in this together," he mumbled.

"You don't get it, even after all this time," McSweeney responded. "Well, I'll remind you again, and for the last time. When you're given an order, you obey it. This isn't a debating society. I've a job to do that's separate from your lot and right now I want to get on with it. So, mount up and get the fuck out of here. Take this shipment to the rendezvous point and continue as planned."

Then McSweeney turned to the other two members of the team. "What are you waiting for? Move it before I change my mind and put a bullet through the lot of you. I'll see you for a debrief at the meeting in the morning. Make sure you're there and ready to listen to orders."

With a quick flurry of activity, the men gathered up the briefcase containing one hundred thousand dollars meant for the purchase of the weapons, and loaded it, along with three boxes of Kalashnikovs, into the back of their van. O'Driscoll muttered something like an apology towards McSweeney and climbed into the vehicle. With a screech of tyres, the van left, and the warehouse was plunged into a ghostly silence.

While all this was going on, the remaining gunman was rooted to the spot, his arms still held high above his head.

McSweeney pushed him across to a corner of the warehouse. "Now my old son, I'm going to ask you a few questions and you're going to answer them truthfully."

It was part of the job McSweeney didn't relish. He needed answers and there was only one surefire way of getting them. He didn't like inflicting unnecessary pain on people, but if that's what it took to get the job done, then that's what it took. He hoped it would be over quickly, but in the end it took almost two hours to extract the information.

The man admitted being part of an Arab group that had been brokering dubious arms deals for more than two years from a base in Chicago. He offered up names and addresses, but only after enduring knife slashes across his arms and chest, and the loss of one of his kneecaps to a high velocity round delivered in the classic punishment style of the Irish Republican Army.

Satisfied he had gotten all that he could, McSweeney ended the man's misery with two shots through the forehead.

McSweeney reported in to his superiors, and over the course of the next few days, he sent another five Arab residents of Chicago to make their peace with Allah.

# Chapter 2
## Chicago – the following day

MIKE DEVON HAD A lot on his mind as he pulled into a parking spot beneath a small block of flats at Forty-First and Cicero.

Standing an inch short of six feet, Devon showed all the signs of a man who paid regular visits to his local gym. Biceps bulged out from a white cotton t-shirt and he walked with the easy grace of an athlete. He had jet-black, shoulder-length hair, a face recently tanned by exposure to more sun than he was used to back home, and a slightly squashed nose, a legacy of his amateur boxing days.

Devon was on his first major overseas assignment for MI6, Britain's Secret Intelligence Service. It was run on the same lines as its American cousin's better-known Central Intelligence Agency – both dealt with external or overseas work, leaving internal Intelligence matters to their other lead agencies, MI5, and the FBI, respectively.

Because Devon worked for Britain's external agency on American soil, he had to deal directly with his host's internal agency. Right now, MI6 and the FBI had a common brief to watch the activities of IRA sympathisers within American borders.

The apartment Devon was visiting was a welcome escape from the building site and rundown bedsit that were the usual bases for his undercover routine. The fact there was a rather pretty brunette waiting for him was one more reason to be glad of the change in surroundings.

He had met Pauline Brown shortly after taking up this assignment. She was a shop salesgirl, originally from London, and working with MI6. Her cover provided MI6 with the chance to keep tabs on her boss, an Irish emigrant who owned a fashionable shoe store in a mall at La Grange. He had known links with the IRA and was suspected of organising many of the large-scale arms shipments from America to Ireland. Her job was to watch for associates and note any suspicious activities especially near the shop's rear storage depot.

Devon joined the small Chicago-based team about six months after Brown. Their first meeting was one of those intangible things, where a spark jumped from one to the other, and they became ardent lovers. The station boss, an experienced operative called Peter Fitzsimons, tried to steer them away from the dangers of an office romance, but gave up when he realised they were hopelessly entangled.

As he took the elevator to her second floor apartment, Devon was still feeling uneasy. A few weeks earlier, the station had picked up on a snippet of Intelligence about Arabs doing a deal for a consignment of Kalashnikov AK-47 assault rifles, of the folding-stock 7.62mm variety, that were appearing all too frequently on the streets of Belfast. When Devon tried to push his workmates for information, he met a wall of silence.

As the days wore on, Devon became aware of a mood-shift among the squad of Irish brickies and labourers he had infiltrated at various building sites across Chicago.

He had been hired under a watertight cover and was made to feel welcome among the ex-pat community, socialising most weekends with them in

Irish bars and dancehalls. He accepted there were times when several of their number excluded him from bogus fishing trips or other made-up absences. Undercover work was about patience and building up trust.

During the past week however, the general mood had changed. Sometimes he felt that conversations dried up when he walked into a room or passed by some of the members of the group at work. At other times he thought some of them were watching him too closely, their eyes shifting away furtively when he glanced in their direction.

One of the group leaders, a big loud-mouthed ex-Cork man named Pat O'Driscoll, had taken to questioning him more and more about his background. At first it seemed innocuous but became more intense as O'Driscoll probed about Devon's opinion of what was going on back in Ireland.

The third degree had cranked up Devon's unease.

He got out of the elevator and moved across to a door second in line down a narrow corridor. He pressed the doorbell and saw a shadow fall across the built-in eyepiece. He heard the rattle of a key in the lock and the door opened to reveal Pauline Brown, dressed in a bathrobe with hair pinned under a pink towel, and a smile to light up a city. She jumped into his arms, pressed her lips firmly onto his, and ran her fingers through his hair.

He moved quickly into the room, raising his heel to slam the door shut behind him. "We need to talk," he told her in a voice that carried coldness and dread.

He took ten minutes to apprise her of his suspicions. He could see the rising fear in her eyes and tried to backtrack a little.

"Look, it may be nothing, but we have to be sure."

She stared at him with those hazel-brown eyes that he had come to love. "Mike, I know you. If you're saying something's not right, then we've got to accept it isn't. Have you been followed at any time?"

"No, at least I'm positive there's been no tail. Maybe I'm getting too jumpy?"

She took him by the hand and drew him towards the only two seats in the apartment living room. "If you didn't spot a tail then there wasn't one, but that doesn't mean they don't have other ways of tracking you. We have to be sure."

"I agree," he acknowledged, "that's why I need to get some answers. We might have to put the squeeze on one of the building site workers, but it will be risky. I'll need to fix up a meeting with the boss at the usual place next Saturday and see if he's up for arranging a snatch."

Her eyes widened in shock. "If any of their men go missing, they'll know we're onto them."

"I know, but I don't see any other way. If they've made me, then my time is up anyway. I just don't see many alternatives."

He watched as she processed the information. She had a cute way of pinching her lips when she got serious and he could tell she was getting ready to deliver another one of her "be-careful" messages. He decided to get in ahead of her. "There's a chance they may know of our association. I need you to take a few days off work until we figure this out."

She stiffened on the seat, her nostrils flaring in anger. "Don't dare try to protect me! If this is getting as bad as you think it is, then we need to pull the plug for everybody. You must tell the boss enough is enough."

Devon moved closer to squeeze her hand. He had gone too far and needed to defuse the situation. "I promise you I'll lay it all out for him at our meeting on Saturday. Why don't we both take a few days off until then?"

"That's the first sensible thing you've said since you arrived. How about a trip to New York?"

He smiled at her. "I wasn't thinking about shopping."

"What were you thinking about?"

He rose from the seat, kicked off his shoes, and headed for the bedroom door. Halfway across the room he glanced over his shoulder. "Aren't you coming?"


Fergal McSweeney had little time to rest after dealing with the last of the Arab gang. He had to admit the response to the treachery at the arms handover had been a bit over the top, but a message needed to go out that you fucked with the IRA at your peril.

It would make future transactions go a bit smoother.

For the previous two months, McSweeney had been working on direct orders to locate an MI6 operation against the movement in the Chicago area. His mission was to identify a suspected mole and shut down the entire Brit operation. Over a painstaking period, he put the parts of the jigsaw together.

The finger of suspicion pointed to a relatively new member of one of the construction crews.

Introduced to the Chicago cell as Bernie McEvoy, this man had worked his way in under a story of being on the run after finishing a short stretch in the Maze prison for his part in the bombing of an RUC station in Belfast.

The man's claims were bolstered by confirmation from one of the existing cell members, Rory Lynch, who had introduced McEvoy as a former friend from the Markets area of Belfast where they once courted two sisters.

It soon became obvious to McSweeney that Lynch had been got to, to provide the neat cover.

McSweeney resisted the temptation to take Lynch into the countryside for a long chat. He knew that to do so would alert McEvoy, and there was too much he still needed to learn. Two teams from outside Chicago were given separate assignments, one to monitor Lynch and one to monitor McEvoy.

At the same time, a request was sent back to Belfast to check on all Lynch's relatives to try to discover what hold MI6 had on him. Were any of his kin in prison in either Northern Ireland or England? Were any of them throwing money around? What was in their bank accounts? Did they go on too many holidays? Everything had to be checked, and the IRA had men in place to do the checking. Bank officials, solicitors, lawyers, and even senior RUC officers were all on the payroll.

The noose tightened around Lynch.

Nothing came back from Belfast. There appeared to be no skeletons in the collective Lynch wardrobes. The break came from London, courtesy of the British Government's own anti-terror legislation, which gave MI5 the right to lift anyone with an Irish background and hold them for questioning without charge for up to fourteen days. One such victim of the regular police swoops was a middle-order member of Sinn Fein, a resurgent political party known to be the public voice of the IRA.

Ever keen to recruit Republicans as informers, MI5 offered all sorts of inducements to their quarry. However, in the case of Timothy Morgan, an over-zealous officer let it slip that among the many men who had changed sides rather than face a lengthy spell in prison, was one such man now living the easy life in America.

"We concocted a sheaf of charges against him," the MI5 man gloatingly told Morgan," "And he knew we could make it stick. He was offered twenty years solitary confinement at the 'pleasure' of Her Majesty, or he could choose freedom. It was an easy choice. All he had to do was tip us the wink if he heard anything we should know about. Now he's running around Chicago as free as a bird and nobody's any the wiser. Now why don't you consider a similar offer?"

After two weeks of telling the MI5 man to go fuck himself, and enduring nightly beatings with a rubber hose, Morgan was released without charge. He immediately contacted local IRA leaders in an Irish pub in the Kilburn area of London and passed on the details of what he had been told. A message was taken to Chicago and arrived during the third week of surveillance on Rory Lynch.

At least now McSweeney knew what carrot-and-stick approach had been used to turn Lynch into a renegade. Lynch would keep for another time. All efforts were immediately switched to tailing Bernie McEvoy.

McSweeney took personal charge of the surveillance and recognised from an early stage that his adversary was good, damn good. He watched the way the man kept checking things happening around him, usually with just casual pretences of reading a paper, or adjusting the cap on his head. He looked the sort who took few chances, someone capable of spotting a tail from a mile away.

So McSweeney pulled his men off any direct surveillance. Working on the age-old principles of covert shadowing, he knew the best way of getting the job done was to be in place when the target arrived at his destination rather than have to tail him all the way there and risk exposure.

They knew where McEvoy lived, where he drank, where he shopped, and where he went for his other social pleasures, including the home of a petite brunette salesgirl, whom he had taken up with some five months previously.

These were the starting points. McSweeney ordered listening devices to be hidden in McEvoy's apartment and tapped the public telephone in the lounge bar of O'Casey's Traditional Irish Pub where McEvoy spent most of his evenings and was recognised as a regular, one of their own.

The IRA unit set him up with a job on a building site on the fringe of Chicago's Chinese quarter. Once again, the nearest public telephone was bugged, and one of McEvoy's co-workers, Seamus Flynn, was told to monitor all his movements.

McSweeney personally briefed Flynn, an out-and-out Republican with an impressive kill record back in Ireland.

"Don't let your emotions get in the way," McSweeney warned. "This man is dirty, and he'll get what's coming, but right now we need to learn a lot more about his contacts. If you balls this up in any way, I'll have you."

He knew Flynn would do as he was told. The man was old school. He would continue to smile and talk to McEvoy and go for a drink with him, even if underneath he wanted to put a bullet through his brain. Flynn begged McSweeney to let him be the one to pull the trigger when the time came.

"We'll see how things pan out," had been McSweeney's non-committal response.

Over the next few weeks, the team picked up snatches of phone calls and watched as McEvoy chatted to different people while he went about his daily life. Twice he received calls asking for a meeting, but the location was not given and McSweeney passed on the opportunity to tail the MI6 man.

The watchers' patience was rewarded when on a Friday night in O'Casey's, McEvoy used the phone and asked a man at the other end to meet him in a small burger joint opposite Flanagan's Gym on West Wacker Drive on Saturday afternoon.

With sixteen hours to go before the appointment, McSweeney swung into action. Two hours after listening to the phone tape, he was sitting in Al's Burger Palace at West Wacker, taking in the surroundings and drawing up a plan of action.

At 3pm the following day, McSweeney's people were in place. At table two a young couple sat holding hands and staring lovingly into each other's eyes, apparently oblivious to the rest of the world. At another table sat a workman in muddied dungarees with a large plate of double fries and a burger that lacked none of the wide variety of dressings for which Al's Palace was famous. At table six near the rear entrance, was a young mother resting from the stress of the Saturday afternoon shopping, and gently rocking a small pram pulled up tightly to the corner of her table.

These were all McSweeney's people. He had coached them for several hours on how to get inside their new personas; how to act naturally while observing what was going on around them.

Across the street, McSweeney took up vigil at a window above Flanagan's Gym. It hadn't been a problem getting in. Art Flanagan, the owner of the gym, even provided a flask of coffee and a plate of sandwiches for his vigil. Gazing directly down and into the front window of Al's Palace, McSweeney had a grandstand view, including a watch on the two cars he had placed at either end of West Wacker. Whoever turned up would be followed this time.

Ten minutes before McEvoy's appointed meeting time, a man, casually dressed in light blue jeans with a contrasting dark blue woollen sweater approached Al's Palace on foot from the corner of Third and West Wacker. What was striking about the man was his constant shifting of attention, first to the footpath behind him, and then across to the opposite footpath, and then to the cars, which constantly rolled by.

It was all done with a casual turn of the head, but it didn't fool McSweeney.

This was a pro, a trained operative who didn't take chances. Aged about fifty and standing at six-one, the frame looked hard and lean. No doubt about it, thought McSweeney, MI6 through and through.

It was expected that one of the operatives would arrive ahead of the appointed time to scope out the place. McSweeney's people had been warned this was a possibility, and they had to keep up their pretence from the moment they entered the burger joint until they set eyes on McEvoy, who would be recognisable from the photos passed around during the late-night briefing.

The first man entered Al's Palace, grabbed a seat near the window, and threw a friendly nod at the dungaree-clad worker at the next table. He ordered a coffee and told the waitress he was waiting for a friend.

Later that evening, a full report on what took place was relayed to McSweeney by Johnny McIntyre, now dressed in more familiar clothes of jeans, sneakers and a t-shirt. He had discarded his dungarees and fluffed his hair back up from the greased down look he wore earlier.

"When this geezer, Bernie McEvoy, walked through the door he made straight for the counter. He pretended to read from an overhead menu, but he didn't fool me. I watched him look in the mirror for his contact and then walk over to where the other geezer was sitting."

McSweeney urged McIntyre to hurry the report along. "Then what happened?"

"At first it was just meaningless chit-chat about work, their families, the weather, and the chances of the Bears winning the big match in the NFL Eastern division play-offs. Then McEvoy leaned closer to the other man and whispered something."

"Did you hear what was said?"

"I just caught snippets, but McEvoy seemed to be saying he was getting strange looks at the building site and thought he might be compromised. Yes, that's the word he used, compromised."

"Anything else?"

McIntyre paused for a moment before continuing. "The other guy said something about cutting their losses and getting out, but McEvoy was having none of it. Said he'd wait until after the weekend and would take someone called Pauline with him."

McSweeney turned his gaze from McIntyre to another man, who was present in the burger bar and who had been ordered to follow McEvoy's contact.

"How did your tail go?"

The second man reported following the contact back to a downtown apartment, two blocks from the Ritz Hotel. "He made it easy by hailing a taxi round the corner from Al's and rode it all the way to the apartment. I didn't hang around, but I don't think he was throwing a ruse at me. I think he definitely lives there," the watcher reported.

McSweeney milked as much detail as possible before dismissing the men with a thanks and an assurance their work would not go unnoticed. Already forming several plans, he wanted time alone to think things through and decide on his next move.

One thing was obvious to him; the girl named as Pauline must be whom they had previously assumed was McEvoy's girlfriend. That being so, she was not his girlfriend, but part of the MI6 operation.

So far that made three people to be dealt with, and in the process, McSweeney reckoned he would uncover yet more names. He decided the man referred to as Peter would be first on the list. He was McEvoy's back up and would react almost immediately if McEvoy failed to make contact, whereas McEvoy would be unaware that Peter was out of the picture.

Second to go would be McEvoy himself. They would interrogate him, but it was McSweeney's guess they would get little. That's why the girl would be last. With her two accomplices out of the way she would be terrified when confronted with the news of their deaths. That would give him leverage.

If she knew anything, he would get it from her. He hoped she would crack early. The thought of inflicting too much hurt on the girl was not one he relished. But the choice would be hers.

# Chapter 3
## Chicago

TWO DAYS LATER, Peter Fitzsimons left his apartment just after 8am to drive across town to his office in the FBI complex at 2111 West Roosevelt. Apart from acting as Mike Devon's handler, he was chief liaison officer between MI6 and the FBI. He spent most of his time in the office and usually got home around 4.30pm.

That afternoon he stepped from his taxi at precisely 4.40pm and climbed the stairs to his apartment. He unlocked the door and immediately reached to disarm the small intruder alarm he had fitted when he took out the lease more than a year previously.

Something nagged at him as he started to enter the four-digit code - the small green light in the console wasn't blinking! Before he could fully react, a voice came from within his sitting room.

"No need to bother with that, Peter. I've disarmed it for you."

He spun immediately to face the direction of the voice. Simultaneously his right hand reached inside his jacket for the shoulder holster.

"Don't make another move, not so much as a twitch."

Fitzsimons did what he was told and froze, his eyes focussed on the silver pistol and suppressor aimed directly at him. Behind the gun he could make out the shape of a man sitting casually in one of his threadbare armchairs.

"What's this about, who are you?" It was obvious Fitzsimons was trying to keep his voice at an even pitch.

The gunman ignored the questions. "Let's get rid of your weapon first. With your thumb and one finger, remove it from your holster and toss it on the floor beside me. I don't care if you're MI6; one furtive movement of your eyes, one attempt to do other than I've told you to do, and I'll send your Brit ass to hell."

Fitzsimons knew there was no wriggle room. The weapon he was staring into was held rock-steady in the two-fisted palm grip of a professional. He retrieved the automatic from the holster and tossed it on the floor.

"Now, here's what's going to happen." The unwelcome guest spoke as if planning a tea party. "We're going to have a chat about your friend Bernie McEvoy, or whatever his real name is, and you're going to tell me everything I want to know."

Fitzsimons cursed himself for allowing his eyebrows to rise at the shock of hearing McEvoy's name. He quickly tried to bluff his way forward. "First, you tell me who wants to know and then we'll discuss how you might continue to live when you leave this room."

The other man smiled. "My name doesn't matter and by now I know you've guessed I'm IRA. What you don't know is that I'm not here to play mind games. I'm here to kill you."

The next thing Fitzsimons knew was that his leg was on fire. He crumpled to the floor, clutching his knee as blood seeped through his fingers. It took him a moment to fight through the pain and for his brain to register that he'd just been shot.

He watched as the gunman rose from his seat and pointed the weapon at the centre of his head.

"I want the names of all those involved in this sick little operation."

Fitzsimons turned to face his attacker. "Go fuck yourself. You'll get nothing from me you IRA scum."

They were the last words he ever spoke. He barely had time to register the flash from the muzzle before his world was plunged into darkness.

Devon left his apartment to head for a usual Monday night of mindless banter at O'Casey's Traditional Irish Pub, hoping tonight would be different than the many that had gone before. He wanted desperately to pick up on something that would help bring his current assignment to an end and take him one step closer to a return to London.

But this is what he signed up for; this is what gave him the much-needed bursts of adrenaline he wouldn't get from behind a desk. The problem was that the nagging doubts at the back of his mind wouldn't go away. Was it his imagination? Maybe he was too long at the game and was getting paranoid?

Almost as soon as he walked into O'Casey's, he knew things were wrong.

For a start, there were a lot more people sitting about in small groups than was usual for an early Monday evening session. Among the regulars, he spotted several of his construction site buddies, who usually did their drinking at the other end of town. He also recognised the faces of Johnny and Raymond McIntyre, two brothers well-known to MI6 from their former exploits on the streets of Belfast, and who he had seen only occasionally during this current operation.

What clinched it for Devon was the stranger sitting at the end of the bar. One look into the man's cold, penetrating blue eyes, told Devon here was trouble, all wrapped up in a brown bomber jacket and blue jeans.

Devon fought an urge to turn and make a bolt for it.

He had no doubt he would make it through onto the street, but outside there was nowhere to run. O'Casey's was located midway on a largely deserted residential street, with lots of doorways behind which he knew there were plenty of sympathisers to the cause of Irish Republicanism.

Fronting it out, Devon walked straight to the bar and ordered his usual pint of Guinness. "Set her on the bar, Tom. I need to take a leak," he told the barman and continued on his way to the toilet block at the rear of the premises.

As he moved past the stranger, Devon gave the faintest of friendly nods, pushed open the creaking wood door, and disappeared inside. Immediately he checked for an escape route, but the fire door to the exterior was heavily bolted shut. He darted into one of the cubicles lined along both sides of the room and locked the door.

Then he clambered on the toilet seat, grabbed the top of the thin partition board, and hoisted himself into the next cubicle. Without pausing he darted across the room into one of the opposite cubicles, this time leaving the door open. He hopped onto the toilet seat and waited, his eyes taking in a rectangular window above his head.

The door leading to the bar area creaked open and he could hear the squelch of boots on the tiled floor. There were at least two, maybe three men in the passageway. Devon pulled a Glock 17 from a holster fitted to the belt of his trousers and sucked in a deep breath.

A figure stepped into view, his back to Devon. He was holding a revolver aimed at the locked door. The man appeared to glance sideways as if to accept instructions from whoever else was with him, before lifting a leg to ram against the flimsy door.

Devon waited until the door splintered open before he fired two rounds into the man's back, aiming for his heart. Then he rose to full height on the toilet seat and peered downwards into the passage where two other men were huddled, their faces still showing signs of shock from the gunfire.

Devon fired a single round directly into the top of the first man's head. As the body crumpled to the floor, the second man turned to run back towards the bar. He made it as far as the connecting door before Devon fired again.

Forcing his attention away from the passage, Devon glanced at the window above and began hammering the glass with the butt of his Glock. He knew he had been lucky to earn a few precious seconds, but he couldn't fight off a sustained attack in such a cramped space. He needed to get outside.

The glass gave way and fell in shards away from him. He continued to attack it to create enough of an opening to squeeze through. Thankfully, the blast of cold air told him the window led to the exterior of the building.

He hoisted himself up to the ledge and peered through the gap. There was a darkened alley leading to the lights of a street about a hundred yards to his left. The place was deserted.

He wormed through the opening and fell heavily onto a cobblestoned surface. His right shoulder took the brunt of the fall, but he ignored the shooting pain, regained his feet, and set off at a sprint towards the streetlights.

Fergal McSweeney had watched his target make his entrance to the bar. The fucker had looked calm as he ordered a drink and headed for the toilets. He even had the barefaced cheek to smile at McSweeney as he passed by!

As soon as the door to the toilets swung closed, McSweeney nodded almost imperceptively to the table where the McIntyres sat with Patrick Connolly, a regular of O'Casey's, and a man known to be a leader of the IRA's cell in the locality. All three got up and moved to the bathroom door.

After a brief pause, they pushed through, ready to deliver a beating to the Brit undercover agent before bundling him into a car parked at the rear of the premises and delivering him to his interrogation and death in one of their out-of-city safe houses.

McSweeney waited patiently for his men to let him know they were ready. Suddenly the quiet of the bar was broken by the unmistakeable staccato sound of gunfire: two rapid small arms rounds, followed closely by two more.

McSweeney leapt off his stool, gun in hand, and rolled across the floor towards the wall alongside the toilet entrance.

The door burst open and Raymond McIntyre fell forward against the bar, clutching at his stomach. Blood trickled through his fingers and he was gasping for breath.

"The fucker shot us, the fucker shot us," he repeated before falling to the ground where he lay moaning and staring wide-eyed at McSweeney.

There were no more sounds from inside the toilet block. McSweeney planted his foot against the door and smashed it off its hinges. As the door gave way, he leapt to his right against the opposite wall, but no further shots came.

Cautiously he peered around the corner and could make out the limp form of Patrick Connolly sitting almost serenely on the floor with his back propped against a cubicle door and looking curiously peaceful despite the gaping hole in the middle of his forehead.

Across from Connolly's body in the opposite cubicle, McSweeney could see a pair of legs jutting out from under the raised door. The black Doc Martin boots were unmistakeably those of Johnny McIntyre.

McSweeney turned towards the figures cowering behind tables in the bar and barked "Outside, quickly, and seal off the back alley. Two of you to each end of the street and wait for my instructions."

As the bar emptied, McSweeney moved at a crouch through the doorway, his Sig Sauer in a two-handed grip sweeping the area. He had already noticed the broken window above one of the cisterns, and the torn piece of material that had been ripped from the MI6 man's clothes as he scrambled through the opening.

Two questions raced through his mind. What had alerted the agent? How had his crew misread the situation so disastrously? These could wait. The priority now was to find the fucker and kill him.

As he turned to race back through the bar,

McSweeney heard more gunfire, this time from the street to the rear of the pub.

The Brit was still at large and killing his men.

Out on the street, McSweeney ran into one of the recruits who had chased around the building on McSweeney's orders. "Jeez, he's got Tommy and I thought I saw wee Geordie go down too!" he told him.

At this point, McSweeney wasn't too worried about the respective fates of two of the volunteers who had been drafted in at the last moment to lend a bit of muscle to the snatch operation on the British agent.

"Which way?" McSweeney screamed before taking off up the street towards the building pointed out by the frightened man.

It was a large tenement block, one building from the end of the street. The front door was lying open as McSweeney cautiously approached. Crouching in the shadows thrown from the six-storey buildings, McSweeney reached the railings around a basement shop directly in line with the open door opposite.

Chances were that the British agent had already bolted through the tenement block and out the other side, but McSweeney wasn't in the habit of rushing in where fools often treaded. This enemy deserved more respect than that.

Just as McSweeney made up his mind to skirt farther up the street and approach the tenement block from the rear, a soft voice, no more than a few feet away, almost made him jump out of his skin.

"Don't move, don't say a word. I'd rather shoot you right here and right now, but first I'll give you one chance to get us both a ticket out of here." The voice was whispered from somewhere on the darkened basement steps below the railing where McSweeney knelt.

The IRA enforcer knew, probably for the first time in his life, there was no way out. How had he been suckered so easily? No, he had to give credit to the Brit agent. Any other man would have kept running, taken his chances in holding off and evading his pursuers until he reached the comparative safety of the busy Chicago downtown area just a few blocks away.

It took nerve to play it any other way, and that was the one factor McSweeney hadn't counted on.

The voice spoke again. "Keep your gun exactly as it is. Don't turn around and listen carefully. Since you're obviously the big cheese around here, I want you to yell down the street to your men and tell them I've given you the slip. Tell them you know where I'm headed, and that you'll handle it from here on your own."

McSweeney laughed lightly. "They're not going to buy that. You're a dead man walking."

"Shut up! Either you make this convincing or I'll pop a 9mm into the back of your head and take my chances out in the street with that bunch of amateurs you rounded up to do a man's job."

McSweeney was raging inside, mainly because he knew the man was right. "Ok," he said back into the darkness. "I'm going to stand up and give the orders."

He raised himself and glanced back down the street. He could see at least four of his men making their way cautiously up the pavements on both sides of the streets. Lights had gone on in a few apartments, but nobody was about to venture out of doors to investigate the commotion. McSweeney knew that in this part of town people learned to mind their own business.

"Listen up," McSweeney yelled. "He's gone. I think he's making a run for his apartment and I'm going to head him off. I don't need any support. Go back and mop up at O'Casey's. Make sure there's nothing for the cops to investigate and I'll see you later."

McSweeney banked on the pursuers knowing better than to argue. He had shown them on previous occasions that he was more than capable of getting the job done. Right now, all they had to worry about was disposing of the bodies back at O'Casey's before the Chicago PD black-and-whites descended on the place.

He watched as they peeled off and retreated down the street towards the pub.

For more than a minute there was complete silence, interrupted again by the voice behind him. "I want you to move slowly towards the top of the steps keeping your pistol pointed to the ground."

As McSweeney started to move, he suddenly stopped and whispered: "Hold it, one of my men is coming back up the street. I'll get rid of him."

"Make sure you do."

McSweeney moved a few feet back out to the pavement and glanced to his right as if to speak to the approaching man. There was no one there, but McSweeney knew it was unlikely the agent hiding on the stairs below ground could see beyond a few yards to either side of his hideout.

He had to time this right otherwise the Brit would shoot him, borrow his bomber jacket, and casually walk away in the opposite direction from O'Casey's. That's what McSweeney would do in his shoes, and he knew this man was cut from the same cloth.

McSweeney raised his left hand as if to stop the approaching figure. At the same time as his arm reached beyond his head, he dropped to the ground in a roll and brought his Sig up to fire into the darkness beyond the railing. Two rounds spat from his pistol, and he heard a low groan before he felt the force of a high calibre round fired almost instantaneous to his own discharges.

Pain washed over him long before the realisation he had been shot. His gun-hand involuntarily flew to his left shoulder where the round entered. He could see blood already seeping through the sweater just above his right nipple.

Instinct took over. He rolled again to avoid more incoming rounds and was surprised to find he was on the pavement at the opposite side from the basement steps. He looked for the cover of a parked car, all the while keeping his Sig trained on the darkness across the street.

Just then the wail of a siren broke the spell. As he glanced down the street, McSweeney could see flashing lights from the top of a car now racing towards him. With a supreme effort, he rose to his feet and bounded up the four steps leading towards the open door of the tenement building.

The hunter had become the hunted.

He ran through the building and found the back door at the end of a long corridor. The original escape route he had considered for the British agent was now his own lifeline, and he wasted no time in pushing through the door and out into wasteland gardens beyond.

One hundred yards of ground lay between him

and the lights of buildings beyond, and he steered directly towards the first door he could see. It was another tenement block. Again, he went through and out the other side, onto a busier street than the one he had left behind.

Luck was with him.

A young man was sitting behind the wheel of an old Chevy convertible idling at the bottom of the steps. Probably someone waiting to pick up his date thought McSweeney, as he walked down the steps and approached the youngster. He leaned in through the passenger window, gave the youngster sight of his gun, and calmly ordered to be taken across town.

Thirty minutes later he was back at his apartment where he discarded his bloodied sweater and applied a first aid bandage. The bullet had gone straight through and he would get better medical attention later.

First, he had a few things to do.

He knew he had shot the British spy but didn't know if his rounds were fatal. The absence of more return fire encouraged him to believe he had finished the bastard off. Either way, he was grateful he had gotten out alive. The Brit was good, better than anybody he had come up against before. The way he had handled himself at O'Casey's, and later got the drop on McSweeney, told the IRA man he was lucky to be still breathing.

It was only his own coolness - not to mention a large slice of luck - that had enabled him to come out alive. In a strange way he hoped the Brit wasn't dead, and that he would get the chance of another encounter sometime in the future.

Two days later, McSweeney was out of Chicago and back in New York recovering from his wound.

Before he left, he paid a visit to the salesgirl called Pauline. She appeared to be packing when McSweeney picked the front door lock of her apartment and walked in on the terrified girl.

There was no time for interrogation. He didn't know whether an alarm had been raised among her superiors, and whether at any minute a Brit unit would come calling to protect one of their assets. Better to get it over with and get out. He shot her with his trademark double-tap between the eyes, ransacked the house, and left without knowing her true identity.

The fate of Rory Lynch was left in the hands of the Chicago IRA unit members. His death came after two days of torture in a barn on a remote ranch in the Illinois countryside. The body would never be found. The gunfight at O'Casey's didn't make front-page news, nor was there any mention of the deaths of Patrick Connolly and the McIntyre brothers. What was reported, was the motiveless killing of a construction site worker in a street close to O'Casey's, and the unrelated homicide of a young salesgirl, apparently robbed in her home by a person or persons unknown.

# Eight Years Later

# Chapter 4
## Dublin 1993

THE TAXI PULLED INTO the parking lane outside the landmark General Post Office building in Dublin's O'Connell Street and a man in a long dark overcoat alighted from the passenger compartment. Out of habit he glanced at the imposing edifice, his eyes picking out several bullet holes he knew had been allowed to remain in the plasterwork as a reminder of the failed Easter Rising in 1916, when a fifteen-hundred strong group calling itself the Irish Republican Brotherhood, stormed the building in a bid to end English dominion over Ireland.

Liam Nolan knew his history. After five days of mortar and cannon fire, the rebels surrendered with four hundred and fifty of their number dead, and another hundred facing summary execution in the following days. Four years later, Michael Collins led the IRA on a merciless and unrelenting campaign of terror against the occupying forces, and by 1921 the British had left Ireland, or at least twenty-six of its counties.

The remaining six counties of Northern Ireland still had to be reclaimed and that, Nolan reminded himself as he crossed the street, was why he was here.

He walked past Clerys department store, turned a corner into Lower Abbey Street, and entered Wynn's Hotel, famous as the venue for the meeting of volunteers who planned that Easter Rising almost eighty years ago.

He strolled into the foyer, past the small concierge desk, and pushed open the door into the downstairs bar. As he walked to the rear of the room, he cut a dashing figure to the small group of residents enjoying an afternoon tipple.

Standing at six foot three, he was heavily muscled and exuded an air of confident authority. He was told often that he reminded people of the actor Liam Neeson. He liked the comparison.

He sat down at a table with a clear view to the lounge door, a precaution that was second nature to him. He removed his overcoat, laid it on a stool beside the table, and patted the shoulder holster beneath his brown leather jacket. He nodded at the barman, who acknowledged his presence with a slight shake of the head and began fixing a drink without being told the order.

Several minutes later the barman approached the table carrying a tray with a pint of Guinness and a cut glass tumbler of Irish whiskey.

"Nice to see you again, Mr Nolan. Hope everything's fine for you."

"Sure, it's grand, Mickey. And what about yourself? The family doing well?"

"Yes sir, thank you for asking."

Nolan placed a fifty Irish Punt note on the tray. "I'm expecting company Mickey, get them three pints of Guinness and keep the change for yourself."

Nolan savoured the first biting taste of Bushmills Black Bush and washed it down with a long gulp of Guinness. Wiping the foam from his lips with the back of his hand, he watched three men enter the bar and make their way to his table.

There were only slight nods of greeting and recognition as they took their seats around the table and waited for the barman to bring their order. Few would have guessed that here were the four leading members of the twelve-strong Provisional IRA Army Council.

Under the title of Commandant, Nolan was the de facto supreme commander of the terror organisation. He glanced at his three lieutenants who were separately in charge of engineering (bomb-making,) logistics (personnel,) and fundraising (racketeering.). Nothing happened in Ireland, North or South, unless rubber-stamped by this quartet.

As usual, Nolan got straight to the point.

"I've had an interesting invitation to a meeting in The Green this afternoon, actually in about an hour's time." He was referring to the St. Stephen's Green city park at the top of Grafton Street.

"What's it about?" asked Patrick Pearse, a forty year-old Dubliner named after one of the 1916 Easter Rising rebels, but with no family connections.

Like all Irishman, Nolan knew Pearse's illustrious namesake survived the Post Office blitz but was executed two days after the surrender. He also knew this Patrick Pearse lived well out of the spotlight. When he wasn't sourcing the latest bomb-making technologies and materials, he liked nothing better than sailing his father's thirty-five foot yacht out of Howth harbour, a yacht that Nolan ensured was used on more than one occasion for other than pleasure sailing.

Nolan switched his gaze to the other two at the table. Francis Dooley, easily recognisable by a heavily pock-marked face, and Joe Coyle, a father of seven, who celebrated his sixtieth birthday three months ago on St. Patrick's Day, and looked more suited to the boardroom of a multi-national corporation than a backstreet pub. They drew their seats forward and waited with anticipation.

Nolan continued: "The Brits are looking for a little off-the-record chinwag through an intermediary who's based at their embassy in Ballsbridge. He's being passed off as a low level clerk, but he'll be Intelligence through and through. They're really stepping up the cold war stuff and it looks to me like they're gagging for peace."

"Aye, but what price do they expect?" asked Pearse.

"It really doesn't matter. We stick to our own agenda. We've got to strengthen our own position and when we get down to the real bargaining, we do so from a position of strength."

Nolan liked the easy camaraderie he shared with these men. He and Dooley grew up together in a twenty-storey flat complex in Ballymun, went to various inner city schools together, and shared prison time at the country's notorious Mountjoy Gaol on IRA membership charges.

At that time, still in their late teens, they were on the fringe of things, but inside the foreboding walls of Mountjoy they met Pearse, who fired their bellies with Republican ideals. On their release, Pearse introduced them to Joe Coyle, the Dublin recruiting officer for the organisation. Within two years they rose through the ranks.

Nolan knew Dooley had always looked to him for direction and was by his side constantly through training and early missions. The pair gained a reputation for ruthlessness and the degree of planning that went into their operations. Despite that, Nolan was surprised by a series of promotions that saw him, at the age of twenty-eight, join the

Army Council, the youngest man ever to be admitted into the upper echelons.

It was Nolan who was behind a series of spectacular successes for the IRA, including high profile bombings in several key English cities, but it was not until he became supreme Commandant, that his vision for forcing a United Ireland really took flight.

His philosophy was a simple one: taking the fight to the heart of the British government, including attacks on the British Army, targeting key political figures, and disrupting the machinery of government by destroying public buildings.

His crowning achievement was just over eighteen months previously with a mortar attack on Downing Street. Three rockets fired remotely from a parked van came within an ace of success, when one of Nolan's operatives, perched on a nearby motorcycle, pressed the red firing pin and launched the missiles on a trajectory that took them over the roofs of the Horse Guards buildings on Whitehall.

One exploded in the back garden of number ten Downing Street, where Prime Minister John Major was presiding over a Gulf War cabinet meeting. The bombproof windows shielded all inside from any injuries, but the sheer audacity of the attack enhanced the IRA's reputation as one of the world's leading terror organisations.

Although Nolan privately seethed at what he considered the failure of the operation to kill or maim, he knew the commission of the attack had struck a devastating blow to the morale of the security forces, and more importantly, to that of the British people in general. There was little doubt in his mind that all the recent overtures for peace from

London were coming on the back of the Downing Street operation. He was convinced that one more similar attack would tip them over the edge and provide his organisation with some real muscle in any talks about an Irish solution.

He had Joe Coyle to thank for the logistics of the operation. His one-time mentor devised the remote control mechanism for the mortars and planned the launch from a white Transit van with its roof removed and covered by flimsy white paper to hide the contents from prying eyes as it was driven from a rented garage in Ealing.

Coyle personally picked the location to park the van, factored in direction, flight path, and the precise explosive charge to control distance to the target. It was said later that the van was abandoned ten yards from the site specified and that the paper covering on the van roof, flimsy or not, had caused a miniscule deviation from target.

But the fact that one rocket landed in the garden, showed Coyle was near perfect on all his calculations.

Nolan had sent him to London the previous month to scope out the target. He knew the dapper little figure, wearing a trademark tan suit and matching loafers, would have blended in well with the usual mix of sightseers, shoppers and workers that thronged London's streets. Staying in one of the top hotels under a false identity complete with full paperwork, Coyle would have raised no suspicions.

In the massive police dragnet that followed the attack, Coyle was already long gone and his name on the hotel register would not have warranted a second glance. The two men who drove and parked the van made off on a motorbike and were in Amsterdam via

Cardiff International Airport before the alert went out.

Nolan rose from his seat, grabbed his overcoat from the stool, and turned to the men still seated. "I have to go now, but I'll see you all later."

"Do you want any back-up?" asked Dooley.

"Nah, this'll be straightforward. They know better than try anything. The fact that they want this meeting on my own doorstep shows they are serious. I'll listen to what they have to say and maybe rattle their cage a bit. I'll brief you later the outcome."

With that Nolan rose from his seat, strode through the lounge, and exited onto the street. The pavements were busier now, as last minute shoppers mingled with workers rushing to catch buses and trains. He pulled the lapels of the heavy coat up to his neck to ward off the chill from a biting south easterly and made his way towards O'Connell Bridge.

He barely noticed the usual array of hawkers dotted along the bridge footpath as he continued past the entrance to Trinity College and onto Grafton Street. He had no time today to stop, as he often did at the Molly Malone statue, or to notice the crowds thronging outside the vast St. Stephen's Green shopping centre at the corner of one of Dublin's busiest roundabouts.

Directly across from where he stood was the Fusiliers' Arch, the main entrance to St. Stephen's Green. Passing under the arch, erected to commemorate soldiers of the Royal Dublin Fusiliers who died during the Boer War, he turned right, along a narrow concrete path, which bordered the interior of the park.

There were fewer souls than usual enjoying the tranquillity of the massive park, and those who braved the elements seemed to be a mixture of power-walkers and dog owners forced out in the cold to provide their pets, rather than themselves, with exercise.

Nolan ignored them, keeping his eyes fixed straight ahead as a circular bandstand, his rendezvous point, came into view.

He stopped under the cover of a tall oak tree about fifty yards from the bandstand and watched for any arrivals. Barely five minutes into his vigil, a voice from a border hedge directly opposite, startled him from his thoughts and he silently cursed at the unmistakeable English accent.

A man emerged from the undergrowth.

"Now that we both know we are alone perhaps we should introduce ourselves."

Annoyed with himself for getting caught in the open, Nolan turned on the intruder and barked "I'm not here to play fucking games. Tell me who you are and what you want."

The man, who Nolan judged to be in his early thirties, brushed some leaves from his raincoat and stepped out directly in front of Nolan. Offering his hand, he said evenly, "Just call me Mr Smith, and I presume you are Mr Nolan."

Ignoring the offered hand, Nolan looked the man squarely in the eyes.

"This thing ends now unless you tell me who you are. You know who I am and I'm damned if I'm going to waste my time with some Brit fucker who thinks he can hide behind a phoney moniker. Spit it out, and no hogwash about you being a lowly gopher."

The man withdrew his hand and studied his opponent for a few seconds, appearing to decide how much to tell him.

"Fair enough. My name is Malcolm Fisher and I do work at the Embassy. All I'll say is that I'm not in the clerical or diplomatic ends, as you would have known, but I'll go no further than that. Whitehall has asked me to set up this little chat to explore how we might be able to take things forward towards a peace settlement and perhaps save both of us a lot of heartaches in the future. I think it would be better if we take a walk around the park rather than stand here looking rather conspicuous."

Nolan shrugged and started walking towards the bandstand and the footpath that bordered a small lake beyond. Fisher got into stride beside him and they walked for a few minutes without conversation.

"It's your show," Nolan eventually broke the silence. "Let's hear what's on your mind."

Fisher, both hands deep in his coat pockets, looked straight ahead as they continued walking. "Look, we've had almost twenty-five years of these so-called troubles. I think both sides would like to see an end to them."

"Easily done," said Nolan, "Just pack up your tents and get the fuck out of Ireland. We can go on for another twenty-five years if we have to."

If he intended to put Fisher off his stride, it didn't work.

"That's not going to solve anything. The British Government will continue to oppose you, and in the end you can't win by the bomb and the bullet. Why not step back and let the politicos have a go at finding a solution that will suit all sides? My Government is not against a united Ireland, but there are a lot of considerations to be taken into account. We are prepared to work with you to resolve these."

"Precisely what does that mean?" asked Nolan.

"Obviously, I don't have a crystal ball. Let's just say that if the IRA announced a permanent ceasefire, you might find my government would be more inclined to look at a thirty-two county solution to the problems of Northern Ireland. We will work closely with the Dublin government to see how things might be taken forward and we guarantee key milestones would be set for the proper transition of the current situation. We've also spoken with our American cousins, and they are more than willing to act as honest brokers to ensure progress is made."

Nolan let out a forced laugh.

"You surely don't expect us to take your word for all this. You honestly think we're just going to roll over with our hands in the air and say we've lost the war? No, history has taught us Mr Fisher, that the only way to get you people out of Ireland is to kick you out, not to talk you into submission. There's no way we'll stand down until this is finished."

"Look, let's be open about this," said Fisher. "You're losing the battle for the hearts and minds of the people. Even the Americans are saying enough is enough. How long do you really think you can go on if the populace turns against you? Nobody's suggesting you surrender or lose face or even take my word for what's possible. We can set up a series of meetings involving Dublin, Washington, ourselves, and your people to explore what needs to be done before any permanent ceasefire."

He paused for a moment before continuing.

"All I want to know is whether, against this backdrop, your side will stop the violence long enough for us to start talking and whether, if the signs of a political solution are there, you will then permanently step aside and let the politicians handle it?"

"That's a very one-sided view," Nolan responded. "From where I'm standing, your own populace is fed up losing its sons and daughters to an occupation they can't understand and want to stop. And now you're repeating the same mistakes in Iraq. How long do you think before the British people tell you to get out? Hell, they've already started. You and I both know that the more we hit you where it hurts, the more this clamour from your own people will gather momentum. If you're suing for peace then I'm ready to talk terms, but don't insult me with ceasefires that will allow you to redeploy troops from Northern Ireland to Iraq if things start up there again."

Fisher stopped at a summer seat and nodded for agreement to sit down. Then he started talking again. "I will admit we cannot continue to keep Northern Ireland as things stand, both in terms of human cost and hard finances. If there's a way out we want it sure, but don't mistake that for weakness. Like you, we'll continue for another twenty-five years, but who does that benefit? Who hurts the most? The plain answer is that it doesn't suit either side. We must find a way out that saves face for everyone.

"I'm sure your own people are saying the same things, Mr Nolan. I'm not trying to come up with answers today. I know there's a long road ahead of us, but if we can agree to make a start, then surely anything's possible if we involve the right minds."

Nolan stared intently ahead and then turned his head towards Fisher.

"You're forgetting the Unionist veto your government has continued to endorse since 1921.

You have it written in stone that as long as Northern Ireland wants to remain part of the United Kingdom, that right will be safeguarded by her Majesty's government. They use that Orange trump card at every turn and twist, and that alone will scupper any attempts by you to do otherwise."

"It's only a form of words, Mr Nolan. Let's say we are agreeable to redrafting or clarifying that commitment in language you can live with. Would that make a difference?"

"Are you seriously telling me you will go on the record and remove the veto?"

"I can only tell you anything's possible. I hope this demonstrates that if we enter these behind-the-scenes discussions we will do so in good faith, and with the express intention of finding a workable solution. I just need to hear that you will go along with us."

Nolan rose from the seat and started walking again along the pathway. He waited for Fisher to catch up.

"This is not a decision for me to make. If you want me to pass it on, I'll be happy to do so, but there's nothing I can say to you that you'll be able to take back to your paymasters."

"As you said before Mr Nolan, let's not fool each other. We know who you are and what you do. I'm not asking you to give me any commitments at this stage, other than that you will let your own politicos engage in the dialogues I've outlined. And, if their feedback is positive, you won't stand in the way of a ceasefire. Just give us some room to manoeuvre on what will be protracted and difficult negotiations. Give us some breathing space to explore the potential of this new situation."

"That cuts two ways," Nolan said with a trace of anger in his voice. "If we do give you this breathing space you ask for, then make damned sure the British Army and its RUC puppets stop harassing the Catholic population of the North. No matter what happens during these talks, you should know that we would retaliate in any way we see fit against any injustices against the North's minority population. That being said, I won't stand in the way of your talks, but they better not drag on."

"That's all I can ask for. I would offer you my hand again, but I've a feeling you won't accept it."

Nolan stared at the man's back as he watched him walk down a pathway that would take him to an exit gate at Kildare Street.

Nolan turned towards the Fusiliers' Arch exit, genuinely baffled by Fisher's overtures. It's not that he didn't know they were coming. There were enough signs in recent months the Brits wanted a parley, but the fact they singled him out, showed they were getting anxious.

He would let the political reps get on with the talking and he would get on with his job, but he couldn't shake off the notion that this probably signalled a sea-change in British attitudes.

He couldn't remember the language of diplomacy being delivered in such a forthright manner and he believed, for the first time, that the Brits really were on the defensive. His job now was to push them over the edge, and he knew what it would take to do it.

He also knew the man who would do it.


At the other end of the park Malcolm Fisher, real

name Mark Garrett, emerged from the park with his own thoughts. He had learned enough from Nolan to realise they were a long way off from establishing a ceasefire and getting down to talks. The only way to do this would be to disrupt the IRA war machine, both in terms of its recruitment and the support it received from the nationalist community. He had long since put a contingency plan in motion.

And he too knew just the man to make it happen.

# Chapter 5
## London Two Days Later

THE DRIVER EASED his black taxi out of a side road to join the early morning flow along Marlebone High Street. Sweeping past the entrance to the underground tube station, he hung a right into Kensington, ignored blaring horns as he cut across two lanes, and pulled alongside an arched pedestrian entrance set between two high-rise office blocks.

His passenger reached across to slip a five-pound note through the gap in the glass separating him from the driver's compartment.

"Keep the change," he muttered as he gathered up his brief case and climbed down onto a footpath crowded by workers hurrying to their desks and counters.

Mark Garrett strode with purpose through the archway, making straight for a glass-fronted building set in the corner of a rectangle forecourt overlooked on all sides by office buildings. His appointment at 9.30am sharp was with three top military advisors to the Government's all-party COBRA committee. An acronym for Cabinet Office Briefing Room A, where the meetings were usually held, the committee is tasked with responding to national crises by advising the Government on a range of counter measures.

He was met in the foyer by a man who had been awaiting his arrival for the past ten minutes. The two men grabbed upholstered chairs in the corner of the visitors' waiting area and were lost in discussion when the elevator pinged open and a stockily-built woman stepped out.

"Captain Mark Garrett," she announced to the handful of people dotted around the foyer.

Garrett rose from his seat, told his companion to wait for him, and crossed over to join the woman. They shook hands briefly and disappeared into the elevator. It rose four floors and opened onto a plushly-carpeted reception area that looked more like the sitting room of a large baronial estate. It was filled with armchairs and tables, and along one side was an open breakfast bar crammed with a variety of foodstuffs.

There was no mistaking the gentleman's club feel to the place.

Garrett was led to the far end, through a door into a medium-sized boardroom.

General Sir John Sandford was seated at the head of a large mahogany table, flanked by two well-dressed civilians, who were introduced as Bernard Mallory and James Foster. Although no other details were given about the men, and they were not known to Garrett, he could spot Civil Service types a mile off.

He had no doubt these two were link men to their respective ministers, most likely the Defence Minister and the Home Secretary. This was what some politicians called the old Whitehall two-step in all its glory. Put in enough layers and create enough distance between the men at the top and the grunts on the ground, and you were left with deniability.

The General motioned Garrett to a seat at the opposite end of the table as the woman left the room.

"Captain, naturally we've already read your assessment, but I want you to give us the shortened version."

Garrett knew Sandford's reputation first-hand, having worked for him on two previous projects, which were euphemistic descriptions for undercover operations. Sandford liked directness, and Garrett decided this was his best approach.

"As you know, I met with the IRA's top man in Dublin and I think we have a real problem. Put simply, I think they're looking to go on an all-out offensive against us."

"So, he didn't bite on an agreement for a ceasefire and political talks?"

"He pretended to, and although he's under pressure to allow a political solution to take place, his agenda is pretty much the same as ours. He wants his people to be holding all the aces when they take their seats at any peace talks. He wants to hit us hard, and he wants to make sure we have no stomach for staying in the fight."

"Put simply, Mark, that is why you are proposing we do the same to them, is it not?"

Garrett nodded his assent. "Yes, General. I have looked at reworking an old plan first tabled almost twenty years ago. May I recap a bit of the background?"

When Sandford signalled him to continue, Garrett spoke of the aftermath of an IRA campaign in mainland Britain in 1974, when a bomb in Guildford claimed the lives of four British servicemen in October of that year, followed a month later by IRA-detonated bombs in two central Birmingham pubs, The Mulberry Bush and the Tavern in The Town. Twenty-one people died and more than one hundred and eighty were injured in the explosions.

The response from the UK Government was to

send the COBRA committee into a week-long series of behind-closed-door meetings.

Within days, the Prevention of Terrorism Act was enacted because of COBRA's deliberations, but away from the public eye other strategies were being considered.

One such plan was tabled by a retired British Army General, Norman "Storming Norman" Brassington. Given the unimaginative codename of Storm 74, the General's proposal was to take the war to the IRA's doorstep – but in a highly covert fashion. He proposed the setting up of a new taskforce, independent and hidden from all other agencies, including MI5 and MI6. Its job was to 'gum up the works' as he put it, by taking whatever measures necessary to defeat the IRA.

"Most of the General's plan received universal support from his colleagues," Garrett explained. "The idea of setting up a 'dirty tricks' department to burrow beneath the IRA psyche, was particularly appealing, as was his specific plans for a new brand of covert Intelligence gathering, including the systematic bugging of telephones, workplaces, bars, restaurants, homes and vehicles."

Garrett paused to take a sip of water before continuing,

"Where the General started to lose his colleagues, was in his determination to introduce a 'shoot-to-kill' policy that included proposed kidnappings, torture and executions. Many believed the prospect of this being uncovered would leave Britain as a pariah in the eyes of the rest of the world. Some considered a watered down version of the more extreme elements of Storm 74, but the risk of discovery was always uppermost in any considerations."

Garrett completed his summary with what he knew was a dramatic statement.

"I now believe it *is* feasible to establish the kind of covert base that was originally envisaged."

Sandford cut in immediately.

"I would remind you Mark that all those earlier reservations about keeping other agencies, particularly the RUC out of the loop, still remain."

"I know sir, that keeping this thing quiet from the RUC will be the most difficult part of the operation. They're no mugs. They would spot an infiltration like this a mile off."

This time it was the man named Mallory who cut in.

"Let me get this right, Captain. Are you saying the Storm 74 proposal is feasible or not?"

"Sir, in my opinion it could work, but only under exceptionally watertight cover. All the usual bases in Northern Ireland would be useless for the Storm 74 project. Its very nature would raise suspicion within days, and I don't think we would have too long to wait for a visit from the RUC's Chief Constable."

"Good God man, are you saying there are leaks in our operations over there?" The question came from James Foster, speaking for the first time.

Garrett cleared his throat and waited for longer than was comfortable before answering.

"I know you understand that security in Northern Ireland is a relative thing. We have five counter-Intelligence Army units and three similar RUC units. Throw in MI6 and it becomes a bit cluttered. They all work as closely as they can, but not all information is shared. This results in a less than efficient way of going about things."

He continued: "Northern Ireland is a small piece of real estate and it's difficult to disguise the movement of security personnel. We have eight major bases – three in Belfast, and one each at Armagh, Portadown, Londonderry, Lisburn and Ballykinlar. With the exception of Ballykinlar they are all situated in highly built-up areas and there are civilian personnel working at each base.

"These people are of course well screened, but screening takes on a different dimension over there. You've only got to look at some of the disclosures made recently by politicians on both sides to realise they are getting leaks from inside the bases."

"From what you're saying," said Green, "it's a wonder we're functioning at all in Northern Ireland."

"Sir, our record stacks up against that of any Army in similar situations around the world, but the truth is we're talking about covert missions in Northern Ireland, and we simply haven't got any that are still current. We've lost seven undercover men in the past five years, and the reality is that we never really got close to the IRA's inner circle."

Foster slapped his sheaf of briefing papers on the table and leaned towards Garrett.

"Are you telling us we should scrap the project? It can't possibly function in the scenario you've painted for us."

Garrett knew he had reached the crunch issue. "Sir, I'm trying to show that Storm 74 can only survive if it works outside normal channels and...."

A polite rap at the top of the table cut him short. General Sandford sat back on his chair and swept the faces around him. Finally, he stopped at Garrett.

"It's obvious, Mark that you have an alternative to offer. I think we would all like to hear it."

"Yes sir," he told the General. "I believe it is out of the question to mount this kind of operation from any of our current bases. Equally it's not practical to stage the show from here, but I think I've found the answer. With your permission sir?"

Garrett nodded to the briefcase in front of him. When the General's eyes flickered an acknowledgement, he rose to his feet and unhinged the metal clasp. He produced a large map, crossed to a noticeboard to his left, and carefully pinned it on top of a few circulars yellowed by lengthy exposure to the sun.

"An outline map of Ulster. These black dots represent Army bases and small posts throughout the province." He tapped out the areas using a gold Parker ballpoint pen, part of his prize for winning a handgun marksman title at Warcop two years previously.

"You will notice two large red-coloured dots, here and here. These are two major Royal Air Force installations at Ballykelly in County Londonderry and at Bishopscourt in County Down on the east coast. I suggest one of these should be home to Storm 74."

There was an immediate stirring among his listeners. The babble of voices grew until General Sandford cut in. "Gentlemen, please. Proceed, Captain Garrett."

The pen was pointed at a red dot near the bottom of the map. "This is Bishopscourt. The entire base covers approximately 76 acres in the heart of the countryside in perhaps the quietest part of the province. The base used to play a key role in the UK's overall military radar network, and it was also home to the Civilian Air Traffic Control Centre.

"The CATCC has been moved to Ballykelly with the result that large parts of the Bishopscourt base are effectively closed down. As you know, the military radar network was streamlined last year to take account of the introduction of an early warning system known as UKADGE, the United Kingdom Air Defence Ground Environment. It was proposed that Bishopscourt should be included, but this has now been dismissed. It now seems unlikely we will need a post in Northern Ireland and my information is that Whitehall doesn't quite know what to do with Bishopscourt."

"Your information, if I may say so Captain, comes under the classified heading." The rebuke came from Foster.

"On the contrary sir, the details can be found on both police and Army files in Northern Ireland. And anyway, it was suggested last year that the Army should take over the Bishopscourt base in the event of an RAF withdrawal. That proposal is still under consideration."

General Sandford seemed to realise the significance of Garrett's train of thought.

"So, what you're saying is that we should acquire this Bishopscourt for Storm 74?"

"No sir, not entirely."

"Then what are you saying?"

"Sir, it's important the RAF remain at Bishopscourt while it's been used for our operations," Garrett told him.

The General countered. "You mean a sort of joint base?"

"I don't think that's doable, sir. What I'm suggesting is that Storm 74 take total control of Bishopscourt and pose as RAF personnel."

That brought an immediate response from Foster. "Preposterous. Have you any idea what you're saying, Captain?"

Sandford ignored the outburst and nodded at Garrett to complete his briefing.

Still on his feet, Garrett walked back towards the boardroom table and took his seat.

"Sir, you will remember what I've said about Northern Ireland security, and the problems faced at our existing bases. Unique to this situation is the RAF, primarily because it has no peacekeeping role. The IRA seems to have forgotten our flier boys exist, with the result that we've never had to deal with a campaign against them. This fact alone makes the RAF the best possible cover against intelligence leaks."

He was in full flow: "Second, RAF Bishopscourt is the most ideally suited of all Ministry of Defence installations in Northern Ireland. The troubles have hardly scratched the surface in that part of the country, and it's known there is no IRA intelligence unit operating in the area.

"The base itself is well hidden and protected. The runways are in excellent condition for the airlift of supplies and personnel, and there is a warren of underground bunkers and stores. Although it is isolated, it is within twenty minutes of the large Army base at Ballykinlar and within an hour from the border to the Republic of Ireland."

Garrett continued to outline a plan to rundown the existing RAF operation and move in the operatives who would form the Storm 74 squad.

"Base security perimeters would be manned by the project's own unit members, who would be required to wear RAF uniforms to mask the activity that would be going on in the background. A fleet of civilian vehicles would be airlifted onto the base, under the cover of darkness, and used for operations off-base with a collection of localised number plates that would be given bonafide entries on the central civilian Vehicle Licensing computer database in Coleraine."

For twenty minutes he continued to outline the precise details of the cover to be put in place, and the logistics involved in the countless operations planned by the project, both in Northern Ireland and in the Republic. Finally, he produced a dossier of names of the operatives who had been selected as potential recruits to the squad.

He sat back in his seat and scanned the faces opposite, trying to gauge reaction to his proposals. He hoped he could count on the General but was unsure about the others. Foster appeared completely negative, and he couldn't get a read on Mallory.

The silence lasted for several minutes before Sandford rose and walked to the large window at the end of the room. Garrett could see over the General's shoulders that Big Ben, London's iconic clock tower, was silhouetted against a clear sky as the morning continued to develop across the city.

Sandford turned back to face Garrett.

"Who are you proposing to head up this project?"

Garrett's spirits rose. "He's waiting downstairs. With your permission I would like to bring him in on the final part of the briefing."

Sandford moved to a table behind him and pushed an intercom. "Dorothy, please have Captain Garrett's guest shown up here immediately."

The boardroom door opened a few minutes later

and the same woman, who had escorted Garrett earlier, ushered a tall man into the room. He carried the poise of a man who knew how to be at ease in any company. Without a word he took a seat beside Garrett.

"Sir," said Garrett, "May I introduce you to our top operative. This is Mike Devon."

# Chapter 6
## Belfast

THE SUN ROSE OVER the Black Mountain hilltop range that guarded Belfast on its north-west boundary, the rays penetrating birch trees standing sentry on either side of an almost deserted Windsor Terrace, a leafy suburb like any to be found in the more affluent parts of south-east England.

Only one car, a silver BMW5 series saloon, was making use of the thoroughfare at such an early hour. Its driver, Terry Mitchell, was taking his time to manoeuvre along the eight hundred-yard stretch.

Mitchell was never one to rush an important assignment. Lives depended on him getting things right.

Beside him sat a leggy woman, draped in a fake foxfur scarf, her face framed by short shoulder-length blonde hair that allowed a view of the two-inch jewel-studded chain earrings hanging almost to her chin. Like everything about her they were also fakes.

God but she was beautiful, thought Mitchell, as he stole a glance at well-rounded knees dropping over the seat close to where his left hand rested on the gear stick. Beautiful, that is, until she opened her gob and then the thick, guttural accent of her native Fermanagh grated on his nerves. It wasn't her fault, Mitchell conceded, that Angela Moore was brought up in family squalor, stopped schooling at the age of fourteen, and ran away to the bright lights of Belfast where she got caught up in the wrong company.

She had told him how things changed for her three years ago when she took a cupboard room in a house in one of the many Belfast ghetto estates, and began a new career that earned her more money than she had ever had, plus a grudging respect from the inhabitants of her adopted surroundings.

Mitchell turned his attention back to the job in hand, absorbing the smallest of details as he passed each of the large stand-alone mansions, screened from the outside world by manicured hedges and long winding driveways. Two cars could barely pass on this stretch of roadway, but at least there were no parked cars to impede progress.

Residents here enjoyed their own off-road parking, either in generous driveways or in standard detached garages that looked bigger and more expensive than the homes Mitchell was used to living in. Not that anyone would have thought so, watching him drive by in his top-of-the range car, and wearing a conservative three-piece striped suit with matching tie and breast pocket handkerchief.

Like his passenger, he too was a master of disguise.

Terry Mitchell had recently celebrated his thirtieth birthday. Unlike his passenger, he had enjoyed a happy childhood and took his education as far as Queen's University where he conquered the complexities of a degree in Modern_Languages and dreamed of worldwide travel. Too many nights spent in the Student's Union in the company of political activists put an end to his planned future as a linguistics professor, and the day after he picked up his degree at the traditional graduation ceremony in Whitla Hall, he was already lost to the world of academia.

Now, as he glanced around with the confident air of a man who belonged among the city's nouveau riche, his memories of student life and early-years idealism were gone forever.

He aimed the BMW towards the far end of the half-mile drive-through, which opened onto the busy Lisburn Road, full of noise and pollution, and a world away from the cocooned residents of Windsor Terrace.

Several hundred yards before they reached the busy intersection, he noticed a telephone engineer emerge from a van and open his toolbox beside a green cast-iron junction box fitted against a wall across from house number eighteen.

"I see Eugene's on time for a change," the passenger offered with a unique nasally-challenged accent, distorted still even more by a phlegmy rasp that betrayed her forty-a-day smoking habit. "Let's leave the rest to him and get out of here. This place gives me the creeps. Fuck their money and their pretentions."

Mitchell's head didn't move, but he snarled in her direction through gritted teeth.

"This is our last run Angela, so pay attention. Keep your eyes on number eighteen and do your fucking job."

He diverted his attention to the driveway at number eighteen as he cruised by. It was the second time that morning this house held a particular fascination for him. As he noted the details of the portico front door and the security alarms mounted on the gable wall, he knew the telephone engineer was doing exactly the same. They would meet later to compare notes.

It was just after 8am and the sleepy suburb was

stirring itself into life. The noise of a rattling bin lid mingled with radio music to signal the start of the day in some households. In the autumn gloom of a September morning, the lights on a stairwell landing came on in number eighteen.

Mitchell saw all he needed. As he gunned the engine, his passenger removed her blonde wig and fur shoulder wrap in readiness for the integration with the early morning city rush-hour traffic. Three times they had repeated this exercise during the past two weeks, each time with a different stolen car, and each time with a different disguise.

Instead of the telephone engineer, the previous occasions had also variously seen the movements of a mail delivery van, and a florist apparently looking for the right address to deliver a bouquet to a birthday lady.

Mitchell couldn't help but think that had anyone been paying close attention on the days he had stalked this estate, they would have known this was a surveillance operation. But nobody noticed. Too busy with their own lives to worry about anyone else. Why buy a secluded multi-million pound home if you wanted to mix it over the garden fence with your neighbour?

Of course, it made his job easier if there wasn't anyone to give a toss about anyone else. Yet, despite the lack of interest and the solitude of the place, Mitchell had gone about his business in a thoroughly professional way. No room for mistakes. The whole idea of Intel-gathering was to be unobtrusive, not to draw attention, don't stand out.

And no organisation taught it better than the Provisional IRA.

A week later at number eighteen Windsor Terrace, the day began like most others for retired Detective Chief Inspector John Turnbull. Up at 8am, he wandered aimlessly around the large empty house, tidying up from the night before, and waiting patiently for the kettle to boil his first cup of instant coffee.

He carried his mug through to the small study area where he devoted most of his time trying to get to grips with the memoirs he was writing of a time spent heading the RUC's anti-terrorist taskforce.

A day just like any other, except that at 8.30am, when he should have been engrossed in his morning papers, he was dead.

Alerted by a neighbour, an RUC patrol found John Turnbull sprawled across the floor on top of a pool of coagulating blood that ran from a gaping wound in the back of his head. Above eyes that were staring vacantly into infinity through a fixed spot in the ceiling, were two neat small holes where high velocity rounds had entered his brain before exploding out the rear on their terrible path of destruction.

It was clear Turnbull's body was then pushed from his seat behind the ornate Georgian two-drawer desk and fell in a grotesque heap against the study wall several feet behind him. Every detail of the murder scene was absorbed immediately by the man now standing over the corpse.

He noted the ransacking, which had taken place in the desk drawers, the large mahogany bookcase, and the single metal filing cabinet. He also stared at the computer lead lying snaked across the desktop where it had been yanked from the silver-coated laptop he knew was kept there permanently by its owner. There was no sign of the laptop.

After completing an initial sweep of the room, the man forced his eyes back to the face of the corpse. It was a face he knew well. John Turnbull mentored him and was his boss for the past ten years before eventually taking late retirement to spend more time with his two grandchildren, and his roses and chrysanthemums.

It was Turnbull who taught him the true values of policework and whose job he took barely five months ago when the 'big man' stepped down. How could he ever forget the attention to detail that Turnbull drummed into him? How could he ever hope to emulate a man who had waged a relentless crusade against the terrorists who had turned his beloved Northern Ireland into a war zone?

The man now lying as an empty shell at his feet was responsible more than anyone for driving the Provisional IRA onto the back foot.

And now the Provos had their revenge. There was no doubt in the mind of the newly promoted Detective Chief Inspector Martin Vennison this was their handiwork.

It was well known that Turnbull was top of their most-wanted list. The man responsible for incarcerating so many of the IRA's godfathers and enforcers couldn't hope to outrun them forever. They had caught up with him in his isolated two-storey home and taken him when he was at his most vulnerable, a lonely widower seeing out his years after a lifetime of dedicated and unselfish service.

The only thing to surprise Vennison was that the killing had the hallmarks of a lone assassin. The Provos usually sent in a two-man hit team, one armed with a shotgun to disable the target with a wide pattern of shot, while a second assailant stepped up to the hapless victim with a handgun to deliver a killing shot to the head.

This time it was different.

Clearly only one person was involved in the murder of John Turnbull and that person knew what he was doing.

Vennison noted the holes in the centre of the forehead. Blood had bubbled to the surface and cobwebbed across the white skin into the furrows of the brow. There was no doubting the classic double-tap technique favoured by anti-terrorist squads such as the SAS, or highly-trained assassins.

Behind the corpse - about four feet up the freshly painted wall - a gouge of plaster was broken away where high velocity rounds must have torn through the victim's head to spend on the concrete surface.

The dead man was lying on his back behind the desk, his left leg incongruously wrapped around the leg of a red leather-upholstered chair that had travelled with him on his flight backwards, suggesting Turnbull was still seated at the desk when death paid its visit.

Why had he not reacted sooner to the intruder? Was it someone he knew and had unwittingly invited into his home? Or had the assassin somehow managed to get up close and personal without detection by Turnbull? The latter scenario sent a chill racing through Vennison. Someone that good would have to be very, very good to best the old warhorse.

At sixty-seven, John Turnbull had shown few obvious signs of his age. A large bear of a man, he still had a shock of white hair and muscles free from the usual flab brought on by advancing years. On the day of his retirement his mind was as razor sharp as ever, and his fitness would have done credit to someone twenty years his junior. Turnbull had not gone out to pasture and would not have been an easy target. Yet someone had made a mockery of that notion, and whoever it was, would take some catching.

As Martin Vennison turned away at last from his old colleague and friend, he recrossed the room muttering silently. Not normally given to grandstand gestures or knee-jerk reactions, Vennison nonetheless swore a solemn oath.

He would get the bastard who did this, and he would get the men who sent him to do it.

If it were the last thing he ever did, he would see them behind bars or face down permanently in the dirt.

Right now, he didn't care which.

# Chapter 7
### Belfast Hotel

FERGAL McSWEENEY SAT alone at a table in the Europa Hotel surrounded by all the trimmings of his favourite breakfast. The plate was heaped with sausages, bacon, mushrooms, and beans, while on a side plate stood two slices each of fried potato bread and fried soda bread. They don't make fry-ups like they make them in Ireland, he reflected.

This was what he missed most during his long absences out of the country. The good old 'Ulster Fry', the staple food of his homeland, had helped cure many a hangover, not to mention pushing cholesterol levels through the ceiling.

As usual after a job, McSweeney ate with a hearty appetite to help replace the adrenalin surge only action could bring. He would remain at Belfast's premier hotel for another three days, attending the annual Motor Show in the King's Hall complex before ghosting back to his family in Ayrshire in Scotland – a family that knew him as a reputable luxury car salesman, who supposedly hailed originally from Glasgow where he was born of an Irish mother and a Scots father.

It had been six months between jobs for him on this side of the Irish Sea. The call to eliminate John Turnbull was received a month ago, making it imperative for him to travel over the previous week, ostensibly to attend the Motor Show. The groundwork had already been done. The movements and habits of his victim were meticulously gathered by the IRA runners and gophers that made up the local Intelligence unit.

McSweeney never met people like Terry Mitchell or Angela Moore, but he knew too well their importance to the organisation, not to mention his own safety. He had come to rely on the detail of their reports and the schematics that were laid out for him.

Nothing had been left to chance over the period preceding the hit. Every day was accounted for until the watchers were sure of the target's daily routine.

During the time they had him under surveillance, it had become clear Turnbull stayed at home alone on Tuesdays and Wednesdays, his weekends taken up by visits to his daughter and grandchildren. On Mondays he never missed a round of golf with his old colleagues at the Royal Belfast Golf Club. Thursdays saw him in the centre of the city doing the rounds of the shops and ending up for evening dinner at the Culloden Hotel, usually in the company of his elderly sister, who also lived alone and made the weekly trip from her home in Bangor to keep in touch with her brother.

Fridays were always the same, a full day spent at the RUC Social Club premises from where he was usually driven home the worse for wear in the small hours of the morning.

The hit had been originally planned for early Saturday morning when Turnbull would be at his most vulnerable. After being dropped off by his driver at around 1am, he would have been in no fit state to defend himself. However, the watchers noticed that because of increased weekend activity around the city, it was not unusual to see RUC patrol cars drive slowly past the Windsor Terrace home at odd hours during the night. Someone probably figured that since patrols were out and about on Friday evenings and early Saturday mornings, they might as well check on the homes of some of their colleagues. No doubt Turnbull's wasn't the only drive-past on their list.

No, it all came down to either Tuesday or Wednesday. Take him in his own den and send out a message that none of the bastards were safe from retribution. That's what had finally swayed the mind of the Officer in Command of the Belfast unit tasked with the assassination.

There had been problems with overcoming the security, both inside and outside the home. The presence of an intruder alarm, motion detection lights and cameras were obvious from the outside, and there was likely to be a "panic alarm" button wired to the nearest RUC station to summon help at the first sign of anything suspicious.

They were problems, but nothing that couldn't be overcome.

McSweeney had decided to make the hit on Turnbull on a Wednesday morning. He chose the time for several reasons, but mainly because he wanted as many neighbours out of the way as possible. It was learned there were several school runs from adjoining houses, with parents driving away shortly after 7am. In all but one case they never returned, continuing instead from the school drop-off to their place of work.

The only neighbour this didn't apply to was a middle-aged housewife who got back at around 9:15am from taking two teenage girls to school and calling in at the local shops.

The main reason for waiting until after daylight

was that McSweeney had been in no position to deal with the automatic light sensors. These would remain on until 8am precisely. Getting past the intruder alarms would be a piece of cake for him.

At exactly 8am McSweeney had walked up the driveway belonging to the housewife neighbour, and around to the rear of the house. At the bottom of the garden was a high hedge separating her property from Turnbull's.

Wearing the overalls of a British Telecom engineer - to match the van in which he had driven up to the entrance to the housewife's home - McSweeney clambered through the hedge and took up a concealed position from which to monitor the target's house.

Within a few minutes, he had seen someone move from upstairs to downstairs. A figure appeared in the kitchen and was immediately recognised by McSweeney as his target. He was a giant of man dressed casually in a black t-shirt that helped to contrast the shock of unkempt white hair.

Almost as if to confirm Turnbull hadn't begun his daily grooming, the figure inside the house moved to a cabinet mirror and began running his fingers through loose strands before moving back to the sink and filling a kettle.

McSweeney maintained his vigil, as Turnbull appeared to be making a cup of tea or coffee. McSweeney watched as the man hoisted a small black bag and walked towards the outside back door. It was a sliding patio type, and as he stepped through to carry the bag towards a wheelie bin, the sounds of a radio news broadcast could be heard from somewhere farther into the house.

Turnbull paused momentarily to look at the

clear blue skies and inhale the fresh morning air before dropping the bag in the bin and returning to the house. He pulled the door closed and walked directly to the sink area. Moments later he could be seen carrying a cup from the kitchen into another room.

It was as McSweeney had guessed. The intruder alarm was disabled for the day. Wasting no time, he bolted from his vantage point and raced to the wall outside the kitchen window. He edged towards the back door and tentatively pulled against the recessed handle. To his surprise it gave way immediately. He slid it noiselessly across its runners.

John Turnbull was sitting at a desk, sipping from a cup, and totally engrossed in the morning edition of the *Belfast Newsletter*, which was delivered daily through his letterbox at 7.30am. In front of him, a small fifteen-inch laptop computer was open and displaying the familiar Microsoft Windows default screen against a pale blue background.

"You must have been expecting me, Chief Inspector. Nice of you to leave the door open," McSweeney said softly as he walked past the desk to stand in front of the shocked figure.

Turnbull jumped in his seat at the sound of the interruption but seemed to recover his composure. He fixed his eyes on the silver gun and snub-nosed silencer in the hands of his uninvited guest.

"Let me guess, you haven't come to fix the telephone. Do I know you? Are you IRA or the Ulster Volunteer Force?"

McSweeney admired the man's outward composure, though he guessed his insides were knotting up with fear.

In a fluid, casual movement McSweeney grabbed a stool resting against a small breakfast table and sat across the desk from his victim, all the while keeping his weapon trained on the middle of the face in front of him.

"You really didn't think we would forget about you. It's time to pay for your crimes against the Irish people."

McSweeney could see furrows appear on the Turnbull's head and knew the other man had worked out who had come to kill him.

"Ah, the penny drops. So, it's Provisional IRA. Is this personal or are you just carrying out orders from those fucking unseen godfathers?"

McSweeney leaned forward and peered directly into Turnbull's eyes.

"I've never met you, and until a month ago, I didn't even know you existed. Of course, over the past few weeks I've gotten to know you pretty well from our files. I must say you've been a busy fucker these past twenty-five years. You've sent down a lot of good volunteers and you've caused us a lot of headaches. Now it's payback time."

Without waiting for a reply McSweeney squeezed the trigger twice and watched as his victim slumped lifeless across the desk.

He moved around the desk, pulled the body roughly back against the seat, and pushed it away. The chair toppled, crashing the body heavily onto the carpet.

After spending no more than five minutes searching the desk drawers and nearby filing cabinets, McSweeney left the way he came, clutching the laptop and a handful of papers that might contain something useful for the Belfast Brigade's

Intelligence gatherers. *Might as well throw in a little bonus for them*, he mused.

Retracing his steps down the garden, through the hedge and along the neighbour's driveway, he was back in the bogus BT van and travelling away from the scene ten minutes ahead of the time he had allowed to complete the job.

He guessed the van would later be found burned out on inner city waste ground.


Three days after the shooting, McSweeney drove aboard the Stena ferry from Belfast to Stranraer. He ate a hearty breakfast in the dining area situated amidships and spent the two and a half hour journey reading a Frederick Forsyth novel.

As the ship steered its way down Loch Ryan, he moved with the rest of the passengers back to the car decks and settled behind the wheel of a dark blue Mercedes Series 3 convertible. His Sig Sauer was safely concealed in a hidden recess, specially built into the floor of the car. It was a purpose-built box that sprung open when a button below the driver's dashboard was depressed, but only if the ignition key was turned on.

McSweeney smiled as he considered the peculiar lapse of security on the part of the authorities. Travel by air from mainline Great Britain to any part of Ireland, and you could expect the most rigorous screening, but go by any of the many ferry routes and security was abysmally slack. Fewer than one in ten cars were searched and even those were perfunctory at best, particularly if you were careful to be amid the initial boarding rush.

As he passed through the small harbour town of Stranraer and took the A21 eastwards along the Ayrshire coast towards Glasgow, McSweeney relaxed and eased into his new persona. A mountain of paperwork awaited him, and he was taking delivery of a new suite of Mercs at the start of next week.

Business was booming in the car trade and he loved the distraction it provided.

# Chapter 8
## Antrim Road, Belfast
## Six months later

THE LONE FIGURE standing under a sycamore tree in a small residential estate off the Antrim Road pulled the lapels of his jacket around his neck to ward off the raindrops spilling from the big leaves above him. He used only his left hand to carry out the alterations to his dress; his right hand was wrapped around the butt of a small Beretta concealed in his coat pocket.

John Kelly's feet and legs were cold and stiff from a twenty-minute vigil, and he knew he could risk exposure no longer.

Wracked with a mixture of fear and anticipation that dialled his senses to their highest setting, he pushed away from the tree and strode quickly along the leaf-covered pathway, his eyes darting from side to side to check he wasn't being watched.

Glancing at his wristwatch, he saw there were a few moments to spare, providing of course everything went according to plan. But why shouldn't it? He had worked on this for three weeks and everything was exactly as it should be. Had he missed something? Did those young bastards make the early morning spotcheck as planned?

The thoughts were pushed from his mind as the whitewashed driveway pillars loomed in front of him. Without breaking stride, he turned the corner and walked past a parked Renault Espace in the driveway, reaching the front porch in less than fifteen strides.

He focussed on the brightly-lit bell button perched high on the door jam. He hit it smartly with the gloved index finger of his left hand. An inside door opened, and then he saw a silhouetted figure grow larger as it approached the other side of the opaque glass in front of him.

His grip tightened on the Beretta.

The door opened to reveal a semi-balding man dressed casually in a mauve-coloured Cashmere sweater and dark blue denim cords. He held the door firmly, allowing a space of just nine inches to peer out.

"Yes, can I help you?"

Kelly's foot pushed violently against the bottom of the door, catching the man off balance, and forcing him back into the hallway. Before the man had time to recover, Kelly stepped into the hallway, used his backside to close the door behind him, and withdrew the Beretta.

The man's arms instinctively leapt up to protect his head as he stumbled backwards into a small chestnut telephone table. It gave way under his weight, sending him crashing onto the thick shag carpet. He was on his knees now, gazing in terror at the cylindrical tube pointed firmly at his head.

"Oh Jesus Christ, please, please, don't kill me. I never bothered anybody. I'm out of that fucking game."

Kelly didn't reply. He moved around the sobbing figure beneath him and pushed the gun into the base of his victim's neck.

"Wait, please wait. Let me say a prayer. I have to leave a note for my wife. She will…"

He never spoke again.

Kelly's finger contracted on the small trigger and the man fell forward onto the carpet, a pool of blood slowly expanding under his head. The body convulsed twice before going still.

Kelly leaned forward to place the muzzle into the man's left ear. This time the sound seemed deafening in the empty space.

The sound of Kelly's approaching footsteps carried clearly to Alan Doyle, hidden in the dense garden undergrowth behind the wall of number 209 Falstaff Avenue on the Antrim Road. He tensed as the sound grew.

Doyle waited for the noises to fade in the opposite direction before risking a look through a bush of green twigs to stare across at a man walking up the driveway toward the front door.

*Ah, Mr Kelly I presume...welcome to the party*, Doyle mumbled to himself as he watched the man push his way into the house.

Moments later came the sound of a shot, followed by another.

Keeping his eyes on the door, Doyle reached into his shoulder holster for a Walther PPK. He was in a squat position, the weapon held in his right hand resting on his knee. All he had to do was wait a few more moments.

The door opened and Kelly re-emerged.

Doyle let the twigs fall back into place and listened as the steps closed on his position. Judging his moment, he sprang to his feet to find Kelly exactly opposite him on the other side of the pavement wall.

With one expert movement, Doyle's left arm

encircled his victim's throat. He yanked hard, bringing Kelly easily over the wall and down into the bush beside him.

As the man thrashed his legs and wriggled his head in a vain attempt to escape the vice-like clutch, Doyle applied more pressure and whispered. "If you don't stop moving, I'll snap your neck."

His words had the desired effect. The struggling stopped and the man sagged into a sitting position on the damp ground.

Using his right hand, Doyle pressed the barrel of the Walther into the side of Kelly's head. "I'm going to release my grip and I want you to turn round to face me. If you make one wrong move, you're a dead man."

Doyle eased away his left arm, keeping the Walther tight to the head as Kelly turned slowly. When the manoeuvre was completed, the Walther was now pushed hard against Kelly's forehead, above eyes that stared in shock at the face-blackened figure before him.

Doyle smiled. "Nice to meet you, Mr Kelly. Bet you're surprised at this turn of events?"

"Who the fuck are you? What's your game?"

The smile faded from Doyle's face. "My game is to put an end to your activities. We knew all about what you were up to this morning and let's just say your murdering days are over. It's time to pay the piper."

As he spoke, Doyle began searching Kelly's jacket. He removed the Beretta before thumbing the magazine-eject button and handing the clip over to a bewildered Kelly.

Kelly's raised his brows. "What's going on.... I don't understand."

The smile was back on Doyle's face. "Don't worry, you'll get the picture. Empty the magazine carefully and hand me the ammunition."

As Kelly pushed the bullets from the clip into his left palm, Doyle held his Walther in the centre of the man's forehead. He glanced at the Beretta in his other hand and checked that a round was still chambered. He pocketed the Walther and placed the Beretta against Kelly's head. "There's still one in the spout, so don't get any funny ideas."

When Kelly finished clearing the magazine, Doyle grabbed the ammo and stuffed it into one of his jacket pockets. Then he took the mag and rammed it back into the Beretta. "Now we wait," he told his captive.

It was exactly five minutes when Doyle heard the wail of police sirens coming from the left.

"Time to go."

He pushed Kelly, still crouching, along the wall towards the driveway entrance. He knelt on the tarmac, shielded by the gatepost, and waited.

The sirens became a raucous screech. Doyle peered around the side of the concrete post and saw two large Ford Granada cars slide to a halt about fifty yards away. He dragged Kelly to his feet and held him crouched below the level of the pillar.

Suddenly, he pointed the Beretta into the air and squeezed off the last remaining round. At the same time, he pushed the weapon into Kelly's hand and gave him a violent shove that sent him sprawling across the pavement and out into the street.

As Doyle wriggled down the driveway to the cover of the side of the house, he heard a distinct shout above the dying echoes of his gunfire.

"He's got a gun!"

What followed was a cacophony of noise created by the familiar language of the RUC-issue sub-machine guns.

Without waiting, Doyle ran down to the rear of the house and made his escape over a six-foot high boundary hedge at the end of a small manicured lawn.

The scene of the shooting flashed on the screen of the portable colour television perched atop a filing cabinet in the corner of the room. As usual, the BBC newsreader was precise and to the point:

*An RUC patrol today shot dead a suspected IRA gunman as he attempted to flee from the scene of a violent murder in Belfast.*

*The shooting took place at Falstaff Avenue shortly after eight this morning. A former Loyalist godfather was murdered in his home by a lone gunman who was then trapped at the scene by a passing RUC patrol. The gunman, who was spotted running away from the house, fired twice at police, and was killed in the exchanges which followed.*

*The terrorist's victim was Billy Young, widely known as a former commander of the loyalist Ulster Defence Association. He served fifteen years in prison for a series of murders in the seventies and was released only last year. He was married and had one son. None of his family was at home at the time of the shooting.*

*In a statement to a Belfast newspaper, the IRA named the gunman as John Kelly, a twenty-one year old single man from the Falls Road area of Belfast. The statement said Kelly was a volunteer and died on active service in the fight for Irish freedom.*

*The IRA also warned that attacks on loyalist activists and members of the security forces would continue.*

Mike Devon rose from his seat, crossed the room, and switched off the set. Then he turned to the man sitting at the side of his desk.

"Nice job, Alan. At least we've fooled the press, and the IRA won't have a clue about what's going on."

"Thanks, Mike. I was glad to get your call. We nearly missed this one. What made them give us the green light?"

Devon looked across the desk at Captain Alan Doyle, a fresh-faced thirty year-old who had crammed more covert operations into his Army career than most men twenty years his senior. Doyle was dressed in an open-necked white shirt matched by smart light blue Farah slacks. Twelve hours earlier his apparel had been in marked contrast as he slouched behind a garden wall in Belfast.

"Not tonight, Alan. I've had a long two days and need a bit of shut-eye before facing up to this tomorrow. We currently have at least a dozen projects to get underway and I need a clear head. We'll have a team briefing in the morning at 0700. Will you fix it up for me?"

Devon knew Doyle would understand his reluctance to go into any further detail. The two had met and struck up an instant friendship on a training exercise in Hereford in the south-west of England almost ten years previously. While Devon later enlisted in Her Majesty's Secret Service, Doyle had gone off to join Britain's famed SAS regiment.

When Devon was asked to head up his latest project the first name on his list was Doyle's. It came as no surprise that Doyle jumped at the chance.

Devon threw a mock salute at his number two and walked across to a large door. Out in the fresh air he gazed briefly at the stars above Bishopscourt, crossed a car park, and disappeared into the sleeping quarters where he had allocated himself a generous three-roomed suite.

Sleep for Devon was a fleeting experience. It washed over him like an incoming tide broken on the rocks by a jumble of images fighting for attention inside his head. The events of the past forty-eight hours kept tumbling back to be analysed again and again. Finally, when he knew they couldn't be checked, he rose to meet them face on.

The bottle of Bells was on the bedside table. With a practiced hand he drew it towards him, unscrewed the cap, and poured a generous measure into a waiting tumbler. The first biting taste of the brown liquid cut through the haze as he walked through to the living room to slump into a fireside chair.

He re-ran the day's events with a recall so vivid he could have been sitting in a darkened cinema watching as the film rolled in front of him.

The call came in mid-afternoon on the day before. He had been helicoptered twenty-five miles and watched as the machine made a slow descent to rooftop height as it approached the familiar outline of Thiepval Barracks, home of Army GHQ in Northern Ireland.

Devon had barely stirred during the brief hop from Bishopscourt, lifting his head only once to gaze dispassionately below at the H-shaped rows of buildings that formed the Maze prison complex, home to the most hardened terrorists from both sides of Northern Ireland's great divide.

The pilot had circled once before setting his machine down on a grass-covered enclosure that was once a cricket square in the days before the overcrowding of troops and machinery.

Devon had crouched under the still swirling blades as he dashed for cover from the sudden downpour of rain that greeted his arrival. Waiting in the overhang of a small storage hut had been Lt. Col. John "Dickie" Henderson, the man ultimately in charge of Devon's Storm 74 project. With him was Captain Mark Garrett, the man who recruited Devon, and was to be the liaison between Bishopscourt and Lisburn.

Only these two men in Northern Ireland were party to Devon's ultimate mission.

The group had walked through to Henderson's office and settled around a small boardroom table.

"We have to be convinced your unit is ready," said Henderson.

"We're as ready as we'll ever be, sir." Devon had told him and then added as an afterthought, "We've been ready for six months."

Almost as if he hadn't heard, Henderson threw his follow-up question. "Will you be able to fully implement the second phase of Storm 74?"

"Yes, sir, we will. As you know Captain Michael Thomas has been on the ground in Dundalk for some time and has infiltrated the IRA's Southern Irish command. We've had to pass on four targets in the last few months and we know of another one lined up in Belfast tomorrow."

Henderson rose from his seat and lifted a small file. "I've been reading about this. Give me your take."

Devon had glanced across at Garrett, and then turned to the older man.

"Well, we know the IRA is to attempt a hit tomorrow morning on an ex-loyalist paramilitary who was once considered a big fish. He's gone to flab a bit after spending fifteen years inside, but he would still be a major coup for the Belfast brigade. We also know that it is to be a single-man operation and the gunman is John Kelly, one of our top forty targets."

Henderson had interrupted: "And there has been no Intelligence leak to the RUC?"

"No, sir."

The Colonel paused to digest the information.

"Now we're down to brass tacks. We can save this man's life if we tip the RUC, but if we do that, we undermine our own project. If we follow through with our plan, the hit proceeds and then we nail the IRA shooter."

"That's about it, sir," said Devon. "The previous four targets we knew about and had to let go were all bomb runs. Two were clearly intended to damage property only and no one was injured. In the other two, we had one civilian casualty and four Army dead. If we had been activated, we could have gotten all the bombers without loss."

"But isn't this rather more different?" Henderson had asked. "The Army casualties were unforeseen. We knew the Provos were planning a culvert bomb, but we couldn't pinpoint the location in time to stop the operation. In this case, however, we know the precise details and we're talking about deliberately throwing a man's life away."

Devon couldn't disguise his sigh and heave of the shoulders.

"Sir, if it weren't for our current project, we wouldn't have the information in the first place. Our whole concept is to undermine the morale of IRA volunteers. If we take out one of them we can throw a real frightener into their works. Our only alternative is to sit back, give the information to the RUC, and let them pick up this bastard on nothing more than a possession charge. He'll be a bloody hero on the inside and be out in two years to take up where he left off."

Still seated at the table, Garrett had decided to intervene. "I think Mike's right. We need to give a go on this."

"Okay," said Henderson. "Give me the details."

It was Devon who had responded. "Sir, we'll have Captain Doyle on the ground. He will take up position in the garden of the house from a few hours before what we know is the time of the hit. When the gunman leaves the house after the shooting, Doyle will grab him and detain him at the scene. Then he'll make sure there's a shoot-out with the RUC."

"Will our man get out?"

"Shouldn't be much of a problem. He has his escape route mapped out."

"Won't the neighbours see what's going down?"

"No. The IRA has planned this well. The nearest neighbour is on a month's holiday with family in the south of England, and anyway there's a screen of wall and trees between the houses that would make it impossible for anybody to see what's happening."

Henderson had then paced across the room, finally stopping in front of Devon. "You've got a go." It was said with a curt nod of the head and a calm authority.

Devon pushed aside his recall of events and rose to turn on the matching recessed lights overhanging the fireplace in his Bishopscourt quarters. It had been quite a day - he had struck the first blow and now he intended to accelerate the pace of attack on the IRA command structure.

He knew the next few weeks and months would be the most intense of his life, but he was looking ahead to the challenge.

He had long ago made a silent promise to the memories of Peter Fitzsimons and Pauline Brown that he would avenge the events in Chicago. Now he was doing just that. A lot of IRA men and women would die because of his mission here, but he would swap them all for a chance to cross paths again with the man with the cold blue eyes.

Somehow, Devon believed they would meet again.

# Chapter 9
## Bishopscourt, County Down

BISHOPSCOURT HAD undergone many changes to its character since the start of the Northern Ireland "troubles" in 1969. A military base it may have been, but its shared role with a civilian Air Traffic Control Centre meant it was an open house to virtually everyone in the small surrounding farming community.

In those early carefree days there were more civilian workers on the base than uniformed personnel. The place was alive with tradesmen, joiners, plumbers, painters, and mechanics, as well as labourers, store hands and office secretaries.

Security was kept to a minimum, and relationships between airmen and their civvy helpers had reached that warm, personal level where house parties, both inside and outside the base, became a weekly norm.

The change was gradual at first and then accelerated under the constant worrying threat of terrorist infiltration. The civilian workforce was eroded under a policy of phased redundancies until, by the mid-seventies, only a small handful of Imperial Civil Servants remained. At the same time the security fencing around the base was upgraded and strengthened, and approach roads were reconstructed to provide the familiar tarmac ramps, which slowed the movement of all vehicles in and out of the camp.

For the first time too, the base was linked to the

joint Army/RUC computer centre, which instantly relayed back information on the registration numbers of cars seen near the base.

It was a slow process of isolation that succeeded in severing links between base personnel and their civilian neighbours. Vehicle checkpoints, or VCPs, were set around the perimeter and led to increased resentment between the two sides.

It also didn't help that constant transfers of staff brought in serving officers unfamiliar with the old ways and old traditions.

For all that, Bishopscourt was a base without purpose, a growing security monolith with nothing to secure. Its future was never quite certain and its role in the overall strategy of the RAF never quite defined. Its only hope of fulfilment was to share in the nuclear defence programme. It soon became obvious however, that it would not be necessary to have a regional centre in Northern Ireland. The UK mainland centres of West Drayton, Bentley Priory and Staxton Wold provided sufficient air cover to complete the radar picture of the United Kingdom without the help of Northern Ireland.

And so began for Bishopscourt a limbo existence, which ended with the arrival of Mike Devon and his Special Forces unit.

For two months Devon concentrated his planners on the task of providing absolute security. Once again, the perimeter fencing was overhauled, this time to include electrification, intruder alarm trip wires and thermal imaging cameras, strategically concealed to keep a wary eye on approach roads and neighbouring farmlands. Maturing evergreens were planted in long thin rows to provide better screening from the outside.

The biggest task was to enlarge and link several of the underground storage bunkers to provide space for the operations nerve centre of Storm 74. Once completed it gave shelter to the massive computer flown in and assembled in just five weeks by a specially-commissioned eight-man panel from Japan.

Around it, in vast glass casings, hung scores of street maps of most of the large towns of Ulster. The homes of known Republicans were shown by green-coloured stick-on dots while those of Loyalist militants were denoted by orange dots. At first glance, these showed up as a proliferation that seemed to cover most of the areas encased by the expensive mahogany frames.

Beside each case was a selection of photographs, a mixture of day and night scenes taken at ground level and from the air. Below these, in one long unbroken wall of steel, were Roneo Vickers filing cabinets, each crammed with the personal data of the men, women and children who lived in the dotted homes.

In the centre of that incredible underground warehouse, were the mapping tables and desks of the men responsible for collating and updating the information culled from the unit's expansive network. Off to the left ran a small winding corridor, opening into yet another chamber, considerably smaller than its parent, but no less frantic with the bustle of men and machines.

This was the radio hub: sending out its tentacles to sweep the entire six counties of Ulster and beyond, for the lifeblood of data to sustain and nourish the Storm 74 project.

There were twelve consoles in front of trained

operators who shared eight-hour shifts with two other colleagues - three men per console making a total of thirty-six operatives keeping an ever-present vigil against any suspicious activity on the airwaves.

Two specialist monitors sat at the head of the room, one tuned in permanently to known RUC wavelengths, another to pick up anything flowing out of Thiepval Barracks, Lisburn. A third monitor roamed the range to home in specifically on Ulster Defence Regiment sound traffic, and a final set was calibrated to listen in on the Divisional Mobile Support Unit, the elite first line riot corps of the RUC.

The constant crackle of static in the room was complemented by the whirring and clicking noise of the line printers and decoders, which intercepted the flow of information from each console on its way down the corridor to the main computer.

More than three miles of cabling and wiring ran back and forth between the rooms. At various intervals clusters of wires could be seen disappearing through the ceiling and into the base of six massive receiver/transmitter dishes rotating in monotonous ninety degree turns every forty-five seconds against the coastal skyline of Bishopscourt.

Together they comprised the most sophisticated land surveillance system in Europe, ingeniously disguised to appear as any other RAF radar installation. The search of the skies, however, had long since been subordinated to the greater need for a search of what was taking place closer to sea level.

In the third of the three underground chambers, was a mind-boggling array of coloured telephones, fixed permanently to a purpose-built wooden bench that ran for thirty feet on one of the long sides of the rectangular-shaped cavern. Four operators shifted constantly along the range of the table, each responsible for six phones and for transferring messages across the room to two coordinators keeping vigil on three vast Plessey Communications Visual Display Units.

Each phone was a link between the base and the twenty-four "Field Collators" who fed the system with a daily drip of news and information, the majority of which was a weighty mass of trivia.

There was an FC attached to each of the nine Army units currently serving in Northern Ireland. Unknown to these units, the collators were transferred in to spy for Storm 74, relaying any information gathered about Republican and Loyalist frontliners. Nothing was overlooked. Movements, habits, girlfriends, regular pub visits, change of car, favourite shops – it was all ingested by the system like a hungry gossip columnist. One report went to their assigned units and one went to Bishopscourt. Sometimes only one report went to Bishopscourt.

One phone sat away from the rest.

This was the Dundalk "hotline" used with care by Captain Michael "Taffy" Thomas, who had infiltrated the notorious Southern East Brigade of the Provisional IRA. He had made a total of six calls to the green-coloured handset since his arrival in the border town via Dublin thirteen months ago.

The first had been to report that his new electrical shop had just landed a major tender to supply circuitry information and training to a group of local businessmen. The following four calls had been to describe how and when the businessmen intended using some of their newly acquired skills.

The sixth call, made just ten days ago, was to

report how his new colleagues proposed to liquidate the business of a main rival based at Falstaff Avenue, Belfast.


Mike Devon rose early and looked below his window to the sprawling grounds of the base. The runways were damp from a heavy overnight mist, and here and there was the incongruous sight of the limp flags of a golf course. The previous occupants had fashioned nine holes out of the generously flat land, even going as far as to install bunkers and plant heather bushes in an attempt to provide it with character.

One of the men had found an abandoned set of clubs and tried his hand at negotiating the first hole. He later bragged about hitting the world's longest tee shot – his wicked slice crossed over the fairway, bounced on a runway, and ended up over a half-mile away!

Beyond the barbed wire perimeter fence, Devon tried to follow the shaded patterns of rolling countryside as it tossed and tumbled its way to the hazy horizons of the County Down coastline. Just discernible to his left were the Mountains of Mourne, a colossus of nature, forever immortalised in the haunting lyrics of Percy French, who lovingly created imagery of rocks sweeping down to a sea washing into the strands of the holiday resort of Newcastle.

But Mike Devon didn't look with the eye of a romantic lyricist.

Many times he had conceded its natural beauty, but always there was an overriding emotion. How could there be such ugliness in a paradise? Every time he gazed admiringly at this beautiful landscape it was a thought that reverberated to chastise him for his weakness. Never forget, he told himself, this God-forsaken country has visited untold misery on the British people stretching back centuries.

And the only reason he was here was to exact a bit of payback for the death of his friends in Chicago in 1985.

The callous way both had been slain and Devon's own narrow escape, was the stuff of nightmares ever since.

He had taken two bullets, one that drove through his stomach, miraculously missing his vital organs, and one that gouged a track across the left side of his head just above the ear. It created a permanent scar, now mostly hidden by his combed over black hair, but once again he had been damned lucky.

He remembered coming round from a state of unconsciousness as two Chicago PD patrolmen stood over him, guns drawn and keeping their distance, understandably wary of the stranger lying at their feet.

They had responded to an emergency call from one of the local residents and found Devon spreadeagled on basement steps and still clutching a Glock 15-round automatic.

After relieving him of his weapon, they handcuffed one of his arms to a nearby railing and radioed in for back-up and an ambulance. Despite Devon's protestations, the policemen refused to believe his story or to call one of the special numbers he provided.

It was an hour later, lying in a hospital bed, that he finally made some headway with a homicide detective who arrived to take a statement.

The detective made the call, relayed Devon's story, and instantly stiffened as a voice at the other end barked out a series of orders. Within fifteen minutes the ward was awash with FBI officers, and the detective was hustled to the side. He was told the matter was one of national security, and the Feds were taking over. They politely thanked him for his help and ushered him out of the hospital.

The following afternoon, FBI Agent Stan Reno visited Devon as he recovered from an emergency operation performed in the early hours of the morning. It was Reno who broke the news about the fate of Peter Fitzsimons and Pauline Brown.

Devon had struggled to keep his emotions in check.

In the weeks and months that followed, the FBI operation ground to a halt. Despite a computer-enhanced identikit photo generated from detailed descriptions provided by Devon, they never found their man. The image was not on any databases accessed by the FBI, CIA, Homeland Security, Interpol, or MI6. Despite being posted in every police station, train station and airport, across Illinois no one came forward.

The mystery man had disappeared.

But his image was burned into Devon's brain. He would not forget in a hurry the cold-blooded stare of a killer. He had no doubt this was the man who had murdered his friends.

When he had been posted back to London at his own request, it was because of a burning desire to hunt down the IRA gunman. Somehow, he had escaped the American net, and Devon was betting the farm he was back in Ireland, most likely in the Southern Republic.

The face of Pauline Brown was ever present in his thoughts. He remembered wanting to take her back to London after the completion of their Chicago mission, to meet his elderly parents. His mother would have gotten on like a house on fire with the effervescent Pauline.

He dreamed of the pair of them taking on a new assignment, living in the capital where they grew up, and raising a family of their own.

His father was ex-military and wanted Devon to follow him into service. But the young Devon had other ideas. At political studies in the University of London he was fired up by a lecture given by a Government spook on world affairs, speculating correctly on the fall of communism, and the potential rise of an increased threat from the Middle East.

Devon underwent an exhaustive training programme, including a spell with the CIA in its Maryland facility, and being seconded to the British Army's elite counter-terrorist investigative unit linked to the SAS.

His job took him around the world, carrying out spying missions in Moscow and extricating colleagues from behind the Berlin Wall before its collapse in 1989.

Before that he was seconded to MI6, for whom he carried out several dirty missions and was highly regarded within the corridors of power as a dependable and lethal operative. It was these credentials that put him initially in the front line against the IRA, firstly on an undercover tour to Belfast, and then to America where he was tasked to break up the supply of support that was providing the lifeblood needed by the terrorists back in Ireland.

It was how he had met Pauline Brown and they

sparked from minute one. She too was a Londoner but travelled a different path that eventually crossed with Devon in Chicago. She had moved back to her father's native Washington, and for a few years had been given low-grade assignments attached to the British Embassy's diplomatic corps.

Slowly her star rose. Her superiors realised they had an exceptional young operative, and she was thrust more and more into the field, working alongside more seasoned veterans.

At twenty-five years of age, she was in the full sparkle of early womanhood, possessing an engaging charm that shone through when she laughed and told stories of her childhood, often garnishing them with made-up fantasies of knights in shining armour sweeping her off her feet.

Devon knew he was her knight. She had told him how she was smitten by his self-assurance and contrasting vulnerability. They had swapped memories of London often as their relationship grew, and she was determined to follow him back there when their current assignment was finished. She never got the chance.

Devon was stirred from his thoughts by the harsh tones of the base intercom sitting on the corner of his desk.

"Mike, I'm calling the troops together for the meeting," Alan Doyle told him.

Fifteen minutes later he was in the main briefing room going through his papers as each of his managers filed in and took their seats. The term *managers* was one he had given to his field commanders as the best way of circumventing the assortment of military ranks that hung uneasily on all their shoulders.

He threw a cursory greeting to the men and studied them closely as they sat in a small semi-circle under the large blackboard wall.

He knew Doyle would be first. The ex-SAS man had a fetish about timekeeping, his life governed almost exclusively by the sweep hand on the twenty-four-hour clock. There was another reason of course.

His successful mission in Belfast yesterday had pushed his adrenaline levels off the charts and he was still grinning like a cat that had gotten the cream! As usual, he was casually dressed. He was every inch the military man of action, but many people had made the mistake of believing he was all brawn and no brain.

Devon knew Alan Doyle was a cool, calculating tactician, hardened by living life on a tightrope. He had fought his way out of many corners during a distinguished career, getting by as much on his wits as by his carthorse strength.

Devon had memorised the personnel files of the rest of the team.

Sitting beside Doyle, and looking positively Lilliputian by comparison, was Mark Webber, a radar and telecommunications expert who ran the operations room. A precise and meticulous man, Webber continually looked out of place among the ensemble of elite fighting men gathered together in that small pocket of Northern Ireland. The starched collar and pencil moustache went well with the squeaky voice, heavily accented by his old Etonian background, but for all that he was popular and well liked by everyone on the base.

Not so companionable was Tony Betts, the only recruit from the Senior Service. His reputation for drunkenness and womanising had brought him to the brink of a dishonourable discharge from the Special Boat Squadron. His career was rescued because Storm 74 needed a man with his special skills.

Betts' genius for explosives was tested to the limit during a period of secondment with the Paras in Londonderry where he twice defused bombs more prudent officers would have left well alone. In one report to his superiors in Portsmouth, the unit's senior medical advisor suggested Betts had reached the point of not caring, a classic case of a man living out a death wish.

John Tully was as usual, fidgeting with his coat sleeve, a habit that irked his colleagues and one that Tully could not control. The only son of a Somerset doctor, Tully led a cloistered existence during his childhood, and had surprised everyone by his decision to join the Army at the age of eighteen.

The Army brought out the best in him and discovered his one true talent in life; he was a deadeye marksman with any weapon. Six years with the Paras and two with the SAS taught him the survival knowledge he needed to make him potentially the most lethal sniper in Northern Ireland. Two years previously in Crossmaglen, County Armagh, he blew a man's head away with a single shot from a range of 780 yards.

Peter Ackmore was the last to arrive, wearing his familiar oil-stained boilersuit, and fidgeting impatiently in obvious annoyance at being dragged away from under the bonnet of one of the base's Land Rovers. As senior mechanic he was kept busier than most and had little time for the silver-spooned officers who had continually made his life a misery by insisting on stupid protocol when all he wanted was to spend his time mucking around engines.

He acknowledged this bunch was different than the rest who had gone before, but he lived a daily dread of being awakened and ordered back to more mundane duties.

Devon waited until they finished their preliminary greetings and small chat before lifting off his cap and setting it down on the desk in front of him. The men recognised it as his way to signal the start of the meeting. Immediately there was a hush in the room.

"First off, congrats to Alan for a job well done yesterday morning."

Devon waited for the round of high-fives to settle down. "We're off and running and you don't need me to tell you things are going to get pretty hectic around here. Alan will update us."

Alan Doyle moved the file on his knee, but as he pulled back the flap cover, he hesitated and let it fall closed again. Everyone in the room knew Doyle had a photographic memory and didn't need the crutch of a bunch of papers.

"We have a list of forty prime targets. Correction, make that thirty-nine as of yesterday," Doyle said with just a hint of mischief.

"Everyone on the list is a known terrorist involved at various levels. We know that if they can be taken out of circulation the IRA's effectiveness will crumble."

"Sir, are all the targets the Provos?" The question came from John Tully.

It was Doyle who answered. "The list includes thirty-four Provos, two from the National Liberation Army, and two from the loyalist Ulster Freedom Fighters. Frankly, the loyalist mob doesn't rate the same kind of attention as the others, and after all, our main job is to force the IRA out of business."

Before continuing, Doyle opened the file in front of him and withdrew a photograph, which he pinned to the backboard. "Top of the list is Liam Nolan. He's the Provos' head honcho and it's fair to say that little or nothing has happened in the North without going through him. He's a slippery customer, never involved in missions himself these days, but he's a shrewd cold-hearted murdering bastard who never passes up the chance for a bit of aggro."

"What keeps him on the loose?" This from Mark Webber.

"As I say, he's never in the field himself. Does all his planning from Dublin or Dundalk and hasn't been in the North that we know about since the release from the general internment lift in 1969. Frankly, I can't see us getting him by any other operational methods."

"We certainly can't leave him wandering around while we're picking off the smaller fish." It was more a definite statement than a rhetorical aside from Devon.

"I agree Mike, but the only alternative is a first strike."

"What's a first strike sir, eh, I mean Mike?"

"That's where you come in, Tully. We simply take a shot at him some night and it's no more Mr Nolan," Devon coldly told him.

Tony Betts cut in. "Won't that jeopardise our mission? Surely the whole idea is to bump off these bastards without anyone having a foggy?"

"Yes, but I'm afraid there's going to be the odd exception and, just to correct Alan's earlier statement, Nolan is not top of the list. There's another with no name and no location, but he's bound to surface sooner or later. He'll be our priority if we hear anything."

There was an immediate stirring in the room, each man looking at the other for any confirmation that someone knew what Devon meant. They looked quizzically at the head of the table, silently urging Devon to elaborate.

"Look, all I'll say now is that there's an IRA specialist out there, and I hope we come across him. He is unlikely to make an appearance unless we muddy the waters enough to bring him out of hiding. When that happens, I want to be ready for him. For now, let's concentrate on the job in hand."

Doyle picked up as if there had been no interruption.

"Leaving that aside, I suggest we take the next six names below Nolan and start working on how we can isolate them. For a start I'll increase surveillance to twenty-four hours, but we'll have to take a decision on planting the bugs. That's Webber's end. What've you got, Mark?"

Webber rose from his seat and walked to the back of the room to retrieve a suitcase he positioned there at the start of the meeting. He carried it forward and placed it on the table next to Devon. Then, as if to increase the drama, he unfastened the locks and gingerly lifted the lid.

"We've developed and perfected a new range of Ex-Ears, which basically means they are devices for exterior listening," he told his attentive audience. "It's out of the question to risk the usual interior techniques such as phone-tapping, concealed bugs etc., so we've gone for the easier and I think more effective method."

He withdrew a flat-shaped, mud-coloured object from the case and held it up for everyone to see.

"This is our prize baby. For obvious reasons we've christened her "mud-in-the-eye" because that's what we hope she's going to do to the enemy. It's fully magnetised and will stick to any metal surface, particularly designed for the underbelly of a car. It will pick up on any conversation from the interior of the car and has a receiver range of one mile. As you can see it's barely the size of a pancake and weighs only six ounces. Should it become dislodged and fall at the feet of one of our scummy chums, it's hardly likely they'll give it a second glance."

Devon took the disc, studied it for a second and then asked, "I take it this doesn't work when the engine's running?"

"On the contrary Mike, old mud-in-the-eye has been designed with that in mind. In plain terms her little micro-circuit is plugged into a rather special receiving computer which automatically separates all the noise patterns and gives them to us in individual patterns. Rather like separating all the instrument sections in an orchestra, which can be done in a cheap music studio with the barest essentials."

"Christ that's incredible. You could make a fortune if you patented that," said Betts, licking the corner of his mouth as if savouring the prospect.

"This is nothing new," Webber continued. "These little buggers, or rather ones very similar to them, have been around a long time. We've simply added a few bits and pieces of our own. I'll give you a demo in a minute, but first I want to explain other aspects of it."

He held one up for all to see. "Although these are ideal for cars, they were actually designed for the family garden. One of these placed in a flower patch underneath a window will pick up voices inside the house. Their effectiveness is restricted to only one room so a number would have to be planted. However, you can see how bloody useful they are."

"You bet, especially when the buggers are having it off with the missus." The interruption by Betts caused guffaws of laughter, but Devon cut sharply in.

"That'll be enough."

Devon still couldn't decide whether he liked Betts. He knew the gruff sailor had personal problems and had chased himself into a bottle to forget a broken marriage and the loss of inheritance from a wealthy stockbroker father. The father kicked Betts out of the home after a teenage scandal when Betts and four friends raped the old man's personal secretary. Devon put the thought out of his mind and turned back to Webber.

"I think we could do with the demonstration now, Mark."

From the suitcase Webber withdrew what looked like a standard transistor radio. He extended two antennae and switched on several dials. He handed Devon a piece of paper and instructed him to read aloud.

Devon cleared his throat and began "I hereby grant the brilliant Mark Webber a year's leave of absence with double pay...."

Instantly Devon's voice echoed back from the transistor sitting on the table beside him, and he stopped reading to peer at the red and black box.

Webber explained. "Before the briefing I took the trouble of placing one of our little friends outside the window. I might also add that it's covered with an inch of topsoil and you can judge the effectiveness for yourself."

"That's incredible."

Webber held up his hands. "Wait. I'm not finished yet."

He lifted the base intercom, pushed a button, and spoke into the handset. "Start her up Tom and give her the treatment."

Into the silence that enveloped the room came the unmistakeable sound of an engine starting and being revved at high pitch from somewhere across the base. Webber twiddled with the knobs on the transistor and after a moment's crackle came the softening sound of Bing Crosby's *White Christmas*.

"So, it plays tunes as well, big deal," said Betts.

"I'm afraid you don't understand. The song you're listening to is coming from a cassette recorder sitting on the passenger seat of one of our half-tonners which is currently having her guts raked out by Tom Bridges in the motor pool. We're hearing it courtesy of a mud-in-the-eye which is fixed underneath the engine mounting."

"That's brilliant, there's no engine noise coming through," said Devon.

"Like I've said Mike, our friend here" – he patted the transistor with affection – "has separated the sounds and discarded the ones we don't want. It's really elementary."

Devon, who had been standing during most of the proceedings, went back to his seat at the desk. For the first time in twenty-four hours, he could now see the road ahead and knew his next moves exactly.

"Alan, get your squad together and work closely with Mark on this one. I want these devices in place and operational by the end of the week. Make out a list of your requirements for the motor pool and get going fast."

Then he turned his attention to Ackmore.

"How are the cars coming along?"

"We now have ten private vehicles, all fully licensed, false number plates, the works. The armoured sheets and bulletproof windows are complete, but there's still some electronic wiring to be done as per Mark's instructions."

"Let's not waste time. Find out how many we need for this week's operation and get them ready. I want an around-the-clock shift on this."

"There's still a fair amount of..."

"Look I don't want to hear problems, just do what you can. The coffee breaks and squash sessions finish right here. We're going to war gentlemen and I want everybody's back to the mill."

Realising his voice sounded too harsh, Devon got up from his chair and walked round to stand in front of Ackmore. "Let me put it another way. We're finally getting the chance to do more than feed silly information through to the RUC's confidential telephones and I want us well prepared. Your job is to make sure we are."

"That reminds me Mike," Webber cut in, "Do we still continue those little calls?"

"Yes but concentrate your operators on updating the info we have on Alan's main targets. From now on anything we get on any of those we keep to ourselves. I'm sure as hell not going to get one of them picked up for pissin' against a doorway in the Falls Road and depriving us of the chance of putting them six feet under."

Suddenly Betts stood up to tower over Devon. "And can someone please tell me what the fuck I'm supposed to be doing while the rest of you are chasing around the countryside playing with electronic bugs?"

Devon met his glare without flinching. "Sit down Betts and for once take the chip off your shoulder. As it so happens, we do have a job. We've just gotten wind that the IRA is planning a car bomb in the Newry area tomorrow evening. We don't know the target, but we do know the route the bombers will take. Your job will be to intercept them."

A buzz of noise swept around the room, but Devon held up his hand in a gesture for silence. "I know this is not one of our top targets, but frankly it's a little nugget we can't just pass up on. It's something we should be able to handle with minimal planning so I'm authorising a go on it."

He leaned down to eyeball the seated Betts. "Just remember to do exactly what you're told and nothing more. One step out of line and I'll have you back where you started, heading for a walk to civvy street."

For a fleeting second Betts seemed ready to explode, but gradually the tight lines on his face eased to make way for a grin. "Okay, you're the boss."

Devon turned his back on him and walked to the head of the room again.

"I think we've covered everything for the day. I'll see each of you individually later, but in the meantime you all know what to do. Let's get cracking."

# Chapter 10
## Dundalk, Southern Ireland

THE BLUE VOLVO jumped out of the side road and into the thin stream of traffic snaking along Dundalk's main shopping precinct. The window wipers fought gallantly to hold back torrential rain beating down from the late evening skies, but they had already lost the battle. The driver was forced to ease off the accelerator as he peered frantically into the darkness to judge the centre of the road.

Mary McKeever was in the passenger seat, fiddling nervously through her handbag, and dragging deep from the cigarette at the corner of her mouth. She was still remembering their lovemaking less than an hour ago and was cursing her ill-luck at having to leave the bedroom to venture out on a night like this.

It was the first time they had made it together. They were not supposed to have left until 7pm, but she had asked him to come round at 5 to go over last minute details. She met him at the door, wearing only a short bathrobe, and when she bent down to hand him a drink on the sofa, she made sure he had a full view down the front of the robe to her well-rounded breasts.

She sank in the seat beside him and crossed her legs in such a way that the robe fell open to reveal the full length of her thighs. He came to her quickly and she slumped back willingly under his embrace, her hands searching for the belt of his trousers as he unravelled the knot on her robe. Then he picked her up like a doll in his arms and carried her through into the bedroom.

Afterwards, as she lay on top of the bed gazing through the curtainless window into the dark night, she talked about the love that had finally erupted between them. The spark of affection was ignited at an IRA meeting in Dublin three months previously, and on their first mission together five weeks later, they kissed and petted on the front seat of a stolen car before going out to shoot dead an off-duty UDR soldier.

"Brendan, do you have any feelings for me?"

"I think you know the answer. I wish to God we could get out of this fuckin' business and away on our own somewhere."

"Are you making an indecent proposal?"

"Jesus Mary, there's nothing I want more than to spend time with you, but you know it's impossible. Our Lord and Master, Mr Liam fuckin' Nolan, wouldn't have any of that nonsense."

"Then why don't we just disappear and forget Nolan and his crap?"

"How the hell can we?"

"Listen Brendan, I have an aunt living in Germany. She could put us up and you could find work. They'd never get us there."

"Stop dreaming darling, they would have to come after us. You know what that bastard Nolan is like."

The topic over, they dressed and headed into the night to begin the thirty minute drive to the border at Newry. The silence continued until the first lights of the town came into view.

"Brendan, why don't we at least ask Nolan? We just can't leave it like this."

"You know what his answer's going to be. He's liable to split us into different brigades to make sure we don't see each other again. High and mighty bloody Nolan thinks he's on some sort of a crusade and nothing's supposed to get in the way. Please Mary, don't talk about it again."

She watched as he eased the Volvo through the deserted customs post and approached the main British Army checkpoint on the outskirts of Newry. Surprisingly, after only a momentary delay, they were waved through. Perhaps it was the heavy rain, she considered, but it's not often the Brit bastards are so generous. It was her experience at this checkpoint to be kept waiting while a thorough document search and, on occasions, a stripping down of the inside of the vehicle, was carried out.

The car swung onto the country road leading to the small hamlet of Hilltown, and ten minutes later turned sharply off into a farm laneway. Brendan's hand flicked the light switch twice and from the hedge at the rear of the car three men emerged carrying large, black plastic bags.

She waited while Brendan climbed out, squeezing his way between the car and the hedge to where the men were standing. Without a word, he opened the boot.

She noticed the considerable exertion the men needed to heave the bags into the car. When they finished Brendan slammed down the lid and the trio ran off into the night. Back behind the wheel, Brendan reversed onto the main road and they continued on their way.

As the Volvo turned a corner three miles down the road, she nearly leapt from her seat at the sight of a menacing red light flickering in the roadway ahead.

"Holy fuck, it's the Brits!"

Brendan looked across at her. "Do you think we should make a run for it?"

"It's too late. For Chrissakes, stay calm. It's only a routine stop. They may not fancy searching anything on a night like this."

As the car slowed to approach the light, she could make out the shape of two Land Rovers parked at an angle across the road, and at least six uniformed figures standing on the grass verges on either side. Brendan killed his main beam and rolled down his window as he brought the car to a stop beside the soldier standing in the centre of the road.

The clipped English accent was unmistakeable. "Good evening, sir. Sorry for the inconvenience, but can I see your driving licence?"

She could see the shake in Brendan's hand as he reached into his jacket, withdrew his wallet, and handed over the licence. The soldier examined it briefly.

"Can I have your name and your passenger's name?"

"I'm Brendan Gracey and this is my girlfriend, Mary McKeever."

"Where do you live, sir?"

"We're both from Dundalk."

"And may I ask where you're going?"

"Eh, yes, we're going to visit relatives in Castlewellan. Mary's sister has taken ill and we're staying with the family for a few days."

The soldier appeared to look towards the rear of the car before responding. "That will be all, sir. Enjoy your trip. I hope your friend's sister will be all right."

She could almost feel the relief as Brendan

rolled up the window and eased the car between the Land Rovers before accelerating into the night.

"We've done it. Christ Brendan I was wetting myself. Stupid Brit bastards."

"That was the closest call I've ever had. I think we should get the fuck out of this business. When we get back tonight, I think we'll talk about your aunt in Germany."


While John Tully engaged the car occupants in the usual formal questions asked at a roadside VCP, Tony Betts slipped out from the hedge at the rear of the car and crawled across the road until he reached under the boot.

From a pocket in his flak jacket he removed a small black box and a lump of putty-like substance, which he pressed against the petrol tank. Then he fixed the box into the putty and carefully burrowed a hole on either side using two short wires. Finally, he flicked a switch on the outer casing of the box and crawled back to his place of concealment in the hedge.

As the car lights disappeared around the corner at the end of the straight, the soldiers at the roadstop were galvanised into action. Both Land Rovers were hurriedly loaded up and Tully jumped into the rear of one of the vehicles. He picked up the handset on the mobile RT.

"Clear at this end."

"Ready here."

He turned to his left and said sharply: "Hit it."

Without a flicker of emotion, Betts nodded an acknowledgment before moving his hand fractionally across the top of the aluminium case on his lap. His index finger pressed down on a small red switch and all eyes in the Land Rover turned towards the distant horizon where a bright orange glow was already lighting the night skyline followed by a sharper, more intense yellowing.

A few seconds later, the noise of the double explosion reached the ears of the huddled group of soldiers and sparked off a spontaneous chorus of cheering.

Betts leaned forward in his seat. "All right, that'll do. Let's get out of here. Looks like that sick sister won't be getting any visitors tonight."

Alan Doyle was back in his favourite environment. Face-darkened and wearing his all-purpose action suit, he was garden hopping in the centre of the Falls Road, the IRA heartland of Belfast.

He was dropped at 3am from a car at a small park close to the Royal Victoria Hospital, making his way through Waterford Street and into Clonard Street. The incessant rain and gloomy night sky kept all eyes indoors, but even in this deserted dusk he took no chances.

It was slow going, crawling through hedges and hand-leaping walls. Every ten minutes he stopped to check with a pencil torch the map concealed under his jacket. It was no ordinary map, and Doyle looked particularly at the little one-inch square colour photographs to check his progress towards the house he was seeking in Dunluce Street.

Finally, he saw the street sign on the gable wall of the red-bricked building opposite. He knew the time had come to break cover and pray no one spotted the dark figure running towards the rear of the little terraced estate.

Three cars in quick succession roared past the small hedge, which concealed him, and in the distance he could hear a dog barking. The silence returned, and he raised his head above the level of the hedge to check his surroundings.

His eyes focused on a shadow beside a doorway of a house a hundred yards away. He reached inside his coat pocket for the night-vision binoculars. He adjusted the sights to discover a large overhanging garden tree swinging in the breeze, and then suddenly his position was awash with a shaft of light.

He immediately dropped down on his belly.

Behind him the door of a house, not twenty paces from his position, had opened. Doyle was aching with the temptation to move his head to catch a glimpse of the intruder, but he knew better. The shaft of light seemed to spread across his entire body and, as the seconds ticked off, he knew he would be spotted.

Then the silence was interrupted. "It's coming down cats and dogs," said a voice at the doorway to no one in particular. This was followed by the clinking sound of empty milk bottles on the step, and almost immediately the shaft of light grew smaller and the door closed with what seemed an unusually loud bang.

Doyle waited a full two minutes before turning to raise his head once again above the level of the hedge to recheck the roadway. Satisfied all was well, he leapt to his feet and bounded noiselessly across the wet tarmac, flattening himself against a three-foot high wall at the entrance to the back alley of a row of terraced houses.

He inched his way down the darkened corridor,

meticulously checking for dustbins and other obstacles in his path. He counted off the green coloured doors leading to the backyards of each of the houses. At the seventh door he stopped, checked up and down the alley, and nervously squeezed the rickety latch.

It gave way under his pressure and he pushed it open. The creaking of the dilapidated hinges sent waves of panic surging through him. He stopped the forward motion to peer through the six-inch crack he had created.

A dim interior light and the sound of a radio told him the house was occupied. He could see no shadows at any of the windows and pushed his way smartly into the yard.

He stood immobile for three minutes, allowing his eyes to become accustomed to the new darkness, and to seek out the entire contents of the yard. He crossed a small patio area at a crouch and knelt beside the back door to listen for any movement within the house. As he knelt, his eyes fixed on two window flower boxes.

He dipped inside his jacket and removed the flat listening device, raising himself from his crouch until his eyes were flush with the top of one of the boxes. He pushed back the damp soil and slipped the device into the hole he created, before carefully replacing the soil.

Back in the alley he allowed himself a deep breath and returned to the wall at the entrance. He knew that was the easy part. It would be much more difficult to crawl unnoticed to the front garden to place the second of his bugs. It took exactly fifty-five minutes to manoeuvre through hedges and over walls to reach his destination barely one hundred and fifty yards from the entrance to the alley. He risked nothing, lying for long periods when he heard any noises that threatened his safety.

Two teenage girls gave him his biggest fright as they walked past his wall and stopped within touching distance while one told of her sex conquest the night before with a redheaded youth called Charlie, who picked her up at a disco in Beechmount.

Doyle waited long after the footsteps faded from his hearing before continuing on his way. Eventually he crawled through three strands of broken wire, which separated the gardens of numbers six and seven.

By now he was aching all over. His fingers, numbed by the long exposure to the cold, were barely able to retrieve the second listening device from his jacket. This time he worked slowly and awkwardly. He attached the device under the wheel arch of a car parked in the driveway and retraced his steps to the generous cover afforded by an over-grown bush in the corner of number five.

He peered at his wristwatch and stiffened as he saw he was already overdue at the pick-up point. He had allowed two hours for the operation - his back-up crew were under strict instructions to vacate the area if he had not returned by 0500. He had now less than twelve minutes to make the hospital rendezvous.

He knew that to be stranded in the Clonard area would be a certain death sentence.

He would have to throw caution to the wind, but even then it would need an Olympic-style sprint down the streets to meet the schedule. A black bicycle, propped up against a wall leading to one of the houses, provided Doyle with his escape route.

If anyone saw the strange black figure hurtling at breakneck speed down the hill towards the Royal Victoria Hospital, they would have sounded mad trying to explain it to their friends.

Legs stuck out from either side of the bike, Doyle whooped and hollered like a teenager oblivious to the world around him. He careered through intersections, thankfully free from night-time traffic, and jumped off the bicycle when he spotted his pick-up idling just inside the hospital entrance road. The bike continued under its own volition before crashing heavily into the brick wall of an old building.

Doyle dove into the back of the waiting car and couldn't stop laughing on the journey back to Bishopscourt.


Fifty miles from Doyle's location, a lonely figure carrying a large rucksack on his back, slipped off the main Drogheda to Dublin Road and was immediately lost to sight by large copses of trees that straddled the hillsides around the A25. He was dropped from an unmarked car close to his present location and began his trek to a vantage point high in the remote hillside.

Twenty minutes later, John Tully crested a ridge and peered down the other side of the small mountain towards open farmland, dotted only by a few homes that would have been expensive to acquire in these upmarket surroundings.

He dropped his rucksack on the ground and removed a night-vision sniper scope from one of the many pockets built into his combat jacket. After adjusting the lens and sweeping the area, he homed in on his target, a single storey ranch-style bungalow with twin garages fed by a sweeping tarmac driveway that afforded access to a private roadway beyond.

From another pocket he slipped out a hazy aerial reconnaissance photograph, showing a design exact in every detail to the picture he had just studied through his green-tinted lens. He double-checked all the terrain features around the site. Satisfied he was on target, he began his preparations.

He walked back and forth for about a hundred yards and decided on a vantage point, which afforded him the sightlines he needed. He unrolled a ground blanket, a double-width sleeping bag and camouflage netting, and started to prepare his weapon.

He unfolded the tripod of a Barrett M90 rifle and pushed it into the soft earth. The weapon was an American-made piece of bolt-action armoury that came with a Phantom 4x60 night vision lens. When the parts and components were tightly screwed into place, he swivelled the barrel towards the building far below his position.

There would be time to check distances and precision in the morning.

Several lights shone from windows to the front of the house, and a Range Rover was parked beside a garage near the front door. The owner of both the vehicle and the home was in residence and - if the Intel was good - he would remain there until 7am the next morning when he left to oversee the various nefarious projects he was involved in on both sides of the Irish border.

Tully checked his watch. Five hours to go and nothing to do but wait. He pushed a small earpiece into position and plugged it into a small alarm clock tucked into yet another pocket of his coat. After munching on a power biscuit and taking a drink of water from a canteen, he settled down to sleep.

Despite what was ahead of him these were nerveless periods for the unflappable ex-para, and within minutes he was dozing.

The vibration in the earpiece brought him instantly to his senses at 6.30am. He stood and stretched the weariness out of his muscles and then relieved himself behind a small bush. He returned to his nest and started his calibrations by sharpening the lens on the front door of the house and reading off the yardage from a gauge running down the side of the screen.

Precisely 603 yards to the front doorbell, which was faintly illuminated by its interior light.

It was an almost airless morning so he would not have to factor in much for windage deviation. The rate of descent of the .50 BMG round would need a variable, which he judged to be about two feet higher than the target area.

The time ticked off towards 7am and he was now on high alert. There had been movement in the house for the past twenty minutes, judging by the number of lights switching on and off.

At 7.05am the front door opened.

Tully watched dispassionately as a man in a dark overcoat stood talking in the doorway to a slightly built woman, who reached up to kiss him on the cheek before returning inside and closing the door. As the man walked to his car, he was tracked all the way by Tully.

The figure below stopped to open the driver's door. High above him Tully's finger squeezed the trigger of the high-powered rifle, releasing its deadly load.

The bullet screamed across the gulf between the two men at a rate of five hundred feet per second, and by the time it obliterated the man's head, the sound of its discharge was still following behind.

Tully calmly began to disassemble the weapon and repack all his detritus, including the shell casing, which he ejected from the breach. Slinging the rucksack over his shoulder, he retraced his path back over the mountain and towards the waiting pick-up on the other side.

By the time he crossed the border back into the North thirty-five minutes later, the first response cars of the *Garda Siochana*, the police force of the Irish Republic, had just arrived at the scene of the murder of one Tommy Boyle, a known high-ranking IRA activist involved in drugs and gun-running.

The first impression of the senior detective in charge of the scene, was that this was the result of factional infighting between the IRA and known Eastern European gangs, who were trying to muscle into the Irish drugs scene. Then again, he thought, it could be a cleaning-house operation by the IRA themselves.

Nothing that would happen in the days ahead would change his opinion, particularly in light of some well-placed disinformation that emanated from Bishopscourt.

# Chapter 11
## Saintfield, County Down

THE TWO IRA VOLUNTEERS driving along the main road from Belfast to the small dormitory town of Saintfield had no idea they were being tailed. Kevin O'Brien and Jim Perry were not exactly blessed with smarts, but they were committed recruits, and were kept busy with a number of fetch-and-carry jobs since their enlistment into the Belfast Brigade from the riots of Short Strand almost four years ago.

Tonight they were transporting a number of handguns and ten pounds of Semtex explosive to a storage bunker in a remote farm belonging to a sympathiser, who didn't mind doing his bit for the cause, just so long as he got on with his own life attending to a small herd of Friesians that would never provide him with a viable dairy business.

The brown envelopes of cash left behind a milk churn every few months, helped keep his head above water.

It was a typical IRA set-up. Equipment was always being moved around. With new shipments coming in regularly from the continent, they needed arms dumps in the most unlikely spots, remote in all respects from the efforts of the RUC to locate them.

At any one time this huge arsenal, dotted around in sites such as the Saintfield farm, amounted to over 20,000 handguns, sub-machine guns, mortars, RPGs, and the more specialised sniper rifles. Add to that an almost endless supply of fertiliser bombs and two ground-to-air missile launchers, and it was easy to understand why they had grown to become the world's leading terror organisation, as much in terms of logistics as in the training skills, and dedication of its membership.

The Saintfield farm dump was in operation for almost ten years. Despite its remoteness in rural County Down, the short travelling distance to Belfast made it one of the IRA's most prized assets. At any one time, almost a quarter of the Belfast Brigade's entire weaponry was hidden beneath the concrete flooring of the large barn that had fallen into dilapidation because of lack of investment by the owner.

Two old and broken down Massey Ferguson tractors joined with an assortment of defunct farm equipment, and putrefying straw bales to litter almost the entire floor area, providing natural camouflage to the riches below the surface.

O'Brien and Perry had made the journey many times without incident. It was just their bad luck that tonight they were being followed. Their names had come out of the hat as worthy of surveillance, and O'Brien had made it too easy for his pursuers. It was known that among his habits, he always had a teatime tipple at Cliftonville Golf Club. His car was parked as usual along the tree-lined avenue outside the club and it had taken only twenty seconds to fit a listening device under the front passenger wheel arch.


Two cars back, Mike Devon and Mark Webber settled into the specially converted Austin Rover Maestro, with Webber cradling a small opened suitcase on his lap.

Devon tailed O'Brien for twenty minutes after leaving the golf club car park. They crossed the city towards Ballysillan, the car ahead stopping at the corner of Silverstream Park, where a man in his forties crossed the road and climbed in. The car sped off down the Crumlin Road and emerged onto the Ormeau Road on its route towards Saintfield.

Devon knew the passenger was James "The Snake" Perry, a long-time friend of O'Brien's, who was often to be seen in the company of the younger man. As the convoy exited onto the quieter Saintfield Road, the conversation so far had revealed little. Devon had almost given up hope when the static was broken.

"Have you heard anything more about what happened to Kelly? The boys are saying there must be a tout about."

"Yeah, there's no way the RUC just happened to be in the neighbourhood, but why the fuck didn't they nail him before he got to that bastard Billy Young?"

The names being mentioned piqued Devon's interest. This was the shooting covered by Alan Doyle, who had let the IRA gunman complete his job before handing him over for execution to an RUC patrol.

A voice broke in again on the transceiver on Webber's lap.

"The guess is that Kelly made a balls-up of the stake-out and somebody got suspicious. The cops must have wet themselves when they arrived for a routine check and saw John Wayne walking up the street trying to do an OK Corral."

Silence for a moment and then: "That's what we

can't understand. He must have heard them coming and had time to hide, and anyway the kid on the bike said it must have been at least five minutes from the time of the shots until he heard the police sirens."

"I think we can forget about the kid. The boys reckon he did a runner and now he's minus two kneecaps."

"If they'd left it to me, I'd have cut his cock off and shoved it down his mouth."

Silence again, this time for about three minutes. The sound of a match being struck, and a few loud sighs were all that filtered through the suitcase receiver. Finally, the voices started up again.

"Let's get rid of these guns and explosives and get back to the social club to hear what's happening."

"Doubt there'll be much happening. Everything's gone noticeably quiet over the past few days. I think everyone's getting jumpy."

The car ahead turned off the main road and two miles later, it took another turn through a gap in a large, overgrown roadside hedge.

Devon watched the headlights disappear into what appeared to be a small laneway running towards farm buildings. He pulled over to the side of the road, threw the gearstick into neutral, and pulled on the handbrake.

"Slide over and take the wheel, Mark. Drive beyond the entrance and wait for my signal."

Without waiting for a response, he pushed open the door and sprinted across the road to scramble through the nearest opening he could find in the hedge.

On the other side a large grazing field stretched before him, and he broke into an all-out run towards the top of a hill. He could see the lights from

O'Brien's car play across the rust-covered, galvanised roof of a barn. He stopped beside a small rickety gate, stuck his head over the top, and checked his bearings.

The farmyard was less than two hundred yards away, but the lights from the buildings threw the laneway into silhouette. He would have to stick to the field.

As he followed the line of the laneway, he spoke into his throat microphone: "Mark, can you hear me? What's happening?"

"Nothing, Skip. Both car doors opened and closed a few minutes ago and they must still be away from it. Everything's been quiet since."

Devon continued creeping towards the farmyard. At a gap in the hedge, he withdrew a pair of binoculars and scanned directly into the barn. He could see two figures kneeling on the floor in front of an old tractor. He knew immediately what he had to do.

Stuffing the binos back into this coat, he withdrew a Glock 17 from his waistband and made for the barn entrance. He could hear murmurings coming from the direction of the two figures and eased his way silently into the interior. Using the tractor as a screen, he crept towards the two figures, and then stood with the pistol aimed directly at his targets ten feet in front.

"Mr O'Brien and Mr Perry, I presume," he whispered at them.

Both men spun and fell backwards as if hit by a charge of electricity, both turning to look at Devon in bewilderment.

"What the...."

"Shut up. I'm holding the gun and I do the

talking."

One of the men tried to sit up, while the other continued to stare into the barrel of the pistol. Devon took one step forward.

"I'm not going to tell you again. Sit perfectly still and don't open your mouths. We're going to take a little drive and then we're going to have a nice little chat about...."

Devon was cut off in mid-sentence as the fidgety man launched himself upwards towards the gun. With a simple sidestep, Devon let his would-be assailant dive past him and then brought the butt of the gun down heavily on the back of the man's exposed head. There was a crack and crunch of bone as the man slumped lifeless to the ground.

"You've killed him, you bastard!"

Devon knelt down to place the barrel of the Glock against the other man's ear.

"I very much doubt it, and didn't I tell you to keep quiet?" he asked evenly. "Now be a good boy and roll over on your stomach with your hands behind your head."

Then Devon spoke again into his microphone. "Mark, bring the car into the barn, we've got a couple of passengers for transportation."

Fifteen minutes later he was on the way back to Bishopscourt. The unconscious man was O'Brien, according to his talkative partner, and was trussed up and lying in the boot of Webber's car, while Perry was behind the wheel of his own car tamely obeying Devon's instructions. The fact that he had a Glock pushed into the bottom of his neck probably helped.

Webber had radioed ahead, and by the time the convoy arrived at the base thirty-five minutes later, there was a reception committee waiting for them.

Devon barked out instructions. "Take these two to separate bunker rooms and get the doc to take a look at our friend with the headache. I want them kept in isolation, with no food or drink until tomorrow morning."

He stopped himself as he turned to leave.

"Mark, get onto the RUC confidential phoneline and let them know about that arms dump in Saintfield. It's no good to us and the boys in blue might as well have a bit of glory. We've got what we want."

Five minutes later he listened as Mark Webber spoke into a telephone console in the main operations room. The call he was making would be routed through more than a dozen exchanges, with no hope of a trace.

In his best Ulster brogue Webber relayed the message:

*I have information about an IRA arms dump. There are all kinds of guns and explosives hidden on a farm at 427 Dalmellington Road, Saintfield. You might want to look under the floor in the main barn. That's all I can tell you.*

As soon as the connection was cut, Devon turned his attention to Alan Doyle.

"Looks like things are really on the move."

"What do you want to do with our guests?"

Devon knew he didn't have the time or patience for a drawn out interrogation. "We'll work on them tomorrow, but if we don't get anywhere, we'll go to plan B tomorrow night."

The noise of the helicopter was almost deafening as

Jim Perry was led out of the underground bunker, his head covered by a smelly, stained sack. He felt the gravel beneath his feet as he was pushed towards the claxon sound of the rotors. He was then bundled into the interior of the beast and made to lay on the floor, aware from the sound of voices that he was surrounded by, at least five other people.

A door slid across, blocking out the worst of the cacophony. He felt his stomach go light as the machine lifted off the ground.

Five minutes later the makeshift hood was pulled from his head. Kevin O'Brien was wedged on the floor beside him, and the face-blackened figures of four soldiers were seated on a bench opposite.

One of the soldiers rose and lifted a large duffle bag from which he started to extract a long chain.

The soldier pointed at O'Brien. "We'll start with you."

Perry watched as the soldier started to wrap the chain around O'Brien's torso. At first, he thought nothing about it, but became concerned as the chain continued to encircle O'Brien's body, down over his hips and thighs, then around his legs and ankles.

He noticed O'Brien was sharing his sense of foreboding. His friend's face was a mask of fear and he began wriggling against his metal bonds.

"What's going on, what's this for?"

The soldier ignored O'Brien's words and withdrew two large locks that he used to secure the chain tightly at two strategic points, one at O'Brien's midsection and the other around his ankles. Already attached to each lock were small weights, flat brown discs that Perry knew were commonly seen alongside scales in a greengrocer's shop.

Perry watched the soldier return to his seat,

smiling at his trussed-up friend as if admiring his handiwork.

Then another soldier, the man who had captured him the night before, leaned forward to talk to O'Brien.

"You're about to take a trip down to the Irish Sea. We've tried to get you to give us the information we need, but it's clear you want to play hardball. Well you won't be the first, and there'll be others after you're gone. I'm done wasting time. Either start talking or make your peace with your maker."

Perry willed O'Brien to co-operate, but nothing doing.

"You're bluffing, you wouldn't dare. We've got rights. I want to see a lawyer."

O'Brien's words caused a chorus of laughter among the soldiers. They all looked at each other before one of them rose and grabbed O'Brien roughly round the shoulders and hauled him to his feet like a rag doll.

Perry was getting a bad feeling about what was going to happen next. He heard the soldier shout into O'Brien's ear.

"I was hoping you'd say that. The thing is, we're almost two thousand feet up and I'm looking forward to seeing how you hard bastards fly. The good news is that there's nothing but water below; the bad news is that by the time you hit the surface you'll be travelling at almost two hundred miles per second. The impact will smash you up like a china doll and, when you sink to the bottom, the sharks can enjoy a midnight feast."

Another man got off the bench and began sliding the door back on its runner. The sudden inrush of wind and noise took Perry by surprise.

"Move him forward."

Perry watched open-mouthed as his friend was bundled to the doorway.

"Are you sure you've still nothing to say?"

"You'll get nothing from me."

The two men appeared to shrug at each other, before stepping around to stand behind O'Brien.

*Oh, Christ, they're going to do it!*

Perry was aware of a growing tightness in his chest. He could hardly breathe as he watched the events unfold.

The taller of the two soldiers pushed hard against O'Brien's back, sending him hurtling out into space. Perry covered his face with his hands in a futile attempt to block out the sickening sight he had just witnessed. Then one of the men closed the door and all eyes seemed to bore into him. He heard words he didn't want to hear.

"Now for the other one."

He curled into a ball as he watched a soldier pull another length of chain from the sack. Something snapped inside him.

"No, no, please don't kill me." As the words came out, he was aware of a warm liquid running between his legs.

"The bastard's wet himself!"

Perry tried to squirm away from the soldier with the chain but knew it would be hopeless.

Then he became aware of another voice, this time a tinny, hollow sound erupting from the helicopter intercom:

"Skip, we've got incoming on our flightpath. We have to descend immediately and return to base."

"Fuck it! Okay boys, we'll have to wrap this up for the night."

It took a while for Perry to understand what was happening. Could he dare to believe he had just been reprieved?

He was aware that one of the soldiers was bent over him and whispering in his ear.

"Don't worry, old son. We'll do this again tomorrow night and next time, you won't be so lucky."

The helicopter banked to the south and landed on the marked-out square within the compound. Devon waited until the engine died and the rotors stopped spinning before opening the doors and issuing orders.

"Take this piece of shit back to his cell."

He watched with a smile as Doyle and Betts dragged the prisoner across waste ground to the underground block. On the trip back he had noticed that Perry hadn't uttered a word, withdrawing into a trance-like state, brought on no doubt by fear and shock.

Just the way he wanted him.

Having spent the previous day grilling both prisoners for hours on end, Devon had concluded O'Brien was the stronger of the two, and least likely to give up information. Whilst O'Brien exuded the confidence of a prisoner of war, demanding rights that he could later wear like a badge of honour, Perry was more a street runner, expansive in his bravado only in the company of more steely men.

Alone he would be a different story and tonight's little show was to nudge Perry closer to cracking.

What Perry didn't know was that O'Brien had not been shoved to his death by the ignominious exit from the chopper. Devon had arranged for the machine to not climb above two hundred feet and for a safety net to be strung between the landing arms to halt O'Brien's staged execution.

He knew that as the chopper settled close to the ground, O'Brien was hauled from the net and whisked away to his own private cell in a separate block before the team had alighted.

There was, of course, no other aircraft in the vicinity at the time of the escapade. The radio chatter was devised by Devon as a ruse to make Perry feel he had been lucky, at least for the time being.

From the moment they picked up both men, there was no doubt in Devon's mind that neither would return to their lives. These bastards wanted a war and now they were getting it. He would milk both of them for everything they knew, and after tonight's brush with death, he had little doubt that both would be extremely talkative.

The following day he left Perry alone in his cell, and at 6.30pm, two hours after darkness fell across the Bishopscourt base, he entered the room with Doyle and Betts. A sack was dumped on the floor with enough force to ensure its contents made a heavy, metallic sound.

Devon stepped forward holding a black hood.

"Time to go for another ride."

"Wait, wait... I'll talk, I'll tell you what I know."

Twenty minutes later Devon entered O'Brien's cell across the compound and pulled up a stool beside the flimsy army cot where the IRA man lay staring up at the ceiling.

"I'll get straight to the point. We put on that little show last night to force one of you to talk. Now we've got what we wanted. Your friend is singing like a canary and we don't need you. You can either join in or we'll execute you. We will repeat what we did last night, but this time you will be dumped at sea. I've no more time to waste. It's up to you."

Devon noted the change in his prisoner straightaway. Unlike the previous evening, there was no shouting or yelling. He continued to stare at the ceiling for almost a minute and then turned to Devon.

"What guarantees do I have that you won't kill me if I tell you what I know?"

Devon stood up and walked back to the door.

"There are no guarantees, but I will tell you this. If you talk you will be treated well, and you will be with us for quite a while as we find things out and ask you to explain them to us. We'll start later today."

# Chapter 12
## RUC Headquarters

HOME FOR THE ROYAL Ulster Constabulary was in the heart of South Belfast. The administrative headquarters was an imposing series of high-tech office blocks in the money-belt area of Knock. This was the force's public face, one that provided a veneer of normal policing activities.

But across the city, in less salubrious surroundings at Castlereagh, was an anti-terrorist operation that dealt with the realities of a vicious guerrilla war.

Hundreds of men and women, picked up for questioning on terrorist-related matters, found themselves within its chilling walls, knowing that normal arrest and interrogation protocols were parked at the door,

On the third floor, high above the warren of underground cells and detention rooms all ominously soundproofed, sat the office of the man who ran the biggest operation of its type in Europe. As always, he was behind his desk.

Detective Chief Superintendent Billy Carter was running down the retirement clock, but he had never known things so bad. He started on the beat and had been through many ups and downs during his twenty-eight years with the force. Things were a lot different now than when he checked lock-up shops in those early days in his native Portadown.

His roots were in Protestant Ulster, a staunch supporter of the union with Great Britain, and a convert to the Free Presbyterianism created by Ian Paisley. Historically and religiously, Carter shared common ground with most of his fellow countrymen – but he differed greatly when it came down to politics.

He knew Ulster's problems could not be solved by a stroke of the pen. Until Protestants and Catholics could live together, each with their own legitimate aims, there would be no future. He determined a long time ago to work towards that goal, hopeless though at times it seemed.

His job was to root out the evil men from both sides and let the talkers get on with talking.

To that end, he was glad of the promotion of Martin Vennison to succeed the legendary John Turnbull, a man who got the job done, and who had ultimately paid for his many successes against the Provisional IRA. The youthful Detective Chief Inspector Vennison shared Turnbull's drive and commitment and had already made impressive returns on the faith that was shown in him.

The two now faced each other across the desk – the wily old campaigner and the young blood that had now become his right arm.

"Martin, I've been reading the reports on the Billy Young shooting and things just don't add up."

The younger man held the stare of his superior.

"Sir, we have firmly established there was another man at the scene. The footprints and markings in the soil tell us a lot, but there are more questions than answers. If this other man was with the shooter, Kelly, he got clean away on an easy escape to the rear of the house. So why didn't Kelly go with him? Why did he run out in the middle of the road in a hopeless shoot-out situation? There's something funny going on."

Carter rose and walked to a noticeboard covered with photographs of the scene of the shooting in Falstaff Avenue.

"Has anyone come up with a feasible explanation as to why Kelly remained at the scene for so long after the shooting?"

"Two of the Scenes of Crime boys think that maybe Kelly was on the job with a look-out and for some reason, this mystery man detained Kelly behind the wall of the house next door until we arrived."

"But what possible motive could there be in that, Martin?"

"It could be that Kelly blotted his copybook with the Provos, but they just couldn't bump him off themselves. He was one of their main recruitment officers and was well liked. I know it's a bit thin, and I certainly don't buy it, but at least it fits."

Carter went back to his desk and opened a file folder.

"It's thin all right. You know the Provos, and you know they're hardly likely to do us any favours. Why should they give us credit for topping one of their bright boys, even if he had turned bad on them? No, we're going to have to do better than that."

He lifted a single sheet from the folder and passed it across to Vennison. "And here's another thing that doesn't add up."

"What is it, sir?"

"Came in late last night, another anonymous tip-off, this time about an arms dump in Saintfield. We did a raid first thing this morning and hit the jackpot. Everything's become too pat in the last few weeks."

"I don't understand."

"Up until three weeks ago we were bogged down. Now in that short space of time we have incidents where IRA volunteers blow themselves to bits, we stumble into a gunman leaving the scene of a murder five minutes after it happens, and we get a watertight tip-off about a respected farmer who seems to be a one-man bloody arsenal dump."

As an afterthought he added: "All that, of course, could just be a coincidence, but I had a team working through the night on the confidential telephone message about the incident. It turns out there's a striking similarity between that message and a host of other messages we have been receiving for the past few months on minor things."

"You mean those messages we discussed last month when we reckoned we had a telephone supergrass on our hands?"

Carter's eyes went back to the file.

"Each of those messages had a kind of clipped efficiency about them. No superfluous details, no pauses, and the most telling factor were the voices. Out of the thirty-eight messages we have assessed as coming from the same source, we have identified five different voices, and all of them with a phoney Northern Irish accent."

This time Vennison rose and walked across the room.

"I'm frankly baffled. Is there another police force out there doing our job for us?"

"That may not be as crazy as it sounds, Martin. I'm convinced somebody is networking a campaign against the Provos. These tip-offs and incidents are stretching too far to be the work of some isolated renegade, and anyway whoever it is seems to be plugging into all the right sources. Is it possible that some of the other Republican factions have got it in for the glory boys of the Provisionals?"

"Sir, there's no love lost between the Provos and the Irish National Liberation Army, but the word is they're trying to agree on a split of territories between them. Anyway, like you said, we're the common enemy and they're not going to do anything to help us."

"Well, do you think any of the loyalist mobs have suddenly got a bit of organisation and decided to give us a friendly hand?"

Vennison smiled. "The Ulster Defence Association is afraid to leave their East Belfast stronghold. Then we have the Ulster Freedom Fighters and the Ulster Volunteer Force who, frankly, are all bluster and no brains. Even if it were possible that any of them were behind this, they would be shouting from the rooftops and holding press conferences every hour to let the world know how they are defending Ulster. I'm afraid we'll have to look in another direction."

Carter nodded an acknowledgement and leaned back on his expensive swivel chair. He had thrown his thoughts at Vennison, knowing he would get the same answers and conclusions he had already drawn for himself. It gave him a warm glow to watch the progress of his young protégé and he marvelled at how both had begun to think alike.

The silence stretched to several minutes before Carter decided to set out his plans.

"Martin, I'm taking you off everything. I want to find out what the hell is going on. Take whomever you need and start wading through files. Somebody is making us look right idiots and I'm not having it.

You've got two weeks to find me the fairy godmother."

"I was hoping you would say that, sir. Can I have McDowell, Green and McCormick?"

"Certainly. Will that be enough?"

"Yes, sir. One more thing, can you get me clearance to do a thorough check through the Army computers? They don't pass us everything they hear, and it might be they missed something of significance."

Detective Sergeant George McDowell was cursing his luck. He had been told he was being brought into a new "priority red" case, and that usually meant a bit of action out on the streets instead of cooped up for hours on end, trying to get blood from a stone in the daily ritual of interrogating suspects before their inevitable release.

The heady days of the "supergrass" informers had passed, and he was back to the long hard slog of rounding up known participants, playing ping-pong with them for the fourteen days allowed under the Emergency Acts, and letting them go with no satisfaction other than having put the bastards through the hoop for two weeks of their miserable lives.

That was why McDowell had welcomed DCI Vennison's call to action of a different kind. However, after two days of monotony behind a mountain of files, his enthusiasm was beginning to wane. To make matters worse he wasn't even sure what he was looking for.

McDowell was a hard-bitten product of Northern Ireland's troubles. He had held down a detective posting on the Falls Road during the worst of the campaign in the seventies, and had survived an IRA murder bid outside his bachelor flat in the Queens's University area after ordering a black taxi to ferry him from a drinking binge in one of his favourite watering holes.

Despite the drink, he was alert enough to spot two shadowy figures walk from a side entrance as he paid the cab driver. With a practised movement he eased the service revolver out from his underarm holster and was ready when a shotgun was raised and pointed towards him.

There was no standing on ceremony, no procedural calling of identity. McDowell dropped to his knee and loosed off every round in the direction of the two assailants.

He remembered the deafening roar of the answering shotgun but felt nothing as he rolled over and over on the wet street. When he eventually lifted his head and focussed on the scene, he saw one figure already two hundred yards away running at breakneck speed down the deserted street. The man with the shotgun was lying in a bundle on the pavement.

McDowell ran to him. Watery eyes stared through the slits of a balaclava, and he could hear faint moans as the chest heaved up and down. He pulled off the hood to reveal a fair-haired youth of about eighteen, who was to die two days later at the Royal Victoria Hospital from a single bullet, which pierced his upper abdomen. The other attacker was never found.

The memory was interrupted by a voice coming from a nearby desk. He lifted his head to look at Detective Constable Maurice "Mo" Green.

"George, why are we getting so fired up about a few tip-offs? If we run this grass to ground, we could lose a bloody good source."

"Look Mo, ours is not to reason why. And anyway, I'm beginning to get intrigued about all this. That tip-off about the farmer with all the guns was quick off the mark. We know two blocks of Semtex were delivered to him on the same night we got the phone call, and yet for that kind of movement, there couldn't have been more than three or four people in the know."

"So, what are you saying?"

"It's simple. If there's a grass in that brigade he would know the timespan is narrow. So why risk getting in touch with us so soon? Another week and the finger of suspicion is much wider; doing it this way he's bound to be rumbled."

"Well, have we got a Provo grass, or haven't we?"

McDowell paused to light his pipe. "Quite definitely not. We're dealing with some-thing else, but I'm damned if I can work it out yet. Let's start at the beginning again and see if we can find something else that might link these calls. The boss is working backwards from the arms find and maybe we'll meet in the middle."

Down the corridor Vennison was with Detective Inspector Tom McCormick behind a trestle table surveying a lone figure seated on a chair in the centre of an interrogation room. The man was dressed in police-issue forensic orange-coloured coveralls that were supplied after a thorough strip-search.

In his early forties with thin greying hair and a greying beard, the man cut a pathetic figure, sitting hunched over with his knees up to his chest.

"You're in a lot of trouble, Mr Lavery," Vennison said evenly. "I'm afraid you'll be going to Long Kesh until you're a very old man. Have you decided to make a statement?"

There was no response.

"Look Lavery, we're getting a bit fed up trying to make you face up to this." McCormick had taken over the questioning. "You know it'll be ten years for possession, another five for membership in the Provos, and then we throw away the keys if any of those weapons match up to murders."

He watched the man shift in his seat.

"They asked me to rent my shed for storage. I couldn't refuse, you know what they're like. I didn't know what they were using it for."

"Come off it, Lavery. You knew who these people were. You knew their game. You're one of them, aren't you?"

"Please, I swear to you, they threatened my wife and kid, said they'd kill them if I didn't do what I was told. I'm innocent."

Vennison saw through the sham but decided to play along.

"All right Mr Lavery, when did this first start and how many times did these people visit your shed?"

"They came at Christmas two years ago, that's when it started. They've come dozens of times ever since, usually at night. They don't come to the house. We've been told to ignore what's happening and to go about our business."

"Have you ever gotten a look at any of the men?"

"No, like I said we don't watch what's happening."

"Mr Lavery, we are trying extremely hard to believe your story, but you don't expect us to swallow that? What about the men who set it all up? What were they like?"

"They were wearing hoods. They came at 2am and they seemed to be young men from their voices, but I don't know any more than that."

"Why didn't you contact the police?"

"I was frightened."

"Why do you think they picked on you?"

"I don't know. Maybe it's because my farm is isolated, and they thought no one would ever find out."

"Do you support the IRA?"

"No, no, no."

"Do you support Sinn Fein?"

"No."

"Do you want to see a united Ireland?"

"I'm not interested in politics. I just care about my family and my farm."

Vennison opened a file in front of him and withdrew a plum-coloured photo album, which he positioned between himself and Tom McCormick. The pages were turned slowly and both men seemed engrossed in their examination, leaving a deathly hush in the room. Finally, Vennison lifted his eyes towards the prisoner.

"Tell me Mr Lavery, do you remember the big Sinn Fein rally in Downpatrick last August on the anniversary of the 1976 internments?"

"Eh, vaguely. I wasn't interested in it, but I read about it in the local paper."

"Were you at the rally?"

"Absolutely not, I was working."

"Then how do you explain this?" Vennison

withdrew one of the photos from the album and passed it over the table.

The prisoner rose, crossed the room, and picked up a black and white print. Vennison noted blood draining from the face and the lean of a hand on the table, as if he were trying to steady himself.

"That is your photograph isn't it, Mr Lavery? That is *you* waving your fists at police and marching in the rally?"

"How, how the hell did you get that?"

"Never mind. The game's up isn't it, Lavery?"

Vennison had dropped the "Mr" and was hardening his voice.

"You're nothing but a dyed-in-the-wool Republican and you're in the IRA up to your neck. You can stop the play-acting and sit down."

The transformation was amazing. The prisoner smiled, straightened up and swaggered back to his chair.

"Go fuck yourself you black bastard. I'll do a possession charge standing on my head. The boys will look after the family and there's nothing you can do about it."

"Are you ready to make a statement?"

"No way! I don't have to tell you anything. I'll wait for my solicitor."

Vennison reached under the table, away from his prisoner's gaze, and pressed a small button. Time to turn the screws, he thought.

McCormick took over the questioning. "You'll have to talk sometime."

"Yeah, when I'm good and ready. You'll get nothing from me."

There was a rap on the door and a young uniformed officer walked in.

"Scuse me sir, this has arrived from the lab." He handed a file cover to Vennison and walked out without glancing at the prisoner.

Vennison opened the cover and began to read a traffic accident report, which had been lying on one of the piles in the outer office. It was a standard ploy. The file didn't matter, but he always wondered why it was accident statements, which were brought in posing as forensic reports. He passed the document over to McCormick and waited until he finished reading before again addressing the prisoner.

"Lavery, we have just matched up two semi-automatic pistols taken from your shed with the murder of two policemen in Newry three months ago. We're playing for real now."

The prisoner's smile faded.

"You're bluffing, you don't have…"

Vennison jumped to his feet and shouted across the room.

"Shut the fuck up. You were complicit in the murder of two of our colleagues and I'm going to see you pay for it. All deals are off. You're going to a black hole and I'll make sure you never see the light of day again. You can forget about your family and your farm. By the time our crime scene boys finish with tearing up your house and sheds, there'll be nothing left. Your bank accounts will be frozen and the RSPCA will be directed to seize your livestock. You're out of business, and your wife and daughter will have nothing to live on. If you think the Provos will bankroll the rest of their lives you're delusional."

Turning to McCormick, Vennison handed over the file.

"Charge him Inspector and then get him the fuck out of my sight."

Tom McCormick rose to tower over the prisoner.

"Michael John Lavery, I hereby arrest you for the double murder and conspiracy to murder Reserve Constable Thomas Patterson and Inspector Patrick Noble at Newry in the County of Down on...."

"Wait, wait! You can't do this. I didn't know! I swear to fuck, I didn't know. I'll tell you what I can, but you have to help me. Those bastards will kill me!"

Vennison watched tears stream down Lavery's face. He spoke through gritted teeth, trying to make it appear the words were hard to come by.

"You'll get one chance and one chance only. If you tell us everything we need to know we might be able to do something but cross me just once and I'll throw the book at you and your family."

# Chapter 13
## Belfast Housing Estate

THREE RUC LAND Rovers were in position at exactly 5.30am, one at the corner of Springfield Road, one at the rear of Clonard Gardens, and one at the head of Cupar Street.

Vennison was in the first of four Ford Cortinas, which swept up the Falls Road, left onto Springmartin and into St. Patrick's Terrace. The tyres screeched as the driver hit the brakes outside the third house. The cars' occupants poured out in a carefully rehearsed move, two plainclothed men breaking left and right to take up crouching positions on the pavement, checking for movement behind the curtained windows of the run-down terraced block.

Altogether eight men squeezed through the gate and up the narrow path at full stride to the front door. The manoeuvre was being repeated at the rear of the house.

A burly sergeant swung a heavy industrial hammer at the flimsy door lock, which surrendered easily under the single blow. The door was pushed back and the invaders rushed in. Vennison led them up the stairs as the back door gave way and more men rushed in to check the downstairs rooms.

The first door at the top of the stairs was yanked open to reveal an untidy broom cupboard, the second door led to a small walk-in toilet. Ahead, Vennison could see Mo Green pointing through an open door and then rush in. He sprinted after him and was in time to see a bare-chested Pat Duggan sit bolt upright on the bed, rub the sleep from his eyes, and stare incredulously at the strangers in his room.

Green grabbed Duggan by the arm and yanked him onto the floor. Not a word was spoken. Duggan curled up in a ball, his hands trying to cover his genitals from the glares of the policemen.

There was a movement on the bed and then the head of a small, good-looking woman emerged over the top of the sheets. Incredibly, she had slept through the commotion and now, as she took in what was happening, she broke into a hysterical scream.

Vennison walked to the edge of the bed.

"Don't be alarmed, Mrs Duggan. We are police officers and we are taking your husband in for questioning in connection with serious crimes. He will be taken to Castlereagh Holding Centre and if...."

"Bastards, you can't do that. He hasn't done anything!" Suddenly the screaming had stopped.

Pat Duggan turned his head towards his wife. "Don't worry Molly, I'll be all right. Get me some clothes."

Molly Duggan hesitated and then flung back the sheets to show she was wearing only a flimsy pair of panties. Vennison rushed to the door and grabbed a man's dressing gown, which was draped over the inside handle. He handed it to the woman. "I'm sorry about this," he said sympathetically.

Without responding, she wrapped herself in the gown, climbed from the bed, and pushed past Vennison. At a small built-in wardrobe, she gathered various items of clothes and retraced her steps towards her husband, who was still huddled on the floor. She helped him dress, stopping every so often to caress his hair and kiss him lightly on the cheek.

When it was finished, Green stepped forward

with a pair of handcuffs, locking Duggan into one side and himself into the other. Throughout the house a team of other policemen were emptying the contents of drawers and containers into large black bags. There was no time for searching. Everything went into the bags.

When an all-clear was given, the group emerged onto the street, less than five minutes after they had entered Duggan's home. There were already several opened doorways at other houses, and room lights were going on every few seconds. But as yet, no sizeable crowd had gathered. This was what Vennison had wanted: in and out and no unruly mob to deal with.

As he slumped in the rear of the car ferrying him back to Castlereagh, Vennison reflected on a job well done. The Saintfield farmer had been co-operative, and after a detailed follow-up interrogation, he had picked out Duggan from a series of mugshots as the man who had requisitioned his farm shed.

Another link in the chain had been exposed, but Vennison knew Duggan would be considerably less forthcoming than the farmer, even if they could tie him directly to the arms find.

But that could wait for another day.


"This is odd," George McDowell said more to himself than DC Maurice Green, who was sitting at the end of the long trestle table they were sharing to pour through a mountain of files and loose document sheets.

"What's odd?"

"We need to check if any Army patrols were operating in the area the night those two IRA volunteers blew themselves up in the car bomb on the Newry Road. We'll ring the two closest bases and then try Lisburn GHQ but make it low key. Give them the old tying-up-loose-ends bit, we're just wondering if by chance etcetera, etcetera. Don't sound too official or anxious."

Mo Green looked quizzically at his colleague. "What am I hoping to be told?"

"Unless I miss my guess, there were no patrols within a million miles of the scene."

"I'm sorry George, but you've lost me."

"I've come across an interesting report from the CID team who were in charge at that end. The following afternoon there was a "did-you-see-any-thing-suspicious" uniformed Vehicle Checkpoint. They talked to a Dublin businessman on his way back from an overnight stop, and he told them he had been waved through an Army VCP near the scene of the explosion the previous night."

"Keep going. I'm all ears."

"I've checked the approximate times, and if this punter is right, then there was an Army presence in the area within ten minutes of the explosion, yet the boys in khaki green aren't letting on about it. And we have no records of having been given prior notice of any VCPs, as is required by protocol agreed between the Chief Constable and the GOC."

McDowell was aware Green was scratching his head.

"What's a GOC?"

"Jeez Mo. You need to get out more. The General Officer Commanding the Army in Northern Ireland.

"So, the records show there was no VCP, the Army has confirmed there was no VCP, and yet we are accepting an eyewitness account that there was. What if the eyewitness was simply wrong and he just mixed his dates up?"

"I can't buy that," McDowell told him. "This was the following day and the man had made only a one-night stopover in Belfast. How could he have been confused?"

"What are you saying? Let's suppose there was a VCP, what does that tell us?"

"Ah, that is the sixty-four thousand dollar question. Let's get the feedback and take this up with the boss." Twenty minutes later, McDowell joined Vennison and McCormick at a small boardroom-type table in Vennison's office. He moved over to a small wall-mounted wipeboard and began to scribble several key headings.

"The first piece in this jigsaw concerns whether or not there was an Army VCP on the Newry Road at or near the time of the explosion, which killed two IRA volunteers. The Army says no, and we appear to have a credible witness who says yes. What do we make of it?"

Without waiting for a response, McDowell continued.

"Don't ask me why, but I think the Army is lying. When I called them for verification, I got the run-around. It should have been a straightforward matter for them to confirm or deny, but I was transferred constantly up the line until I got to their security liaison officer, Mark Garrett. He said he had no knowledge of a patrol but would check and let us know what he finds when he meets with the Chief Super for a regular briefing tomorrow."

When he finished, he watched Vennison put down the report and move to a wipeboard where he wrote the words *Army VCP* inside a bubble circle. Then he turned back to his colleagues.

"And now we come to another piece of startling information. I asked forensics to do a rerun through the wreckage of the Newry explosion and to consider what would happen if an explosive device had been placed on the exterior of the car. I've gotten back a lot of jargon about implosions and explosions. There was hardly anything left of that car to work with, and so it's all theory and inconclusive, but the bottom line is it could have happened that way...."

McDowell was about to say something but thought better of interrupting the briefing.

"Apparently, they did discover some pieces of metal, which had been subjected to a different kind of explosion than other parts. At first, they assumed the bombers were carrying several different kinds of bombs, with at least two separate timing devices. It's not unusual for the Provos to haul several homemade bundles for different targets. Anyway, one piece of metal near the petrol tank appears to have been blown inwards rather than outwards, which would support the theory about a device on the outside of the car. However, it is pointed out that with a number of unstable explosive packages they tend to go off at different intervals and so one explosion could blow the bottom out of a car while a follow-up, triggered by the first detonation, could act on the fragments in an inverted way."

"So, what do we know for sure?" McDowell asked.

"I know it's a bit muddled, but of the two theories, the scientists say they would be happier with the one which has an explosive device on the outside."

Vennison again lifted a marker pen and drew on the board the words *car bomb not accidental*. Then with a flourish he drew circles round both sets of words and joined them with a two-way arrow. On top of the line of the arrow he wrote *British Connection?*

He stood back from the Board and moved forward to draw another arrow downwards to another circle that he sketched. Inside the circle he wrote *Arms dump – British tip off?*

There was silence in the room before McDowell stood up and motioned to Vennison's hand where he held the marker pen. "May I, sir?"

He took the pen, drew another arrow to another circle and wrote the words *Belfast shooting – British Involvement?*

# Chapter 14
## RUC Castlereagh

MARK GARRETT HAD a lot on his mind. His weekly briefing meeting with the RUC was usually just a matter of formality, but today was going to be a lot different. The constant enquiries that had come in about an Army VCP near the scene of the IRA car explosion were too insistent to be brushed aside.

The police were on to something, and he had to get them off track as soon as possible. He knew Devon's squad had carried out the car bomb, but for the life of him he couldn't figure out what the RUC knew about it.

He roped in Captain John Dawson, in charge of a small detachment of SAS personnel based in Lisburn and outlined his ideas for blaming increased surveillance on Dawson's group. He knew he would have to go big to get the RUC to drop any further meddling. The best way to achieve this, he figured, was to involve the SAS.

There were always official and unofficial denials of an SAS presence in Ulster, and Garrett reckoned that if the RUC were able to wriggle the information from him, they would be happy to keep a lid on things.

At least that's what he hoped.

"Chief Superintendent, I believe we owe you an explanation," said Garrett as he held the gaze of Billy Carter.

"I believe Captain, you know Chief Inspector Vennison," Carter replied.

Garrett ignored the formal tone and extended his hand to the young aide.

"Good to see you again, Martin. Gentlemen, this is Captain John Dawson, who is here to help clear up a few things."

The handshakes were polite and formal, and the senior policeman waved everyone towards a row of seats surrounding his large desk in the Castlereagh office. When they all had settled, he turned to Garrett.

"Captain, we seem to have a rather odd conflict of stories about an Army roadstop and I think we need to clear up the confusion."

Garrett tried to take things in his stride. "Sir, I can now confirm there was a VCP on the Newry Road on the night of the bar bomb explosion, but even we at Lisburn had to do some digging to get confirmation of this. What happened was that Captain Dawson's unit was just recently posted to Ulster and he took it on himself to put together a patrol to see the lay of the land. Captain Dawson is unfamiliar with the procedures of logging out patrols and there was no paperwork available when we tried to answer the earlier enquiries from your officers."

"What time was the patrol logged out at and why was it on the Newry Road?" asked Vennison.

Garrett referred to a typed sheet. "The patrol left Lisburn at 6:00pm and was back in barracks again at 9.00pm. The choice of route was purely random. Captain Dawson wanted to see Newry town and the border security post there."

"Was Captain Dawson's unit aware of the car bomb? Did they hear or see anything?"

"As I understand it, the bomb exploded at around 8.30pm, but the unit had already lifted its impromptu roadstop in the area at just after 8.00pm and was on its way to Belfast at the time of the explosion."

Vennison shifted in his seat to look directly at Dawson.

"Tell me Captain, why you didn't immediately report your presence in the area when you heard of the bomb. This information was vital to us and frankly a lot of our time has been wasted trying to get to the truth of the matter."

Dawson spoke for the first time, his broad Cornwall accent evident in the clipped nature of his reply.

"I'm really sorry about that. Being new to the province I just didn't add the two together. I thought the patrol was logged out and in by the barracks gate personnel. I just didn't know the patrol leader had to fill in a bunch of forms. It won't happen again."

Superintendent Carter took over.

"And tell me why it was important that your unit went out on this fact-finding tour. There are plenty of personnel at Lisburn who can brief you on all parts of this country and who should have accompanied you on a properly logged patrol."

"We work as a closed unit to protect our independence from other units."

"Just what are you telling me?" What regiment are you attached to and what precisely is your job here?"

Garrett decided to jump in.

"Sir, Captain Dawson heads up a fast response unit that's been put together to help regular units requiring assistance. It's something that was tried in Kuwait and it worked well there. We're still trying to assess whether it can be applied in Northern Ireland."

"Captain, I've heard some fairy stories in my time, but this takes the biscuit. Do you honestly expect me to swallow this hogwash? You're going to have to do better than that."

"Sir, you know that much of what I can't say is classified information and...."

Carter almost exploded. "Listen boy, this isn't a fucking game we're playing and if you've come here without the full answers, then I'll just have to go over your head until we get those answers. Is that clear?"

Garrett feigned uneasiness. "Er, yes sir. Captain Dawson is with the Special Air Service."

"Oh, is he now? And what brings the SAS to our little corner of the globe? We've no Iran embassies here. Maybe they want to play themselves against the little fish?"

Garrett was amused by the hard-nosed humour of Billy Carter. He liked the man, always did. Carter was a copper's copper, a good friend to have in your corner, but an implacable foe if you stood against him.

"Sir, I know the information about the patrol was important to you, but when the first enquiry from your officers was innocently denied by our admin office, we were unsure about how to follow up without compromising Captain Dawson's unit. Naturally, we had to get it to you."

"Naturally," said Carter with what Garret knew was a trace of annoyance.

"Our problem was how best to confirm your information and let you know the unit had nothing to report about the car bomb. It happened a long time after they had left the scene."

"And I have your word on that?" Are you sure

there's nothing to be gained by my officers interviewing Captain Dawson and his men in case they missed something?"

"Sir, I personally briefed all the unit members and there's nothing they can report. They only stopped a few cars to get the feel of a regular roadstop and then moved on. They didn't see or hear anything untoward."

Once again Carter appeared to be on the verge of a tirade.

"Mark, we've known each other for a long time, and although we both play these little games, I thought we had at least established a mutual trust about these kinds of matters."

Dawson cleared his throat and interjected.

"Well, actually sir, it was my fault. I had a bit of pressure put on Captain Garrett to keep us out of it and that's why there was the initial delay in responding to your officers."

"So why the change of heart in coming forward?"

"Not to put too fine a point on it, Captain Garrett persuaded us that you would smell a rat if we didn't come clean."

"What about the little charade at the start of this meeting?"

Garrett held his hand in front of Dawson to signal he would answer.

"I'm sorry, it was worth a try. We knew we would have to eventually tell you the full story and that's why Captain Dawson came with me today."

Billy Carter stood up from his desk and walked round to face the two soldiers.

"I want to know what other operations Captain Dawson's team have been involved in."

"None sir, and that's the truth. You have my word on it."

"How long will the SAS be staying with us?"

Dawson spoke up. "We were sent here for exactly one month for familiarisation. We leave next weekend."

"What form of familiarisation, and I don't want any bullshit?"

"No sir, we're here to get to know the general lay-out of various places such as the border country, Belfast and Londonderry. It's no more than a low-key drive-around operation to give some of our men, who have never been posted here, a chance to see the countryside."

"How do you travel?"

"In unmarked cars provided by Captain Garrett. The episode with the Army Saracens at the roadstop was a one-off to get the feel of what faces our regular troops."

Carter put out his hand. "Let's shake on this being the end of the matter. We're supposed to be co-operating and it's better if we all work together. And from now on, Captain Dawson, no more little jaunts unless we know about it in advance."

"No sir, I promise."

As Garret turned to leave the room, Vennison called after them.

"Just one more thing. Have we been getting all the proper Intel and tip-off messages that go through Lisburn?"

Garrett was thrown by the question.

"Yes, Martin, we have a clear daily protocol of checking all logs and ensuring they are passed to you in the usual way. Why do you ask?"

"No particular reason, just trying to cover all the

bases."

"Lying bastards! Who the hell do they think they are?"

Billy Carter had spent the last forty minutes pacing up and down the room, stopping every so often to repeat the same expletives, followed by a lengthy diatribe on the merits, or more particularly the demerits, of the British Army.

Vennison watched curiously as his chief built to a climax. He had seen these tempers before, but never this sustained or passionate. The old man of course, had every right to be in a rage. They both knew Garrett and Dawson had sold them a dummy story, and Vennison hoped they both believed they had gotten away with it. What he needed was time to ferret out the right story. This would be best achieved if the Army was kept off guard.

"Sir, I'm convinced that Mark Garrett is as much in the dark as we are. Oh, I know he was here today doing someone's dirty work, but I get the feeling he's not fully clued up."

"What makes you say that?"

Vennison was nursing a folder of names, which Garrett had supplied at a meeting earlier in the year. He tapped it lightly as he answered.

"You remember we discussed with Garrett the possibility of increased surveillance on at least four IRA volunteers."

"What are you driving at?"

"It was Garrett who was enthusiastic about the idea of getting better Intel on the regular comings and goings of some of these boyos, so why would he want a joint approach with us if at the same time one of his units had an operation of their own in mind? No, he would at least have tried to steer us away from the idea rather than positively encouraging it."

"Maybe he's a lot cleverer than we give him credit for."

"Sir, I don't doubt Garrett's abilities for one minute, but this kind of double-bluff wouldn't add up."

"Well what does add up?"

"I think the unit or units behind this are operating outside Garrett's control, or at the very least, he's not part of their command structure."

"Are you saying this *is* an SAS job?"

Vennison leaned back on his chair. "To be honest, until today's meeting I was betting the shop on SAS involvement, but I now rule that out. There's no way Garrett would have brought Captain Dawson along to own up to an SAS presence unless they were totally out of the picture and had nothing to lose by admitting guilt. No, Dawson was clearly a smokescreen, and what bothers me is that if the SAS are nothing better than a smokescreen, then something very heavy indeed is going down."

"So, what you're saying is that an entirely new outfit, definitely undercover, has been started up without our knowledge or consent, and they intend to keep us in the dark living off scraps."

Vennison nodded agreement. "What really puzzles me is that if there is such a unit, I can't figure out how they could be operating out of any of the Northern Ireland bases without Garrett being fully briefed on everything they do. I mean he is the senior army security liaison officer, after all."

Carter returned to pacing the room. "Where does all this leave us? I'm not going to the Chief

Constable with a lot of ifs and buts, and I don't want to send this underground before we've had a chance to work out what they're up to. One whiff that we're onto them will send the rats scurrying for cover. We both know the Chief Constable wouldn't be tactful over a matter like this."

"I know he doesn't much like the Army GOC and would just love the thought of taking him down a peg or two."

Carter continued almost as though he hadn't been listening to his aide, "...and the end result would be that we would be told to butt out and get on with other pressing matters while the braid brigade sunk their teeth into our work. They'll get the file all right, but only when I'm good and ready. So where do we go from here?"

Vennison reached across the desk to lift another folder and turned to face Carter who was still standing in the middle of the floor.

"Before the meeting with Garrett, we were discussing the theories behind the discovery of the Army patrol on duty the night the two Provos were blown up in their car outside Hilltown. Let's go with the assumption that that unit did a hatchet job on the car occupants."

"Is that not too much of a stretch, Martin?"

"Not if you consider the nonsense we just heard from Garrett and Dawson. And another thing, throw in the series of gilt-edged tip-offs we've been receiving. Everything comes back to a surveillance operation, and the possibility the Army has brought in some sort of a hit squad to eliminate some of the Provos' most active people."

"But why the tip-offs? Why keep us out of the picture and then help us with catching these people if they have, as you're suggesting, another agenda in mind?"

"George McDowell has advanced the best theory on this. He believes that if there is a new unit, it's not a stretch to imagine they've been here quite a while, learning the ropes and getting their house in order. During this period, they obviously stumbled across a lot of Intel they couldn't use so they let us have it. Then someone pressed the action button and things started happening, including the car bomb."

Carter looked perplexed.

"For that theory to hold up they would stop sending us confidential messages, but we got one only the other day about the arms dump in Saintfield. Why not just go completely cold with us and get on with whatever it is they are intending to do?"

"With all respect sir, these are scraps. Yes, I know the arms dump is proving to be one of the most significant breakthroughs we've had for years but consider it from the Army's perspective. They've no use for a farmer storing weapons for the IRA; they're after bigger fish to fry. Maybe they've gone for the men who use the weapons; maybe they didn't expect us to get the info so quickly on Pat Duggan, who we picked up at his home, after the farmer spilled the beans."

Carter returned to his desk.

"The more we talk about this the worse it gets. Let's turn our attention to what we're going to do about it."

A loud rap on the door broke the tension. The door opened and Detective Sergeant McDowell stuck his head through the gap.

"Sorry for the interruption sir, but this is very

important."

"Come in Sergeant," what have you got?"

"I've just come from forensics. They've been going through Pat Duggan's belongings and his car that we took from outside his house yesterday morning. He's the man we got the tip-off about from the arms dump farmer."

"I know," said Carter, "we've been talking about him. Carry on Sergeant."

"Thanks, sir. Well the thing is we've hit paydirt. The boys found something curious in the engine compartment and they believe it's a remarkably high tech listening device."

"The hell you say!" Carter jumped to his feet. "Go on, go on."

McDowell referred to a single sheet of paper he was carrying. "They're still examining it, trying to be careful to keep it intact. What they've been able to tell us so far is that they've never seen anything like it. It's shaped like a piece of shit, but it's one of the most advanced bits of kit they've ever come across. It's been disabled, but whoever put it there might have been listening in to our people before they cottoned on to what it was."

"What else do we know about it? Can we trace its origins? Can we track it back to its source?

"From what I gather, there's no chance of that. They don't yet know whether it's satellite-linked or whether it has only short-range capability. They're betting on the latter, but frankly it's got them baffled. They have found a rather sophisticated nuclear-powered battery unit, barely the size of a pinhead, but capable of giving it a long shelf life. They hope to know more when they run full diagnostics on it."

"When will that be?"

"Sir, they've had to call in some specialist communication technies and hope to prepare a full report by tomorrow."

Carter slumped back in his seat. "This is an interesting development, very interesting indeed. Okay Sergeant, keep me posted. I want to know the minute they have any more details."

McDowell turned towards the door and then turned back again. "One more thing. I asked them to guess at origin, and although they were non-committal, they agreed with me that it could only have emanated from a very heavily sourced and funded facility. They're going along with me in guessing British-made, probably MI6 or some offshoot."

The pause that followed was broken by Carter. "Now there's a surprise."

The news shocked Vennison. Things were going off in different directions and he needed to come up with something positive. He came to a decision and turned to Carter.

"Sir, with your permission I'm going to put McDowell and Mo Green on a little bit of surveillance of our own. I think the key lies with Garrett. Let's check him around the clock and see what turns up. He may not be directly part of this, but sooner or later he'll lead us to the man who is. I also suggest we get in touch with our country stations to check out whether there have been any strange happenings or increased activity in their areas."

"Are you hoping Garrett will lead us to a base of operations somewhere in the countryside? Surely that's a long shot?"

"I don't think so. We've already agreed this

phantom unit is not operating from any of the main Army bases, but they've got to be somewhere. We need to turn them up."

"Okay Martin, but we need answers, and we need them yesterday."

# Chapter 15
## Dublin Housing Estate

THE FOLLOWING AFTERNOON, Francis Dooley opened the front door of his detached bungalow in a moneybelt estate at Finglas, north of Dublin. He nodded for Liam Nolan to enter and showed him into a small drawing room where Joe Coyle and Patrick Pearse were already seated, each holding a mug of coffee.

Nolan filled them in on his meeting with the British Government agent at St Stephen's Green.

"I've no doubt these bastards are planning something. They know as well as we do the value of negotiating from a position of strength when it comes to peace talks. I think they're looking to hit us hard over the next few months."

Dooley responded. "That just confirms what you've been saying. We hit them first and we hit them harder."

"Quite so," Nolan said with a smile. "Now you know why I've been trying to piece together the operation in England. Tell me where we are on this."

Dooley lifted a small notebook from the coffee table in front of him.

"As we all recognise, this is going to be our hardest assignment yet. We have fully researched the location and know the ins and outs of everything that goes on around the place. We have the complete itinerary on the resident staff and bodyguards, but the biggest variable we are facing is finding out when the target will be at the chosen location. His time is split between his offices in London and Belfast and he doesn't make it home to Epsom on very many weekends. When he does go home, he takes the London train direct to Epsom where a car is waiting at the station to pick him up. Two minders travel with him at all times and he has a private compartment on the train. One of our people travelled the route two weeks ago and reported that it's impossible to get to the carriage because it is sealed off from other passengers. That rules out an attack on the train."

Dooley turned a page in the notebook.

"The distance from the train station to his home in Epsom is only four miles, but a good stretch of it is a minor country road, which could easily be landmined. Alternatively, his house is visible from the eleventh tee at the golf course, and the back garden could be accessed from the course, which is on the boundary of the garden."

Coyle cut in. "As to when he will next be there, I think we've come up with the answer. Next Friday Parliament is sitting for a full day on the Gulf War debate and is not expected to rise before 4pm. With a number of Government backbench dissenters, a three-line whip is imposed so our man will have to attend. The odds are that he will most certainly go straight to Epsom when the debate ends."

Nolan shifted on his seat and turned towards Dooley.

"Good work, Francis. Now I've some news for you. We're not going with a road bomb and we're not going to attempt a strike on the train. We're going into the bastard's house and we're going to assassinate him and his minders."

There was a general stirring among the other

three, and it was Coyle who spoke first.

"That's going to take some doing. Even if we access the rear garden, we have the problem of getting past the house security. There's also bound to be motion detectors and cameras in the grounds leading to the house."

"This has all been factored in," Nolan told him. "I've had one of our experts look at the security that's in place and he's confident he can get past it. I've just had the full rundown from him and I'm impressed by his thinking. He intends to get into the house through an adjoining garage shortly after 5pm and remain hidden until the target arrives, probably around 6 or 7pm, given the train schedules from London to Epsom."

"Who are we using?" asked Pearse.

"Our friend from Scotland."

"Oh. Him. I see now why you're so confident."

Nolan nodded an acknowledgement. "I'm leaving nothing to chance. We need this. If we pull it off, it will send shockwaves reverberating around Westminster. I want this to be our biggest headline yet."

"Yeah," said Coyle, "I can just see the headlines now: *Northern Ireland Secretary of State murdered in his bedroom.*"

# Chapter 16
## Bishopscourt

JIM PERRY STROLLED out of his cell, down a short corridor, and into a large room serving as a makeshift canteen. He crossed to a trestle table, filled a mug of coffee, and walked towards three men seated near the entrance.

"Okay if I sit here?"

"Go right ahead, Jimmy boy. Are you not having something to eat?"

He recognised the man as the soldier who had wrapped the chains around O'Brien in the helicopter.

"Nah, too much alcohol last night. I knew I should have stayed away from the wine. It doesn't agree with me."

What a transformation in four days! Perry acknowledged he was a shivering wreck when the men came into his cell on that second night. There was no chance in hell he was going the way of O'Brien, so he did the only thing he could.

He started talking.

And once he started, he couldn't stop. He let the floodgates open, determined to demonstrate his willingness to co-operate. He held nothing back, often volunteering information where it wasn't asked.

He added detail to everything, almost to the point of boredom, but figured anything was better than incurring the displeasure of these dangerous men.

He was amazed by the volume of information

they had gathered. Every few hours one of them would come to him with transcripts of conversations they had somehow managed to pick up. He knew they must be bugging a lot of people's homes or telephones, but he wasn't about to stick his nose in.

He provided his captors with a complete command structure of the Provisional IRA in Belfast, adding in addresses, the names of wives and girlfriends, favourite drinking haunts, and details of protection rackets across the city. He passed on rumours about informers working in civilian positions in police and army stations and named several lawyers who were in the movement's pocket.

He was promised a new life in America with money to burn and believed them when told he would be taken there within a few weeks. In return, he was given the freedom of the block in which his cell was housed, and each night at around ten o'clock, he was allowed outside for exercise.

He believed too, that he had forged friendships with the men around him, and even empathised with their own desire to get back home.

As to his own future, he was convinced that all he had to do was co-operate. He was not a brave man, but neither was he a coward. He liked to think he had always gotten by on his wits, but this present situation was way beyond his comfort zone. There would be no lawyers here, wherever here was, and he wouldn't be going in front of a judge anytime soon.

He knew from his night-time exercises that he was in the heart of the country, no lights to be seen for miles around, and the odd mooing from faraway grazing cattle was not a sound he was used to in Belfast.

He enjoyed listening to the peculiar noises of the

countryside. Being given these privileges must mean he was winning the battle. Hell, he was even sharing their canteen, and everyone was friendlier towards him.

From time to time the leader, who called himself Mike, would walk into his cell and ask him about particular people who had come to his attention.

Many of the names were known to him, and those that weren't, could be easily tied to others he knew. During most of these sessions he was able to add value to what Mike knew, and each time he was sure this sent his stock soaring.

He had just returned to his cell and was skimming through a book from the small supply left on a locker beside his bed, when he heard footsteps on the corridor outside, and the man named Mike put his head around the corner.

"I see you've had breakfast. Are you up to running through a few things with me?"

Perry swung his legs off the bed and planted them on the floor.

"Sure Mike, what do you need to know?"

He waited as the man crossed the room, grabbed the single chair that completed the furniture of the cell, and straddled over it.

"There's a name that keeps coming up and I was wondering what you can tell me about him."

"Sure, who is it?"

"Liam Nolan."

*Oh Christ, not him, not Nolan!* Perry knew his reaction must have been obvious. "That's the devil himself, you don't want to go messing with that fucker."

"Tell me about him."

"He's the big cheese, the boss of the outfit, a bit

like yourself Mike. I don't mean you're like him, just that, you know, you're the boss and he's the boss."

"You mean the boss of the IRA in Belfast?"

"Oh, he's much more than that. He's the boss of the whole fucking outfit in Ireland."

"You mean the Capo di Tutti Capo?"

Perry didn't understand what had just been said. He stared blankly at Mike, waiting for an explanation.

"Never mind; tell me what you know about him."

"To be honest I don't know much. I think he's based in Drogheda or Dublin, but I've never met him. He directs all our, I mean the IRA, operations and they say he's killed about twenty Brit soldiers...oh, sorry about that Mike."

"Keep talking."

"There's not much I can add. Like I said, I've never met him, but the word is he's a hard bastard. Doesn't care about anyone but himself. They say he's already topped six of his own people and wouldn't care if there were civilian casualties in any of the things he plans. What I do know is that nothing is done unless he says so, even the top boys in Belfast have to wait for his permission."

"Who does he run about with?"

"I honestly don't know. It's a pity you killed Kevin O'Brien. He could have told you more."

"What do you mean?"

"Well I know O'Brien was with a few of the Belfast boys who met Nolan in Dublin in August. He wouldn't tell me anything about it, says he was sworn to secrecy, but he did let drop that something big was going down."

For a moment, Perry thought he had said

something wrong. Mike jumped from his seat, sending it flying across the room. But instead of moving towards Perry's position, he turned and bolted through the door.

Perry expelled a long breath as he heard the footsteps running away from his cell.


Across the compound, Kevin O'Brien was lying on a cot staring at the ceiling and trying to make sense of his situation.

He didn't mind admitting his nerve went the moment they had shoved him out of that helicopter. He kept trying to console himself that there was nothing he could do but co-operate with these people. Any man in his position would do the same, he reasoned.

At first, he tried not to be too forthcoming, but the odds were stacked against him. He was shocked by the volume of information held by these men and several times he found himself having to confirm various names and events.

He had no doubt that Perry was squealing and knew he would also have to play ball if he wanted to continue living. These were the hardest group of bastards he had ever come across, and his chances of getting out alive were remote. He guessed they must be SAS, and he'd heard enough about those fuckers to know they didn't play by the rules. Just keep your wits about you, he kept repeating to himself, and give them enough to want to keep you alive.

He was startled by the noise of a key rattling in his cell door and then it was flung open by two men who roughly pulled him to his feet.

"The boss wants to see you," one of them said as

they dragged him out into the corridor.

O'Brien was ushered into a spartan room and made to sit on a rickety wooden chair. His warders left without a word and he forced his eyes up from the floor to look at a man behind a desk. He recognised him as the leader of the outfit - the fucker that held his life in his hands.

"I hope they're treating you a bit better, Kevin. If you continue your co-operation, we really can make things very comfortable for you. I should tell you that your friend has been extremely helpful and has been rewarded accordingly."

"What, does he get an extra sausage for his breakfast?"

O'Brien was startled by the noise of a slap against wood as the man brought his fist down on the table.

"Enough! You're on thin ice here. Unless we start moving things forward, then I'll have to assume you're no longer any use to us. Do I make myself clear?"

"Yeah, I'm sorry; it was just an attempt at Irish humour. I've already told you I'll co-operate, but I need to see a way out for me."

"There are no guarantees, but what I can tell you is that Jim Perry is already packing his bags and heading for a new life far away from this country. It's up to you whether you follow him. Now, are we ready to start?"

"Go ahead."

"Okay, two months ago you met with Liam Nolan in Dublin. I want to know who all was at that meeting and what was discussed."

The news took O'Brien off guard. *Fuck Perry, what's he landed me with now?*

"Come on, come on," the man yelled, "I haven't got all day."

O'Brien stared at him for a few seconds and then came to a decision.

"I was asked to do minder for Pat McStravick and Tom Bell who had been ordered to Dublin for a meeting with Nolan. They were there for about two hours and then left. I drove them back home."

"Details, details. Where was the meeting and who was there?"

"They met in the foyer lounge of the Gresham Hotel, that's the big one on O'Connell Street and, can you believe it, they had afternoon tea with little triangle sandwiches and miniature cakes. God, you should have seen the delicate china cups and the fancy silver teapots..."

The man held up his hand in mock surrender.

"Okay, when I said details, I didn't mean you to write me a Michelin dining guide."

"Oh, sorry. Right. Where was I? We were introduced to Liam Nolan, I've never met him before, and there was another man with him, called himself Francis Dooley, an ugly fucker, his face was all full of marks. They all seemed to know each other, but I was the odd one out. Like I said I was just there as a driver and minder. Anyway, Nolan shook hands with me and said he heard I was doing good work and told me to keep it up. Then he asked me to leave, said the meeting was private. I was allowed to sit across the foyer at another table; they even sent me a plate of sandwiches."

"Were you able to hear anything that was said?"

"I was too far away."

"What about on the way home in the car?"

O'Brien forced himself to think for a moment.

"They were very secretive, kept saying things like 'you know that job we were talking about' or 'we'll talk about that later', but they didn't really give anything away."

"You must have picked up something better than that."

O'Brien noted the exasperation in the man's voice.

"I know there must be a big job on. Nolan wouldn't be meeting these boys down in Dublin for an ordinary meeting. It must be something big. And they kept mentioning the word 'job' like it was what they were there to discuss."

"No indication what the job was?"

"No, but I got the impression it would be very soon."

"The meeting was, what, six weeks ago? But nothing's happened since then, so when is it to be?"

"I don't know, honestly I don't, but they don't usually rush into things. My guess is that it was something planned a few months ahead. Maybe something in the next few weeks."

"Anything else?"

"No, no I don't think so...wait, there was one thing. They did mention something about someone from Scotland."

"Scotland? Are you sure? Is the job to be in Scotland?"

"They mentioned 'our Scottish friend' said he would be the man for the job, but I don't think it will be in Scotland."

Devon continued to push. He knew he was onto something and he needed O'Brien to tell him what he knew. There was an edge to his voice as he moved forward on his seat and shouted into O'Brien's' face.

"Why do you say that? Don't think about holding anything back."

O'Brien tried to remember. He knew from the man's reaction to the news that a can of worms had been opened unwittingly. He needed to come up with more information.

"They said something about how this Scottish friend has carried out some of their biggest jobs and that he was brilliant in the operation in Belfast last year."

"What operation?"

"They didn't say, just referred to it as the operation in Belfast last year."

"If this latest job is being planned in Belfast, would you know about it? Would McStravick and Bell be involved in the planning? Would they know about it?"

"I guess so. They are, after all, the big wheels in the city. They would have to be involved, wouldn't they?"

Devon got up from behind the desk and walked round in front of O'Brien.

"Good man, Kevin, you see how easy it is. Now here's what I want you to do. I'm going to put you in with one of our sketch artists and I want you to help draw up a photofit of this Liam Nolan and Francis Dooley. Then I want you to sit down and write me up everything you know about these people, just stick to plain facts, a line at a time. I don't need it to read like a story, but I want full details of everything you can tell us about them. Now, do you think you can do that?"

"Yeah."

"Okay, here's what we'll do. How about we move you to a more comfortable room, maybe get you a few beers, and give you a bit more freedom around here? Like I said before, play ball with us and we'll play ball with you."

The man turned towards the door but glanced back at O'Brien.

"First things first, let's fix you up with a decent bath and a change of clothing."


Back in his office, Devon was met by Alan Doyle, who was already seated in front of the desk and looked up as Devon entered.

"Sorry for the intrusion Mike, but there are a few things here you need to know about, pronto."

Devon sensed the urgency in Doyle's voice. "Spit it out."

"It seems one of our bugs has been found by the RUC...."

"How the fuck did that happen?"

"A bit of bad luck really. You know that arms dump we discovered in Saintfield? It seems the farm owner they brought in for questioning must have talked, because the next thing we know the RUC has mounted an operation on one of our targets, a certain Pat Duggan, who it seems was responsible for the arsenal. They have him in for questioning and they impounded his car for forensic testing."

"Jeez, and they found the bug?"

"Looks like. Peter Ackmore told me this morning the bug suddenly went cold, stopped transmitting, or whatever it does. When I checked back through the record, I found the transcripts of messages between the RUC during the lead-up to the raid on Duggan's house. The timing all fits."

Devon fell into his seat and began rubbing his

chin with the ball of his right hand, a habit that always seemed to be a reflex to a situation that worried him.

"That's all we fucking need. What will they be able to make of the device? Will they be able to tie it to us?"

"Ackmore doesn't think so. There's nothing like it out there, but that alone will raise suspicions. It's not as if this thing is available on the open market, so that will rule out any possibilities the police may come up with about factions spying on each other. They're bound to suss sooner or later that this is an Intelligence operation and they'll probably put MI6 in the frame."

"And this helps us how?"

"It doesn't really. The last thing we need is for them to be asking awkward questions, and if they show the device to MI6, they won't be long in tracking down its origins."

Devon stared out the window trying to gather his thoughts.

"We'll have to bring Mark Garrett in on this. If anyone can head off the posse, it's him"

"Interesting you should say that. I've had Garrett on the blower when you were in your interview with our friend... by the way, how'd that go?"

"Later. What did Garrett want?"

"Apparently he'd just come out of a meeting with the RUC and says he needs to see you urgently. I've pencilled him in for tomorrow morning. He's coming here at 0900."

"They couldn't be on it that quick. Did Garrett give you any indication of what went on at the meeting?"

"No, just said he needed to see you soonest."

Devon swivelled in his chair and then turned back to face Doyle.

"Right, here's what we'll do. I'll buzz Garrett and see what's going on, but in the meantime I want you to get the team working on two names, Pat McStravick and Tom Bell. I want all our resources concentrated on them. They were on our original list but check if we have bugs at their homes and in their cars. If we haven't, then get them installed as a matter of priority. I want round-the-clock on these two. I want to know every move they make over the next few days."

"What's the flap, Mike? Did these come from your little chats with our two guests?"

"Yes. Something big is going down and these two are in the middle of it. I don't know how long we have, but it could be imminent. If nothing shakes loose from surveillance over the next two days, I want them lifted and brought here. Brief the team and get them working a-sap. Let's call a full meeting tonight at 2200."

As Doyle turned to leave the room, Devon halted him.

"One more thing Alan, see if we know anything about an operative in Scotland. We haven't got a name, but he could be a specialist used by the IRA. Whatever's going down it looks like he's also involved. We need to find him."

"Is he the specialist you referred to at one of our earlier briefings?"

Devon was dumbstruck by the comment. He slumped back in his seat and stared at the ceiling, finally turning back towards Doyle.

"Fuck me, Alan. Until you mentioned it, I didn't

make any connection."

At that he rose and crossed to a filing cabinet, withdrawing a folder from the top shelf. He removed a single sheet of paper, stared at it for a long time and then passed it across to Doyle.

"That's a photofit from a good few years back, but it's a great likeness, or it was then," Devon explained as his thoughts wandered back to a Chicago street.

"Get copies made of that and make sure all our people are familiar with it. This is one dangerous motherfucker, and if we ever come across him, we'd better be on our toes."

Doyle studied hard at the pencil-and-ink sketch.

"Seems like you've already come across him, Mike."

"It's a long story. Let's just say we left each other with something to remember. I don't know if this ties in with Scotland, but for the moment it's all we've got."

Long after Doyle left his office, Devon was still deep in thought, remembering Peter Fitzsimons and Pauline Brown, his rage growing as he again recalled the events in Chicago. Eventually he stirred from the memories and grabbed the telephone. After being put through by the main switchboard at Lisburn GHQ, he heard a scrambler being activated, and then the voice of Mark Garrett.

"What's up, Mark?"

"Thanks for getting back to me, Mike. We need to talk face to face. The RUC has gotten wind of the roadstop near Newry and are asking some awkward questions. I've headed them off for now, but I'm guessing they'll come back to it."

Devon let the news sink in and decided to go

straight to the point.

"No mention of one of our listening devices?"

"No, why do you ask?"

"We think they've found one."

Devon went on to explain what had happened, and for a while the line went quiet.

"Mark, you still there?"

"This isn't good, Mike. Chances are they'll start to tie the two things together. I need to come see you. Let me think about this overnight. You still all right for the morning?"

"Yes, I'll see you then."


Mark Garret was oblivious to the rolling countryside as he travelled through the market town of Ballynahinch, into Downpatrick, noted as the last resting place of St. Patrick, and onwards towards the Bishopscourt base. It was a unique landscape, daubed by geographers as the "basket of eggs" county because of the upturned-saucer fields, each one seemingly rising from the descent of its neighbour.

All around could be seen every facet of rural life. Fields turned over by the plough stood in stark contrast to the lush, green grazing acres populated by countless heads of sheep, and the herds of Friesians and Simmentals most favoured by the indigenous farmers.

Here and there nature's pattern was broken only by the ugly rising arms of telegraph poles, and the more acceptable whitewash of the many small cottages, which hugged the roadways.

It was a county noted for its share of labourers' cottages, built in the thriving post-war period to house the migrant workforce who earned a meagre living from the land. Many of the cottages had now lost their original shape, a sad sacrifice to the demands of modernisation and the spread of urban dwellers into the countryside. But sufficient still stood in their former glory to present an exquisite insight into an era long since passed into history.

County Down was still an agricultural belt, but fewer big farms remained and even fewer of the large workforces who tilled the land and breathed life into the soul of the area.

It was the county from which St. Patrick began his Christianisation of Ireland, and left his indelible mark on its heritage, sprinkling it with the ruins of small meeting places and churches that would be forever synonymous with his name.

A statue, built in his memory on the most commanding of the hills of Down, near a hamlet known as Saul, looked over the vast network of roads and country lanes sweeping below as far as the eye could see.

Eight miles away, the stony features of Ireland's Patron Saint, standing sentry over his domain, were clearly visible from the road linking Downpatrick and Bishopscourt.

Visible to all, that is, but Mark Garrett, pre-occupied as he was with his thoughts about the meeting ahead.

His car swept off the main road into the approach to Bishopscourt. Garrett was met by a heavily fortified avenue of concrete sentries, road ramps and watchtowers, and had to pass through two separate checkpoints before being admitted to the base compound.

As his car disappeared around the corner of one

of the many large base buildings, a dark blue Vauxhall Cavalier crept past on the main road, the occupants just about noting the brake lights of Garrett's car, as it was lost to view.

"Now there's an interesting turn up for the books," said Detective Sergeant George McDowell.

"Curiouser and curiouser," intoned Detective Constable Mo Greene, as he gunned the engine and sped away from the base.


It was Garrett's first visit to the base since he helped launch its new use, and he was impressed by the work that had been completed in such a short timespan. He noted the additional security measures, including the perimeter patrols of two-man teams, each dressed in RAF uniforms to maintain outward appearances.

Across the compound he could see a fleet of civilian-adapted cars parked under a gigantic hangar and watched briefly as a group of men were put through tough hand-to-hand combat exercises in a drill square screened off on three sides by high walls.

As he stepped beneath a porch into the main administrative building, he was met in the lobby by Mike Devon, and escorted to a first floor office. As they mounted the stairs the two men engaged in the usual pleasantries, but as soon as the office door sprang back on its hinges, Garrett set the tone for the meeting.

"We've got a problem and frankly I don't know how to deal with it. What we're facing could jeopardise the entire operation."

"I don't underestimate the seriousness of the situation, but I need you to buy us some time. Is there any way you can keep the RUC running in circles for a few weeks?"

"Mike, I've thought about this every way from Christmas, but no matter what I come up with, it's only a matter of time before the shit hits the fan. The thing with the road check at Newry is manageable, and taken in isolation, would not cause us too many worries. But this thing with the discovery of the listening device adds a whole new dimension."

He paused as if to add dramatic impact to his next words.

"Frankly, if they add two and two together, they could blow us out of the water."

When he finished speaking, he studied Devon's reaction. As usual, all he saw was a poker face.

"It can't be that bad. Can't you get MI6 to take the heat off us? There must be some plausible Intel gobbledegook you can spin that will stop them digging any deeper. It's your job to run interference for us."

Garrett was on the verge of snapping back, but the two men had a history of friendship stretching back many years. He knew Devon's mood swings, knew how committed he was to this project, and knew deep down that he wouldn't want to work with anyone else.

"You know I'll do whatever it takes. It's just that this was so unforeseen I can't find any reasonable way out. I know I've got to get to MI6 before the RUC does and trust me, they *will* get around to it sooner rather than later. I'm finding it hard to come up with a scenario that MI6 can use to make the RUC stand down."

"Look Mark, I'm sorry if I came across all high and mighty. I know if it weren't for you, I wouldn't be here. It's just that we're so close to something really big, and I don't need to be sidetracked at this stage."

Garrett's brow furrowed and he looked across the desk at his friend, looking for a hint of what was coming. "Is there something I should know about?"

He listened as Devon filled him in on the information wrangled from the two captives, taking him through the references to Liam Nolan, the possibility of an imminent major IRA operation, and the existence of an IRA specialist in Scotland.

Finally, he told him everything about his experiences in Chicago, and handed him a copy of the identikit he completed all those years ago. "I know this last link is a bit thin, but what is certain is that the IRA is planning something big, a headline that will curl our toes. My guess is that it's a contract on the mainland, but at this stage that's only a guess. We have a couple of prominent leads and if we're left clear to follow up on them, I can guarantee results."

Garrett whistled through his teeth, drew forward his seat and asked Devon to go over everything again.

Two pots of coffee later, he outlined a strategy he believed would fly.

# Chapter 17
## Glasgow

FOUR MILES PAST the main entrance to Glasgow Airport, on the M8 heading towards the city, is a sprawling, forty thousand acre industrial estate, home to some of Europe's leading brand retail and wholesale conglomerates.

Marks and Spencer, Sainsbury's, and Tesco's sit alongside IKEA, B & Q, and Toys R Us in a delirium of out-of-town shopping choices. The estate is criss-crossed by generously wide internal roads, and more parking spaces than can be found in the centre of any major city.

One sector is reserved for car dealerships, every marque represented beneath a sea of colourful flags fluttering from large poles stretching as far as the eye can see. Vast sites are taken up by Renault, Peugeot, Ford, Vauxhall, Toyota, and other leading manufacturers.

Tucked in one corner is an attention-grabbing complex, noticeable for the sight of a Rolls Royce Silver Shadow mounted on a hydraulic platform at the gateway entrance to an enclosure comprising two large showrooms filled with the world's iconic car brands.

Stretching across the front wall of the main showroom, in eight-foot Gothic-embossed blue lettering, is the legend *The International Quality Car Centre*. Beneath the main title in much smaller green lettering is a self-explanatory subtitle, *Importers and Exporters of the World's Leading*

*Automobiles.*

Behind a sea of shimmering glass stands a Porsche Boxer, a Ferrari GTS, an assortment of Mercedes-Benz models, and in the centre of the showroom mounted on a three-foot high plinth, an Aston Martin DB5 under a banner that read *Welcome to the World of James Bond.* Only 983 of the DB5 models were ever made at a factory in Newport Bagnall from 1963 to 1965. Although the model on show was not the one used in the Bond film, it was deceptively represented as being so in the glossy literature.

It was an enthusiast's paradise that attracted a mixture of serious buyers, wannabee owners, and the downright curious. Each model on display - in total more than sixty - carried above it a crisp marketing message similar to that of the Aston Martin and designed to push a customer over the line between wavering and buying.

The man behind the development of the centre was at that moment standing at the window of his second floor office, looking across the compound as visitors alighted from cars and made their way into the showrooms below.

He could always tell the potential from the nosey. After ten years of growing the business into a multimillion-pound annual concern, his instincts were usually right.

Dressed in a light tan suit with an open-necked brown dress shirt, he was the epitome of a successful entrepreneur. Short fair hair was swept back in a salon-coiffured John Travolta style, and he wore designer spectacles that gave him the look of a studious businessman. A weave-patterned gold necklace hung around his neck, and a Rolex wristwatch with a similar woven gold strap could be seen peeping through the left cuff of his shirt.

He idly twisted a wedding ring with the thumb and index finger of his right hand, his thoughts as usual on Mary and two-year-old son Jackie, back at home in Paisley, a short twenty-minute drive away.

He turned back from the window, crossed to his desk, and opened a large envelope couriered to him earlier that morning. He removed his glasses, the plain lenses nothing more than a prop, and set them on the desktop.

*"One more job, just one more job."*

Fergal McSweeney was sick of hearing the mantra, and this time it had taken some persuading for him to finally agree to construct a workable plan.

During a series of phone calls over the past week from Dublin, he had made it clear that's all he would do. He would not carry out the mission himself.

His life had moved on considerably over the past five years. He knew that meeting Mary Halloran was the start of a turnaround for him. He remembered the petite Glaswegian blonde walking into his life at a friend's Hogmanay party, and now he couldn't imagine a time without her.

It was love at first sight, although he admitted she worked harder than he did to make the relationship work. She had turned him from a cold social fish to an outgoing, friendly person, more comfortable in the presence of others than at any time in his life.

He came to rely on her background in the world of advertising. It had helped open up new sales opportunities, as they worked together to build the business to what it was today. Gradually they formed a true partnership, in both their private and professional lives.

Marriage became inevitable, and with the arrival of a son his world was complete.

But a dark cloud hung over him. Over time he told her about his past, about the things he had done, omitting some of the unseemly acts he knew even she would not understand or forgive.

Mary came from a staunchly Irish Republican family herself, but cocooned in a conservative Glaswegian upbringing, he realised she could have no comprehension of the bitterness fuelling the troubles back in Ireland.

Nevertheless, he marvelled at the way she coped with his revelations, providing an outlet for his nightmares, and helping him see a way out to a new life without the shackles of the past.

He knew it wouldn't be easy. The once-in-never-out commitment that was given to the IRA could not be broken, though thankfully over the past few years, he had been called on less and less to carry out the demands of his masters.

Maybe, he reasoned, the success of the business in diverting funds into IRA coffers had become more important to them than risking the future of an active operative. Other younger men had surely stepped in to take on these roles, and a time would come when they left him alone in his own little private space.

After taking on the assignment to assassinate the retired RUC man John Turnbull, six months ago, he had heard nothing from them. They had promised then that would be his last act in the field, and he believed them.

He had believed them right up to the first phone call he received last week.

It was, as usual, Liam Nolan at the other end of the line. He outlined in general terms what was planned and how he expected McSweeney to come up with a foolproof mission operational design when he received the package of Intelligence reports that were being delivered to him. Nolan brushed aside McSweeney's reservations and assured him that a successful operation would result in them all putting their feet up for good.

But McSweeney was having none of the fancy persuasions, and the first two conversations blew up into angry exchanges.

It was during the third call that Nolan had delivered his ultimatum. "Turn your back on us at your peril. If you do, you can forget about your life and that of your wife and son."

The mention of his wife and son hit McSweeney like a hammer blow to the stomach. Until now he had thought his decision carried only implications for himself. He had never considered the possibility of his family becoming involved.

It introduced a new element into his feelings for Nolan. He fought a rising anger and beat away thoughts of rushing to Dublin to kill the fucker.

Instead, he composed himself, bit his lower lip, and delivered a calmly chilling message. "That will be the first and last time you threaten me or my family. You know me and what I'm capable of. If you can't accept my terms, then I guess that will make us enemies. If you make a move towards me or my family, I will see you coming, and I'll make you wish you hadn't been born. I'll kill you and everyone around you. I'll blow your organisation so far apart it'll never be able to pick up the pieces..."

"Do you *know* who you're talking to?"

McSweeney ignored the question. "I'm not finished. What I've said only holds good if you continue to issue threats against me or my family. I put you down for a smarter man than that. I'm still as committed as ever, but things have changed. There are lots of ways I can serve the movement, and all of them are ten times way better than most of the idiots you've got running around. Are you willing to listen to my proposal?"

There was a brief silence before Nolan responded. "I'm all ears."

"Consider this. I'll continue to run the car business and divert more and more funds into your war chest. I've built up a lot of contacts across the world, particularly in America, where very wealthy and influential men stand ready to help the cause. I'll keep developing these contacts, and ensure they put more and more political pressure on the White House to force Britain into a final settlement. On top of all that, I'll continue to help your military strategies, and the planning of individual operations."

"How far are you prepared to go with the Epsom operation?"

McSweeney crossed back to his desk and sat down. "I'll put together a full plan. I'll personally visit the site, check out all the options, and ensure there is a successful mission, no matter who you get to carry it out. You know how I operate, how I plan things down to the last detail. A blueprint from me is a guarantee."

He waited while Nolan considered his words.

"All right, McSweeney, you've got a deal, but

with a few conditions."

"Such as?"

"I want this in three days. I want all the bells and whistles in place by then, and I want you to brief me personally on what you come up with. I want to go over your plan face to face, and I want you to talk me through the critical pressure points. I want to see for myself that you put your best efforts into this."

"I've no problem with that," McSweeney countered. "Where do you want to meet?"

Again, there was a short silence. "I'll come to you."

With that the line went dead.

McSweeney stared at the handset for a few seconds, and then brought his eyes back to the package on the desk. He started rifling through the contents and spent two hours going through the photographs and maps of an area around Epsom in Surrey.

The target had taken his breath away. He now knew Nolan wasn't exaggerating when he said the success of the mission would change the course of history.

As his staff haggled over price deals in the room below, he started formulating a plan of action. As usual it was in three parts – how to travel to the target area leaving no trace of his journey, how to carry out the mission, and how to get safely back to Scotland.

Three hours later he was still at it when his secretary interrupted his flow with an internal call to tell him they were locking up for the night.

He gathered the papers, stuffed them back into the envelope, and crammed the package into a briefcase. He descended the stairs and made his away across to his Mercedes, all the while thinking about what he was going to tell Mary.

It was a thought that stayed with him as he joined the early evening traffic and was still with him when he pulled into the driveway of his home.

The following day McSweeney was in the car park at Fulbrighton Golf Club just outside Epsom. He crossed to the pro shop and enquired about playing a round on the pretext he was in town for a business conference and had a free morning.

Tee bookings were slow on Tuesdays, and he was cleared to start immediately.

After buying a playing ticket and a course planner, he returned to his car and removed a golf cart and bag from the boot. He had started to play just over two years ago, more because of business contacts than the true vocation of the Sunday morning amateur and was unable to get below the eighteen handicap he started with.

After playing through the first five holes, he was delighted to note the course ahead of him was clear of other players. He looked at the planner, a small printed notebook that set out the shape and design of the course and walked across an adjoining fairway to where he guessed the 11th tee would be sited.

He knew from Intelligence passed to him in Scotland that the garden of the target house swept down to the edge of the golf course at the 11th hole, a four hundred and forty yard par four with an out-of-bounds fence running down the left side, close to a number of grand houses perched on a rise overlooking the course.

After hitting his tee shot, he deliberately aimed a few wedge shots to the left until he reached the garden of the fourth house. He looked carefully around before proceeding to hook a shot over the fence into a boundary hedge beyond.

He made a show of looking for his ball, all the time taking in the features around him.

He spotted a small gap in the hedge and muscled his way through into an overgrown weedy patch that led to a rockery climbing up an incline towards the house. Without pause, he scrambled through the weeds and up the side of the rockery, keeping close to an internal boundary hedge.

At the crest, the rockery gave way to a well-kept lawn, dotted with several flower patches sweeping all the way to what appeared to be a patio area at the back of the house. He could chance going no farther but removed a small pair of binoculars from his pocket and began a slow sweep of the entire area. He committed every detail to memory, including security measures on doors, windows, and exterior walls.

It was then he heard dogs barking in the patio area. There was a breeze in his face coming from the direction of the house and he knew they could not have picked up his scent. The presence of dogs was a good sign for him, rather than one more security detail to worry about.

For one thing, dogs would not be allowed to roam in the garden, or any area immediately surrounding the house if there were motion or trip sensor security measures in place. *Scratch that worry.*

He also couldn't understand why there was more than one dog. When one dog barks it could be a sign of trespass or danger, but with more than one making a noise it could just be playful games between them. The delay in reacting to the noises of more than one animal was precious time wasted by any security detail.

*Mistake number two.*

He focussed on the garage adjoining the house and noted the doorway leading from the rear to the patio area. It was likely that through that door there would be another door leading directly from the garage to the house itself.

*Possible entry point number one.*

Just as he was shifting his gaze away from the garage door, it opened to reveal a tall, ginger-headed man dressed in an unimaginative white shirt and dark coloured tie. Everything about him said security, but the real telltale was the underarm holster strapped around his shoulder and secured with a belt running across his midriff.

*Where did they get these people from?*

An hour later he was back in his car and driving past the front of the house along a generously wide, but secluded roadway servicing the exclusive properties. A short squat man was walking across the front of the house as McSweeney drove by, and there was time for him to note enough detail to be sure this was a second member of security.

He gunned the engine and headed home.

The next day he was at Glasgow International Airport and settled into an early morning transit train to Epsom Downs, the most direct route he could find to get quickly and safely to his target area. The wheels of planning were firmly in motion, and he needed to plot in precise times and movements both to and from the job.

How far from the train station to the house? What form of transport to use? How to get the equipment he needed on site? How to make his getaway after the job was finished?

He spent most of the day travelling around the area in either taxis or walking from one location to the next. During this time he improvised a few disguises, simply swapping between overcoats or jackets, using, and not using spectacles, and on occasions wearing a variety of headwear.

Satisfied he was not attracting any attention, he constructed the various strands of his plan.

He had decided to work the plan in reverse from his movements today. Whoever was chosen for the job would drive down from Glasgow in a stolen car to be abandoned in the Golf Club park. A ticket on the Epsom Downs to Glasgow International rail link would be purchased in advance, to afford only a short window of opportunity between the time he left the scene and the time the train started from the station. He knew the dragnet would close in rapidly, and that travel by road was out of the question.

It was also clear to him that if the man missed his train time, it was unlikely any more trains would run, and he would be trapped in Epsom.

Even if the police tracked the movements of a man back to Glasgow International Airport, McSweeney knew they would be chasing a ghost. Changes in disguise would see to it that CCTV would be useless in tracking individuals.

But - and there was always a but - he had to prepare for every eventuality.

He accepted that the weakness in the scheme was the need to time the action close to the departure of the train from Epsom, and to make sure the assassin was on that train. If the man failed to board, he would be left stranded, having to scurry around Epsom looking for a bolthole that wouldn't hold up to the intense follow-up police search.

His plan B would have to involve alternative transportation out of the area. He would arrange for two separate cars driven by volunteers. The first would act as a transport from the target house to the train station. If the man missed the train, McSweeney would switch to another car already parked there, and make his way out of the area as fast as possible towards London.

Back in his office, McSweeney poured over the details, immersing himself in every aspect of the plan. He subjected it to constant challenge and change and eventually settled on a workable solution.

On Thursday evening he left work as usual, and headed home. The lights were on in most rooms and he knew Mary would be in the kitchen preparing dinner and trying to keep Jackie amused in the playpen, where the boy was put to avoid the kinds of domestic accidents that can happen when mums are moving hot saucepans around the room.

At the sound of his entry, his son became animated in the playpen, jumping up and down on the toy-strewn bottom and mouthing the word "Daddy" over and over again. It was a sound that always melted his heart.

He moved to his wife's side, gave her a gentle peck on the cheek as she ladled cabbage from a pot into a serving dish, and then stooped to pick up his son. He hugged him tightly and then flung his squealing son up in the air several times, delighting in the laughs it drew from the toddler.

Mary McSweeney was an accomplished cook and he usually looked forward to her midweek three-courser. As he looked at her, she turned from the cooker, her face smudged in flour, and smiled in a way he found totally disarming.

"How did your trips go?"

He shot her a worried look. "Mary, we need to talk."

Two hours later the dinner dishes were washed and put away. They both supervised putting their son to bed and walked back downstairs. Mary carried two glasses of red wine into the sitting room.

"What's wrong, Fergal?"

He took her through his conversation with Liam Nolan three days earlier. He held nothing back, including his trips to Epsom, and the detailed plan he had put together for the assassination of the Secretary of State. When he finished, he noticed the colour had drained from her face, and she was staring open-mouthed.

Finally, she spoke.

"This is too much. You can't do this. That poor man is only doing his job. He doesn't deserve this. This is murder. You have to call the whole thing off."

McSweeney took her hands in his.

"I can't call it off Mary. Even if I wasn't involved, they would go ahead. They've been planning this for months and nothing can stop it."

The tears started to flow down her face.

"When will it all end? Will they leave you alone after this? Will we ever have a normal life? At least you won't have to go on risking your life. I'm proud of the way you stood up to them and made them agree to stop using you. Will that truly mean you will be out of the action?"

McSweeney had thought a hundred times about how he would tell her the next part. In the end he just let it tumble out.

"Listen Mary, I don't think it will end here. No matter what Nolan agreed to, I don't trust the fucker. We'll always be looking over our shoulders. Nolan's used to getting his own way and he won't take kindly to me giving him an earful and threatening him."

"But you said he agreed you could take a back seat." It was more of a question than a statement.

"That's only because he needs me for the planning. When this is over, he's going to start thinking differently."

"What are we going to do?"

"There's only one thing we can do, Mary. We've got to up stakes and go to America. I have friends there who will help us with a new identity, a new life. We can bring up little Jackie away from all this madness."

McSweeney stared at his wife waiting for a response. When it eventually came, it surprised him.

"Let's do it! I've always wanted to live in America."

# Chapter 18
## Dublin Hotel

LIAM NOLAN WAS IN a foul mood as he watched his men file into the downtown hotel lounge and walk towards his table. He waited patiently while they took their seats before he addressed them.

"This arms dump find in the North is a bitter pill to swallow. Is there still no trace of the two operatives? Have they turned supergrasses? We've got to find out what's going on and plug the leaks."

His eyes fell on Patrick Pearse.

"I've been in touch with Belfast and they have exhausted every angle, but there's no sign of O'Brien and Perry, that's the two that transferred a shipment to the dump the day before it was raided by the RUC. They've dropped off the map and we can't find any evidence they're being held by the authorities."

"Are our sources in the various RUC stations coming forward?"

"Yes. They tell us there's no mention of the boys, and if they were held anywhere in the country, they would know about it."

"What about," Joe Coyle interrupted, "if they had planned this for months with the security forces and were already set up with a new identity."

"To be honest, it's the only thing that makes sense, but Belfast can't understand it. These two were dedicated volunteers and had given no inkling of disaffection. Naturally, we've interrogated the families and friends, but they are as bewildered as we are."

Nolan ran the fingers of his right hand through the crop of mousey brown hair that topped his aquiline features. "This has come at a bad time for us. We need to get this sorted, find these fuckers, and move on to the real business at hand. We've been taking too many hits lately and I'm beginning to believe the Brits have stolen a march on us."

"What are you getting at?" The question was from Joe Coyle.

Nolan beckoned the group closer.

"Remember what I told you after the meeting with the Brit agent? I said the fuckers intended to do what we're planning to do, and that's hit hard before any talks start. All these reversals of late are too coincidental. I think the Brits are behind everything we've been suffering."

It was Coyle who spoke next. "Now that you say it, all these things started happening not long after your meeting. We lost two operatives in a car bomb, we keep getting press nonsense about informers, and then O'Brien and Perry go missing. Our biggest arms dump in the North is uncovered, Pat Duggan gets arrested, Tommy Boyle is assassinated, and John Kelly is killed by the RUC during the hit on that loyalist fucker."

Nolan didn't need a full commentary, and his annoyance was evident in the sharp reply. "And what have we been doing in the meantime? I'll tell you what we've been doing. Absolutely nothing!"

Dooley cut in. "We're nearly there with our biggest ever operation. When we finish the job at Epsom, we'll be way ahead of the Brits."

Nolan smacked him affectionately on the knee. "You're missing the point Francis. We've dropped everything to prepare for the Epsom job. The media thinks we're on the run. Hell, even our own troops are beginning to get disheartened. We're leaving ourselves wide open!"

"This is leading somewhere. What's on your mind, Liam?"

"It's really rather simple, Joe. The Brits would know we intend to up our game. They'll have been waiting for the start of something, but so far we haven't delivered..."

Coyle finished the sentence for him "... and the longer we wait the more they'll know we're planning something big."

"Joe, I can always count on you to weigh up a situation. You're bang on the money. They'll be guessing by now that we're planning something big and that will put us at a disadvantage. They'll be looking at things they never looked at before. They might even stumble on what we intend to do."

"I can guarantee that our security is watertight. They couldn't possibly get wind of our operation."

Nolan struggled to keep the anger from his voice. "I was talking generally rather than specifically. What if they simply looked at the possibility of a ministerial hit, I mean a hit on any minister, not specifically our target? They would start altering security procedures, change planned appointments, anything to get a jump on us."

"Do you think that's possible?" The question came from Pearse.

"Yes, and it's our own fault. We should have been throwing up smokescreens, putting them on false trails instead of sitting on our asses. Well that stops right now. I want to launch one of the biggest, most sustained periods of activity we've ever had, and I want it to start right away."

He paused to take a sip of whiskey before turning to Dooley, "How long will it take to replace the equipment lost at the dump?"

"There's no doubt this is a body blow, but it won't hamper our operations too much. We've enough in other stores and dumps and we hope to be getting a fresh shipment from our Libyan friends within the next two months. It depends on what you have in mind."

Nolan was staring off at the distance. He still couldn't get his mind around the assassination of Tommy Boyle. He knew that the death of the popular head of the movement's racketeering in Dublin had caused mayhem in the rank and file members. People were looking over their shoulders wondering who was next, despite assurances from high command that this was not a hit sanctioned from the inside.

This wasn't going to go away anytime soon, and Nolan knew he needed to start turning their fortunes around at perhaps the most crucial period for his leadership. He turned back to face the group of men seated around the table.

"Here's what we'll do. I want every brigade commander to come up with a number of operations designed to bring the North to a standstill. I don't care what they do. Give them a free rein. I want car bombs, drive-by shootings at police stations, hoax bomb alerts, anything that will point to a major offensive by us. I want the Brits to think this is our response, I want them to concentrate their resources one way while we operate another way."

His words led to animated conversations between the others. They were all nodding agreement at Nolan's plan when he held up his hand to stop the talk.

"There's one more thing. We've had a slight hitch with the Epsom job. Our Scottish friend has gotten cold feet, but it's nothing that can't be handled."

For the next thirty minutes he outlined what he intended to do.

# Chapter 19
## Bishopscourt

MIKE DEVON WAS MORE and more convinced that the mysterious Scotland figure talked about by the prisoner, O'Brien, was the one and same person he had encountered in an Irish bar in Chicago all those years ago.

He contacted Mark Garrett and asked him to investigate what O'Brien had described as "a Belfast operation" sometime the previous year. There was practically nothing to go on, but Devon helped Garrett to narrow down the search.

"This guy will not have been involved in any run-of-the-mill nonsense. He's a specialist and will have been brought in only for a difficult or high profile op. We're looking for an unsolved, something that made the headlines, but didn't get off base one in the follow up investigations. Put everything you have on this Mark, this could be our best lead to tracking down a real sonofabitch."

The following morning he had his answer. Garrett called on the secure line and briefed him with his findings.

"There were a few cases that could fit the bill of the calibre of operative you're talking about, but there's one that really stands out. In September last year, a retired RUC Detective Chief Inspector by the name of John Turnbull was murdered in his home. It was classic covert stuff, no forced entry, no clues left behind, and the victim despatched with a double tap."

"What do we know about the RUC's investigation?"

"As you would expect, there was a monumental deployment of resources. They shook every tree, rounded up all the usual suspects, but came up dry. The word at the time was that none of the Belfast boyos were involved, but nothing could be proved one way or another. The investigation just ran out of steam."

Devon pondered the details and came to a conclusion. "We need to run a cold case review on this. The detectives at the time would not have known about the Scottish angle, but if we plot this into the equation, we might get farther than they did."

"What precisely have you got in mind?" Devon thought for only a moment. "What about looking at airline passenger lists, hotel bookings in Belfast, car rentals, business meetings, and conferences, anything that ties a link back to Scotland around the time of the killing?"

"That's too much for us to handle. We would need to bring in the RUC to break down the kind of doors you're asking to be opened. It's not easy getting hands on passenger bookings for airports and ferry terminals, let alone putting together the kind of resources needed to sift through the mountain of paperwork these types of enquiries engender. It's just not possible, Mike."

Devon considered the options, before coming to a decision. "Okay, let's bring in the RUC."

"Do you know what you're saying? This could get out of control extremely fast. For one thing, how do we explain the information?"

The wheels in Devon's brain were already

turning. "We've come too far to let this get in the way. Tell the RUC you picked up some radio traffic or some such bullshit but get them on board and let's see if they can turn over a few stones. Also, I think it's time we let them have a copy of the police composite picture from Chicago. It might help them trace back to a passport or driving licence. It might also help if they pass the composite to their counterparts in the Scotland terrorist unit. We've got to run this guy down."

He spent another ten minutes going through with Garret, the best possible way to approach the RUC.

When they reached the end of their conversation, there was a pause before Garret spoke again. "I have to ask you, Mike. How much of this is personal and how much is really to do with why we set up this operation in the first place?"

The question stunned Devon, not least because he hadn't thought of it from that angle. "You deserve an honest answer, Mark, and I'll give you one. Sure, I want this bastard badly as payback for Chicago, but up until a few seconds ago my thoughts were only on the current mission. I know what this bastard's capable of and if he's coming in to play again, you can bet your bottom dollar he'll leave a trail of bodies all over the place. If we let that happen, then everything you and I have worked for over the past year will count for nothing. That's the reason why we have to find him."

# Chapter 20
## RUC Castlereagh

BILLY CARTER LISTENED intently to Martin Vennison's report of events over the past twenty-four hours. Of most interest was the revelation that military liaison officer, Mark Garrett, had been tailed to Bishopscourt, an RAF base supposedly outside the remit of the Army.

Try as he could, Carter couldn't come up with a logical explanation for Garrett's visit.

His thoughts were interrupted by a flashing red light on a nearby telephone console. He grabbed it, listened for several minutes, and then spoke gruffly into the mouthpiece. "You'd better come over right now."

He rested the handset back on its cradle and turned to Vennison. "This is getting real interesting. Speak of the devil and he appears."

"What is it, sir?"

"That was Captain Garrett and he says he needs to see us urgently with some vital information. He wouldn't elaborate over the phone but suffice to say he has credible Intel about one of our high profile cases and is on his way here."

Thirty minutes later, Carter listened as Mark Garrett spoke from a seat opposite him at the conference table in his office.

"I'll get straight to the point, Detective Chief Superintendent. One of our satellite listening systems picked up on some chatter, which we believe could be extremely critical in your investigation into the murder of your former colleague John Turnbull last year."

Carter felt as though an electric shock had just passed through his body. "The hell you say. Spell it out boy; tell us what you've got!"

He listened as Garrett explained about a satellite listening station picking up what appeared to be a conversation emerging from a telephone landline somewhere in Belfast. The listeners hadn't been able to trace the origins of the call, but they were alerted by the mention of Turnbull's name and a reference to a Scotland-based shooter who carried out the hit.

Carter interrupted the flow. "How did Turnbull's name raise a flag?"

"The names of all murder victims in the United Kingdom are listed in satellite data-mining databases, which trigger a transcript of any conversation using the pre-loaded alert words."

Garrett stopped speaking to hand a sheet of paper to Carter. "This is the exact transcript of the conversation that took place just over a week ago. Since then it has gone through several channels before landing on my desk. I've brought it to you as soon as I realised its significance."

Carter's eyes ran down the lines of type, and when he finished reading, he handed the note to Martin Vennison. Then he turned back towards Garrett. "I suppose there's little point in asking you where exactly this came from."

"I'm sure you understand the use of this technology goes way beyond the usual security measures. Other than not being able to identify the satellite or its use, I can confirm this is all we have."

Vennison cut in. "You say this was recorded over a week ago, so how come it has taken so long to reach us?"

"There's nothing mysterious here, Inspector. More than one thousand automated transcripts are processed every day. These are screened by low-level operatives, ranked in order of potential importance, and passed progressively up the line to different Intelligence agencies. Other than trans-cripts that contain trigger words such as 'bomb,' it usually takes quite a few days to ensure that credible transcripts reach the right destination."

"And there's no way of tracing where this emanated from other than the general area of Belfast?"

"No, this is not real-time surveillance. The chatter that goes on in telephones, CB handsets and a host of other devices using the airwaves, is filtered through the satellite databases. When a trigger word is identified, a transcript is prepared and sent to the monitoring station in much the same way that fax machines work. As you can imagine, the data printer is working overtime and more than ninety per cent of notices are eventually discarded. At the moment, the technology is not in place to trace back to the source, although that is expected to be available over the next few years. The Americans are leading the way through NASA, but we still have a bit to go to refine the various systems. In the meantime, we make do."

Carter was shaken by the news but tried not to let it show by dropping his head and rummaging through papers in front of him. "So how did this transcript get to you?"

"The original report was sent for review to MI5, who pulled the file and traced the name back to a Belfast murder. As I'm sure you're aware, I am the MI5 liaison for Northern Ireland, and so it was forwarded to me. I admit I sat on it for a few days while I tried to gather additional Intel that may be of use to you...."

"You mean you wasted valuable time in contacting us."

"On the contrary, sir. The mention in the transcript of an IRA specialist based in Scotland gave me an idea to contact a few of our own operatives who may have come across the term or who may know something about specialists, either working directly for or hired by the IRA."

Carter eyed Garrett closely as he delved into a folder and withdrew another sheet of paper. "What have we here?"

"This is a composite photo of a man who was working for the IRA in America a number of years ago. We know he was responsible for several deaths, including two of our own operatives, but he escaped the dragnet and went to ground. At the time, we believed he was either back in Ireland or living somewhere on the continent. Nothing else was heard from him."

Carter stared at the grainy image, trying to come to terms with what he was being told. "Why wasn't this sketch circulated at the time to the RUC?"

"Back then, the manhunt was concentrated in America and it was over a year before the authorities concluded that the fugitive had fled the country. The trail went cold and the file remained within MI5 until now. It was judged that this operative had probably been retired and would not surface again, although of course, he was kept on the watching lists of both the FBI and MI5."

"And nobody thought the RUC might be able to put a name to the sketch?" The anger in Billy Carter's voice was thinly concealed.

"Sir, I don't have all the answers and frankly I've gone out on a limb to get this information to you."

"What makes you think this man is responsible for the murder of John Turnbull?"

"Frankly, I don't know whether he is or isn't the man you're looking for. The very mention of the word 'specialist' matched the term used by our American operatives at the time, and I believed it was worth drawing your attention to it. The fact there is a specialist IRA hit man based in Scotland makes it a credible line of enquiry and is one that will be pursued by MI5. I thought you might want in on this."

As was his usual habit, Billy Carter rose from his seat and started pacing the room. Eventually he turned back to Garrett. "Can we interview any of the operatives who were originally involved in the American operation?"

"Out of the question." Garrett's unequivocal tone left no room for further debate.

"Can we get our hands on any details or notes on the operation?"

"No chance."

"What can we get?"

"Basically, what you have, which is pretty much what we have. Look, we could all be barking up the wrong tree, but you've got to admit this takes you farther along the road than you've previously gotten with the Turnbull case. From our point of view, it might also reopen an avenue that's been closed for a long time. We also lost good people, and like you, we want this bastard."

"Okay," said Carter. "What can you tell us generally about the American operation?"

"Off the record, we were tracking down a number of IRA arms shipments and had identified all the players in a unit operating in the Chicago area. We were closing in on the top men when this new figure emerged from literally nowhere and started cleaning house. Somehow, he learned the identities of our operatives, killed two of them, and almost got a third before skipping the scene. He was not run of the mill, which is why he was described as a specialist in our reports. Flimsy though it may be, that is where I've made this connection. It's up to you to decide how you're going to proceed."

# Chapter 21
## Glasgow

THE JOURNEY FROM Dublin to Glasgow was relatively stress-free, but extremely circuitous for Liam Nolan. He knew his name and face was at the top of all security force watchlists throughout Northern Ireland and mainline Britain. Because of that, he needed to take extra precautions.

One of his many disguises and stock of false papers was always guaranteed to get round cursory checks, but the real guarantee of beating detection was to avoid the risk of being stopped. To do this he travelled north to Belfast, taking one of many routes that crossed the border away from main roads - on this occasion being handed over to a local farmer, whose tractor took him across an open field, starting in the Republic of Ireland and ending up in Northern Ireland. Here he was met by a car, which taxied him into the centre of Belfast.

Nolan loved the eccentricity of the field. There were no walls or hedges, no signposts or tracks to demarcate its international boundaries. It was one of many such anomalies on the border and one of the reasons why he was able to move his IRA volunteers so freely between the two jurisdictions.

Once in Belfast, Nolan boarded a bus to Larne harbour and became a foot passenger on the Larne to Stranraer ferry. A Northern Ireland driving licence was produced at the ticket counter to match with the telephone reservation made in the name of his alias. He was shown immediately to the passenger terminal.

Just under three hours later he walked off the ferry and made his way to a short-term passenger car park where a local recruit was waiting to transport him by road across Ayrshire and into Glasgow.

By agreement, he met with McSweeney at his car sales business. It was early evening and only a skeleton staff was on duty for the last part of the sales shift, due to end at 9pm. It wasn't unusual for the boss to hold evening meetings or to stay on the premises after they had locked up for the day.

Nolan entered the showroom and was shown to the upstairs office where McSweeney was seated beside a coffee table.

Nolan shook McSweeney's hand and asked after his welfare. When the junior salesman, who had escorted Nolan to the room, left and closed the door firmly behind him, Nolan immediately dropped the façade.

"This is some mess you've landed us in Fergal. How the fuck are we expected to come up with another operative to take your place at this late stage?"

"Look, Nolan. What's done is done. You must have someone in mind otherwise you wouldn't have made this trip. So, tell me what you want me to do."

Nolan considered for a moment before responding.

"It so happens I have someone capable of stepping in, not that you're off the hook for turning your back on us. I won't forget this."

Nolan watched McSweeney's eyes narrow. He knew those penetrating slits were windows into the soul of a dangerous and highly skilled assassin; one the IRA had expended considerable time and resources to hone to perfection. He had hoped his words would evoke a response, maybe even lead to McSweeney losing his temper. If push came to shove, Nolan fancied his chances.

Nolan's right hand was pushed deep into the pocket of his overcoat, his fist wrapped around a small-calibre Beretta. He waited for the slightest wrong move.

When McSweeney eventually spoke, the calm words surprised Nolan.

"I'm not going to pick a fight with you. I thought we'd already been over that ground. If my previous terms are not acceptable, then just say so and we'll take it from here. Oh, and just so that you know; I can get across this table and snap your neck before you have time to clear the weapon in your right-hand pocket. So, what's it to be?"

Nolan weighed the options. Nothing would give him greater pleasure than ending this here and now. The idea that McSweeney could get to him before he cleared his pocket was laughable. He could spring back from the seat and get off two shots before McSweeney got even halfway.

But he had bigger things to worry about. Getting trapped in Scotland while he evaded a murder scene was something he simply couldn't risk. McSweeney would keep for now.

He withdrew his hand from the coat and held the empty palm towards McSweeney.

"I haven't come here for a pissing contest. We don't have time to waste on personal feelings. Let's just go through this plan of yours and hope you've covered all the bases."

Deep down Nolan was seething, but held his temper in check and spent the better part of three hours delving through maps and crude diagrams until he was satisfied he knew all that he could about the terrain, and the approaches to the Epsom target house.

He didn't have the benefit of McSweeney's on-the-ground feel for the area, but with detailed probing he constructed a full mental picture of what was involved.


Three hundred and fifty miles due south from where Nolan and McSweeney were finalising their plans, a dark blue Ford Mondeo Estate pulled into a deserted supermarket car park close to a train station entrance. Francis Dooley reached across to the passenger seat, activated a stopwatch, and set off again on a journey through the sleepy suburbs.

He kept his speed at thirty miles per hour and observed the red stop at two sets of traffic lights. He crossed a main road leading towards the town centre and drove uphill towards a row of exclusive homes set into the hills of a countryside blanketed by unspoilt greenery.

It was late at night and he made mental notes of obvious time delays that would be caused by early evening traffic. Adjustments for this could be made later.

He passed one of the large houses and continued to the end of the road, emerging eventually onto the main road. He headed towards the town centre and then signalled right to follow a sign embossed in yellow lettering. Two miles farther, he again signalled and turned left to follow a similar sign, indicating a golf club was one mile along a narrow road framed by hedgerows.

Five minutes later, he pulled into the club car park and reached across to depress the button on his stopwatch. There were a few cars scattered around the park, but no one in sight to watch as he wrote down the time shown on the watch. He reset the timepiece, manoeuvred out of the park, and followed a sign for the railway station.

Within twenty minutes, he pulled into the station's customer car park and again depressed the stopwatch. After scribbling a few lines in his notebook, he alighted from the car and walked to the station entrance.

At 3am the place was deserted as he headed for the main timetable noticeboard and scanned the information until he found what he was looking for. The first train to Glasgow was not due until 7.30am.

Dooley returned to his car, removed his jacket, and made a pillow as he settled across the two front seats, knowing a commuter waiting for an early morning train would attract no attention. He settled into a light sleep.

The early morning bustle of a busy station woke him from his slumbers at just after 6am. He noticed the car park had started to fill up. The angry noise of a diesel passenger train roared away from the station as he crossed to the ticket office. He bought a one-way ticket to the Glasgow International terminal and noted with relief that the station café was open for business.

He would pass the next ninety minutes sitting over a light breakfast and several mugs of tea before setting off on the next leg of his journey.

The car would be left in the park and eventually reunited with its owner. It was stolen from a driveway the previous evening, the theft unlikely to be discovered until the man was on his way to Glasgow.

Nolan was grateful to take his leave of McSweeney. He had insisted on staying the night at the sales showroom and waved off offers to drive him back to the airport. He had an appointment in the morning and needed to lie low until then.

He was provided with one of the salesroom's used Mercedes and explained where he could leave it to be picked up later. With little more than a curt farewell, he drove out of the industrial estate and merged with the early morning rush-hour traffic. He followed the signs for Glasgow International Airport.

At the short-stay car park thirty minutes later, he settled to await passengers emerging from the busy train station close to the main terminal entrance.

A man wandered away from the main throng of people milling around the terminal and threaded his way through the rows of parked cars. Nolan recognised the pock-marked face, climbed out of the car, and stood with his hand holding open the driver's door as he tried to get the man's attention.

Eventually the man noticed the gesticulations and changed his direction. Nolan climbed back into his seat and waited for the passenger door to open.

Dooley pulled back the handle and sank into the generous seat. "I've got everything you asked for."

Nolan didn't mind the absence of greetings and small talk. It was what he had come to expect from a man with whom he had spent most of his adult life. "We're good at my end. Let's get back to the ferry and head home."

# Chapter 22
## Dundalk Hotel

MIKE DEVON HOPED it was the breakthrough he had been waiting for. He had pressed undercover operative Taffy Thomas to take all steps to find what he could about the Dublin hotel meeting that was revealed during the recent round of interrogations.

A response had come through on the green-coloured handset that was set up exclusively as Thomas' link with the base. It was a cryptic message demanding an urgent meeting at a small hotel just across the border outside Newry.

When Thomas walked into the hotel's lounge bar, Devon was struck by the transformation in the features of the former demolitions man. The mop of brown hair was cut short and showing more than a few signs of heavy greying. It sat over a gaunt face that was once rounded and wrinkle-free. Gone was the sparkle that was always a feature of his eyes.

Devon knew that anywhere in the world, under-cover work was not for the faint-hearted. In Ireland, it was foolhardy at best, suicidal at the extreme.

As he watched Thomas stride across the room, he knew that the lack of contact with family and former friends, the ever-present threat of discovery, and the constant lies and subterfuge had taken a heavy toll. The features and hang-dog demeanor told Devon that Thomas had probably lived two lifetimes over the past eight months.

He tried to erase the concern from his face and voice. "Taffy, you're looking good. How's things been for you?"

Thomas shook Devon's hand warmly, gripping tightly as if it was the only human contact he had had for some time. "Mike, I can't tell you how good it is to see a friendly face. I've been going stir-crazy sitting in that one-room apartment of mine, and letting those fuckers push me this way and that. I think I've got some news for you, but it may have come at a price."

Devon leaned forward to pour a cup of coffee from the pot he had ordered before Thomas's arrival. "What do you mean, Taffy?"

"I know you said this was urgent and that I should push as hard as I could. Well, I might have pushed too hard. I think I've aroused some suspicions. I don't know Mike, maybe I'm just getting paranoid."

Devon cut him off. "Taffy, I've been there before. I once thought I was being paranoid. It ended up with two particularly good people getting killed. Sometimes you've just got to go with your gut. Tell me what's happened."

Thomas seemed glad to unburden some of his thoughts and fears. He explained that from the moment he had arrived in Dundalk to set up a wholesale electrical supply business as an advance part of the Storm 74 project, he had been forced to literally switch off his old life. No contact with friends or family, worm his way into the trust of his country's enemies, and somehow keep up the front for as long as possible.

Devon listened as Thomas related his story.


Taffy Thomas seemed an ideal choice to go

undercover in Ireland. The planners wanted to set up an electrical business and who better than a man who had spent four years training with elite bomb-making and bomb-disposal squads based with the SAS in Hertfordshire.

Thomas constructed a legend for himself that centred on fictional time served overseas with the French Foreign Legion. He liked to tell casual acquaintances that as a true-blooded Welshman, he couldn't serve in the British Army, the choice offered to him by magistrates, who were threatening to send him to prison after a string of misdemeanors in his native Cardiff.

His story was that he jumped bail and headed to Morocco to enlist with the famed regiment. After doing fifteen years with the Legion, and seeing very little sun or sand, he decided to make a new start in Ireland, the birthplace of his grandfather.

It all seemed very plausible, especially when the planners were able to come up with a "grandfather" who had no other living relatives in Ireland, and conveniently died in America after emigrating forty years ago. It was not a story that could be tracked down.

Those same planners also bankrolled the electrical shop for Thomas. Apart from the fact that electrics were his area of expertise, and he would therefore be comfortable with his new persona, it was hoped the shop might draw in some customers looking for the kind of circuit boards, remote switch units, or reels of electrical wire that could be used for things other than those intended.

He kept his head down for the first three months, drinking in popular bars and trying to make as many friends as he could with the locals.

Gradually a few men began to talk more openly, usually about how well the IRA was doing in the war against the British.

He knew they said these things to check where his sympathies were. He always made it clear the fucking Brits should never have been in Ireland and should be kicked out as soon as possible.

Things took a dramatic leap forward one night when Thomas answered the doorbell of his flat above the business. Two men he knew well from socialising in the local pub, told him they had an emergency and needed his help. They took him to a small out-of-town storage depot and showed him a bomb, which had been discovered under the bonnet of a van.

They had spun a story that their mate was caught up in a small drugs war with a notorious rival gang and had found the device when he was servicing the vehicle earlier that day. They didn't know what to do and hoped Thomas might be able to help.

He knew that what he was being told was a load of balls, but also knew he had to react the right way. These were not the kind of men who would simply allow him to say he couldn't help and walk away as if nothing had happened. It was a test, and one Thomas simply had to pass.

One glance at the bomb told him that disarming it would not present any problems, but he had a feeling it was more than his skills they were testing.

"Look, I want nothing to do with drugs," he had told them. "I don't mind bombs, Christ I've seen enough of them with the Foreign Legion. I'll disarm this thing, but don't ask me to do anything that involves drugs."

The response had seemed to appease the men.

One of them stepped forward. "We just want this thing disarmed and out of the way. Do that for us and I promise we'll never ask you to get involved with drugs."

Thomas had set about making the crude device safe. He had recognised the small block of Semtex 10, a Czechoslovakian plastic explosive that had become synonymous with terrorists the world over and was a particular favourite with the IRA.

The explosive had been moulded around the vehicle's starter unit, with a detonator cap attached to a wire leading to a small timing device tied around a fan pipe. The timepiece was still set at zero. Thomas had pulled the detonator from the explosive and removed all the other parts.

"Someone forgot to set the timer," he told the men who were waiting a safe distance away. "You could have driven this thing to Kingdom come and the bomb would not have detonated."

He knew the device had been set deliberately this way to ensure there would be no accidents for any of the men involved.

The following night the men had called again with Thomas to take him for a celebratory drink. Over the course of the evening, he had allowed them to take the conversation where they wanted it to go. By the time they had finished their last drink, he was the IRA's newest recruit. From there it had been a case of building trust, although he knew he would never be fully accepted. Undercover operatives were taught to understand that an outsider would always be an outsider - there would be many discussions he was excluded from, and many people he was not allowed to meet. He had to learn to live with what he got.

Devon listened as Thomas filled him in on snippets of his life over the past six months. It was like someone unburdening themselves in a confessional, seizing an opportunity to talk without the gut-wrenching fear of tripping up. Devon had been there and had experienced the isolation of living on a tightrope.

He let Thomas talk it all out before deciding to bring him back on track. "Taffy, I need to know what you've found out about Nolan."

The figure across from him seemed to snap out of his melancholy. He sat upright and began talking in a measured voice. "I started out by pushing some of the lesser lights for information about Nolan and the other names you supplied. Everyone was happy to talk as if they were all bosom buddies, but few of them knew anything of substance.

"Then I get to drinking with one of the higher ups and he tells me a few interesting things about a big job coming up and that he might be part of it. Says it will not be in Ireland, and that the world will sit up and take notice."

"Anything else?" Devon was unable to keep the impatience from his voice.

"I'm coming to it, Mike. I started to get the feeling I pushed too hard because every time I tried to bring up the subject, there was nothing. Nobody wanted to talk. Then one of my regular drinking buddies said something interesting."

"What was it?"

Thomas looked around the room as if checking for anyone who might be listening. "Right out of the blue this guy asks me why I'm so interested in the assassination operation."

"He used the word 'assassination'? Did he say who?"

"No, but I got the impression that it was someone from the Government. This guy kept referring to teaching ministers a lesson about trying to run the affairs of Ireland...."

Devon suddenly raised a hand from the table and motioned to Thomas to stop. He had noted the earlier appearance of two men coming through the hotel front door and into the lounge. Something about them marked them as worth watching. Now he was sure his instincts were true. A third man had just emerged from a rear corridor that led to toilets, according to a sign on the wall.

"Taffy, don't turn round. Is it possible you were followed here?"

"I took all the usual precautions, but you just never know. What's going on?"

Devon told him about the new arrivals. Two men, one in a suit, the other wearing a green tweed sports jacket, seated at the right side of the bar. The third, wearing dark horn-rimmed glasses and making a lousy pretence of reading a paper, was opposite them at the left side of the bar. "Taffy, without making it obvious, see if you recognise any of them."

Thomas swivelled in his chair and raised his hand as if to attract the attention of one of the waiters before turning back to Devon. "Can't see the face of the man behind the paper and I don't recognise the man in the suit, but I do know the one in the green jacket."

"So, we can take it you're compromised?"

"I guess so. I'm sorry, Mike. I shouldn't have let

this happen."

"Nonsense, Taffy. This was my doing. I was the one who asked you to push the boat out. What's done is done and, anyway, this might be a blessing in disguise."

"What do you mean?"

Devon walked him through a plan that was forming in his mind. They had to extricate themselves from what was a potentially lethal situation and, if they could get one of their visitors to talk, it might just be a bonus. He quizzed Thomas about his knowledge of the hotel layout and tried to weigh up the risks of starting something inside the premises or taking it outside to the car park.

He was still assessing the angles when a shadow fell across the table.

"This looks very cosy." It was the man with the newspaper.

"Got something in mind friend?" Devon asked in a matter-of-fact manner.

The man nodded down to the newspaper folded across the bottom of his right arm. Protruding from the fold was the snub-nosed shape of the barrel of a revolver. It was aimed directly at Devon's head.

Devon noticed the two men at the bar rise from the seats and walk towards the foyer to take up station either side of the entrance doors. The man in the suit had an overcoat draped over his arm and made a great show of suggesting he too, had a concealed weapon. Green jacket kept his hands buried into his pockets.

The man with the newspaper spoke. "We're going to take a little walk to one of the guest rooms. We just want a chat, but if you try anything stupid, we will have no hesitation in killing you. Do I make myself clear?"

Devon didn't respond. He knew they were well and truly boxed in. One wrong move would lead to a firefight they couldn't possibly win. He remembered his training instructor's old mantra: *Don't be impatient, wait your time and an opportunity will present itself.*

"I said, do I make myself clear?"

"Yes," Devon intoned, "there are no heroes here. I'm sure this is just a misunderstanding that can be cleared up." He nodded his eyes fractionally to the right and then to the left. He hoped Thomas wasn't out of practice and would read the message correctly.

He stood up and walked towards the lounge entrance, with Thomas falling in step alongside. The newspaper man kept just enough distance to avoid being sideswiped whilst ahead, the two men in the foyer kept their eyes rigidly fixed on their quarry.

Devon scanned the entrance. It was a double-door opening with both sides pushed flat against the foyer side and hooked to the wall. No chance of slamming a door into faces.

As the group approached the door arch, a teenage waiter carrying a tray of drinks walked away from the bar and was cutting a path towards them. Devon paused and signalled for the youngster to go ahead of them. As he walked across their front, Devon shot out a leg and tripped him.

The tray of drinks was momentarily suspended in air as the waiter tumbled towards the carpet. Devon ducked his head as if to avoid the flying glasses. In the same motion swivelled on his right foot and aimed an extended left-footed kick at newspaper man coming behind him.

It was not a kick designed to hurt or disable, but

Devon was satisfied the glancing blow from his toecap midway down the man's right leg caused him to jump back, lose balance, and tumble towards the nearest table.

Devon continued his swivel through ninety degrees and rose to look down on the gunman. He had fallen downwards against the table but recovered his balance and was on his way back up, his right hand still clutching the revolver and bringing it to bear on Devon.

The newspaper tumbled to the floor, but the man's posture meant he was now looking up at Devon, exposing his neck. That was all the opening Devon needed. He drove a straight-arm jab, tight fingers fully extended, into the man's throat.

It was a lethal blow delivered with the full weight and momentum of Devon's thrust, the fingers tearing into the exposed flesh and horribly crushing the vital airway passage.

The man collapsed under the weight of the blow, sending tables and chairs flying among the other bar patrons, who were still trying to understand what was happening.

The man clutched vainly at his throat trying to force air through the closed passage. The terrified look on his face remained as he struggled on the carpeted floor for another twenty seconds and then went still.

By that time, Devon had already turned towards the doorway to assess the threat from the other two assailants.

He was glad to see Taffy was quick to react to his attack on the gunman. He had clearly remembered the eye movements meant *I'll go right, you go left.*

As the unfortunate waiter fell to the ground,

Thomas had made as if to catch him. He grabbed the youth around the waist and ran him towards green jacket standing to the left of the door.

The last thing Devon remembered was all three figures collapsing to the ground. By the time he had dealt with his own gunman, Devon was horrified to see Thomas emerge from a melee of limbs on the foyer floor to stare down the barrel of a compact Smith and Wesson pistol being held by the man in the green jacket.

Devon tore through the doorway, his hands already grabbing for a Glock jammed into a waistband holster at the back of his trousers. Even as he raised the weapon to aim towards the second gunman man, he knew he was too late.

Devon let out a fierce scream in the hope of drawing the man's attention away from Thomas, but to no avail. The gunmen calmly squeezed the trigger and Thomas fell backwards over the bodies still squirming on the floor.

Devon squeezed off three rapid-fire shots on the run towards the gunman and noted with relish that all found centre mass. As he rushed past the falling body, he knocked the pistol from the man's grip and aimed a fourth shot directly into the man's face.

Green jacket was now struggling to his feet. Devon couldn't risk shooting towards him, not with Taffy lying so close. It was not that he would miss at such close range, but he knew a through-and-through round would hit Taffy as it exited the target's body.

Instead, Devon turned the gun in his hand and aimed a vicious swipe with the handle at the side of the man's head as he ran past him. There was a satisfying crunch of bone. Green jacket collapsed unconscious against the young waiter, who was prostrate on the carpet, his hands covering his head as protection against the flying bullets.

Thomas was face upward, his eyes blinking, and his chest heaving as Devon cradled him in his arms. A red stain was growing across the front of Thomas' t-shirt as Devon gingerly opened his jacket to assess the damage. The bullet had torn in through the upper chest, but Devon had no way of knowing what internal damage it had caused.

He yelled at shocked staff to fetch a towel and had to aim his pistol at the barman before a towel was eventually produced.

He set his weapon on the ground and pressed the towel into Thomas' shirt to stem the bleeding. Then he quickly released his trousers belt, which he fastened around his friend's shoulder in a crude tourniquet.

He picked up his gun, sat back on his haunches, and tried to assess his options. He was in the Republic of Ireland and couldn't just summon up an ambulance. There would be too many questions. In any case, he himself couldn't hang around to deal with the fall-out.

He would have to risk driving Thomas back to Bishopscourt. He knew the chances of the Welshman making the journey were slim to say the least, but there were no other choices. He was not prepared to leave him behind.

He waved the gun again at the staff and ordered two waiters to carry Thomas out into the car park. He supervised the men in placing Thomas delicately across the back seat of his car, wrapped a car blanket over his friend, and shouted for onlookers to get away.

He climbed into the driver's seat, started the engine, and was already making a call back to base by the time he screamed out of the car park, causing traffic on the main road to swerve to avoid a collision.

# Chapter 23
## RUC Castlereagh

THE PAST FEW DAYS had been a hive of activity at the RUC offices of Martin Vennison. The composite picture supplied by Mark Garrett was circulated to all stations, although the chances of anyone putting a name to the line drawing were remote in the extreme.

It was nearly a decade since the composite was put together and the natural ageing of the subject, combined with any manner of disguise, was likely to render it virtually worthless. But it had to be tried.

Most of Vennison's resources were concentrated on the connection to Scotland. He had ordered George McDowell and Mo Green to backtrack through the days and weeks leading up to the assassination of DCI John Turnbull. If someone travelled from Scotland to carry out the hit, they might have left a trail, which was a piece of the puzzle not available in the original investigation.

Hotel reservations for up to one week before the assassination were being checked as were all airline and ferry passenger lists. They were looking for someone who made the journey up to a week before the killing, and a return journey up to a week afterwards.

Vennison's gut told him the assassin would get in and out quick. They would pay particular attention to the time period of three days either side of the hit, but he knew he couldn't leave anything to chance.

Airline passenger lists were easier to obtain,

with only a handful of scheduled flights operating daily between Edinburgh and Glasgow to Northern Ireland's two airports. Playing the Prevention of Terrorism Act card was always guaranteed to override any concern about warrants, and within two days he had full printed lists from British Airways and British Midlands.

For the moment he set these aside. In an initial brainstorming session with his team, he concluded the profile of their suspect was someone who worked alone and would want to maintain a certain degree of independence from the security risks of meeting and dealing with local assets.

He believed this type of man would look after his own travel arrangements, which meant he was more likely to make the journey by car. And that meant he would use one of the ferries.

Getting full lists from the two main ferry operators on the Stranraer to Larne and Belfast to Cairnryan routes was a little more troublesome. Vennison was aware most ferry tickets were sold direct through their own booking offices, but often they dealt with last-minute passengers who turned up knowing these boats were rarely fully booked for foot traffic. Car bookings were a different matter and usually had to be confirmed within three days of sailing. Eventually exhaustive lists arrived at his office.

Knowing that all angles had to be covered, he set up two sorting groups of detectives. One group dealt with car and passenger bookings, isolating those with only a driver listed on the booking. He judged it was likely the shooter was a loner and would not travel with anyone else or as part of a group booking.

The second group dealt with passenger-only

bookings, discarding all bookings by females and those involving groups.

The initial task was to concentrate only on trips that originated in Scotland. Passengers leaving Northern Ireland and then returning could immediately be discounted as being the subject of their search.

After almost a day of sifting through the lists, he ordered his detectives to assemble separate smaller lists, which he then assigned to individual officers.

Male car owner bookings produced a list of one hundred and sixty people who had travelled within the timeframe. An additional two hundred and ten names were added from the lists of male passengers who did not book a car.

Vennison put DC Maurice Green in charge of assessing the second list. Working from the addresses given against each name, he was told to cross-check Scotland's electoral register, available to the RUC through an online secure database.

The second name Green checked turned out to be eighty-year-old retired miner from Arbroathshire and this gave him an idea to fast-track through the list. After discussing a possible cut-off point with Vennison, it was agreed to divide the names into three separate groups – those aged thirty and under who were most likely to be within the range of their quarry; those aged between thirty-one and fifty who were marked as possibles; and those over fifty who could be discounted as unlikely subjects.

Vennison decided to concentrate only on those who made both the outward and inward trips.

Three hours of sifting the electoral register finally produced what he was after. The list was now whittled down to twenty-eight people aged thirty and under; one hundred and forty aged between thirty and fifty; and forty-two confirmed as over fifty.

Using the same methodology, Vennison directed the team to break down the new list to highlight single males who had booked a car. They soon discovered that only eighteen men fitted the thirty and underage profile.

They now had a total of forty-six possible suspects between the two lists.

Believing it unlikely the man they were looking for stayed at known addresses, Vennison's next task was to check local hotels. This couldn't be done over a telephone. He broke up the desk research and sent the team home for the evening.

The next day would be a hard footslog around the city's many hotels.


Maurice Green assigned the Europa Hotel to himself. It was the largest in Belfast and he loved the upstairs business lounge where they served some of the best coffee and croissants around. No sense slumming it when he could treat himself to a bit of luxury while he rummaged through guest lists.

True to form, the hotel manager set Green up at a discreet corner table and brought him the reservation lists he had asked for. It was not unusual for Belfast hotels to receive requests from the RUC about their guests, and the manager didn't raise an eyebrow when Green told him what he was after.

Green had barely finished his first cup of coffee when he spotted a name that appeared on both his list and the hotel's register. It brightened up his mood and he started to attack the remaining names with relish. After more than two hours of checking and rechecking, he discovered another two names.

Vennison watched as the detectives filed back into the conference room. The tour of hotels had generated nine names of men who had travelled from Scotland at various dates shortly before John Turnbull's murder, stayed in one of the city hotels, and left again for Scotland up to a week after the event.

Unfortunately, none of the staff at the hotels could identify the photo, which was shown to them. It was pretty much as Vennison had expected.

Vennison scrawled the nine on a large incident whiteboard at the head of the room, before turning to fire a series of questions at his team. What was known about the men? What was known about their movements? Could any relations be discovered in Northern Ireland? Had they any form?

He had already ascertained none of the names were known to the RUC. The next step would be to check with Strathclyde police, but Vennison wanted more work done before they pursued that avenue.

He tasked each of the team members with one name and he took the remaining name for himself. The allocation was purely random.

The job now was to check social security records, tax records, bank accounts; vehicle licensing, the Passport Office, anywhere the names might show up and provide some background on the suspects.

As the team filed out of the conference room, Vennison allowed himself a deep sigh. There was nothing like the thrill of a chase, but he was too long in the tooth to get carried away. He knew that if they drew a blank, then they would have to start on the next list, and then the list afterwards. So much of detective work was down to mind-numbing deskwork. He knew there was rarely one of those television-type plots that always seemed to provide a conveniently neat clue to a Colombo or a Taggart.

As agreed, the team reassembled in the conference room at 6pm. Vennison had arranged for the canteen to send up a platter of mixed sandwiches and enough coffee and tea to keep them going during what promised to be a late evening.

The feedback began positively. Two of the nine names were immediately scratched from the whiteboard. One was shown to have died in a motorcycle accident shortly after returning to Scotland, while the other was in the Beatson West of Scotland Cancer Centre living out his last days.

The remaining seven names produced a visiting University Fine Arts lecturer, who regularly travelled between Glasgow and Belfast; a Church of Scotland minister who was hotly tipped to be the next Moderator; a freelance journalist who specialised in magazine articles on the state of British shipbuilding; a bricklayer whose name popped up at various construction sites in the Edinburgh area; a nondescript footballer who played for one of Scotland's third division teams; an unemployed scaffolder; and a car salesman who dealt in luxury motors.

Copies of passport photos or driving licences were produced for all nine men. After studying the images against the photofit, Vennison agreed with the team that at least three of the suspects had the same cranial shape and facial bone structure, but there was no striking resemblance that would stand up in a court of law.

A fair amount of animated discussion followed, with each of the detectives putting forward views to discount some of the names. Most didn't believe there was any need to pursue the minister, not from a religious standpoint, but because there was information to show he had never spent any noticeable time away from his flock. It was certain therefore, that he would not have been shooting up the streets of Chicago all those years ago.

Equally, Vennison agreed to discount the footballer whose career could be traced to one team after another during the past ten years.

The freelance journalist and the unemployed scaffolder also didn't strike any chord with the image in the photofit. That left three names.

Vennison listened as his detectives expounded a variety of theories.

A professor travelling between the University of Glasgow and Queen's University in Belfast would be perfect cover for an out-of-town operative, who was required for occasional wet work on behalf of the IRA. The same could be said of a nomadic bricklayer, who seemed to pop up in a variety of locations. What better cover than to say he was in Belfast looking for work?

Then there was the luxury car salesman, who would be able to show ample innocent reasons why he should travel freely around the British Isles. The detective in charge of researching this suspect was able to add that the Belfast Motor Show was staged at the time of the man's visit. Was this just coincidental or was it the perfect front for murder?

Vennison knew there was enough to go on with all three subjects. Was it possible one of these men was responsible for John Turnbull's death? The only way to find out was to eyeball them directly, get a look behind the poker-faced one-dimensional passport photos, and try to assess the soul of the man.

The more he thought about it, the more convinced he became that he had to travel to Scotland and meet each of these men. His copper's instinct would take over.

The only problem he faced was convincing his boss he should make such a trip, let alone doing so without the knowledge of Scotland's Strathclyde police. He knew DCI Billy Carter wanted Turnbull's killer caught above all else on his agenda, but would be go for what Vennison was planning?

He believed the old man would back his play and would be anxious to know what could be gleaned from face-to-face meetings with Angus Stewart, the University Professor: John White, the unemployed brickie: and Fergal McSweeney, the luxury car salesman.

# Chapter 24
## Dundalk

DEVON PULLED OFF the main road into a narrow laneway, which appeared to lead to a distant farmhouse. He was still on the Republic of Ireland side of the border and needed help getting through the main Army roadblock just outside Newry.

For the past ten minutes, he had to listen to faint moans coming from the back seat. He knew Taffy Thomas couldn't take much more of the bumping around that he was subjected to since the quick getaway from the hotel.

He drew up alongside an iron gate leading into a field. Jumping from the car, he pushed the rusty gate back as far as he could and climbed back behind the wheel. He manoeuvred the car into the rutted tracks of the field and parked it tight against a hedge that screened it from the laneway.

Using a special two-way radio, he relayed his position to the men in the fake ambulance tearing towards his location from the Bishopscourt base. It was one of the stock of vehicles held on the base, and he knew Alan Doyle and John Tully would be aboard, uniformed in the garb of the Northern Ireland Ambulance Service.

They would tell the Army roadblock privates that they had been called to the scene of a traffic accident and would be back this way soon to ferry a critically injured man to the Daisy Hill Hospital on the northern side of the border.

Devon was aware of such mutual arrangements

existing between the health authorities on either side of the border. The hope was they could return with the injured Thomas and be waved through.

The ambulance was still twenty minutes away.

Devon climbed into the back seat and removed the blood-soaked towel and tourniquet. Thomas stirred and tried to speak.

Devon cut him off. "Not now, Taffy. Keep your strength, old son. Help is on the way. We'll have you up and running in no time."

The lips moved fractionally and a barely audible whisper escaped. Devon had to lean over.

"Mike, I need to tell you something.... It's something I overheard.... something about Epso..."

"For fucksake Taffy, shut up and conserve your energy." Devon hadn't meant it to be so harsh, but he was getting more and more worried about Thomas.

"...it might be important...something that was said Eps...Epsilon...I think it might be..." The voice went still as Thomas again lapsed into unconsciousness.

Devon kept compressing the towel against the wound whilst cursing for the ambulance to hurry up. Then he heard a diesel engine somewhere in the laneway. He leapt from the car and edged along the hedge to the gateway.

Risking a glance down the lane, he noticed the welcome sight of the blue and yellow livery of an ambulance. He pulled open the gate and waved at Alan Doyle who was behind the wheel.

The ambulance pulled up alongside and Doyle jumped from the vehicle clutching a medical bag. "How bad is he?"

Devon nodded his head towards the deserted vehicle. "He's in the back seat. Lost a lot of blood and we need to get him back as soon as possible."

Doyle sprinted towards the car whilst Devon shouted at Tully to get behind the wheel of the ambulance. "We need to get this thing turned around ready to go. Pull into the field and do a one-eighty. Hurry, hurry."

The words had barely left his mouth when he noticed Doyle climb back out of the car, his usual square shoulders looking a bit drooped. "I'm sorry, Mike. He's gone."

The death of Taffy Thomas hit Devon hard. The journey back to Bishopscourt was uneventful, and he spoke few words to Doyle and Tully. As expected, the ambulance was waved straight through the Army border checkpoint.

He had left the car in the field, removed the number plates, and set a timed charge against the fuel tank. He reckoned there was a fair chance at least one John Citizen had taken note of the number plate as he fled the hotel car park, but there was no sense in making life easy for the police. Within twenty minutes of their departure, the charge would detonate, and the resultant fireball would leave little more than a charred chassis.

Devon used the trip back to base to run through several options arising from Thomas' death. The timing couldn't have been worse. It could lead to the kind of scrutiny Devon could do without.

Taffy was unmarried, but his father and mother were still living in Cardiff and he had a sister somewhere in the South of England. They all believed Taffy was off serving overseas on a peacekeeping role in Rwanda and would want to know every detail about how he met his death. It wouldn't be too difficult to construct a plausible story, able to stand up to the local scrutiny that the residents of Cardiff would put against what they considered to be the death of one of their heroes.

They might have to bury Thomas in Bishopscourt and continue a charade with the family about him being unavailable because he was taking part in some sort of hush-hush mission. Devon dismissed the idea as a non-starter.

At the very least, Taffy deserved a full military funeral with his proud family in attendance.

By the time he arrived back at base, he had constructed a story about Taffy being involved in a fatal accident. He would be dressed in full uniform before being flown back to Wales. It was unlikely the family would inspect the body already prepared in the coffin.

Devon decided to contact Mark Garrett to make the immediate arrangements. In the meantime, a special service would be held at Bishopscourt to give the squad the chance to say its own goodbye.

For most of the night Devon tossed and turned, unable to shake the images of Thomas reeling in the hotel foyer from the gunshot that took his life. He blamed himself for what happened. He pushed Taffy too hard to break his cover in the pursuit of information and had failed to save him when he made his play against the gunmen.

Could he have done anything differently? Could he have reacted a split second earlier and neutralised the man in the suit before he brought his weapon to bear on Taffy? The questions wouldn't go away, and he rose from the bed to make coffee.

As he waited for the kettle to boil in the small

kitchen area of his room, his eyes fell on the bottle of Bells whiskey. He uncapped the bottle, lifted an upturned glass from the draining board and poured a double measure. He lifted the glass towards the ceiling, muttered "Here's to you Taffy," and downed the contents in one swallow. He slammed the glass back on the draining board, prepared a mug of coffee, and settled into an armchair.

For the next two hours, he replayed the information Thomas provided before his death. The big operation planned by the IRA appeared to be against a politician, a minister no less, and appeared to be scheduled for somewhere in Britain. But they didn't know who the target was or where the operation was planned for.

They didn't know jackshit, he almost screamed at himself.

And what was all that nonsense about Epsilon? Taffy said he heard the word used, but what the fuck was that about? Was it a codeword for the IRA operation? Was there any historical event that had similar undertones to the grandstand event planned by them, something to hit the headlines all over the world?

# Chapter 25
## Dublin Farmhouse

LIAM NOLAN STRETCHED out on a chair in the living room of his farmhouse in Dublin's southside. Across the room Francis Dooley was doing the same. There was no one else at home. Nolan's wife Margaret had left him six years earlier under the pressures of a marriage, wrecked by her husband's absences.

At first, she handled the prison terms that seemed to come every other year, but in the last few years, when Nolan was climbing fast through the ranks of the IRA, she rarely saw him. When he did come home, there was little for them to talk about and they simply drifted apart. She knew there was no other woman. He didn't have time for such distractions, and when she announced she was leaving, he understood fully her need for a new life.

He helped her buy a modest bungalow and provided enough money to keep her comfortable. Thankfully, there were no children in the marriage.

Nolan had arrived back from Scotland with Dooley the previous night and had spent hours bent over a coffee table littered with scraps of paper, road maps, and train timetables. They walked through all aspects of the plan originally set out by McSweeney, noting any changes that could be made and cross-checking against their own information.

The shrill tones of a telephone broke Nolan's concentration. It was sitting on a small table in the hallway and he rose reluctantly to answer its insistent call.

He was sorry he did.

Five minutes later he slammed the receiver back into its cradle and stormed into the living room. "You're not going to fucking believe this. Two of our men have just been shot to death, and we seem to have a fucking informer in our midst!"

He lashed out with his foot, sending a small stool across the room to collide with a plant stand. The ornament teetered for a second before collapsing on the floor, spilling its contents of soil and flowers across the beige carpet. Nolan stared at the mess and then slumped into the armchair.

He regained his composure before filling Dooley in on the telephone call. "That was Frankie Denvir in Dundalk. He's just told me that the fucking Welshman Taffy Thomas was a plant, and that he was trailing him along with Paddy Spence and Terry Cochrane when they got involved in a gunfight in the Crescent Hotel near Newry. Spence and Cochrane are dead, although he's pretty sure Cochrane got Thomas before he went down."

Fucking hell Liam, how did this happen? That bastard's been at the centre of Dundalk operations for almost a year. That might explain a lot, all this bad luck we've been having. The bastard has been feeding the Brits, but why?"

"Use your fucking head, man. He's been feeding them because he's one of them. How did we not spot it?"

Dooley looked uncomfortable. "We should have known it was too good to be true, an experienced explosives expert turning up at our door and virtually offering his services. I remember Frankie Denvir telling us he had vetted the man and was sure he was genuine. The idea of an English-hating Welshman returning to the roots of his grandparents was all very believable."

"Well it's not very fucking believable now, is it?" yelled Nolan.

"What happened to make them suspect something was wrong?" Dooley asked.

"That's the worst part. It seems the bastard was doing too much sniffing around this job we've planned. Loose talk must have triggered his curiosity and he couldn't help but shove his oar in. Denvir started getting suspicious and he had him constantly followed for the past few days. When he unexpectedly announced he was closing his shop for the afternoon, with some bullshit story of having to go to the wholesalers for re-stocking, Denvir assembled a team and followed him."

Nolan relayed the rest of the story as told to him by Denvir. As he spoke, Dooley constantly shifted in his seat waiting for an opportunity to speak. When Nolan finished the story Dooley dived in.

"That means the job's compromised. We can't go ahead."

"No," Nolan retorted emphatically. "Denvir is adamant that any talk in the Dundalk circle was all general stuff. No details were known by his crew. We go ahead as planned."

Dooley leaned back in his seat. "I still don't like the idea of you doing this, Liam. There are plenty of men we can use without risking you."

Nolan had earlier broken the news that he would be taking McSweeney's place, and the two men argued over it through the first few cans of beer. He had hoped Dooley would drop the subject once and for all. "I'm not going there again, Francis. There's no one else we can trust. I'm doing it."

"At least consider letting me help you," Dooley pleaded.

As Nolan looked across at his long-time friend, a smile spread across his face. "No Francis, I've something extra special that I want you to take care of."

# Chapter 26
## Bishopscourt

THE MOOD AMONG THE men had been sombre all morning. The special service arranged for Taffy Thomas was conducted by a Presbyterian Minister, who was flown across by helicopter from the Lisburn Army base. He was accompanied by Mark Garrett and a regimental funeral team who had prepared Thomas's body and placed it in an ornate teak coffin they had brought with them.

The coffin remained open during the short service, and when it was over the men filed by, offering a last salute to their fallen comrade. Many did not know Thomas because of the nature of his undercover work, but they knew he was part of the team, one of them.

The lid was placed on the coffin and it was carried silently out to the waiting helicopter. It would be transported back to Lisburn and taken from there on a transport plane to Wales.

Devon watched until the helicopter disappeared into the clouds before turning on his heels and beckoning Garrett to join him in the Mess.

Men sat around trestle tables, staring at untouched plates of food. Devon could understand their loss of appetite and the awkward silence that replaced the usual noisy banter.

Devon heard banging coming from the rear of the room and could see Peter Ackmore thumping a beer bottle on top of the table. Ackmore normally did his best to remain inconspicuous in the company of others, but this time there seemed to be a confident set to his jaw as he rose to address the group.

"Is this any way to be remembering Taffy? Unlike most of you, I knew him well from our earlier days in training and I can tell you he would be turning in his coffin at the sight of the lot of us. Taffy liked nothing better than a good laugh, and he always said that when his time came, he would want a bit of pretty music and everyone having a good time. Let's celebrate the life of a good man, a true friend, and one of the bravest people you'll ever meet. Here's to you Taffy!"

The men followed Ackmore's lead, raised their glasses and shouted, "Cheers" in unison. At a corner table, one man started up a chorus of 'For he's a jolly good fellow' and within seconds, the refrain was picked up by everyone.

When the singing stopped, the stories began, with everyone clamouring to relate some of their funny memories of a fallen comrade. The room descended into shouts and laughter and Devon nodded for a case of beer to be brought into the middle of the room.

"Might as well let them get it out of their system," he told Garrett seated alongside him.

For more than an hour he watched as the camaraderie of men in a close-knit environment took flight. The empty case of beer was replaced with a fresh one and the gloom lifted from all their shoulders.

Devon tuned into Ackmore, who was telling a story about Taffy's early military career.

"Remember the time he fell into the Colonel's prize rose garden on his way back to barracks from a bender? The poor sod slept the night there and was only discovered the next morning at reveille. He was covered in thorns and had a terrible rash on his face and arms."

The room descended into laughter.

"Wait there's more. The RSM made him take a bath before parading him on a disciplinary charge in front of the Colonel."

"I'll bet he really smelt of roses after that," guffawed Mark Webber.

"No," said Ackmore, "the old bastard made him take a bath filled with Epsom Salts." With that he fell into a fit of giggles.

The words hit Mike Devon with the impact of a sledgehammer. *Epsom? Could it have anything to do with Epsom?*


Devon punched Garrett on the shoulder, pushed his way through the melee of men, and ran towards his office. He was starting to sort out papers on the desk when Garrett arrived breathless at the doorway.

"What's going on, Mike?"

Devon held up a piece of paper. "It's no wonder we couldn't make sense of Taffy's reference to Epsilon. What if he was trying to say Epsom?"

"It's a bit of a stretch Mike, going from the Greek word Epsilon to Epsom."

Devon was scribbling furiously on a notepad in front of him. "Look, Taffy was in a bad way, barely able to speak. I struggled to understand what he was trying to say as he lapsed in and out of consciousness. What if what he was saying was 'Epsom, Epsom'?"

"I grant you it's possible. But what's so significant about Epsom? We are really no farther forward."

"What if," said Devon, "the town of Epsom had a physical connection to the intended target? What if the target lived in Epsom, or was likely to pass through it sometime soon? What if Epsom was the place chosen for a bomb at a political party rally, or a fundraising garden party? Hell, there could be all kinds of connections. We need to find out what we can about any important people or events connected with Epsom."

"You know," said Garrett, "you might just have something there. Let me see what I can find out." He grabbed the telephone and made several frantic calls to Ministry of Defence Intelligence colleagues in London, each time pushing hard for immediate answers to several questions.

He told Devon several sources promised to ring back as soon as they had any answers.

The two sat looking alternately at each other and at the phone sitting on the desk between them. Ten minutes after the last call, the phone buzzed. Garrett snatched it off the cradle and listened intently. He never interrupted, eventually said an enthusiastic thanks, and replaced the phone.

"What, what?" Devon couldn't keep the impatience from his voice.

"You're never going to believe this. The Secretary of State for Northern Ireland has his family home in Surrey, in Epsom no less."

Devon stared blankly, trying to assimilate what had just been learned. He could come up with only one conclusion. The IRA's so-called big operation, the target of their attention, was none other than the Secretary of State.

He turned towards Garrett. "Okay, I think we

know who and we know where, but we don't yet know when."

Garret thought for a moment before responding. "Most of the top politicians spend weekdays in London, or in the Secretary of State's case, commuting between London and Belfast. That leaves little time spent at home. We need to get hold of his diary for the next few weeks and find out when he's going to be in Epsom."

"That begs a question. How the fuck does the IRA know when he'll be in Epsom? These guys don't leave anything to chance. They will be sure of their target's movements, but how?"

"Right now, I don't know and I don't care. That's for another day. We need to get on top of this. I'll need to fly to London and brief MI5, MI6, the PM's office, the Metropolitan Police Special Operations bodyguards, and God knows who else."

"Wait just a minute, Mark," Devon interrupted. "This is our show. I want the chance to nail this bastard. Don't think about keeping us out of the loop."

"Are you out of your frickin' skull? This is too big; there are too many agencies that need to be involved. This must be handled from the mainland. I'm sorry Mike, but there's no other way. We've got to pass this up the line."

Devon saw the logic and knew Garrett was right. But he also knew he couldn't just sit back in Northern Ireland sucking his thumbs while one of the biggest operations of his career was played out in England. His only chance of getting involved was to persuade Garrett he had something to offer.

"Okay, at least take me with you. I can add a lot to any discussion about the Intel we've received, and don't forget, I once had the pleasure of running into the man they'll be hunting for."

Garrett stood up from the desk and stared at the floor for a few seconds before appearing to come to a decision. "All right, but we'll be there strictly as message carriers and to answer any questions. The decisions will not be ours to make."

He walked over to the office door, paused before opening it, then turned back to Devon.

"Better get a bag packed. We'll leave within the hour."

# Chapter 27
## Edinburgh

DRESSED IN DENIMS, a loose woollen sweater and a zip-up sports jacket, Martin Vennison pushed his finger against the bell of a door in the rundown Pennywell housing estate in Edinburgh. Within seconds it was opened by a heavy-set man, whose trousers had long since given up the fight to stay around the massive beer belly that pushed them down around his hips.

"I'm looking for John White," Vennison told him in a mock English accent.

"Well you've found him. What do you want?" The thick Scottish brogue was barely understandable to Vennison.

Despite first impressions, he decided to go through with his cover story and attempt to learn more about the man. "I'm opening a new building site in Glasgow and I'm looking for good brickies. I'm told you're one of the best."

The flattery had the desired effect. The menace dissipated from the man's features and he allowed a smile to drift across the chubby, alcohol-inflamed cheeks. "Whoever told you that knows what they're talking about. Come on in stranger and wet your whistle."

Over the course of the next thirty minutes, Vennison set out his sham plan to build a new office block. Under the pretence of checking out White's job history, he was treated to a warts-and-all account of the man's life, which included barely-believable tales of his sexual escapades, his single-handed construction of a 100-house estate in Sterling, and a brief period working on North Sea oil rigs. All told with the bluster of a man who half believed in his own stories.

The smell of dog piss mingled with tobacco and alcohol fumes almost made Vennison heave, and he was glad finally to take his leave with promises of contacting the man again within the next two days and arranging transport for him to Glasgow.

Outside in the welcome fresh air, he smiled at the thought of White standing in the front room of his house two days from now agitatedly staring out through the curtains for a minibus that wouldn't be arriving.

Scratch one name from the list.

Vennison climbed into a rented Volkswagen and set out on a journey to meet an arts professor at the University of Glasgow. He had arrived at Edinburgh Airport on the early-bird 8am flight and allowed himself a full day in the city to track down White. Working only from the address on the electoral register, he fully expected not to find the man at home and would probably have to make several trips to the house in the course of the day and evening.

The fact that he hit it lucky meant he was almost a day ahead of his planned schedule.

It was now nearly midday on Wednesday, and he calculated he could make the fifty-mile trip to Glasgow in just a few hours, allowing time for a lunch stop. He might get lucky again and catch the professor still at university. If not, he would book a room for the night and try in the morning. He couldn't think of a plausible story for visiting a professor at his home so if he missed him today, it would have to wait until morning.

He drove his car into the thinning university car park shortly after 4pm. The traffic across country was heavier than he anticipated and he stopped for longer than planned at a Little Chef roadside café. After tucking into a hearty Aberdeen Angus steak pie and chips, he sat for forty minutes over two cups of coffee, and that morning's well-thumbed complimentary issue of *The Scotsman*.

He climbed from the Volkswagen and walked through the imposing doors of the main university building, stopping to talk to the nearest student, or at least he assumed he was a student judging from the youthful appearance and the prerequisite scarf roped around his neck.

He asked for directions to Professor Angus Stewart but was met with a blank stare and a shrug of the shoulders. He listened as the youth lectured him on the size of the university, the numerous faculties housed in more than thirty buildings, and the need for students to know only the names of the lecturers assigned to them.

Vennison felt like giving the young twerp a clip around his self-important ear. He settled instead for a "thanks-for-nothing" look that flew miles over the youth's head, turned on his heels, and sought out the next unhelpful soul.

As it was, he was mistaken.

A girl, who looked to be still in her teens, flashed a big smile when he stopped her. She pointed him towards a room to the left of the long entrance corridor. He thanked her and strode off towards a sign that read "Dean of Faculty's Office."

He knocked and entered a busy secretarial office. A woman seated nearest the door looked up and motioned him over. When he told her who he was looking for, she lifted what appeared to be a large diary and thumbed through various pages. Finally, she lifted her head toward him. "I'm afraid you're out of luck. He's at a conference in Edinburgh and is not due back until tomorrow afternoon. He is taking a lecture at Hall Ten at three o'clock so you should be able to catch him then."

Cursing his luck, he returned to his car and noticed signs for the Hunterian Museum and Art Gallery. If he was going to talk art with a professor, he might as well bone up on a few facts. First, he would look around for a decent hotel close to the university and kill an hour or so in the museum.

As it turned out, by the time he found accommodation, the notion of venturing out again had left him. He settled for a meal in the hotel and retired early to bed.

The next afternoon he was back at the university, seated in the lobby awaiting the expectant return of Professor Stewart. The long clock arm had just ticked past the three mark when a bearded figure swept into the foyer followed by a small entourage of students vying for his attention.

Several were handing him plastic-covered folders, no doubt last-minute submissions of their assignments, while the professor frantically struggled with trying to tuck the material under his arms, at the same time as holding on to a heavy-looking briefcase.

Vennison let the scene play out for a few minutes before approaching the gathering. He had recognised the man from a large picture adorning the hallway along with those of other members of the faculty.

Vennison held up his warrant card and ushered the puzzled professor away from the group.

"What can I do for you, Chief Inspector? I'm in rather a hurry to prepare for a lecture. Can we walk and talk and the same time?" With that he took off, leaving Vennison with no option but to follow.

Vennison decided to take a direct approach. "I need more than a few moments, sir. You may be a witness in a murder case I'm investigating back in Belfast and I could order you back there if I thought it necessary."

The bluff had the desired effect. "This is preposterous, what are you talking about? I know nothing about a murder."

Vennison smiled benevolently. "Look sir, just a few minutes. Is there anywhere we can speak in private?"

The professor ushered Vennison into a small room off the main hallway. When they were seated, Vennison began a casual interrogation. He spun a story that the professor may have been a guest at the Europa Hotel at the same time that a man stayed there, a man who was since wanted in connection with a murder. It was part true, part fancy, but it gave Vennison the time to assess his suspect.

From his pocket Vennison fished a copy of the identikit sketch provided by Mark Garrett and asked the professor whether he recognised the man.

At the same time, Vennison used the opportunity to again look at the sketch and compare it against the man sitting opposite. Quite apart from a beard, which could have been added since the sketch was done, there wasn't the slightest resemblance between the two.

It was hardly surprising either that the professor

couldn't identify the sketch, but Vennison kept up a barrage of questions, trying to understand the professor's trips to Belfast, tracking his career and movements over the past few years, and learning more about the man's devotion to the world of Egyptian art.

It seemed that when he wasn't busy as an eminent visiting lecturer in universities throughout the British Isles, the professor was off every summer on field trips to Egypt or Africa.

The man was a walking, breathing antithesis of the kind of man Vennison was after.

Ten minutes later, Vennison was back in the forecourt of the university, punching a number into his mobile phone. "Is this the International Quality Car Centre? Could I speak to Mr McSweeney?"

The voice at the other end told him the owner wouldn't be in today and most likely, not until tomorrow afternoon. Dammit, thought Vennison, he would have to visit the man at his house in the morning.

# Chapter 28
## Glasgow

MARY McSWEENEY WRAPPED young Jackie in his favourite tartan scarf and carried him out through the hallway towards the front door. She turned her head to look up the stairs and shout at the empty space. "I'm just going to the shop before you head to work. Won't be long. Do you need anything?"

The muffled out-of-tune singing behind the bathroom door continued, and she knew her husband hadn't heard. She smiled down at Jackie and told him, "Let's leave Frank Sinatra in his own wee world." She laughed, and as if in understanding, the child giggled with her.

Outside, it was mind-numbingly cold. As forecast, an Arctic wind had raced down from the north during the night, giving forewarning of the heavy snowfalls trailing in its wake. Thankfully, Mary had booked off this Friday from her teaching job to enjoy a rare long weekend with her son. It was a day for the central heating and a bit of leisurely home baking.

First, she needed the ingredients. The shop was only ten minutes' drive away, and she told herself the crisp morning air would put a bit of colour into her cheeks.

The Mercedes was parked frontwards as usual facing into the driveway. She hated having to reverse out through the pillars onto the main road, but to be fair to Fergal he would have turned the car last night if he had known she was going out this morning. The home baking and the shopping trip was a last minute whim when she realised it would not be a day for pushing a pram in the park.

She clicked the button on the key fob causing the lights to blink as the door locks disengaged. Holding the youngster in her arms, she wrestled open the back door and placed him into his own special seat. By the time she finished with the straps, the cold had crept through her clothing, making her shiver, and regretting her decision to venture out from the warmth of the home.

She climbed into the driver's seat and made all the usual adjustments, tilting the rear view mirror, pulling the seat forward, and turning the handle to raise it to a proper size for people to see out. Satisfied she was as comfortable as she could be, she buckled in and inserted the key into the ignition switch.

Today was going to be a good day, she thought.


As Mary McSweeney turned the key clockwise it created an electrical pulse, which shot towards the starter unit. A millisecond before it brought the unit into life, it veered off on a secondary course, down a wire looped around the oil sump and fed along the undercarriage to an odd-looking black box.

The box was crudely duct-taped to a large square of putty-like material shaped against the underflooring on the driver's side.

The electrical pulse completed a circuit. The small black box gratefully grabbed at it and sent it down a small length of det cord, which ended in a cylindrical metal tube pushed deep into the putty material.

The Semtex did what it was manufactured to do;

it exploded with all the concussive force and destructive power that was built into its hideous DNA.

The blast pushed upwards, tearing through the flimsy framework of the car and propelled it almost ten feet from the ground. It ran along the length of the car, collapsing and disintegrating everything in its path before finally rupturing the fuel tank. That created a fireball, which only added to the carnage, leaving the car a twisted lump of burning metal.

The two occupants were long gone, neither having time to comprehend what had happened, nor to feel any sensations from the phenomenon that had extinguished their lifeforces.

But the concussive wave was not yet spent. The awesome energy wrapped inside the invisible tornado changed the molecular structure of the air around it and created a vortex that attacked anything in its path. The windows of homes up to three hundred yards away were shattered as the wave cut through the residential area, randomly setting off car alarms and knocking over brick walls.

Back at the seat of its power, it blew the front door of the McSweeney home clean off the hinges and raced up the conveniently placed stairway. The bathroom door suffered a glancing blow that was enough to knock it open and throw it against the figure standing with a shaving brush in front of a mirror.

By the time the wave reached him, Fergal McSweeney was still trying to understand the initial thunderous noise outside his home. His head was pummelled against the wall mirror and he collapsed to the tiled floor, blissfully unaware that the blast had forever taken away his wife and son.

The remainder of the wave shattered open the bathroom window and dissipated into the morning air.


The black Volkswagen was waved to a stop by a police roadblock on the A749 East Kilbride Road. The occupant was well used to seeing such sights back in Northern Ireland, but the stop and search powers of the local constabularies in England, Scotland, and Wales didn't have the same Emergency Powers Act flexibility that their RUC colleagues enjoyed in Belfast.

It was a surprise therefore to Martin Vennison, to come up against one near the centre of Glasgow.

Over the roofs of the chimneys of the houses, which stretched down East Kilbride Road, he noticed a thick pall of smoke, another sight more common on the streets of Northern Ireland. Could be nothing more than a house fire, he told himself, as he waited for the constable to reach his open window along the small queue of traffic that had formed ahead of him.

The policeman kept it formal and to the point. He explained there was "an incident" ahead and the roads in the area were being cordoned off. Vennison was told to wait in his car until he was directed to turn around and drive out of the area.

"I'm trying to get to Sheridan Avenue," Vennison explained. "Is it near here? Can I turn off somewhere and detour to it?"

The big traffic policeman suddenly eyed Vennison suspiciously. His whole demeanour had changed. Vennison noticed the right hand wrapping itself around a nasty-looking truncheon tucked into his belt. It was a moment all coppers recognised, a moment when you thought you had something, the moment when a suspect lets slip something he shouldn't have.

"Know someone in Sheridan, do we, sir?" the patrolman asked in the tone of a schoolteacher scolding the dunce of the classroom.

Vennison didn't know what he'd stumbled into, but whatever it was, it was not something he wanted to get involved in. He needed to think quickly. "Not at all officer. I'm heading for Cowglen Golf Club and got a bit lost. A man on the other street told me there was a short cut to the club through Sheridan Avenue."

"Aye, right enough there is," said the policeman, who seemed to relax his defensive posture and removed his hand from the truncheon. "You'll not get through there either I'm afraid. All the streets in this area are being closed off. There's been a gas explosion and we're wary about other leaks until the whole system is shut off."

A short while later Vennison was on his way again, this time retracing his journey towards the main road. At a small church car park, he left the Volkswagen and set off on foot back towards the plume of smoke. He skirted away from the road where he was stopped earlier and walked through a narrow housing street until he came to a group of bystanders at the head of a major road junction.

At least five police cars could be seen blocking off all approaches to the junction. Directly across from where Vennison stood, a sign on the gable wall of a house pointed to Sheridan Avenue.

"Is that where the gas explosion is?" Vennison asked an elderly man standing in a huddled group.

"Gas explosion? Yonder's no gas explosion! I

saw the damage before they pushed us back here. There's been a car bomb down at number twelve."

Vennison's heart pounded. Number twelve Sheridan Avenue was the address he had for Fergal McSweeney! He asked the next question with a certain amount of trepidation. "Anyone killed or injured?"

"Aye," said the man, "heard them say there were two bodies in the car, not that they could recognise much. Looks like it must be the wife and child, poor things."

"Why do you say that?" Vennison couldn't keep the urgency from his voice.

The old man turned to take a better look at Vennison. "Cause they just stretchered an injured man from the house and rushed him away in an ambulance."


The lights were everywhere, hurting his eyes and sending screaming jolts of pain through his brain. A weird constant droning noise grated on his teeth and made him want to cover his ears. But he couldn't move. His body wouldn't respond to the various jumbled signals that were being subconsciously sent to his motor senses.

Gradually he had the feeling of rising to the surface from a bottomless crater. He could now hear voices. Through a furry glaze across his eyes, he could make out the shapes of people standing over him. It seemed to take forever for the fog to clear from his vision.

A man in a white coat was holding a clipboard. He recognised the uniforms of two nurses who stood either side of the man, listening to what he was saying. One of them glanced his way. "He's coming round, Doctor."

White coat bent over him, shining another bright light into his eyes.

McSweeney turned away. "Where am I? What's happened?"

"Take it easy, Mr McSweeney. You've had a nasty bump. There's a fair amount of concussion and we need to check for any internal injuries."

"What happened?"

"You were caught up in an explosion, but you've been very lucky."

Explosion? His mind tried to sort out his memories but could only deliver snatches to him. He had been in the bathroom, but how did he get here? He had heard the front door slamming and then the car doors. He remembered thinking why was Mary going out? Was she coming to visit him? What was that bang? *Holy fuck!* He had seen at first hand too many car bombs not to understand what his brain was trying to hide from him. The realisation hit him hard.

"Where's my wife? Where's Mary?"

The doctor put his hands on McSweeney's chest, pushing him gently downwards on the bed. "I'm sorry, Mr McSweeney, but I'm afraid she's gone."

"What do you mean gone, where's she gone to?"

Even as the doctor gathered the courage to utter the words, the full awful truth hit McSweeney. He still needed to hear the words.

"Your wife is dead. I'm deeply sorry."

McSweeney turned away, rolling his body out of the bed before the doctor could stop him. As he planted his feet on the floor, a wave of light-headedness washed over him, making him lose his balance. He stumbled backwards, catching the metal guard of the bed to prevent himself from crashing into a locker. It was only then he noticed he was wearing a standard hospital gown, his naked buttocks exposed to the two nurses.

"Where's my clothes? I need to get out of here."

The doctor's sympathetic tone was replaced by a harsher, authoritative voice. "Out of the question. We have quite a few tests to run. You are in no fit condition to go anywhere."

"I have to get home to my son."

The look of horror on the faces of the nurses stopped McSweeney in mid-sentence and sent a cold shiver running through his body. He looked pleadingly at them, willing them to tell him everything was all right. But deep down he knew it wasn't.

The doctor leaned over to speak, but McSweeney didn't want to hear the words that were coming. He turned away as the doctor spoke. "I'm sorry to be the one to tell you, but your son is also dead."

McSweeney couldn't help himself. He let out a loud, animal scream and pounded his fists on the bed shouting "Jackie, Jackie," his head buried in the sheets and his entire body wracked by uncontrollable shaking.

He was aware of falling back into the bottomless crater. And then darkness.

Sometime later the light came back again and he tried to move on the bed, this time noticing he was now between the sheets and hooked up to a metal stand that delivered tubes into his arm. He glanced around the room. He had a ward to himself, the glass door closed against the noise of the normal hustle and bustle of a busy hospital. Outside in the corridor, he noticed a uniformed policeman sitting on a chair at the doorway to his room.

The grief he felt about Mary and little Jackie started to take hold, but he fought back the feelings. What were the police doing here? Were they here for his protection or did they have other reasons? Gradually he started to work through the events of the morning.

That he had been targeted by his erstwhile colleagues in the IRA, he had no doubt. He told them he wanted out and the only way they would let that happen was by making sure he was permanently out. After all he had sacrificed, after all he had done for the bastards, and this was his reward!

Well, they had missed their chance to kill him. They had robbed him of the only people he ever really cared about, and they would pay dearly for it.

He swore a silent, solemn oath. Liam Nolan would die a slow, painful death.

He knew the attempt on his life had also obliterated his cover story. The police were no mugs; they would figure that a seemingly upstanding, innocent car dealer would not be a random victim of the IRA. The car bomb would have left a typical forensic signature, and they would want to know how McSweeney was mixed up with a terrorist organisation. He would have to get out of here.

He looked around the room for his clothes but couldn't see any. He sat up in the bed, removed the catheter from his arm applying pressure to stop the bleeding, and swung his legs onto the floor. He shuffled towards an en suite bathroom, making sure he made just the right amount of noise.

The door to the ward was thrown open and the policeman burst in. He looked too young for the job and sported a mop of curly ginger hair that must have been the subject of a lot of micky-taking. He put an arm on McSweeney's shoulder.

"You shouldn't be out of bed, sir. Let me fetch a nurse."

"There's no time," McSweeney said in a weak voice, "I'm going to be sick. Quick, help me into the loo."

The young copper looked nervously over his shoulder and then grabbed McSweeney around the waist, allowing the sick man to lean against him. He pushed open the bathroom door and guided McSweeney towards a high-standing wash-hand basin.

McSweeney's left arm was resting on the policeman's shoulder. He wrapped it around the youngster's neck, swung him around, and slammed the top of his head into the wall. The man slumped to the floor unconscious. He pulled the bathroom door closed and fumbled to undress the policeman. The exertion of constantly moving the limp body brought on waves of nausea and he had to pause twice to clear his head. He pulled on the ill-fitting uniform and rifled through the pockets until he found a set of car keys.

He inched the door open, checking no one had heard the commotion. The door to his ward had swung closed, and people could be seen moving up and down the corridor, oblivious to what was happening.

He moved to the window and looked out for the first time. Thankfully, he was on the ground floor, grateful he didn't have to shinny down drainpipes. He felt unsteady on his feet but shook aside the urge to sit down. The window opened easily to his touch.

He pulled it aside, clambered out one leg at a time, and dropped to a garden below.

Making his way along the building, he came to a pathway leading to a car park at the front of the hospital. He spent more than five minutes trying to find the police vehicle, but to no avail. In exasperation, he took off the policeman's jacket, rolled it in a ball, and used it as a cushion to ram his elbow against the driver's side window of a Ford Escort. The glass shattered easily, and he reached in to lift the lock switch.

Sitting behind the wheel, he calmly broke the plastic surround to the steering column, fiddled with the jumble of exposed wires, and rearranged the circuitry. The car came to life when he touched two exposed wires together.

He shoved the gear lever forward, reversed from the parking space, and made his way to the large pillared entrance. His intention was to get to the car showroom where he kept spare clothes, fake passports, and a rainy-day wad of cash. From there he had to get out of Scotland. He had to stay one step ahead of the police, and most important of all, he had to settle a score with Liam Nolan.

As he reached the hospital entrance, he had to swerve to avoid a blue taxi, which was rushing through the pillars, a sombre-looking man in the back seat.


Vennison got caught up in queues almost as soon as he left the scene of the car bomb. Traffic in the area was gridlocked, with drivers dodging off into side streets to avoid the confusion. He didn't know the area and couldn't risk losing directions to the hospital that the old man had provided him with back at the road junction.

But sitting in a slow-moving queue, he was getting nowhere fast. What he needed was a local pilot.

He abandoned the car at a kerbside outside a block of flats and made his way towards the main road several hundred yards away. He stood for more than twenty minutes trying to get the attention of a taxi, finally succeeding in hailing a blue Datsun minibus with a familiar sign attached to the roof. He told the driver to take him to the Southern General Hospital on the Govan Road.

Within fifteen minutes, thanks to some expert driving and constant darts down side roads, they pulled up at the hospital entrance. Vennison instructed the driver to wait for him, dashed out of the vehicle, and made his way to a large, circular reception desk.

The nurse on duty was adamant there were no admissions from the bomb incident. Yes, she had heard of it and yes, this was the nearest hospital, but she had been on duty all morning and there were definitely no emergency admissions.

She must have seen the concern in his face and assumed he was a relative of the victims. "I'll ring around for you," she offered without prompting.

Vennison paced the reception area as she made a number of calls, finally gesturing him over as she put down the telephone. "The Glasgow Royal Infirmary has admitted a man who was caught up in that bomb...."

Vennison was running for the door before she had the chance to finish telling him her information.

Back in the taxi he fidgeted, as the driver again

manoeuvred against the clustered traffic. There was now no doubt in Vennison's mind that the man at the hospital was the man he was after. A car bomb at his home was just too much of a coincidence, and Vennison didn't believe in coincidences. He couldn't begin to guess what had happened, maybe a falling out among thieves, but it didn't matter.

What mattered was that he had to get to Fergal McSweeney before he signed himself out of hospital before he disappeared again into the shadows of a double life.

Ahead he could see a large sign for the hospital. The driver signalled a turn towards the entrance, swung across an oncoming line of traffic, and aimed his vehicle between two large pillars. As they entered the hospital grounds, the driver blared his horn at a Ford Escort that had partially crossed into his lane, heading in the opposite direction.

As the two cars passed, Vennison noticed a white-faced man behind the wheel, wearing what appeared to be the shirt epaulettes of a police uniform. The taxi pulled to a stop in a brightly painted yellow box at the hospital entrance. Vennison pulled a handful of notes from his wallet, thrust them at the driver, and was out of the vehicle before the man had time to count them.

Inside the hospital, he was directed to a long corridor leading off to his left. He started sprinting down the linoleum-covered floor, his shoes squeaking on the polished surface. Ahead, he could see several people in an agitated state gathered around a doorway. He pushed past them and watched a nurse applying a bandage to a ginger-haired man sitting on the bed, dressed only in Boxer shorts and a white vest.

"What's happened here?" he shouted in a voice dripping with authority.

"This poor man's been attacked by a patient," answered the nurse. "He stole his clothes and...."

The penny dropped with Vennison. He leaned over the young constable. "Listen son, I've no time to explain everything. Tell your people the man drove away from here in a battered red Ford Escort. I'm sorry, but I didn't get the number plate. Call in now and tell them it's imperative this man is caught. He's an extremely dangerous terrorist. They'll know what to do."

Without waiting for a response, he bolted from the ward, running back at an all-out sprint towards the reception area. He needed transport. There was only one place McSweeney could be heading.

# Chapter 29
## London

THE PAST TWENTY-FOUR hours were a blur to Devon. He had flown with Garrett into Northolt shortly after 7pm and was whisked immediately by car to Whitehall. One meeting followed another throughout the night, with neither man able to grab more than two hours sleep on makeshift beds in an MI5 office.

They were quizzed incessantly by a variety of suited men, some known to Devon from his former postings. They were challenged time and again about the credibility of their Intel, with more than a few awkward questions for them to work around concerning how they came about the information now in their possession.

Devon was glad to see the appearance of General Sir John Sandford, who moved the dis-cussions along into what he called more relevant matters.

It was now 8pm on Wednesday evening and a fresh round of discussions was set up in a conference room deep in the bowels of the large building. When he entered the room, Devon was surprised to see that the Home Secretary and the Secretary of State for Northern Ireland attended the top of the table.

General Sandford was there and obviously chairing the proceedings. "Gentlemen, I'll get straight to the point. We now know that a credible attempt is to be made on the life of the Secretary of State for Northern Ireland, and that it is to be made sometime soon, at or around his home in Epsom. We can also confirm that the only planned stay by the Secretary of State at Epsom is this Friday evening."

A murmur of voices ran around the room, but the General held up his hand to signal silence. "Yes, I know its short notice, but thanks to Captain Garrett and Mr Devon, it's better than no notice at all. As I see it, we only have two options. The first is obvious. We cancel all the Secretary's arrangements for Friday and wrap him up in a protective shield that even a mouse couldn't get through. That leaves us free to hunt around Epsom for any would-be attackers. The downside to this is that we might be spotted and the IRA mission could be aborted."

The General lifted a glass of water from the table in front of him, took a generous drink, and set the glass back down with a determined thunk. "The second option is to let the Secretary continue with his planned visit home, and then see if we can smoke out the bastards."

He deliberately let the idea hang in the air.

Several people clambered for the General's attention. "I know you all have points to raise but let me finish and then we can decide how best to proceed. As we understand it, any planned hit on the Secretary will take place at Epsom. That means it could be anywhere – the train station, the route to the house, or the house itself. We have put together a plan to take care of all three scenarios. I might add that this plan has the full backing of the Home Secretary and the Secretary of State. Now let's have those questions."

For more than an hour the discussion raged. Every angle was discussed and debated, every possibility explored, and each counter-action agreed on. Finally, the General signalled for the proceedings to stop. He looked around at each of the faces at the table.

"Gentleman, there are only two questions that remain unanswered. Who is to head up this operation and who is to take part?"

Again, there was a stir around the table before the General continued. "We have decided to put together a multi-jurisdictional taskforce involving all our agencies, MI6, MI5, the Metropolitan Counter Terrorist Unit, and the SAS. Overall control is being given to Major John Breen, of the CTU. He has already drawn together a list of personnel he wishes to use and will go into a detailed planning session with Heads of Department immediately after this meeting."

With that, the General started gathering together several papers strewn in front of him. As he started to rise, he turned back to the group, almost as an afterthought.

"Oh, I should have said that Major Breen has specifically requested the inclusion of Mr Devon. Given Mr Devon's unique background to this operation, I concur totally."


Devon could have kissed the old General. He thought it unlikely Major Breen had made any such request, but rather the idea had been foisted on him by the General. Devon knew the General was behind setting up Storm 74 and would want to make sure it was in the thick of the action. This was a major coup and he had no doubt the General would be reminding the powers-that-be of that very fact long after the dust settled.

Devon was concerned, however, that the Major

might resent his involvement and keep him on the sidelines as much as possible. His fears were allayed soon afterwards.

Breen called Devon to the side of the room, away from the small groups that were forming. He put out his hand as Devon walked forward. "Good job, Devon. A lot of people are in your debt. Are you up for seeing a bit of action on this one?"

Devon was taken aback. "Thanks, sir and yes, I'm ready to do anything you need."

"That's the spirit. We need to talk privately. I have things for your ears only. Meet me in the Nelson Room on the second floor in twenty minutes. I have other things to attend to first."

With that he was gone into the crowd, leaving Devon more than a little confused. At the very least he had expected a fight to stay on board.

Now he appeared to have just been offered a key role.

# Chapter 30
## Glasgow

McSWEENEY AIMED THE stolen car across Glasgow in a blur of speed, blaring horns and jumping lights. He pulled into the industrial estate and made his way to the entrance of his car business. A single chain hung across the gateway and he could see a sign hanging from its centre. It read simply: *CLOSED DUE TO A BEREAVEMENT IN THE FAMILY.* It was less than three hours since the bombing and he silently thanked the showroom manager for his thoughtfulness.

He alighted from the car, removed the chain, and climbed back behind the wheel. He drove to the rear of the building where the car would be hidden from view. He hoped all the staff had gone home after hearing the news. He had things to do and he didn't want to go through the emotional turmoil of dealing with condolences and questions.

At the top of the rear steps, he punched a code into the door lock and stepped inside. Someone had set the interior alarm and he entered the deactivation sequence before it started squealing. The alarm meant no one was around.

He made his way through the building to his first floor office. In a room off the office, he changed clothes. Because of frequent late night meetings, he always kept a small, spare wardrobe consisting of fresh underwear, several shirts, a black suit, and matching black shoes. He pushed back a large wooden box to reveal an underfloor safe and extracted most of its contents.

Into the inside pockets of his suit jacket, he rammed four bundles of cash, three containing thirty thousand pounds in sterling and one containing ten thousand Euros. Next, he sorted through a small pile of fake passports and two fake driving licences. He decided to take them all.

The last things he collected were a Sig P226, together with three spare ammunition clips, plus a Ka-Bar straight-edged combat knife, which he strapped around his lower left leg.

Back in his office he searched through his desk drawers and removed the keys for a silver Mercedes he knew would be parked outside as a test-drive model. He was about to rise from the seat when his eyes fell on a picture frame in the centre of the desk.

The faces of Mary and little Jackie stared back at him accusingly.

He slumped back in the chair, hands clasped against his head. He had to fight for breath as the anguish burrowed deep into his very soul. This was worse than any physical pain he had ever had to endure, including the sensation of a bullet tearing into his shoulder all those years ago in Chicago.

It took him more than two minutes to stop the shaking that attacked every part of his body. Was this delayed shock, or just the horrible realisation, probably for the first time that day, that he was never going to see his wife and son again?

The darkness was lifted by another gripping sensation. The anger seemed to start from his toes and worked its way up through his body, finding release only in a scream that reverberated off the walls of the empty office.

He knew what he had to do. He looked at the

clock on the office wall. There was no doubt in his mind that Liam Nolan would involve himself in the assassination of the Secretary of State. That meant he knew where Nolan would be in about six hours from now. Time enough for him to get to Epsom.

Time enough to pay a debt for Mary and little Jackie.

# Chapter 31
## London

THE BLACK LEXUS pulled into the kerb outside the entrance to Waterloo Station, ignoring the no-parking signs and causing pedestrians exiting the station to move their luggage away from the pavement. A heavy-set man jumped from the front passenger seat to open the rear door, holding it backwards to allow another man to alight.

The unmistakeably portly figure of Giles Partridge, Secretary of State for Northern Ireland, looked imperiously around before following his bodyguard, who was cutting a path through the early evening rush hour crowds. A second bodyguard fell in step behind.

Partridge wore his characteristic wide-brimmed black Fedora hat, pulled low over a chubby bespectacled face. His strides were short and rather ungainly, and he struggled to keep a firm grip on the familiar ministerial red leather case that he kept with him at all times.

Despite a plummy voice and a background steeped in England's old-world aristocracy, he was a politician well-liked by the masses. He was the champion of many causes, including the introduction of successful strategies to tackle inner-city deprivation, and reducing joblessness among the country's young people.

He was seen by many as a future Prime Minister, unafraid to turn down some of the messier jobs in Government, including the poisoned chalice of what many in Westminster referred to as "the Northern Ireland Portfolio." The job was considered to be tantamount to an exile posting. Not so Partridge. He believed he could make a difference to that troubled province.

As the trio approached platform three, the train was already prepared and accepted passengers through a line of opened doors. At the rear of the train a guard stood beside a closed door, opening it only as the group approached. He nodded recognition at Partridge, and then closed the door firmly behind the group.

Inside the private carriage, one of the bodyguards slid a bolt across the door. The blinds on the windows were already drawn.

The carriage consisted of a generous seating area and a small bathroom. There were six large armchair-type seats bolted to the floor and a longer seat, covered in cushions that could serve as a bed. A small refrigerator sat in one corner and a coffee vending machine in another. All three men settled in their seats and waited for the train to move.

Partridge considered the events of the past twenty-four hours. He had helped the security services tie down the likely date for the planned attempt on his life. It was a Bank Holiday weekend and his only engagement on Friday was an afternoon House of Commons debate on Northern Ireland. After that he was scheduled to address a constituency meeting back in Epsom early on Saturday morning, before heading for a mini-break to the Channel Islands.

It wouldn't need rocket science for people to know he would travel back to his home and remain there overnight in preparation for the Saturday morning engagement.

All that was needed was to show he was following through with his plans. For any counteraction to be mounted he had to get on the train, despite the obvious risks involved. He was no hero, but he was realistic enough to know that if the operation against him was called off, there would be another attempt down the line on him or someone else.

And next time they might not get the chance to do something about it.

Almost on time the train pulled gently out of the station shortly after 5:30, picking up speed as it headed for the country.

Ten minutes out of London, the bathroom door opened from the inside and a tall, well-muscled man walked calmly into the middle of the carriage.

The man sitting in a car overlooking the passenger exit archway at Epsom Station was nursing a mobile phone in his lap and looking furtively around him at the comings and goings in the large customer car park. The phone pulsed, causing him to jerk involuntarily upright.

No name appeared on the screen. He didn't expect one. He hit the receive button and listened to the curt message, *"The bird has flown."*

His response was an equally abrupt one-word reply, "Okay."

He knew the train journey from London was just under forty minutes. His job was to wait, relay a second message to another phone, and then drive to a pre-arranged destination. He glanced at his watch, all the time scanning for a distinctive brown Land

Rover that should be arriving shortly to pick up the VIP passenger. Fifteen minutes to go. He shifted impatiently in his seat.

At 6:05 the Land Rover pulled into the car park, manoeuvred around the two rows of parked cars, and reversed into a reserved spot less than fifty yards from the archway.

Even through the tinted windows the man could make out two shapes sitting in the front of the vehicle.

The whining noise of a decelerating train signalled the arrival of the 5:30 from Waterloo. Most of the passengers had already disembarked and filed through the arch before he recognised the black Fedora, flanked by two minders. The distinctive ministerial case could be seen hanging from the man's right hand, as he made straight for the back door of the Land Rover. He jumped in, followed by his minders, one climbing in through the left hand door, the other using the same right hand door the Secretary of State had used.

Almost as soon as the doors slammed, the vehicle shot away from its spot and exited the car park in a cloud of dust.

The man called up a pre-recorded message on his phone and sent it down the line. It read simply, *"The bird has landed."*


Heavy rain fell in a constant pour as a figure in black squeezed through a hedge, dispersing a miniature torrent of droplets that had formed on the foliage. The weather suited his purpose. The dark, overcast sky blotted out any available light from the moon, meaning he could move without presenting a silhouette to anyone watching through the windows of the large house on the high ground.

He made his way gradually along an inside hedge, rapidly ascending the steep incline towards a rockery at the crest. He paused at the first rocks and scanned ahead.

The ground was level at his point and he could distinguish the interior lights of the house and the shadows they cast over the lawn. There was no sign of the guard dogs. He settled down and waited.

The sound of a door closing at the front of the house brought him fully alert. He could hear the grating jangle of a garage door swinging outwards. Then the cough of an engine and the lights of a vehicle illuminated the front driveway. He could make out a brown Land Rover as it rolled away from the house and roared off into the night.

He was on his feet immediately, sprinting at full speed to the gable wall of the garage. He edged his way along the wall and paused where it ended at the front of the house. He noticed the garage doors were still open.

He darted inside and waited in the shadows behind a discarded fridge. His mobile phone vibrated in his trouser pocket. He retrieved it, flipped open the lid and accessed the message. It was what he had hoped for: "The bird has landed."

He inched his way across to a door linking the garage to the house, depressing the handle, and looking relieved when it gave way. He was of course, prepared to tackle it if it had been locked, but this just made the job easier. Gradually, inch-by-inch, he pushed the door inwards, all the time alert to any movement or noises.

The door led into what appeared to be a small

utility room cluttered with a dishwasher, a washing machine, and two chest freezers. Ahead lay another door, this one slightly open, and providing a view into a generously sized kitchen. He crossed the space between the two doors, paused for just a moment, and ran noiselessly into the room. He bent behind a central food preparation counter and listened again.

The kitchen opened into a long well-lit hallway with rooms running off at both sides. The sound of music playing somewhere ahead concentrated his focus. It was hard to judge the source, but it appeared to be from one of the rooms to the left. He rose from his hiding place and crept silently across to the hallway entrance.

From his jacket pocket he extracted a Glock 17, already fitted with a noise suppressor.

Foot by agonising foot he made his way along the corridor, all the while prepared to shoot at any figure that might emerge from any of the rooms. At the end of the hallway, the corridor turned into another smaller hallway and at the end of this, he could see the start of a stairwell.

Once again, he moved slowly down its length, this time having to check both ways for any signs of trouble.

He squatted at the bottom of the stairwell and counted off fourteen steps to a top landing. The stairs were heavily carpeted and should mask the sound of his footfalls. He sprinted upwards, taking the steps two at a time. When he reached the top, he pressed his back against the wall and waited. There were no lights on in this part of the house.

He moved along the first floor hallway, pushed open the first door, and then closed it again when he noted it was a bathroom. The next room appeared to be a master bedroom. He entered quickly, closing the door silently behind him.

Using a pencil-thin torch he scanned the room, his eyes stopping at what appeared to be a large double-doored wardrobe. He stepped inside, pushing aside a rack of suits and jackets.

He pressed his back against the rear wall of the wardrobe, rearranged the clothing back into order and settled down to wait.

The mechanical Council roadsweeper edged along the kerb picking up the dirt and debris that littered the small rural highway. It was a scene all too familiar on Britain's roads, which were a depository for the casual dispersal of sweet papers, cigarette ends, and all manner of litter flung through car windows by an uncaring public.

No one would have thought to question why the sweeper was in action so late on a Friday afternoon.

In the gloom of a wintry evening, no one would also have noticed a small robotic arm extending from the side of the vehicle over the footpath. Inside the cab, the driver's mate nursed a rectangular metal box displaying a glass screen, housing a single shaky needle.

In the darkness of the cab they wouldn't also have noticed that the passenger wore a set of earmuffs attached to the box and capable of picking up the noise of any signal sent from the boom outside.

This was a rather fancy piece of kit. Its sole function was to pick up the distinctive signature emitted by the full range of commercial explosives. Sensors built into the head of the boom were designed to do the same job as police sniffer dogs. If any Improvised Explosives Devices were planted on the Secretary of State's route from the train station, they would know about it.

This was a final run-through of several measures that were taken immediately after the discovery of the planned IRA hit. Early on Thursday morning, not long after midnight to be precise, a first similar sweep was carried out along the entire route from the station to the Secretary's house.

At the same time, twenty heavily-camouflaged men from 22 Special Air Services were deposited at various vantage points along the route, taking shelter in trees, ditches, and hedges, away from the prying eyes of the public. Ahead of them stretched a cold, isolated vigil. Their job was to pick up on any unusual activity and report back to a command base established in a first floor office at the train station.

The room in which the command centre was established was specially fitted with one-way glass, affording watchers a view of the station car park. From there they had earlier spotted a man in a parked car acting more than a little suspiciously. They watched as the man fidgeted inside the car for more than an hour, made a call on his mobile phone, and left the park shortly after the departure of the Secretary of State's Land Rover.

Two members of the Metropolitan Police Anti-Terrorism Unit followed closely behind in an unmarked armoured car.


The brown Range Rover swept into the drive and drove straight into the opened garage. The five men alighted and moved single-file through the house.

They stopped in the front living room, ostensibly to pass pleasantries with the bodyguard who had remained in the house. Few words were spoken.

The bodyguard pointed them to the television screen, which was hooked to a number of unseen cameras, fitted hastily the previous day by a tech squad from MI5. The cameras, with lens no bigger than a coat button, had been attached to lampshades, picture frames and flower vases. The group watched as images of recordings taken less than thirty minutes ago were played back.

They followed the progress of a black-clad figure as he emerged from the garage and made his way, with the movements of a highly trained professional, to the first floor bedroom. They watched as he secreted himself in the wardrobe and received confirmation that he was still there. The men spoke among each other, communicating as much by gesture as by words.

Mike Devon, dressed in the clothes of The Secretary of State, and still wearing the Fedora, broke away from the group and exited the living room. The heavy clomping of his footsteps could be heard on the hallways, as was his feeble attempt at a tuneless whistle rendition of Dean Martin's 'That's Amore'.

He flicked light switches as he made his way upstairs, pausing at the top to shout backwards: "I'm going for a shower. Have some food sent from the local Chinese restaurant in an hour."

He was aware that the group he left behind in the living room would be checking their weapons. Like himself, they each carried a Heckler and Koch MP5 machine pistol capable of spewing out eight hundred 9mm rounds per minute.

They would wait sixty seconds before leaving the room and making their way towards the stairs, two men on either side as they inched upwards.

Inside the bedroom, the figure in the wardrobe peered out through slats in the wardrobe door. He had adjusted them to provide sufficient view of the room without betraying his presence.

He watched as a man in a Fedora swaggered into the room, panting over the exertions of his climb up the stairs. There was no mistaking the bulk of the figure, or the ministerial case he casually tossed on the bed on his way to the en suite bathroom.

He watched as the man walked through into the bathroom, still whistling that annoying tune. Several seconds later he heard a shower running, followed by the rustle of clothes falling on the floor. He pushed open the wardrobe door and made his way across the room.

His pistol, held in a two-handed grip at eye level, was pointed directly at a two-inch gap in the bathroom doorway. He used the toe of his boot to push the door slowly inwards, his eyes trying to penetrate a fog of steam.

A large bathrobe hung over a glass-partitioned shower area. Added to the steam, it made it impossible to distinguish any shapes behind the screen. He moved forward, bringing his aim to bear on the cubicle.

Suddenly, the bathroom door swung viciously towards him, knocking hard against his gun hand. He held tight to the weapon as he fell backwards, slipping on the polished wood floor of the bedroom.

Fuelled by instinct and adrenaline, he recovered

his bearings in time to move his gun arm in the direction of a blurred figure closing in on him.

He was a fraction too late.

A man, dressed only in an open-necked shirt and slacks, was standing over him, aiming the wicked-looking barrel of an MP5 directly into his face.

He couldn't disguise his look of astonishment as he tried to understand what had just happened. More particularly, he couldn't figure out why his assailant was definitely not the Secretary of State for Northern Ireland.


Mike Devon was equally astounded to gaze down at a face he didn't know. The pock-marked features below him were not those of the man he expected to meet, the man he confronted in a street in Chicago all those years ago, the man he had come here to kill.

He tore himself from the trancelike state, planted his left foot on the man's gun arm and ordered him to remain still. The look on his captive's face was now replaced by one Devon knew well, it was a look that combined fear, anger, and desperation.

It was a look that told Devon the man would not be taken meekly.

Ignoring the machine pistol held steadily in Devon's hand, the man lashed out with his feet and squirmed to free the arm trapped under Devon's foot.

Devon jumped back to avoid the flailing feet, all the while keeping the MP5 directed at the prone figure's torso.

The man freed his gun hand, and despite

knowing it was a race he couldn't win, he looked ready to fire.

Just as Devon prepared to kick the weapon from the man's hand, he became aware of the bedroom door opening and several figures rushing into the room.

He watched in horror as the first figure aimed an MP5 at the man on the floor.

"No!" Devon shouted.

The man squeezed the trigger and a six-round burst stitched across the back and side of the body lying on the floor. Devon looked down at a large pool of blood already forming around the corpse.

"For fucksake! I wanted to take him alive!" Devon screamed at the shooter, not sure that that was what he really wanted.

"It looked like he was getting ready to fire," the man retorted.

"I had it covered; we needed to interview him..." Devon let the rest of his words drop off. He turned to the shooter, placed a hand on his shoulder and told him: "Never mind, you done good, soldier."

He stooped to examine the corpse, trying to recall where he had seen the distinctive pock-marked face before. He tried to visualise the photos pinned on the noticeboard back at the base, running through the images of the men identified among his top forty targets. There it was, close to the top! It was among the group that was part of Liam Nolan's inner circle.

What he couldn't figure out was why Francis Dooley was carrying out such an important hit instead of the man he had expected to meet.

Pat McStravick heard the gunshots as he sat in his car at the end of the secluded roadway. He was less than five hundred yards from the house where Dooley should have entered more than thirty minutes ago. His job was to wait here, pick up Dooley, and transport him direct to the train station. If Dooley didn't show by 6:15, it meant he was taking an alternative escape route and McStravick was to hightail it out of there.

But those were clearly gunshots he heard. Didn't Dooley say he was using a silenced weapon? Well there was nothing silent about what he had just heard; that was machine-gun fire. What was happening? What should he do?

McStravick was in too much of a panic and staring too intently ahead of him to notice dark shapes emerge on either side of his car. The side windows exploded in a shower of fragmented glass. The next thing he knew was that an arm was around his throat and he was pulled through the opening created in the window, his clothes and flesh tearing on ragged shards of glass.

At least three men were now on top of him, smashing rifle butts into his head and torso. The last thing he remembered before passing out were his arms being twisted behind his back and cold steel wrapping itself around his wrists.


Less than a mile away, another car was parked up with a nervous occupant constantly glancing at his wristwatch and staring out into the gloom of empty fairways. He never noticed that he had been tailed all the way from the train station, or that the car behind him swung into the side of the road to provide a clear view of his vehicle turning into the golf club car park.

Metropolitan Police Officer John Bickers

sported earplugs connecting him to the operational command centre back at the railway station. The static through was broken by a simple short command.

"The threat has been neutralised. Close in and clean up."

He knew the message meant the planned attack on the Secretary of State had been stopped.

Bickers nodded at the colleague in the passenger seat, opened the car door, and held an MP5 one-handed by his side as he began walking towards the entrance to the golf club.

He took up station against a single pillar, which anchored a two-bar swing gate. A lamp mounted on a metal pole threw enough light for him to pick out the detail on the handful of cars, which were stationary in various parts of the park. It didn't take long to spot the vehicle they had followed from the train station.

He signalled to his colleague to move left, taking advantage of the cover of a parked minibus. Bickers went right, using the shadows thrown across the park by a large boundary hedge.

The intention in the pincer movement was obvious.

Bicker reported later that he wasn't sure what alerted the car occupant. One moment the man was sitting there, the next he was scrabbling furiously at the steering wheel. The engine coughed and the car shot forward in a U-turn manoeuvre across the park. It crashed into a car parked in a spot reserved for the Club Captain, righted itself, and turned to face Bicker's colleague.

A gun appeared through a gap in the car's side driver window.

Bicker could hear his colleague shout: "Stop! Armed police officers!"

Gunshots broke the silence of the night as the car driver open fired in the direction of the officer, who dove to the ground and rolled away from bits of asphalt thrown up from near the spot where he had stood.

The engine revved and the car headed straight towards him.

Bickers ran towards the speeding vehicle, firing on full automatic at the passenger side window as the vehicle passed. He continued depressing the trigger and watched as the car appeared to judder as if about to topple. Instead, it flew straight at the boundary hedge, burrowing its way almost through its full width of ten feet. It was stopped by the dense thicket and came to rest with the back wheels still spinning and smoke rising from the damaged bonnet.

Bickers approached the vehicle carefully. The smell of smoke and gasoline was almost overwhelming. He had a view through the shattered glass. One look told him the occupant was dead.

Most of the top of the driver's head was missing.


Back at the command centre, a steady stream of information was flowing in from the men on the ground. They now knew one man was killed at the Secretary's house, while another was arrested on the approach road outside.

News of a second death at the golf club car park had still to reach them when Major John Breen, the man in control of the operation, received an odd call from his headquarters back in London.

The voice was that of General Sandford, who was in the COBRA offices monitoring the action.

Sandford got straight to the point. "We've just received a message passed onto us from the RUC in Northern Ireland. It seems one of their men was near the scene of that car bomb attack in Glasgow this morning and is following what he has described as a high level IRA target driving on the M6 heading in the general direction of London."

The General went on to explain that the RUC man had telephoned back to his own base from a pursuit car and asked that the message be routed instantly to the Anti-Terrorist offices in London. The RUC had requested roadblocks and back up.

Instead, the General had issued instructions for motorway patrols to watch out for the vehicle, but to keep a safe distance.

"The thing is," said the General, "I've given instructions not to intercept. Call it a gut feeling, but I think this vehicle is heading to Epsom."

"Isn't that a bit of a stretch, sir?" Breen asked.

"I don't believe in coincidences, Breen. Doesn't it strike you as odd that on the same day we have the biggest IRA operation mounted in Britain, we also have a car bombing and one of their so-called high-level operatives heading in the same general direction? If I'm right, then he's heading into the funnel of your operation and we'll have him like a rat in a barrel. If not, we'll still have him under surveillance and can pounce at any time we like."

"Sounds fine to me, sir. I'll keep the troops on the ground and circulate a description of the vehicle. Shouldn't we tell the RUC to back off?"

"Already taken care of," the General retorted.

Breen ended the call and was about to issue

instructions when an operative sitting close to him passed over a radio handset. "It's for you, sir. It's Mike Devon and he says it's urgent."

Breen grabbed the handset. "What is it, Devon?"

"Sir, the man we nabbed at the scene is not who we thought it was. There's at least one other target out here unaccounted for, and he's their top man. Everything pointed to him being the one who was supposed to carry out this hit. We need to throw a cordon around the entire area, stop every train, bus, taxi, and car leaving the Epsom area. We need to bottle up this place so tight that...."

"Just a minute, Mike. Let me update you," Breen interrupted. He filled Devon in on his discussion with General Sandford.

Breen waited patiently for a response, but after almost a minute, there was still silence.

"Are you there, Devon?"

"Sorry sir, just trying to understand what this is all about."

"Tell me about it. I'm keeping all teams on alert in the area. If he's heading our way, I want him caught with his trousers down around his ankles. Keep me posted."

"Wait, sir," Devon pleaded before the connection broke off. "Do we know the name of the RUC officer following the suspect?"

Breen searched for the note on his desk. "A Detective Chief Inspector by the name of Martin Vennison. Do you know him?"

"Yes, sir. Can you get me the number of his cell phone? I need to speak with him."

# Chapter 32
## Dublin

NOLAN WAS BACK IN his home in South Dublin. Throughout the previous evening he had argued with Francis Dooley about switching their respective roles in the planned events of the day. His loyal lieutenant and friend eventually persuaded him that he was too important to the movement to risk exposure in such a high profile operation. If he were captured, or worse, they simply could not fill the gap at such a crucial stage in their history.

Nolan finally relented when Dooley painted a picture of the in-fighting and power struggle that would rage in Nolan's absence.

When they took the ferry to Scotland late on Thursday evening, it was agreed Dooley would continue onwards on his own, taking the train from Glasgow to Epsom and meeting up with a small hand-picked team of volunteers who would provide back-up to the operation.

For his part, Nolan would do the job he had assigned to Dooley. It had become clear to him that Fergal McSweeney was past his sell-by date, worse still he believed he could dictate his own terms to the organisation. Nolan was fed up with the assassin telling him what he could and couldn't do. He was fed up listening to the *"I-want-out"* whining that was becoming like a stuck record needle every time they contacted him for a job. Who did this fucker think he was? This was a lifetime vocation, a once-in-never-out commitment, which couldn't be broken.

News of any such betrayal would spread through the ranks like a plague. There was only one solution.

After shaking hands with Dooley and watching him disappear into the Glasgow airport train station, Nolan drove to the home of a local sympathiser. There he assembled a Semtex bomb, waited in the man's house until after 2am, and then set off towards Sheridan Avenue.

Few lights shone from any of the houses in the area. Nolan parked up in the next street, grabbed a case from the back seat, and made his way under the cover of darkness into Sheridan Avenue. He approached number twelve, a detached two-storey building with a generous front garden. The Mercedes stood in the driveway close to the front door of the house.

It took less than ten minutes for Nolan to attach the device to the underside of the car, loop the wires around the exhaust, and run them up to the starter motor.

He retraced his steps, picked up his car, and headed back towards Stranraer to catch the early-morning ferry back to Northern Ireland.

During the long drive to Dublin, the car radio told him the sketchy news of a bomb exploding in central Glasgow. At various stages of the journey, the BBC Radio News updated him with confirmation that the bomb was now known to have been placed under a car. Later still, the station read a short statement from a Strathclyde Police spokesperson that was able to confirm at least two fatalities caused by the explosion.

When Nolan arrived at his farmhouse home, he dashed inside. He switched on the television, flicked his satellite remote control, and stared hungrily at the screen for the latest news.

According to the announcer, it was now known two people had died in the explosion and that a man was rushed to a local hospital. The condition of the injured man was not known, but it was considered his injuries were not life-threatening.

Nolan's concern grew with each bulletin. At first, he reasoned the man who survived could have been a passer-by, just some unlucky jock in the wrong place at the wrong time.

Little by little the constant updates throughout the morning confirmed his worst fears. McSweeney had survived.

Television reporters, speaking to people near the scene, were now piecing together a story of a mother and her son dying in the explosion. Interviewee after interviewee was telling of their sorrow and condolences for the father, who was taken to hospital.

There was now no doubt in Nolan's mind that the wife and child were alone in the car that McSweeney should have been in. He also knew with certainty that if McSweeney were alive, he would come looking for him.

Nolan spent a restless day, pacing through the house and cursing at the clock in the mantelpiece to move faster. His thoughts had now turned to the operation in Epsom, and as the time drew near, he could picture Francis Dooley making his way into the garden from the golf course, creeping along the hedge, and gaining access through the garage door.

He saw himself stepping out of the wardrobe, pointing the gun at the fat bastard's head, and sending him to meet his maker.

It was 6pm. Nothing. No coded message, no

news of the success of the operation. Dooley should be out of the house by now, should be on his way to the train station, and should have called in. Even if something had happened, the getaway driver at the end of the road should have relayed a message, or the back-up driver in the golf club car park.

He had muted the television button for most of the afternoon, sickened by the continued confirmation of McSweeney's survival, but as he glanced across at the set, he could see a new ominous red banner flashing across the bottom of the screen.

BREAKING NEWS: FATAL SHOOTING INCIDENT REPORTED AT EPSOM.

Nolan hit the sound button and stood over the television set, urging the anchorman to provide more detail. Finally, the man stopped wittering on about cuts in the Health Service.

*"And now we return to our breaking news. Police have confirmed that at least one man is dead in a foiled terrorist attack in suburban Epsom. It is believed armed police were involved in a number of incidents in the area, but details are still coming in. More when we get it."*

Nolan reeled back across the room and slumped into an armchair with a force akin to being punched. Foiled? Did he say foiled? He kept trying to replay the words in his mind, all the time thinking of Francis Dooley. No, no, not Francis! It must be a mis-take. He didn't realise he was muttering aloud to himself, all he could think of was his friend lying dead in a country he hated. Maybe it wasn't Francis. Maybe it was one of the others?

Francis dead? McSweeney alive? Could this be really happening? He forced himself out from under the gloom of his thoughts. There was work to be done, not least preparing for a visit that he now knew was inevitable.

# Chapter 33
## Glasgow

VENNISON REACHED THE entrance to the industrial estate where he had an address for the car dealer, when a silver Mercedes tore past him and joined the flow of motorway traffic. The driver didn't glance his way, but Vennison recognised the face of the man who was wearing a policeman's shirt when he last saw him leaving Glasgow Central Hospital.

Vennison executed a neat handbrake turn in his hired Volkswagen and took off in pursuit.

He had lost valuable time waiting for a taxi to take him back across the city to where he had abandoned the car, but knew he had to have his own transport if he intended to run down his quarry. Twice he was caught in traffic queues that seemed to be going nowhere, and he cursed his luck when he realised he had missed McSweeney by only a few minutes.

He exited the industrial estate into the three-lane motorway and crossed to the outer lane. Ahead, all he could see was a line of traffic, his vision obscured by a high-topped van that was hugging the fast lane. He blared on his horn until the van driver moved across to the middle lane, allowing Vennison to accelerate up past eighty.

There was no sign of the silver Mercedes, but thankfully he had passed no exit roads where he could have missed the car turning off.

He drove for twenty minutes at the fastest speed the traffic ahead would allow. As he entered a low dip, he noticed the Mercedes climbing out the other side about thirty cars ahead. He started to close the gap, oblivious to the anger caused to other drivers as he menaced them out of his way.

He noted they were heading onto the M8 towards Stirling and Carlisle, the gateway to England. For more than an hour he kept up the pursuit, turning onto the M74 at Carlisle, and then joining the M6 to the south.

Vennison knew he was isolated and would need help. After weighing up his options, he lifted the mobile phone and called direct to Chief Superintendent Billy Carter. He brought Carter up to speed on what had happened and suggested he call the anti-terrorist unit for support. He had earlier gotten close enough to read the number plate of the Mercedes before dropping back behind four other cars.

Vennison guessed Carter would be astounded by the events and it was little surprise when he ordered him to stay back until help arrived.

"I'll be careful, sir."

Ten minutes after his conversation with Carter, the mobile buzzed on the seat beside him. He lifted it and pressed the green button. A voice boomed out through the receiver.

"Is this Detective Chief Inspector Martin Vennison?"

Vennison acknowledged his identity.

"Good," said the voice, "I'm General Sir John Sandford. You seem to have stumbled into one of our little operations and we're grateful for your support. We'll not waste any time discussing how you've come to be where you are, but you need to tell me your exact position and whether you are still in contact with your target."

Vennison waited for the nearest motorway sign, relayed the information back to his caller, and confirmed he still had vision on the silver Mercedes.

"Good show," the caller told him. "Here's what I want you to do. Keep your distance for the next thirty miles and watch out for the turn-off to the M42. If your man takes the route towards London, you are to stop your pursuit. I have unmarked vehicles standing by to pick up from you."

"But sir...."

"No buts, Detective. We have a serious situation on our hands and frankly we can't have you in the middle of it. Just let us know if there are any deviations before you reach the M42, otherwise we expect you to drop off. Do I make myself clear, Detective?" The voice carried an authority that left no room for debate.

Vennison was fuming, but knew he had no alternative. "Understood, sir."

He flung the phone down on the passenger seat and fought to control his emotions. Within minutes the familiar noise of an incoming call snapped him out of the angry trance. Maybe the General had changed his mind?

He grabbed at the handset with expectation, but the voice on the line was a different one.

"Am I speaking to Martin Vennison?"

"Yes, who is this?"

"My name doesn't matter Mr Vennison but suffice to say that I'm part of the anti-terrorist operation currently being mounted around Epsom. I'm curious as to how you've come to find yourself in pursuit of an IRA suspect along the motorways of England."

Vennison gathered his thoughts. "You need to tell me a bit more than that otherwise this conversation is finished."

"Just what I would expect. We have a mutual acquaintance in Captain Mark Garrett. I need you to tell me if the man you are following matches the identikit photo that Captain Garrett supplied to you a few days ago."

The question momentarily threw Vennison. It was only now that he thought of the identikit. The man in the sketch was the last of the suspects he had to visit, and he had been so wrapped up in the car bomb and the events afterwards, that he hadn't even thought of confirming an ID. The fact that there was a car bombing and that the man had fled from hospital, meant he was probably the man he was looking for, but what about the face? He had gotten a fleeting look at the suspect, firstly on leaving the hospital and later at the industrial estate but hadn't even thought to tie it back to the image produced by a sketch artist a decade ago.

He now reran the two images in his mind. One was of a long-haired youth, the other of a man in his thirties, short hair, more distinct bone structure, less chubbiness in the cheeks. The eyes, those piercing eyes, they were unmistakeable. They matched!

Instead of confirming what he just realised, he tried to draw out the conversation, all the while keeping an eye on the silver Mercedes which was now five cars ahead of him.

"And how do you know about the identikit?"

The mood of the man on the other end of the line seemed to change. "Look, let's not fucking dance around here. I'm looking for this man because he murdered two friends in Chicago a long time ago, and you're looking for him because he probably killed your boss in Belfast last year. I don't know how you did it, but you've unearthed the sonofabitch and we need to continue to help each other."

"So, you're the man Garrett told me about, the man who helped put together the identikit. To tell the truth I thought he was selling me a line on that one."

"Well he wasn't. We passed on the sketch and the Scottish connection in good faith, and obviously it's helped you to track him down. I have to congratulate you for doing in a few days, what MI6 and MI5 couldn't do in ten years."

Vennison accepted the compliment at face value. "I got lucky. I was working my way through a list when the car bomb went off this morning. I just happened to be in the right place at the right time. So, tell me, what's happening at Epsom, is that where our friend is heading?"

"Answer my question first. Is it the same man? Is it the man in the sketch?"

"Yes," Vennison told him unequivocally, "It's the same man."

After a moment's silence the voice spoke again. "Can you tell me your precise current location?"

Vennison read off yet another of the endless stream of signs that flashed past his speeding Volkswagen. The little rental car was under pressure from the long foot-to-the-pedal motorway journey; the temperature control needle having long since moved into the red, and the fuel gauge was beginning a periodic bleeping warning.

"Tell me your name."

"Names don't matter."

"You know all about me. It's only professional

courtesy to return the compliment." Vennison was beginning to get a strange feeling about his caller. He decided to risk a theory. "Apart from helping us with the information on Fergal McSweeney, I think I should thank you for that tip-off on the arms dump and various other little scraps that have fallen into our hands lately."

The reply took a few seconds to come through. "You're fishing. Let's just leave it that we're both on the same side. My father always taught me never to look a gift-horse in the mouth. Nice to talk with you, Mr Vennison."

With that the call was disconnected, leaving Vennison with a jumble of thoughts. Whoever the mysterious caller was, he hadn't denied the reference to the arms dump.

Vennison knew of the man's tie-in with Captain Mark Garrett and of Garrett's strange comings and goings to the Bishopscourt RAF base. Just what was going on behind those fences and barricades? Better still, what kind of strange unit was based there?

One thing was for sure, he told himself, the RAF hadn't suddenly involved itself in covert terrorist operations.

The turn-off to the M42 loomed ahead and he followed the silver Mercedes up the off-ramp to a wide roundabout. He watched as the vehicle took the exit for London, but he drove reluctantly past it and parked on a generous service slip area.

The Met boys could take it from here. He didn't spot any obvious signs of the presence of other pursuit vehicles, but then again, he didn't expect to.

He lifted his cell phone and again called his boss. It became clear that RAF Bishopscourt needed a full-scale investigation. He needed to know what was going on there – and he knew there was no better man for rattling cages than Billy Carter.

# Chapter 34
## Motorway in England

FERGAL McSWEENEY WAS undergoing an out-of-body experience. For more than five hours he had driven relentlessly past blurred traffic and countryside, which seemed to merge into one continuous line of unbroken green.

His mind was elsewhere, re-running images of his wife and son in an endless loop of memories. There was total vivid recall of their awkward courting days, of their wedding and honeymoon, of little Jackie's birth, of all the intimate moments they had shared as a family.

The image of Liam Nolan gatecrashed his thoughts, gradually taking more and more shape until all he could see was the figure of his hatred.

The pictures of Mary and little Jackie faded away.

It was the thoughts of Nolan that brought him back to the present. He could now hear traffic and noticed, for the first time, the white knuckles of his hands clenched against the steering wheel. His entire body ached from its long confinement in the car seat. He wriggled to get comfortable but knew he couldn't sustain the soreness and drowsiness for much longer.

He glanced at the small clock mounted in the car's dashboard. It was just past 5pm. He forced himself to concentrate.

He wasn't sure how long he had been driving in the stupor-like state from which he had awoken.

Realisation washed over him that he didn't know where he was. He needed to get his bearings. Five minutes later he saw a large motorway sign ahead. He slowed his vehicle and crossed to the inside lane for a better look. It told him what he didn't want to know.

He was eighty miles from his destination, with no hope of intercepting Nolan at the planned assassination location or at the train station getaway.

*Fuck it! Fuck it!* He banged the steering wheel in frustration.

He noticed the sign also indicated a service station stop two miles ahead. He would have to pull over, stretch his legs, and plan his next moves. He signalled for the off-ramp, left the motorway, and pulled into a large forecourt dominated by parked trucks and a handful of cars. At the centre, was a large building advertising restroom facilities and a twenty-four hour cafeteria.

He parked up, climbed from the car, and tried to stretch some feeling into tired limbs. He locked the Mercedes and crossed towards the building, already anticipating the recuperative effects of a large mug of coffee.

The interior offered generous seating areas, but although most tables already seemed taken, he found a window seat.

The young waitress took his order – a pot of black coffee and two roast beef sandwiches. He didn't feel much like eating but knew the value of reviving energy and storing up sustenance.

Twenty minutes later he had scoffed the sandwiches and was into his third mug of coffee. He began to take in his surroundings, studying the faces around him and tuning into various conversations.

Old habits die hard.

Looking idly out the window across the forecourt, his gaze fell on a brown Ford Sierra, parked at the rear of the forecourt away from the cluster of other vehicles. His instincts went on high alert. There was nothing strange about a car parked out of sync, but it struck him as odd that there were two figures clearly visible in the interior.

Why pull into a service station and just sit there? It didn't make any sense, unless of course whoever was in that vehicle had their minds on other things.

Without looking directly at the car, he studied it closely in his peripheral vision for ten minutes. He could make out that the occupants were two men, one of who was dangling a lit cigarette through the passenger door window. Was it possible they were tailing him?

After he fled Glasgow, it seemed logical the police would circulate the number plates of any cars in his possession, and that would include all those from his garage. That would have been the first place they would have looked for him. It wouldn't have been difficult to rustle up the staff to ascertain whether any vehicles were missing.

But – and it was a big but – if they were looking for him, the car outside would be a marked traffic unit vehicle. They would have flagged him down before now, and they certainly would have approached him inside the cafeteria.

He cursed himself for letting his mind wander on the long trip down from Scotland. Had there been a tail he would have spotted it, even the two or three-car leapfrogging routine much beloved by surveillance instructors. The fact that he had allowed his mind to tune itself out from reality during large parts of the trip meant he was no better than a fucking novice.

If the two gents sitting in the Ford Sierra were indeed after him, then it was obvious they were from some plainclothes department or other. He didn't intend to wait around trying to figure it out.

He was trying to decide what to do when he picked up a Cockney accent from the next table. "Like I was sayin' the missus always packs me enough sandwiches to last a week, even though I'm only doing the Holyhead-Dublin route in a day and a half. Taste bleedin' awful too."

He was a small ferret-faced man, dressed in a leather-patched coat that had seen better days. His ears were squashed by a dirty woollen hat that looked as if it was glued to his head despite the heat of the cafeteria.

"What are you carrying?" asked his table companion.

"Bleedin' load of fake furs from a sweatshop in Watford. The Paddies probably think they're getting the real thing." With that he burst into an uncontrollable fit of laughing. The man beside him did his best to pretend it was as funny as the speaker seemed to think it was.

"How many of the things are you carrying?" The man cut in more to break the embarrassment of the moment than any real desire for information.

"You wouldn't bleedin' believe it, but there's more than five thousand coats of all shapes and sizes on board. That's me rig out there," he pointed to a large twelve-wheeler with fold-down canvas covers tied off at various sections. There was distinctive orange and blue lettering bearing the faded name of the haulier.

McSweeney rose from the table and made his way to the counter. As the waitress took his payment, he asked for directions to the toilets. She pointed him to a hallway running to the rear, thanked him for a generous tip, and turned towards the next customer.

He entered the toilet block and locked himself in a surprisingly clean cubicle. He checked his pockets, making sure the money and passports were still on him. The Sig Sauer was wedged into his rear waistband. Thankful he had left nothing of importance in the car he emerged from the toilets and made his way to the rear of the premises. The door to the outside was a simple push-bar emergency door.

Outside he took stock of his situation and made his way to the side of the building. He knew he was on the opposite side to the area where the Ford Sierra was parked up, making it impossible for the occupants to notice him as he peered around the corner. There were enough cars and trucks to provide cover for him as he crept towards the Londoner's rig.

On the vehicle's offside, he unravelled a rope running between two metal hooks, which held the canvas in place. He raised the canvas to peer into a compartment full of large cardboard boxes. Using one of the wheel arches for support he hoisted himself up, pushing and squeezing several boxes before he made a hole big enough to scramble through.

Once inside the truck he reset the canvas as best he could. He turned on a small pencil-torch that was built into his key fob. It provided enough light for him to see the compartment was not fully laden.

The cartons stood about four feet high and were lashed together for stability by nylon straps. A small aisle ran between two rows of boxes that stretched from the driver's cab to the rear of the vehicle. He spent five minutes trying to wedge a gap large enough for him to crawl between two boxes. As an afterthought, he cut open one of the boxes using his Ka-Bar and pulled out a pile of fur coats. He laid them in the space he had created and settled in for a comfortable ride.

McSweeney knew his hiding place was unlikely to pass more than a casual inspection, but it would have to do. He also hoped the driver would not check his tie-downs before setting off. He didn't have long to wait.

The noise of the cab door opening, and closing was followed by the roar of an engine. The big vehicle shuddered, and he could feel the movement beneath him as it picked up speed. He settled into the furs and was fast asleep in minutes.

# Chapter 35
## Epsom, Surrey

"HOW THE FUCK could they have lost him?" Devon screamed down the phone at Major John Breen, who had delivered the news of McSweeney's escape.

"You mean to tell me," Devon shouted, "they sat on their asses in a car park for over an hour and just let him walk out of there? One of them should have had an eyeball on him at all times!"

Breen continued as if he wasn't listening to Devon's intervention. "Apparently they could see him seated at the window of the cafeteria. At one stage he appeared to go to the toilet, but that was the last they saw of him. They kept a watch on the Mercedes and it never moved. Eventually they checked out the whole place and there was no sign of him. The car has been abandoned."

"With respect Major, he didn't just set off on foot across the fields or up a motorway. He must have hitched a lift. Have they checked on any vehicles that left the area? Maybe he had arranged for a contact to meet him there?"

Breen was quick to respond. "It was a motorway café with lots of truckers coming and going. He could have thumbed a ride with any number of rigs that left the park during the time he was there. The surveillance boys are adamant though, that they watched all vehicles leaving and all of them were driver-only."

Devon thought for a moment. "He might have sneaked into one of the rigs or left the park by foot and thumbed one after they had driven out of the park. Christ, he could be anywhere by now. What are they doing about a follow-up? Have roadblocks been set up along the routes leading from the service area?"

"The officers at the scene have been interviewing everybody inside the cafeteria for the past thirty minutes. They're trying to establish whether any of the truckers or staff can remember any regulars who were there at the time, who they drive for, their normal routes, and all the usual stuff. Frankly, I don't hold out any hope of a positive lead."

Devon was furious and he didn't care about letting it show. "The thing I can't understand is how the hell he spotted the tail. I thought we were using top men on this operation?"

"No need for recriminations at this stage, Devon. We'll get to that later. For now, we have to concentrate on running down our quarry. To answer your earlier question, we have established roadblocks at ten, twenty, and forty-mile intervals both ways from the service station. I've also given orders for blanket security at all rail depots. I doubt whether he's intending to head back to Scotland, so the likelihood is that he could be trying to make his way into London. From there he can go anywhere, but we've put extra men into the Channel Tunnel rail and bus links and all airports in the London area."

Devon's mind was racing, trying to evaluate the events of the past twelve hours. An idea jumped to the front. "Just a moment Major, we need to look at this from another angle. It's obvious the car bomb this morning was intended for this man, Fergal McSweeney, and from that we can surmise there's been a falling out within the ranks of the IRA. It was our information that McSweeney was to make the hit on the Secretary of State, so why was he not there? Why was he the target of a car bomb eight hours before the planned hit?"

"Where's this leading, Devon?"

"Bear with me. Let's for a moment say that McSweeney refused to undertake the assassination assignment. The plans were too advanced for the IRA to pull out, so they sent in a substitute squad. But they couldn't just ignore McSweeney getting an attack of conscience, or cold feet, or whatever, so they decide to take him out as a lesson to all their conscripts."

Breen interrupted. "That's a bit of a stretch. From your original briefing, we were led to believe we were dealing with a determined, calculating individual, certainly not someone who would get cold feet."

"I agree. I must admit I don't buy that bit of my theory, but there was a falling out for some reason, and that led to the death of this man's wife and child. What would you do if it happened to you?"

The line was silent for few seconds before Breen responded. "Are you suggesting this man came down to Epsom hell bent on revenge?"

"It's what I would do." The coldness in Devon's voice was obvious.

"But his timing was all out. If he were in on the original plan, he would have known the time of the hit and would have known he could not have made it here in time to...."

"Yeah, but what else could he do but try? He had to get out of Scotland; he would have known the car bomb put him in the spotlight. As for his timing, we must remember this is a desperate man, and he could have set off from Glasgow without thinking things through. Or it could be that the original plans included the provision to lie low in a safe house nearby."

"Are you suggesting we keep a tight cordon around the Epsom area in the event that he still might show up here? Surely he must know by now that he couldn't get through the dragnet we've thrown up."

"That's one possibility, Major. This is one resourceful fucker and we can't take the chance that he won't try."

"You said one possibility. Are there any others?"

Devon was still trying to put logic into his thoughts, and he left the Major holding as he rationalised the conclusion he had reached. Eventually he spoke again. "Yes Major, I believe there is."

"Are you going to enlighten me?"

Devon's voice was laced with more confidence than he actually felt. "I think he'll try to make his way to Ireland. If our Intel is correct, the man behind this operation is Liam Nolan. I think McSweeney is on his way to Dublin."

There was silence from the other end, but Devon could hear muted background voices. Eventually Major Breen came back on the line. "If you're right, then his obvious route to Ireland from where we lost him, is to cross into Wales."

"Why Wales?" Devon asked, already knowing the answer before it came back to him.

"Because that's where the Holyhead to Dublin Ferry is located."

McSweeney was awakened by banging sounds. He

immediately tuned into the surroundings, taking in the jumble of fur coats and the stacked cardboard boxes. He realised the truck in which he had been travelling was now stationary, and he could hear the unmistakeable grating of metal rollers being opened and closed somewhere beyond his hiding place.

Using his knife, he carefully made a slit in the canvas wall and peered out into a gloomy night of dark roiling clouds and heavy rainfall.

He saw the lorry was in a queue of vehicles stopped in a large car-park area. Several hundred yards ahead, the scene was lit up by a mobile searchlight sitting atop a small pick-up. More than two dozen men, many of them in uniform, were weaving around the various vehicles, shining torchlights into cabs, or inspecting papers handed to them by irate drivers.

He made his way to the rear of the truck, shouldering aside cartons to make a narrow passageway. Using the Ka-Bar, he cut a slit in the canvas and noticed a large truck had pulled up tightly behind it. The cab of the rig was empty and he could see a group of men standing around smoking under the shelter of a hut, no doubt cursing the delay and waiting for the queue to start moving.

He rammed the knife into the opening he had created and drew the blade down the full length of the canvas. He pushed his head through the gap.

The group was standing with their backs to him, and he could see no other figures. He wriggled through the opening, using the cab of the second truck to steady himself. He jumped to the ground, squeezing along the tight gap, and emerged on the side away from the huddled drivers.

Uniformed figures were making their way along

the queue, about twenty vehicles ahead of him.

To his right stretched a car park, sparsely populated with about fifty vehicles. The interior light of one of the vehicles came on, highlighting a man wriggling into a fluorescent jacket, with a clipboard wedged in his teeth.

Without wasting a second, McSweeney took off in a crouching run between the parked cars, his exposure helped by the lack of lighting at this end of the park.

Approaching the driver's window, he rapped it forcefully and gestured at the startled occupant to roll down the window.

Instead of opening the window, the man pushed open the door. "Wha's the matter? You nearly give me a heart..." He never got to finish the sentence.

McSweeney rammed a wicked punch into the side of the man's head. The blow, delivered to the softer bone and cartilage structure just above the ear, was calculated to temporarily immobilise the victim. It did its job and the man sagged across the passenger seat.

McSweeney bundled the unconscious figure out of the driver's seat and jumped in, closing the door, and knocking off the interior light.

He looked through the rain-covered windscreen to the queue of vehicles beyond. No one moved. No one saw what had happened.

The man in the passenger seat moaned. McSweeney stuck his thumb forcefully into the side of the man's neck, cutting off the blood supply in the carotid artery. He didn't want to kill him. He knew that would be the easy thing to do, no doubt the sensible thing, but just enough pressure could render the victim unconscious for up to two hours. More time than he needed.

He removed the man's fluorescent jacket and put it on, before ripping off an identity badge that hung around the man's neck to identify him as an employee of the Holyhead Port Authority. The clipboard, which had slipped into the passenger footwell, contained a small sheaf of papers filled with lines and tick-boxes.

Probably starting a night shift, McSweeney surmised. Perfect.

He climbed from the car and walked confidently across to the queue of vehicles, making his way past several uniformed policemen checking what appeared to be driving and shipment documents handed to them by drivers.

Other policemen, helped by men dressed in the same yellow-coloured jackets as McSweeney now wore, were clambering into the backs of trucks. It was clear this was a major search operation.

Holding the clipboard in front of him, McSweeney strode confidently through the search area towards a row of vehicles that looked like they had been cleared for embarkation. In the middle of these he spotted a luxury coach, the windows heavily misted by a crowd of passengers. On the rear window he noticed a large sticker announcing *Manchester United Supporters on the Road*. The bus was starting to move towards a tunnel that must lead to the ferry.

McSweeney broke into a trot and caught up with the bus before it entered the tunnel. He rapped the passenger door, which opened as the driver pushed a button on a panel in front of him. "What is it now?" the exasperation dripped from his words.

"Nothing at all," McSweeney said with a forced

grin. "As a United Supporter myself, I'm here to make sure you guys aren't delayed any more. I'll stick with you until you're safely aboard. Drive on."

As they drove onto one of the two ramps leading to the ferry, McSweeney spun the driver a story about going to Dublin to visit his mother. He told the man he had just come off an eighteen-hour shift and would he mind if he grabbed a few hours' sleep on the back seat of the coach when the passengers alighted to enjoy the journey in the ferry's generous lounges? McSweeney knew he couldn't risk milling about with other passengers.

"Help yourself," the driver told him. "When we get to the other side, we can drop you off in the centre of Dublin on our way through."

Devon raced into the car park past the queue of trucks, flashing his badge at any uniform that waved him down. He abandoned his car near a tunnel entrance and went searching for the man in charge.

He found a large, ruddy-faced figure directing several policemen towards vehicles still being processed in the queue stretching back towards the park entrance. Devon introduced himself.

"So, you're the bugger that's caused all this mayhem," the man said good-humouredly. "We're drawing a blank at the moment, but we've still some way to go."

"Don't take this the wrong way," said Devon, "but are you sure your men have been thorough with every vehicle that has come through?"

The man introduced himself as Inspector Tim Little from North Wales Police. "No offence taken," he said pointedly. "My men know what's involved here. We've pulled apart every truck and car and everything is as it should be. We even made three Bishops get out of their car while we searched luggage and checked ID. Hope my missus doesn't find out. She's Roman Catholic and so were the Bishops."

Devon excused himself and headed for the shelter of the tunnel to watch the remainder of the operation unfold. His mood gradually worsened as each vehicle was cleared to proceed through the tunnel towards the ferry entrance ramps.

The final truck in the queue passed him, leaving an empty roadway space filled with policemen and yellow-jacketed port authority workers. All seemed to be looking accusingly in his direction.

He ignored them, turned on his heels, and marched purposefully down the tunnel. Somehow McSweeney had avoided detection, but he knew the action was now switching to Dublin. He decided to hitch a ride on the ferry.

As he walked, he removed his mobile phone from his jacket and hit a speed-dial button to take him directly through to Alan Doyle. He spent several animated minutes issuing instructions for a team to rendezvous with him at Dublin's Dun Laoghaire Harbour.

He knew the drive time from Bishopscourt would be about the same as the ferry-crossing time. Two hours from now he would have his elite team with him. Two hours from now he could start the final part of his revenge mission.

# Chapter 36
## Dublin Ferry

DEVON SPENT THE first hour of the journey walking the entire length of the ferry several times. He stopped to examine the faces of people seated in the numerous passenger lounges and picked his way through two separate dining areas where queues were waiting for service.

Only twice did he stop to take second glances at two men who could match the image he had of McSweeney, but on each occasion he dismissed the likenesses as superficial.

Finally, he gave up the fruitless search, grabbed a coffee, and sat in a generously sized chair with a clear view down one of the ferry's main passageways. You never know, he consoled himself; I might spot the bastard strolling about. *Yeah, chance would be a fine thing!*

He was so intent on reading the faces of scores of men who passed up and down the aisle, that he ignored what was going on in his immediate vicinity.

He was distracted by an elderly woman who rose from a seat beside him, blocking his view as she gathered up knitting accoutrements. He waited as she stuffed balls of wool and different-sized needles into a large handbag that could just as easily have been a hold-all.

Almost as soon as she walked away, a man flopped into the vacant chair.

"Mind if I join you?"

Devon looked at the stranger with a total

absence of curiosity. "Go right ahead. You paid the ticket same as me."

"Actually, I didn't pay, and I suspect neither did you."

That got Devon's attention.

The man opposite was in his thirties, grey hair already fighting for attention through the close crop of black around the ears. He looked lean and fit, dressed casually in light blue denims and a contrasting dark blue sports jacket.

"I'm sorry," Devon said," but do you know me?"

"Couldn't help but notice you pulling up as I sat in the queue leading to the ferry. You seemed to be in charge of something. What was that about?"

"What was what about?"

"No prizes for guessing it was some sort of a security flap," the man replied evenly. "That being so, then I think we're in the same game."

Devon's interest needle had just swung into the red zone. "At the risk of repeating myself, do you think you know me?"

The man returned his stare. "Let's put it this way. Before I spoke to you, I was just following a copper's hunch, but your voice has certain characteristics that even a short mobile phone conversation can't disguise. I think I now know who you are."

Devon became fully alert. He replayed the man's words, recognising his admission that he was a copper, and stopping at the reference to the mobile phone conversation.

Reality dawned. "You couldn't possibly be Detective Chief Inspector Martin Vennison," he offered, more as a statement than a question.

"You have me at somewhat of a disadvantage. I still don't know your name. You were rather curt about that when we last spoke."

"Names don't matter. Can I ask what you're doing on this ferry?"

"It's quite simple really. I needed to get home in a hurry and didn't fancy driving back to Scotland. This ferry was the handiest after I was ordered to lay off the pursuit of our mutual friend. I still have a hire car to return to Scotland, but all things in their own good time. Was that security cordon at Holyhead part of the operation in Epsom?"

"I don't see how that's any of your business, Detective."

"Don't tell me our friend got away from you."

Devon eyed the policeman, trying to get a read of his intentions. He had already proved his resourcefulness, and Devon knew he was not someone to be taken lightly. He eased off the abrupt manner. "Look Detective, you're a bit out of your jurisdiction. I'll admit we've temporarily lost our target, but we don't need your help to pick up his trail again. You've been a great help, more than you know, but right now I'm asking you to back off."

"You obviously think you can pick up the trail again in Dublin, otherwise you wouldn't be here."

Devon considered how much more he could tell Vennison. "I was convinced he was heading for this ferry, but he's either slipped through the cordon, or he's making his way by another route. Yes, one way or another, I think he's headed for Dublin."

"What makes you think you can find him in Dublin? I could also say that's a bit out of your jurisdiction."

"He is linked to a man in Dublin; a man I believe was responsible for the murder of his wife and son in that car bomb this morning."

Vennison sank back into his seat. "You can't just go around Dublin knocking on doors until you find him. Or could it be you have an address for the man he's searching for?"

"Let's just say I have a fair idea where to look."

"You can't do this on your own. You'll need back-up."

Devon fought to keep his voice low. "If you're volunteering to help, forget it. I have things to do that you don't want to be a part of. Besides, there'll be a team waiting for me at the other end."

"That wouldn't happen to be a team based at Bishopscourt?"


Alan Doyle stared at the passengers descending the pedestrian gangway into a glass tunnel, leading from the ferry to the reception building where he was positioned. There was no sign of Devon. The boss had made it clear he had abandoned his car in Holyhead, so this was the only exit he could use.

When the last of the stragglers emerged into the tunnel, Doyle knew something must have happened. To his right, a continuous line of vehicles were disgorged from the belly of the ferry, and now even those had dwindled to a trickle.

Bewildered, he reached for his mobile phone and scrolled through for Devon's name on the contacts panel. At that moment, he became aware of a hand on his shoulder.

"Looking for me?" He turned to see Devon standing with another man.

"What's going on, boss?"

Devon turned to the other man. "Alan, I want

you to meet Detective Martin Vennison from the RUC. He's with us."

Doyle couldn't disguise his surprise as his eyes flickered between Devon and the other man. "I don't understand. What's going on?"

"All in good time, Alan. We're in a hired Volkswagen. Where is the rest of the team?"

"We have two cars in the short-term car park. Everybody's booted and suited. Your gear is in the trunk."

Devon started walking towards the exit door. "Okay Alan, you're with us. I'll explain everything on the way."

# Chapter 37
## Dublin Farmhouse

LIAM NOLAN'S HOME WAS once a working farmhouse, a three-storey Georgian mansion overlooking the rolling hills of Meath to the front, and a large sprawling courtyard to the rear. Several unused farm sheds surrounded the courtyard. Machinery and livestock had long since disappeared.

Until Nolan came along, it was a working farm handed down through three generations engaged in the breeding of cattle, pigs, and sheep. The generous package of more than a hundred acres that went along with the farm was now split into scores of smaller holdings, either sold or leased to neighbouring farmers.

Nolan was an only child, with no interest in farming. Throughout his younger years, he waged a constant battle with his father to escape the drudgery of farm life, finally finding approval from the old man to pursue his political activities. The father was old-school IRA and took a certain pride in his son's ambition to help make Ireland united.

When his father died, Nolan wasted no time in selling off all the assets. It made him a wealthy man. He retained the house and ten acres surrounding it.

Access was by a long, winding laneway that snaked off the main Dublin to Curragh Carriageway, one of Ireland's busiest routes. Set almost a half-mile back, the house was surrounded by tall poplars that hid it from view and blanked out the noises from the roadway beyond.

Four men were in the house with Nolan. His trusted Lieutenants, Joe Coyle and Patrick Pearse shared the living room with Nolan, while upstairs two volunteers were positioned at windows overlooking the front and rear of the property.

Outside, another man was posted in the loft of a former hayshed. An opened shutter door provided a direct line of sight down the darkened driveway. Two more men patrolled the grounds beyond the courtyard, hidden from view by unkempt hedgerows.

All carried crude short-range walkie-talkies.

All were armed to the teeth.

"What makes you think he'll come?" It was about the fourth time Joe Coyle had asked the question in the past twelve hours.

Nolan, tensed by the hours of waiting, continued to pace the room without answering. His gaze fell on an empty armchair that had been a favourite of Francis Dooley's. He still couldn't get used to the idea Dooley would never again sit in it. The constant stream of news bulletins had confirmed his worst fears: that Dooley was dead in Epsom, and the attempt on the life of the Secretary of State had failed miserably.

An already foul mood continued to sour by the hour.

"Course he'll come," Patrick Pearse was answering Coyle. "He's one lucky fuck to still be alive, but now he's got nowhere else to go. He'll want his revenge and he won't mind going out in a blaze of glory."

Nolan turned from a window to glare at the men. "That's enough you two. We don't need to keep going over and over this ground. It's just a matter of time and we need to be ready. Go check everyone's still on their toes."

A two-car convoy pulled up at a narrow country road about a mile from Nolan's property.

Devon pulled a map from a pocket and waited for the others to join him. Vennison and Doyle were first, joined immediately by Mark Webber, Tony Betts, and John Tully.

The team had spent most of the afternoon in a downtown hotel, booking a conference room under the guise of businessmen closing out some deal or other. Apart from wheeling in flasks of coffee and plates of sandwiches, the staff respected their privacy and left them alone for the four hours of booking time their money had bought.

After leaving the hotel, Devon had ordered the group to change back into combat gear before setting off. It had taken less than an hour to drive to their present location.

Before scrambling over a gate into a field, Devon scanned the faces. "Okay. Everybody knows what they have to do. We go on foot across the fields and approach the property from both flanks. Alan will lead team Alpha with Mark and Tony. I'll have team Bravo with John and Detective Vennison. Remember, keep your earpieces and throat mics attached at all times. Nobody moves without my say-so. If we can nab McSweeney alive, that's all well and good. Otherwise, what we have here is a terminate-with-extreme-prejudice operation."

Vennison moved as if to speak, but Devon cut him off. "Listen Detective, I'm still trying to convince myself about taking you along. Part of me wants to leave you here, trussed up like a turkey, so if you still want to come, you'll do what I say when I say it. Are we clear?"

He watched as Vennison opened his mouth to speak but seemed to think better of it. He smacked his lips together, shrugged his shoulders, and turned away.

Daylight was fast fading, just as they had expected. Devon nodded a good-luck signal to Doyle and set off.

Less than twenty minutes later, he heard Doyle's familiar voice through his earpiece.

*"Alpha has eyeballs on the front of the property. The place is lit up like a Christmas tree, but so far no sign of any tangos."*

Devon acknowledged the signal about the tangos, the jargon for opposing forces. Through the gloom he could see the lights of the building, and knew he was less than a few minutes from taking up position at the rear of the premises.

Devon signalled Vennison and Tully to stop at a ten-foot high hedge. Through the thinning twigs he could clearly see a forecourt, with outbuildings dotted around.

He motioned Tully to creep fifty yards to his right, close to the entrance to the largest of the out-buildings. He nodded at Vennison to follow him to the left, towards the rear end of the house. Several minutes later he issued a comms message to everyone to settle in for a patient wait.

The only breaks in the monotony came when Devon acknowledged various radio messages from the other group. Apparently, tangos could be spotted at two points around the rear forecourt, and figures were seen moving across windows in both the ground floor and first floor levels.

*The scene is set*, he thought to himself.

# Chapter 38
## Dublin

THE COACH PULLED INTO the kerbside on Dublin's O'Connell Street. The large doors swished open, allowing McSweeney to step out onto the pavement. He thanked the driver and waved goodbye to the jubilant football supporters, who had kept up constant enthusiastic chants of "C'mon you Reds" despite travelling a long distance to see their beloved United humbled at Old Trafford by a slick-passing Tottenham Hotspur side.

As he walked, he removed the yellow jacket taken from the unfortunate Port of Holyhead worker and dumped it casually in the nearest waste basket.

He crossed the road into Clerys department store, spending the next hour buying a new wardrobe, including a multi-pocketed black zip-up jacket, black jeans, a black turtleneck sweater, and a pair of sturdy black Doc Marten boots.

The store was happy to take his sterling notes, converting the Irish Punt into over three hundred pounds. Jesus, he thought. How do people here afford these prices?

He crossed the road, walked down Parnell Street, and turned into Jury's Inn Hotel. Striding across the large foyer with the confidence of a resident, he made his way to the gents' toilet block. He stripped in a cubicle and dressed in his new gear.

When he was finished, he transferred the Sig Sauer, spare magazines, passports, and currency into the various pockets of his new jacket. All the old clothes, together with price labels and packaging, were stuffed into the Clerys shopping bag.

Within ten minutes he was back in the street, disposing of the bag in the nearest bin he could find. He set off looking for a hire-car office.

By mid-afternoon he was parked in the grounds of a small hotel to the south of the city. He had been to Nolan's house for a briefing several years earlier and knew where he was heading. For now, he wanted food and the chance to pass a few hours until night-time. Darkness presented many advantages, not least that it offered shadows in which he could operate. He had already decided on a full-out assault, and for that he would find no friend in natural light.

At 6:30pm he rose from the dining table and made his way back to the car. Before setting off he checked and chambered the Sig, laying it across the passenger seat within easy reach. He gunned the motor and followed the signs for the Curragh.

He twice drove past the entrance, his memory of the location confused by the addition of new roads and higher hedges along the stretch he knew was the setting for Nolan's property. Eventually he recognised the opening and manoeuvred into the driveway. He lifted the Sig, placed it on his lap, and pressed the accelerator.

He tore into the rear farmyard and circled the perimeter, noticing that lights were on in the house, and surmising that Nolan had surrounded himself with protection goons.

The opened door of the large barn looked a good place to start.

He braked heavily, grabbed the Sig and was out through the driver's door in a flash. He tuck-rolled into the barn and sprinted for cover behind a stack of rotting hay bales.

Above him he could hear running feet across the wooden rafters. He smiled. *Some people just never learn.*

He waited until his night-vision adjusted to the gloom of the barn, then hoisted a bale across the room. It landed with a dull thud and was greeted by two pistol shots.

The flashes came from McSweeney's right, from the top of a flight of dilapidated wooden stairs. A leg could be seen lowering itself onto the topflight, followed by another. Despite the creaking noise of the wood, the owner of the legs continued to repeat the process down another two steps.

Gradually, the full length of a body was visible to McSweeney from his hiding place. He raised his Sig, steadying his aim against the remaining bales.

The man on the stairs was looking away from him, towards the part of the barn where he had fired. McSweeney was confident that even if the gunman glanced in his direction, he would not be able to discern anything through the gloom and shadows.

The sound of running feet on the concrete leading to the barn didn't distract McSweeney's concentration. He squeezed the trigger. The noise boomed across the empty space as the single round tore through the side of the man's head. The legs crumpled, and the body pitched forwards, creating a series of dull thuds as it bounced off one step after another. Finally, it came to rest on the concrete floor.

McSweeney dived over the bales and turned to bring the Sig to bear on the threat coming from the front of the barn.

The footsteps outside stopped. There was a short, sharp whistle, followed by another, and then a second set of running feet. There were now at least two people outside, both crouched somewhere near the opened entrance, but not daring to show themselves.

McSweeney acknowledged they were displaying a bit more smarts than their dead colleague, and he tried to put himself in their shoes. What would he do he if were outside, knowing he couldn't rush a hidden gunman inside?

He looked through the opening, noticing that his abandoned car offered only a few feet of clearance to enter the barn. Reasoning that the men outside were likely placed against the wall of the barn, he knew what he had to do.

He moved out from the cover of the bales into the centre of the barn. Crouched like an athlete in the starting blocks, he surveyed what lay ahead before springing up and tearing across the floor in a full-out run, the sound of his movement cushioned by the rubber soles of his boots.

He leapt over the bonnet, allowing the side of his body to slide across the shiny surface, and came to a halt in a kneeling position, his arms already extended towards the right hand side of the barn.

Just as he had figured, a single gunman was flattened against the corrugated walls, and was turning to fire blindly at the shadow passing across him.

Knowing that he risked taking fire from the second gunman, and possibly from occupants of the house across the forecourt, McSweeney ignored the incoming rounds, held his stance steady, and fired a three-round burst at his assailant.

The man crumpled, and McSweeney dived for cover behind the car, just as incoming fire from his left splintered the car's back window and tore strips of metal from the roof.

He moved around to the front of the car, aware that he was now vulnerable, not only from the gunman to the left, but to anyone wanting to take pot-shots from the house.

He knew that unless he moved soon, he would be trapped in a deadly crossfire.


Devon heard a car engine on the driveway leading to the house. It was travelling at a fair rate, its headlights washing across the house as it entered the rear courtyard. The car completed a full anti-clockwise circular sweep of the yard, and was just beginning a second sweep, when the brakes squealed it to a stop in front of the large barn.

Devon watched as the driver's door burst open and a black-clad figure leapt out, diving in a tuck-roll through the opening to the barn.

There were two pistol shots, followed by a delay, then a third shot from a different calibre weapon. Then came the sound of thuds from within.

Devon watched a man emerge from the exterior shadows. This new arrival put his fingers to his mouth and let out a short, piercing whistle. Another figure came into view, not far from where Devon was hidden, and advanced on the barn door from the opposite side to his partner.

The next thing Devon saw was the extraordinary sight of a man running through the barn door, vaulting the car, and squeezing off a short volley at the man to the right of the barn doorway. The man crumpled and his colleague immediately opened fire on the killer.

Devon activated his throat mic. *"I think our friend has just arrived. He's creating a nice little diversion at the rear of the building. Move in at the front and gain access. Go, go!"*

Devon was aware of Vennison leaning against his shoulder. "That looks like the man I saw in Scotland. I think he's got himself pinned down."

The words flicked a switch in Devon's head. His first instinct was to empty a magazine into the back of a man who had cast a shadow over the past ten years of his life. But even as he thumbed the MP5 full auto, he knew he couldn't do it. *Not like this, you bastard. I want you to see what's coming; I want you to know this is for Pauline and Peter, and all the other innocents you've murdered.*

He lowered the weapon and shifted his gaze to the IRA gunman still crouched to the left of the barn doorway.

Vennison again whispered in his ear. "What are you doing?"

Devon screwed a suppressor into the MP5. "No reason why we can't give our friend a helping hand."

He lifted the weapon, pushed his arm through a thin piece of hedge and took aim at the gunman who had just loosed off another volley in the direction of the parked car. Devon squeezed the trigger.

The dull *whumf, whumf* noise of the discharge could be heard a nanosecond before the sound of the gunman's cry, and the noise he made as his body fell back against the corrugated tin. Then all went silent again.

Devon watched McSweeney rise from behind the car and sprint across the forecourt in a zigzag run. He crouched behind two half-barrel flower holders, his arm extended towards what appeared to be the kitchen window. Two shots were fired through the window into the interior of the kitchen, before McSweeney was up and running again, this time to the side of the building.

Devon tapped Vennison on the shoulder. "Let's go." With that he was off in a sprint towards the other side of the house, anxious to use the diversion created by McSweeney.

Just then, Alan Doyle's voice came into his earpiece. *"Alpha One inside. We can hear noises from one of the rear rooms, and the sounds of at least two sets of footsteps on the floor above. Everyone appears to be attracted to the rear of the building."*

Devon acknowledged and gave orders to move through the house. *"Be advised Alpha One that I'm approaching from the left side of the house and Tango One is moving in from the right."*

*"Roger."*


Mark Webber advanced on the doorway leading from the lounge, Doyle on his left, Betts to his right. He pushed down on the door handle and inched it open. It hinged outwards.

He could see a wide hallway, in the centre of which was a coat stand struggling under the weight of at least six garments. To his left was an ornate front door, with a stain-glass window panel. He advanced his head through the door, trying to get a glimpse to his right.

His eyes swivelled through a semi-circle arc, taking in various hall ornaments, two landscape paintings and a large full-length mirror. They stopped at the gaping barrels of a shotgun held less than six inches away from him. He didn't have time to shout a warning.

Inside the room, Doyle was barely two feet behind Webber when he saw his friend's head disappear in an explosion of pink spray. Bits of bone and droplets of blood assaulted Doyle's face. He let out an animalistic roar, charged against the door and sent it hurtling backwards on its hinges.

He could hear the soft connection of wood against human flesh, but in his haste he tripped over the fallen body of Mark Webber and went flying into the hallway, coming finally to rest with his back against the coat stand.

The garments waved across his face as the stand rocked back and forth before collapsing on him. As he struggled to push the clothes aside, a figure emerged from the swaying door opposite. He could see the man throw a shotgun to the ground and reach for a revolver tucked into the waistband of his trousers.

Doyle's pistol arm was snagged in a long overcoat. As he fought frantically to wrestle free, the man fired twice, hitting him centre mass, just below the breastplate. The last thing he saw was an ever-decreasing circle of light. Then darkness.

The assailant slammed the door shut on a shocked Tony Betts, who had watched the entire scene from the centre of the inside room. Betts activated his mic. *"Man down, man down, no, no two men down, need assistance!"*

Devon recognised Betts' voice. The frantic message could only mean that Doyle and Webber were injured, or worse. It was time to stop pussy-footing about. Without uttering a word to Vennison, crouched beside him, he extracted a hand grenade from his vest, and sprinted to the back of the house, intending to clear a passage one room at a time.

As he ran, he pulled the pin, heaved the grenade through the gap that used to be the kitchen window, and ducked below the brick ledge with his hands covering his head. As soon as the explosion ripped through the inside of the house, he was on his feet crashing against the door, and entering the ruined remains of what was once a typical farmhouse kitchen.

He was aware that Vennison was following but refused to break speed as he leapt over the debris of smashed tables and cupboards.

Ahead, he could see through to the front of the house. He caught a glimpse of a figure at the end of a hallway, turning right and disappearing from view. He heard footsteps on stairs, and knew the man was seeking refuge on higher ground.

He moved down the hallway and stopped dead in his tracks. To his left he could make out what was left of Mark Webber, identifiable only from his clothing and the shape of the ruined body.

To his right he saw the lifeless form of Alan Doyle, sprawled awkwardly on the floor with much of his body covered by a heap of clothes. Rage started deep inside his soul and worked its way through to the surface. The knuckles of both hands gripping the MP5 turned a ghastly white.

Devon stood to his full height, drew in more air, and set off at a run towards the staircase. He turned the corner to look up about a dozen stairs and set off, sprinting them two at a time, his hand depressing the full-auto trigger and sending more than twenty rounds chipping into the walls on either side of the stairwell.

At the top he dropped on his belly, ejected the spent magazine, and rammed home a new one before peering cautiously down an empty hallway. Rising slowly, he began a standard advance, the weapon held up to his face, scanning for any threat.

He lifted one hand from the weapon and checked each closed door with a careful twist of the antiquated knobs. His gun arm dipped as he went through the manoeuvre.

As he turned the handle on the third, he became aware of a figure leaping into the hallway at the far end. Silhouetted against a small gable-end window, Devon saw the man already had his gun raised and pointed in his direction. By the time he could turn fully towards the threat, Devon knew he would be a half-second too late.

He shouldered the door open and collapsed into a tiny bedroom at the same time as a hail of bullets peppered the walls where he had been standing.

He didn't quite make it unscathed.

A burning sensation speared the top of his right thigh, gouging a chunk of flesh and sending an excruciating pain shooting across his body.

He landed on his back and slammed his leg against the opened door. It crashed closed as Devon wriggled across the room to prop himself against the far wall, his weapon aimed two-handed directly at the door.

If the gunman were stupid enough to rush, he would be ready for him.

Outside in the hallway, Patrick Pearse inched his way

to the door, constantly checking ahead and behind for any threat. He thought at least one of his bullets had found a target, but he was too wily to believe he had immobilised his quarry. With his back pressed against the wall, he twisted the handle, and was greeted with two rounds that splintered the wood about chest-high.

Using his left hand, but keeping his body protected by the wall, he pushed the barrel of his gun into one of the bullet holes created by the man inside. Pearse emptied the rest of his magazine through the gap.

As he reloaded, the heard a heavy thud followed by the tinkle of smashing glass. He waited a moment before cautiously turning the handle and letting the door fall open. He chanced a quick peek inside.

The small bedroom window was shattered, and he could see fragments of clothing hanging on shards that were still embedded in the bottom of the wooden frame. He knew then that his quarry had escaped through the window.

He rushed into the room and crossed to the window. Pushing his head through the torn gap, he noticed a small bedroom dresser lying in pieces on a concrete path about ten feet below where he stood.

To his right, the pathway stretched about twenty yards to the rear courtyard, to his left was half that distance running towards the front lawn. Nothing. The man couldn't have made it clear after that drop in such a short space of time.

A floorboard creaked behind him, and Patrick Pearse knew, with all the hopelessness and finality of defeat, that he'd been suckered.

The noise came from immediately behind and slightly to his right, but even as he twisted his body back through the gap and into the room, he knew he couldn't make it.

He had turned less than ninety degrees when he caught sight of the figure kneeling beside the bed, arms extended in his direction, and a look of pure calm on the features of a man who was content with what he was about to do.

Pearse tried to finish his turn. He almost made it when a burst of 9mm Parabellums tore into his chest. The kinetic energy of the rounds pushed him backwards against the broken window, his body disintegrating the wood and glass remnants before spinning through the gap.

Devon raised himself into a squatting position on the bed. He had already removed his jacket to create the torn material on the window glass, and he now used the remnants to tear off crude strips, which he fashioned into dressings for his wound.

It hurt like a bitch, but at least no arteries were severed. He tied off the strips to staunch the flow of blood, and then hobbled towards the hall doorway.

There was still work to be done.

# Chapter 39
## Farmhouse Sitting Room

NOLAN ALMOST LEAPT from his skin at the noise of the car screeching into his farmyard. Any doubts he had about who the visitor might have been were dismissed by the sounds of gunfire. The fact that the radios remained silent only served to worsen an already fragile state. He turned to Patrick Pearse. "Go to the kitchen and see what the fuck's going on!"

Pearse sprang from his seat, grabbed a shotgun, and eased his way out of the front drawing room. Several minutes later, the sound of a shotgun blast told Nolan that Pearse had engaged the enemy.

He had taken up station with Joe Coyle in the drawing room, standing on either side of a bay window overlooking the lawn beyond. Nolan didn't want to be caught in the middle of the room by an attack from outside.

The sound of an explosion shook the building to its very foundation. Glass ornaments jumped from shelves to smash themselves at Nolan's feet. He could now hear the muffled thumps of footsteps in the corridor outside.

He came to a decision and whispered across to Coyle. "Something tells me we'd be better outside than in." He nodded at the large window openings. "Let's work our way back to the rear and see what's happening."

Nolan carefully eased back the curtains and lifted the latch on the nearest window before stepping easily onto a small pathway bordering the lawn.

He was gripping a Bernadelli P-018 Italian-made pistol, holding a magazine of sixteen 7.65mm rounds with an extra round already chambered. He had three spare magazines stuffed into the belt of his trousers.

He knew Coyle favoured the Smith & Wesson Sigma.40, loaded with a fourteen round magazine, though he never carried spares. Nolan doubted if Coyle had ever fully used one complete magazine. He was a planner, not a doer, and always felt uncomfortable around firearms.

Nolan noticed Coyle's hands were shaking and sweat glistened on the pores of his face.

The sound of gunfire assailed his ears from inside the house. Then came the sound of breaking glass from an upstairs room. Nolan turned the corner of the house in time to see the body of Patrick Pearse fly through the air and land with a sickening thud, just a few yards from where he now stood.

The sight seemed to put Coyle over the edge. The gun fell from his grasp, and he stumbled back against the gable wall of the house. By the time Nolan reached him, Coyle was rigid, his eyes glazed over, and his lips trembling. Nolan knew he was going into catatonic shock.

He grabbed Coyle by the shoulders, shaking the smaller man like a rag doll, but to no effect. He slapped him hard across the face. No response. Coyle just stood staring off into space, mumbling incoherently to himself.

"Oh, that's just fucking great!" Nolan roared into the Coyle's face. "It's all very well putting together bombs to blow people to smithereens, or sending someone else out to do your dirty work, but when it comes to manning up for yourself, what do you do?

Turn to jelly that's what, you spineless fucker!"

For a moment, Nolan thought about killing the pathetic sight shivering in front of him. Instead, he bent to pick up the discarded pistol, pushed past Coyle, and headed for the rear of the building.


Tony Betts was still standing behind the closed door, listening to the footsteps outside, and hearing gunshots throughout the house. The sound of the grenade could only have come from Devon, but where the fuck was he? He thumbed his throat mic. *"Boss, boss, what's going on, where are you?"*

*"First floor. Where are you?"*

*"Still in a room to the front of the building. Alan and Mark's bodies are just outside the door."*

*"Get your fucking ass in gear and get out of there. Watch out for our copper friend. I left him near the bodies."*

Devon's voice stung Betts out of his panic. He pushed the handle of the door and cautiously peered out. He forced his eyes away from the mutilated body lying across the doorway entrance, and noticed a figure bent over the prostrate body of Alan Doyle.

Betts lifted his MP5 and was about to pull the trigger when the figure turned. He recognised the face of the Detective.

Betts could see the policeman ripping open the front of Doyle's jacket and undoing the waistcoat of body armour. Doyle was lying at full stretch, his head raised by a makeshift pillow of coats.

"Is he alive?"

"Just coming round now," Vennison replied. "The armour took the full blast, but nothing penetrated. Knocked the wind from him, but he should be okay 'cept for maybe a few broken ribs."

Doyle coughed, blinked his eyes open, and became alert instantly. "Give me a sit-rep."

Betts told him what he knew of the events of the last five minutes. He waited as Vennison filled in the blanks, while Doyle raised himself to his feet, one hand against the wall for support.

"Looks like all the action's upstairs. What do you want us to do?" Betts asked.

"I'll lead, Tony you bring up the rear... wait has this other room been checked?" He pointed at the closed door to the drawing room.

Betts shrugged and looked at Vennison for confirmation. When he shook his head in the negative, Doyle grabbed his MP5 and rushed the door.

Startled by the sudden movement, Betts was slow to follow. By the time he reached the room, Doyle was standing beside the opened windows.

"Looks like whoever was here has flown the nest."

Doyle pushed past Betts and out into the hallway, running towards the stairwell before stopping at the bottom to activate his mic.

*"Boss, it's me. I'm at the bottom of the stairs ...."*

Betts could hear the tinny reply. *"Jesus Alan, is that you? I thought you'd bought it!"*

*"Not bloody likely. On our way up."*

# Chapter 40
## Farmhouse Exterior

McSWEENEY WAS AS confused as at any time in his life. He had heard the muffled shots that neutralised the gunman pinning him down behind the car. Where had they come from? Who fired them? Could they have been wild shots from the house, or could someone have mistaken their target? None of it made any sense.

He used the opportunity to sprint to the side of the building and was creeping under the height of several windows when he heard the faintest of noises behind him. He ducked behind a large oil tank, listening to the rustle of the boundary hedge as someone forced it apart.

McSweeney found a narrow slit where the tank fed a delivery pipe to the ground below. He could make out the figure of a man, clad in combat gear and armed with a rifle. He let the figure come closer.

As the black shape passed the oil tank, McSweeney sprang. His right forearm wrapped easily around the throat, turning the man's neck to the left, and then snapping it back in the opposite direction using his free hand. There was a sharp crack of bone. The man went limp, and McSweeney trailed the body out of sight behind the tank. He flung the MP5 over the hedge into the adjacent field.

As he turned to continue his reconnoitre of the side of the building, he noticed a drainpipe running invitingly from the roof to the ground. Without hesitating he started clambering upwards. He heard a shotgun blast followed by sporadic gunfire and a grenade explosion.

He completed the ascent to the roof and sprawled across the tiles, trying to make sense of what was going on. It was as if he had walked into a private feud. All the better, he thought; *The enemy of my enemy...and all that.*

He began looking around for a skylight. He reasoned there had to be one, and if not, he would take the drainpipe back down one level and try entering an upstairs window.

The roof was tented at a few sections, creating small walkway gullies that he could easily traverse. Within minutes he came across a skylight.

He stared through the window into the gloom for several minutes but could see nothing. Using the pencil light from his key ring he swept the area below, and could make out a small attic room, cluttered with the usual detritus of storage boxes, plastic bags, and discarded toys. The skylight hinged from the inside, with no chance of prying it open from where he stood. He would just have to risk the noise.

He removed his jacket, held it against the window, and hammered against it with the butt of the Sig. It gave after four blows, the glass falling in thick shards to the floor below.

Without waiting for anyone to come investigating, he reached in, pushed down on the hinge handle, and eased open the window. He backed in feet first and dropped noiselessly to the floor.

He moved to a small doorway, cut at an angle to match the sloping contour of the ceiling. It was made of flimsy plyboard and pulled inward easily. He peered out and noticed the room was at the head of a small ladder-like structure of stairs leading directly to another closed door. He descended and opened the second door.

He looked into an unlit hallway that seemed to have several doorways on both sides, and a turning point at the end. There was an eerie silence throughout the house. The gunfire had stopped.

He knew he would have to clear this floor before attempting to go down one level.

Ten minutes later he had reached the end of the hallway, finding nothing in the three rooms on this level. As expected, the hallway led to a set of stairs running down to the next floor. He started his descent.


The two IRA volunteers stationed on the first floor were standing together in the master bedroom, arguing about what to do. They were seasoned enough to know a full-scale battle was in progress, and that it had reached their level. They also knew that McSweeney must have brought a ton of back up, judging by the various sounds of weapons discharging throughout the house.

The grenade attack only served to unnerve them even more. They just didn't know what out there, or how many forces was were arranged against them.

Paddy Brown was the senior of the two, and was urging caution on his younger compatriot, Jimmy Casement, who wanted to rush the corridor. Brown had tried their mobile radio units, but all he monitored was static.

"Useless, fucking toys!" he shouted as he flung one of the handsets across the room.

He saw Casement move to the door. "I'm not waiting here for some fucker to lob a grenade in our laps. I'm going out." With that, he depressed the door handle and stepped out into the hall.

Brown rushed to take up station behind him. They stood back-to-back covering both ends of the narrow passage.

Casement watched in horror as a hand shot out from the recessed stairwell, and a grenade bounced its way down the carpeted floor towards him.

His first and natural reaction was to jump away. He clattered against Brown, lost his balance, and fell awkwardly to the floor in a tangle of legs.

The grenade rolled into his lap.


Devon heard footsteps. There were at least two men, judging by the whispered arguments echoing in the hallway. He pulled a grenade from his jacket, and flung it, still connected to its pin, towards where he judged the men to be.

He knew the sight of the explosive would be enough to cause panic without having to wreck the hallway. In an old house like this, the blast could bring the roof down, and he didn't fancy having to escape from the debris.

He waited for a reaction to the grenade and then stepped into sight, with his MP5 aimed along the corridor.

He saw the flailing bodies and was about to depress the trigger when he became aware of another figure, standing twenty feet beyond the flailing bodies at the opposite end of the corridor. There was something familiar in the man's cold stare behind the sighted pistol.

Devon's memory bank went into automatic rewind, taking him back through time, back through countless thousands of images, back to piercing blue eyes, all the way back to a bar in Chicago.

Finally, he was face to face with his nemesis.


McSweeney had just reached the last step when he heard the noise of people entering the hallway not far from his position. He steadied his Sig and stepped into the passage ready to deal with any threat he found there.

He watched bemused as the two men scrambled about and then fell to the floor.

Then he became aware of a third man at the opposite end of the hall.

There was just enough light from a single bulb in the hallway to pick out the features of a face he had seen before. But where? There was something about the way the man smiled at him that dragged up a distant memory, something that had gnawed at him for a number of years.

He ignored the MP5 pointed in his direction and continued trying to place the face. An image jumped into his brain; an image of a British agent walking past him in a Chicago bar. Now he remembered!

A single word escaped from his mouth. "You."

The realisation dawned on him at about the same time as one of the figures on the floor lifted a gun in his direction. He dropped his aim a fraction and fired twice, both bullets smashing into the man's face.

He was aware instantly of a simultaneous short automatic burst from the far end of the corridor and watched as the second figure on the floor writhed and went still.

He lifted his gaze to the other end of the corridor. The man there was staring at him. Ten seconds passed, then another ten.

McSweeney broke the trance. "I've no fight with you. I've come here for one reason, and one reason only, and that's to kill Liam Nolan."

"I know why you're here. You should know that I'm also here for only one reason, and that's to kill you."

McSweeney continued to stare at the other man. He knew there was a moment in situations like these that only the elite few can read; the point at which one knows for sure that the other is going to pull the trigger.

McSweeney was taught where to look. The signs are there, not in any obvious movement of the hands or fingers, not even in the most imperceptible of eye movements. It comes with an almost unseen relaxation of the facial muscles, a point at which you realise your opponent has reconciled himself to the fact that there's no more talking to be done.

He could see now in the other man's face that the moment had arrived.

# Chapter 41
## Farmhouse Kitchen

NOLAN MOVED BACK into the house through his wrecked kitchen, careful not to make any noise as he picked through the debris. He had felt trapped in the one-door living room and had wanted to flank his opponents, who were still searching at the other side of the house. Ahead in the hallway, he could see three men moving towards the stairs. He ducked behind a ruined cupboard as the man in the rear glanced back in his direction. He waited for several seconds before chancing a look. The three figures had disappeared up the stairwell.

Nolan sprinted silently up the carpeted hall, stopping before he reached the stairwell entrance. He knew the three men would be tight together, and at their most vulnerable. He stepped into the gap and aimed his weapon at the mass of bodies above him.

The man at the rear turned back towards the shadow just as Nolan opened fire, discharging all seventeen rounds, and stopping only when the slider on the pistol locked on empty.

He moved behind the cover of the wall, completed the exchange of magazines, and was preparing to step out again when a long burst of automatic gunfire peppered the walls around him.

He retreated down the hallway, determined to get away from the scene.

Vennison watched Tony Betts take most of the force

of the assault, a succession of bullets striking his armoured vest. However, one ploughed into his wrist, and another entered his throat less than an inch from where his protective suit ended.

There was a terrible gurgling sound before Betts fell, his body slipping down three steps before coming to rest.

Vennison had just enough time to see blood spray from Alan Doyle's right elbow before he felt three hammer blows in the middle of his back. He was propelled face downwards, his forehead catching the angle of one of the steps.

He knew the body armour had absorbed most of the impact of the bullets that struck his back, but it didn't stop it from hurting like hell. He shook off the pain, and scrambled around for his weapon, knowing he wouldn't be so lucky if another fusillade assailed their position.

He became aware of another burst of gunfire, this time from behind. He swivelled to see Doyle holding his weapon left-handed as he raked the bottom of the stairwell.

The big soldier shouted towards him. "Shake yourself, we've got to get after him!"

Vennison looked at Doyle's bloodied right arm dangling at his side. "You're going nowhere."

Keeping a wary eye on the bottom of the stairs, Vennison removed his belt and cinched it above Doyle's elbow. Then he lifted Doyle's arm and delicately squeezed his hand into an opening in his jacket. He raised the zip to form a crude sling.

Vennison had to give the man credit. The pain must have been excruciating, but not a sound came from Doyle's lips.

He lifted his Glock, placed it into Doyle's left

hand, and then grabbed the MP5. "I'll be needing this more than you." He ejected the magazine, fumbled in Betts' clothing, and retrieved a fresh one. He rammed it home, raked the slide, and set off down the stairs.

Vennison turned the corner. No one there. From the rear courtyard he could hear a car engine, and remembered the vehicle left by McSweeney, when he had pulled across the opening to the barn.

He raced down the hall, through the kitchen, and out into the courtyard in time to see the wheels spinning and the car shooting forward. Fortunately, it had been abandoned facing away from the laneway, and he could see the driver struggling to turn the wheel through an almost three-sixty circle.

The face behind the wheel was well known to Vennison. He had seen enough covert shots of the IRA's most senior Godfather to know this was Liam Nolan.

This was the man who had ordered the hit on Chief Inspector John Turnbull.

Vennison calmly raised the MP5 and raked a sustained burst through the windscreen as the car hurtled towards him. He sprang out of its path, rolling several times before coming to his knees, ready to fire again.

The car continued on a straight path into the wall of the house, crumpling itself from the front bumper almost to the driver's compartment.

Vennison gingerly approached the wreckage, placing the barrel of his weapon through the shattered driver's window, and forcing it tight against Nolan's head.

For a moment nothing happened. Then he could hear a groan as Nolan lifted his head from the mangled steering wheel. Blood was oozing from several facial cuts and gashes, but miraculously the man was still alive. The head turned towards Venison. "My legs are trapped, get me some help."

"Fuck you and your help." Vennison spat. "The only help you'll get is a long ride to prison."

"Who the fuck are you?" Nolan asked, as if seeing the man for the first time.

"I'm Detective Inspector Martin Vennison of the RUC, and I'm here to take you in for crimes against the people of Northern Ireland."

"The fuck you say. What are you doing in my country? You don't belong here, copper."

Vennison could hear the total disdain in the man's voice. "I'm just as entitled to be here as you, and when I get you back across the border, I'll make sure you're put away for life."

Nolan started laughing, a low smirking giggle that gradually built to an all-out side-splitting roar.

"What's so funny?"

"I'll tell you what's so funny, copper. Even if you could get me across the border, and even if you get me locked away, I'll be back on the streets in less than a year. Don't you know there's a peace coming? Don't you know our boys will only agree to a peace when all our political prisoners are set free? That's what I'll be, a political prisoner, and a free one at that." He started laughing again.

Vennison knew with certainty that Nolan was right. Knew that if he were locked away, he would be king of the hill, the head bull living a life of luxury until what would be a certain early release.

He also knew that he couldn't live with himself if John Turnbull's murderer was running around free. He casually thumbed the notch on the MP5 to single shot.

Nolan heard the noise and turned towards the raised gun. "What the fuck do you think you're doing?"

Vennison's answer was cryptic. "Say hello to the Devil for me."

He pulled the trigger once and walked away.

# Chapter 42
## A Long Awaited Meeting

MIKE DEVON KNEW this was a classic Mexican stand-off. As soon as he fired his weapon, the chances of walking away were zero. No matter how he played it, nothing could prevent the man facing him from getting off his own shots.

He didn't need telling that the eyes behind the sight of the Sig were the eyes of a marksman. He had heard enough about McSweeney's reputation to know the man wouldn't miss a clear target.

Resignation settled over him. He didn't look for a way out; didn't want one. He had undertaken the whole Storm 74 project with but one thought in mind. He had wanted so badly to kill McSweeney, and now here was his chance. The time had come.

He looked down the musty corridor and prepared himself for the worst. The words came out louder than he intended. "This is for Pauline."

Doyle struggled up the last few stairs. He could see Devon above him, aiming his pistol down the second-floor hallway. He thought he heard him shout something into the gloom before squeezing the trigger.

Doyle stared unbelieving as he watched Devon slump backwards against the wall. The body slid to the ground and was still.

He raced to the top of the landing and looked down the hall. Two men were lying still midway along, and at the far end a third figure was sprawled against the wall.

Doyle ran past the bodies in the middle, kicked away weapons and an unused grenade, and reached the man farthest away. He could see blood pooling around the body. He stooped to pull a Sig from a lifeless hand before turning to run back to Devon.

He knew Devon was wearing a bullet-proof vest, but he still hadn't stirred. No blood was visible as he began to tear off Devon's jacket to check for signs of damage outside the body's protected area. Devon's eyes flicked open, and his mouth hungrily sucked for air. Doyle helped him into a seated position.

"You were gone there for a minute, boss."

Without waiting for an answer, Doyle examined the vest he had torn from Devon's body. Three rounds were evenly grouped, and all hit their mark within four inches of the heart. At a distance of nearly thirty feet, it was pretty impressive shooting by any standard. "Boy, that's some shooting! You're lucky to be alive."

He caught Devon looking at his ruined arm. "Where's everyone else?"

"Webber and Betts have bought the farm. I can't raise Tully, haven't seen him since we split up."

"What about McSweeney? He was at the other end of this hall."

"You got him, boss. You got him good!"

"I need to see him"

Doyle used his good arm to help Devon to his feet.


As Devon approached the body, he could see the eyes were still blinking faintly. He knelt beside

McSweeney and noticed where his rounds had traced a path from the man's navel to his right shoulder. The damage was gruesome.

"We meet again," McSweeney gasped.

"Yeah, small world."

McSweeney spoke again. "Pity I didn't get the chance to get Nolan."

Just then Martin Vennison walked up the corridor. "Did I hear someone mention Liam Nolan?"

Devon turned. "Seems like you know something about him?"

"He's dancing round Old Nick's fire about now."

Devon nodded and swivelled back to McSweeney. The news of Nolan's death seemed to bring new vigour into the dying man's face.

McSweeney glanced over Devon's shoulder and spoke to Vennison. "That really is good news. I don't know who you are, but I'm grateful to you."

"Well, don't be scumbag. You were next on my list, but I see someone's beaten me to it."

Devon was taken aback by the ferocity in Vennison's voice. He put it to the back of his mind and leaned towards McSweeney.

"There's just one thing I need to know. Why did you go for a body shot? Guy with your training wouldn't take the chance on me having a vest. You could have put your rounds anywhere you wanted, so why not go for the head?"

McSweeney fumbled in a breast jacket and removed a photo of a smiling young woman and a fair-haired boy of no more than two or three years of age.

"Let's just say that I owed it to two people to do the right thing before I meet them again."

With that, his head lolled to the side.

Devon stood and gazed down at the body below him.

He watched as Fergal McSweeney died with a smile on his lips.

# Chapter 43
## RUC Castlereagh

SUPERINTENDENT CARTER was trying to come to terms with the way in which Vennison had stumbled across the chief suspect in a year-old murder hunt, and then became embroiled in a major anti-terrorist operation.

What was uppermost in Carter's mind was Vennison's startling revelations about the events at Liam Nolan's house, and the part played by a group who were undoubtedly based at Bishopscourt.

He knew he was working purely on conjecture, suppositions, and hunches, but that was the stuff of his profession and he was ready to follow his instincts.

The knowledge that Captain Mark Garrett, a supposed military Intelligence officer, was followed to the RAF base on several occasions, took on a different meaning when added to his connection with the no-name operative who had tracked John Turnbull's murderer to Nolan's farmhouse.

They now knew this man was the MI6 operative who had run across McSweeney in Chicago and who fed the identikit and Scotland link to the RUC via Mark Garrett just three days ago. It was hardly a stretch to wonder about the mysterious Army roadblock that just happened to be in the same area several months ago when an IRA team was conveniently blown up by their own bomb.

Add that to the significant tip-offs the RUC had been receiving lately, including uncovering a major

IRA arms dump in Saintfield, and the subsequent arrest of a number of the IRA's top men. Then there was the sniper assassination of another IRA man near Dundalk, and the mysterious disappearance of two of its lower-level volunteers in Belfast.

One major break piled up after another had nothing to do with luck, Carter surmised. In the past days alone, there was a gunfight in a south of Ireland border hotel, a car bomb in Glasgow, and a foiled assassination attempt on the Secretary of State in Epsom. Something sinister was working in the background to make these things happen, and Carter was beginning to get an ominous feeling of what that could be.

Following investigations into the unaccounted-for Army roadblock, Carter knew Garrett had attempted to blindside them with a frankly less than believable story of an SAS leader's desire to see the countryside. At the time, he was convinced Garrett was heading up some new Army covert operation from the main barracks at Lisburn.

But what had continued to puzzle him was that if such an operation was mounted out of Lisburn, he would have known about it through the normal liaison officers who were based there, or from the regular briefings that took place between the Army GOC and the RUC's Chief Constable.

They simply couldn't hide it.

The RUC, as the lead civilian and political organisation, had the primary role in Northern Ireland security. The Army's function was to provide back up when required. They couldn't just operate off-base without RUC say-so.

It all pointed to the fact that there was a covert group operating independently, not just from the

RUC itself, but also from the Army. The more Carter thought it through, the more convinced he became that he needed to open the doors at Bishopscourt.

He had arrived back in his offices from a late-night meeting with the Chief Constable and two of his Assistant CCs. He had put his case to them, listening at first to their refusal to contemplate such a move, then to discussions about treading lightly.

Carter told them in no uncertain terms that he had treaded lightly enough for the past few weeks and was not prepared to stand on the sidelines any longer.

He faced down several veiled threats to his job and pension, and icily reminded his superiors that the lives of Northern Ireland citizens were at stake.

"Yes, some of those citizens are IRA Godfathers, and yes, the world would be a better place without them, but they were nonetheless citizens who were under the jurisdiction of the RUC and entitled to due process."

His words made it clear he wouldn't have it any other way, and he challenged his senior officers to say otherwise.

Needless to say, they didn't.

After more than two hours arguing through a series of planned next steps, the four men in the room agreed what had to be done.


At 3:10am, the General Officer Commanding the British Army in Northern Ireland was rousted from his bed and ordered to a meeting in Stormont Castle. The order came directly from the NIO Security Minister, who in turn had conferred with the Secretary of State, by now sequestered in a London hotel because his Epsom house was cordoned off as a crime scene.

The GOC wrote out an authorised entry to Lisburn's Thiepval Barracks where Captain Mark Garrett was to be visited at the first opportunity. Captain Garrett would be asked politely to accompany officers to RUC headquarters in Belfast.

If he refused, he was to be arrested under the Anti-Terrorism Act and frogmarched back the whole way if necessary.

A second signed order, this time from the NIO Security Minister, was also handed to Billy Carter, allowing him to enter the Bishopscourt RAF base, carry out any searches he deemed necessary, and take into custody any persons he believed were operating outside the law.

The HMSU, the RUC's elite Headquarters Mobile Support Unit, was given orders to mobilise by 0600 hours. Six groups of six men, each rigged in full battle dress and carrying Uzi sub-machine guns, stood by armoured Land Rovers at 0500 hours in the police compound at Castlereagh awaiting the green light.


General Sir John Sandford was not one of those people who objected to having his sleep disturbed in the middle of the night. He had long since learned there was little point in shouting down the line at the source of the interruption. There was usually a good reason for it.

This time was no different.

He listened with growing incredulity as he was filled in on the events in Northern Ireland. He cursed the lack of backbone shown by the GOC, but he was at least due some credit for immediately reporting what was going on.

When he was sure he had the full picture, Sandford cut the conversation and immediately dialled another number. He was walking towards his study, struggling one-handed into a silk dressing gown, when the call was answered.

He spoke with all the urgency he could muster. "Listen up, don't say a word. Just do what I tell you to do."

Two police Land Rovers rolled down the security laneway of ramps outside the Thiepval Army compound at Lisburn. They came to stop in front of a heavily fortified concrete sentry station located outside two large swing gates. The gates were firmly shut, with a *No-Entry-Beyond-This-Point* sign hung across them.

The soldier on duty peered out through a glass grill, cut into the concrete just above the height of the driver's side window of the Land Rover. One of the vehicle's seven occupants made some remark about it being like ordering at a McDonalds drive-through.

Billy Carter watched his driver pass a note across to the soldier on duty. The man stared it at it for several minutes before speaking. "I don't understand, sir, I'll ring the base commander."

Carter was having none of it. "Get your hand away from that phone, sonny. Perhaps you didn't read the order correctly, or maybe you didn't see the signature at the bottom. Take your time, read through it again, and then open the gate sometime in the next thirty seconds."

Carter could see the young soldier wavering, not sure how to proceed. He would have been under strict standing orders that no admissions were to be made to the base without the authorisation of the commander. On the other hand, he now held an order from the highest-ranking British officer telling him he had to do precisely that.

"I'm waiting, sonny," said Carter, knowing that the mocking use of the term would rile the soldier even more.

The face behind the glass grill continued to stare at the Land Rover for another five seconds before the occupants could hear a mechanical click and the gates started to swing open.

As soon as a wide enough gap was created, the first Land Rover driver tore through the opening and accelerated towards a building set about two hundred yards to the left. Carter knew from earlier, more social calls, that this was the main administrative block.

When the vehicles came to a rest, the back doors burst open and twelve men jumped out onto the tarmac. Carter and the driver joined them from the front cab, and together the group climbed four steps, pushed open a swing door and entered a well-lit lobby.

Inside, they were greeted by Lt. Col Dickie Henderson, standing in full-dress uniform, flanked by two MPs, standing legs astride, hands on holsters, in a clear defensive pose. Carter knew there must have been a tip-off about his visit otherwise the Colonel would have had to have been roused from his bed. He cursed the closed-rank jungle drums mentality of the military.

Both senior men glared at each other. Carter

spoke first.

"You are no doubt aware that I hold here a warrant for the arrest of Captain Mark Garrett...."

"Chief Superintendent, let me save you some time and effort," Henderson cut in. "Captain Garrett is no longer with us. He's currently serving overseas on a mission of the utmost national security. I'm afraid you've had a wasted journey. You really should have called me in advance."

"It's clear someone called you in advance." Carter was unable to keep the anger from his voice. "I want to see Captain's Garrett's quarters immediately and I want my men to carry out a search of this entire base."

Henderson looked at each of the MPs standing alongside him. "These men are responsible for maintaining base procedures. They will accompany you - and you alone - to Captain Garrett's erstwhile quarters, but there will be no searching of this base."

"May I remind you that I have an arrest warrant together with authorisation from your GOC to be here?"

"As you say yourself, Chief Superintendent, you have an arrest warrant, not a search warrant. This is a military base and therefore not subject to civilian rule. And as for your authorisation, it stops at just about the spot you're now standing on."

Carter knew he couldn't press the issue, but he couldn't let the matter rest as casually as the braided pipsqueak in front of him seemed to think he would.

"I'll tell you this Colonel, and I'll make it simple. If I find out later that Captain Garrett is in fact still on this base, or if it turns out you were in any way an accessory to helping him evade this warrant, then all the fancy ribbons you've covered your chest with, and all the other fancy ribbons in this visiting Army of yours, won't stop me coming after you and nailing your sorry ass to that flagpole outside."

For the first time Henderson's confident demeanour seemed to evaporate. "You can't threaten me..."

"Oh, believe me Colonel, that's not a threat. It's a fucking promise!"

Henderson made as if to respond, but Carter held up his hand to stop him. "Enough, I've heard all I want to hear from you. Now stand aside and have these gentlemen escort me to Garrett's quarters."

Carter turned to his officers, nodded at them to wait, and set off with the MPs in close attention. He knew that all he would be treated to would be an empty footlocker and a rolled up mattress in a sanitised room.

Although it rankled deeply, he knew that for the record he had to make the empty gesture.


Detective Sergeant George McDowell was in the first of four Land Rovers, which turned off the main road and rolled onto the Bishopscourt base entrance avenue. They were greeted by a series of barriers, five in all that comprised long iron poles positioned horizontally across the driveway and hinged into solid-looking concrete blocks.

Each was set about twenty metres apart and between them, he noticed familiar "stinger" strips of iron teeth designed to rip tyres to shreds.

As soon as his vehicle came to rest, McDowell jumped from the passenger seat and approached a group of armed men, four on each side of the first barrier, each wearing RAF uniforms under heavy bullet-proof vests.

He had to admit that as a show of security, it was quite impressive.

As if to increase their menace, the men behind the barrier unshouldered MP5s and aimed them directly at the advancing McDowell.

At the same time, the doors of the Land Rovers opened and disgorged twenty-four heavily armed policemen who ran to the front of the lead vehicle and squatted in an offensive semi-circle formation around McDowell.

"Aye up, you better have a good reason for being here," a grating Yorkshire accent announced to no one in particular. A man, displaying Sergeant stripes stepped towards the barrier, thrusting his face directly against McDowell's. It was a classic intimidation move

It was also a wasted classic intimidation move.

McDowell held up a single A4 sheet of paper. "I have here an order signed by the Northern Ireland Security Minister allowing me to enter this base. I intend to do so immediately, and I advise you order your men to stand down, open these barriers, and remove that rubbish from the ground."

"The fuck you say," the Yorkshire voice responded. "Nobody gets through this gate. Why don't you coppers go play somewhere else?"

He laughed and turned to his mates in an obvious search for support. Smiles passed across all their faces.

McDowell pushed the typed sheet into the man's chest. "You've been duly served. Any moves by you or your men to prevent us entering these premises will be unlawful from this point onwards. Under the terms of the piece of paper you are now holding, I can take whatever action I deem necessary to restore law, and that includes placing you and these men under arrest. If I were you, I would be very careful about what I do next."

The RAF Sergeant grabbed the warrant paper in a reflex action, but deliberately ignored reading it.

McDowell stepped back one pace and nodded to the men around him. They rose and advanced in a line to stand beside him. The men behind the barriers shifted uneasily, but gradually moved forward to mimic the actions of the policemen.

Tensions ran high and McDowell knew one wrong move on either side could literally trigger a major incident.

He decided to help the RAF squad.

Pointing back to the lead Land Rover, McDowell spoke again to the barricade minders. "Our vehicles are fitted with cameras which are providing a live feed back to our base and to the security office at Stormont. Every word that's said and every move that's being made here is being watched and recorded. I order you for the last time to lift these barriers and clear our passage onto the base."

The Sergeant's gaze shifted uneasily from McDowell to the unseen cameras. "And what if we don't?" he asked in a voice that seemed to McDowell to carry a lot less conviction than earlier.

"Then you will leave me with no choice but to enter by force."

McDowell let the seconds tick by. He kept telling himself to give the man time to come to his decision. And pray to God he made the right one.

More than a minute passed.

Finally, the man spoke. "No need for a falling out here. If this paper says you can come in, who am

I to stop you?" With that he nodded to the men around him, and they started to pull the stingers from the roadway. The barriers began rising, one by one.

McDowell waited until he climbed back into the cab of the Land Rover before expelling a grateful sigh. Seated behind the wheel DC Maurice Green turned to him and spoke quietly out of the side of his mouth. "What cameras were you taking about boss?"

McDowell broke into a grin. "You know there are no cameras, and I know there are no cameras...." There was no need to finish the sentence.


An eerie silence greeted the RUC's elite squad when they alighted again from the vehicles in a large concrete compound. McDowell could see two garage-type depots with up-and-over doors opened onto empty spaces. Immediately in front of them, was a stark two-storey administration building constructed in cinder block and painted with a grey coating that had long surrendered to the ravages of the sun.

There were no lights on, and no movement behind the uncurtained windows.

McDowell issued quick instructions to his squad. Six men peeled off and raced to the garages, six others were sent to check smaller bunker-type constructions on the perimeter of the forecourt. McDowell and his remaining men headed for the administration building.

As he approached the opened door, McDowell noticed that the soldiers who had manned the barricade walked onto the concrete square and stood in a casual group eyeing the movements of the policemen. That silly, grating smirk was back across the face of the Yorkshireman.

The RUC men entered the building, their heavy-duty combat boots sending echoes down a number of hallways that radiated from a small foyer. Under McDowell's direction the squad split into each of the hallways, moving down their length, kicking open doorways and briefly checking the interior of rooms before moving on to the next door.

Five minutes later they were back at his side, each shaking their heads in confirmation the building was empty.

A whistle from the far end of one of the corridors alerted McDowell, and he ran to the source. DC Green was standing beside an open doorway, pointing to steps that appeared to run down to another level underground.

McDowell called for the rest of his team, posted two men at the doorway, and signalled for the rest to follow him down the steps.

They emerged into a large tunnel, lit by old-fashioned steel-covered fittings, housing glass containers caked in dust. The effect was to dissipate the light that could penetrate the glass, creating hundreds of finger shadows across a concrete walkway that seemed to stretch forever.

The men advanced, stopping at the first door – a reinforced mahogany structure secured by a cast-iron bolt mechanism through which hung a heavy closed padlock.

"Shall I go ask one of our friends for a key?" Green offered.

"Fuck them," McDowell told him. "Go get the gear. If they want to play silly buggers, so be it."

Ten minutes later, after an assault by a combination of electric cutters and heavy hammers, the door swung open into one of the largest rooms McDowell had ever seen. He directed a dozen of his men to attend to the other doors along the tunnel and then stepped inside the room.

The area was awash with thick electrical cords and cabling, dangling like streamers from the roof. The ends of each strand of wire were crudely cut and left hanging over rows of work benches that could have seated fifty men. Around the walls there was evidence of fittings being torn away, leaving jagged holes in the whitewashed surfaces.

Seats were strewn across the floor like flotsam, and large noticeboards were stripped of whatever had been pinned there. Bits of paper could still be seen trapped by hundreds of coloured tacks.

McDowell noticed most of the streamers were Cat5e cabling, used exclusively for computers and telephony. He inspected a bunch of wires hanging closest to him. There was no dust, no signs they had hung for long in their current state. Somebody had left this room in a hurry. And not too long ago.

The searchers found another similar room and more than twenty smaller rooms. The sight that greeted them was much the same wherever they went - desks with drawers strewn across worn carpet, filing cabinets hanging open, and cot beds upended. Whoever was formerly in residence in Bishopscourt was clearly no longer here.

McDowell grabbed at an upended seat, righted it in the centre of the room and sat down. After a few minutes he came to a decision and beckoned Maurice Green to his side. "I want those so-called sentries disarmed and placed into custody in one of the upstairs rooms. I don't expect too many answers, but I intend to sweat them for everything they have.

Next, get a full Scenes of Crime unit here at the double. I want this place dusted for fingerprints and anything else they can find."

As an afterthought he added, "And I want someone from our Science department to try to piece together what might have gone on here."

Green turned to leave but was called back. "Wait Maurice, there's more. I want a team going over the entire grounds of this base. Get them to use whatever it is they use, but I want to know if there are any surprises out there. Maybe they had to bury equipment or files before they left. If it's out there I want to know about it. See if there are any smouldering fires; find out if some careless bastard dropped something. Don't leave any stone unturned. Find me something."

# Chapter 44
## Hillsborough Castle

THREE DAYS LATER the Chief Constable of the RUC, Sir Trevor Ormerod, was ushered into a plushly decorated drawing room on the east wing of Hillsborough Castle, the official residence of the Northern Ireland Secretary of State. He was greeted by Giles Partridge – who broke off from talking to two other men unknown to Ormerod – and crossed the room to offer a warm handshake.

No introductions were made.

"Sir Trevor, I'll get straight to the point," Partridge told him. "This operation of yours at Bishopscourt has gone on long enough. It's time to pull your men out. I've arranged for the base to be formally handed back to the RAF, and I've agreed to the issue of a Press Release informing the public that the base is to be closed down. The land and all the buildings will be sold off to the private sector."

Ormerod had expected no less, but he was damned if he would give up without a fight. "With respect, Mr Secretary, we haven't finished our investigations."

"Come, come man. Your own progress reports show nothing has been found. If we allow this to continue, the press is bound to get wind of something. We simply can't have unnecessary and damaging speculation at such a delicate time."

"May I remind you," said Ormerod, deliberately dropping the politician's address handle, "that at the very least we have sufficient grounds to believe this base was used as some kind of multi-agency, anti-terrorist operation that was deliberately withheld from the RUC. It is also our firm belief that a whole raft of illegal activities emanated from there, and I include murder among those activities."

Partridge's face reddened and the raised voice was full of anger. "You have no proof of that. And furthermore, you have no hope of finding such proof. You will pull out of that base immediately and transfer all files, tapes, and whatever else you have pertaining to Bishopscourt. This investigation will be taken over by MI5 away from the spotlight of Northern Ireland. This is not a request, it's a direct order."

Ormerod jumped from his seat. "The hands of MI5 are all over that base. It's like asking an accused criminal to investigate his own crime. This is a whitewash, and I'll have no part in it."

One of the two men, who had remained silent throughout the exchange, set down a folder he was holding and spoke directly to Partridge. "Perhaps you think our time would be better spent investigating the various charges of collusion, which have been laid at the door of the RUC?"

Ormerod struggled to keep his composure. "This is outrageous, just what are you implying? Don't think for one minute that I'm going to stand here being blackmailed by a Whitehall spook."

The man spoke again. "No, Sir Trevor, you'll sit and listen. We all have our skeletons, but it serves no useful purpose to start rattling the cupboards. You can have my assurance that any so-called illegalities at Bishopscourt will be dealt with. This matter is being investigated under the Official Secrets Act to which you are a signatory. You will step back, and you will forget about Bishopscourt."

It was the third item on the following morning's BBC Radio Ulster News:

*The Ministry of Defence has announced that the RAF base at Bishopscourt has closed down. Evacuation of personnel and equipment was completed within the last few days. A MoD spokesman said defence budget cuts meant it was no longer possible to justify two RAF bases in Northern Ireland. The second base at Ballykelly will remain open for the foreseeable future.*

*Local politicians from all sides have welcomed the announcement, particularly the MoD's commitment to return the land to private and public use. There is already speculation the area could be used as a civilian airport, although many believe it will be an ideal location for much-needed housing projects.*

# EPILOGUE
## London – Two months later

THE DORCHESTER HOTEL in London's Park Lane has a small dining balcony overlooking some of the most expensive real estate in the nation's capital. Renowned for the over-the-top opulence of its afternoon tea fare, it is one of those places where, if you have to ask the price, you shouldn't be there. Yet that's where Devon found himself during a busy afternoon in the week before Christmas. He didn't much care about the prices - the man opposite was footing the bill.

General Sandford looked every inch the quintessential Englishman, dressed in a checked sports jacket, a yellow cravat hung around his neck, and a pair of spectacles dangling at his chest on an expensive-looking gold chain. He polished off his third miniature apple sponge cake, topped by fresh cream and a large strawberry. He looked content with the world.

"As I was saying Devon, the operation in Northern Ireland was a blinding success. The peace talks are now into the second month, and by all accounts the progress is quite encouraging."

"I can't believe that what we did made much of a difference, apart from saving the life of the Secretary of State. I think they would have gotten round to the peace without any help from us."

"No, no dear boy, you're missing the big picture. We all knew the peace process was inevitable, but it was important Her Majesty's Government was seen to go into these talks in good faith, and not because of a public backlash against more IRA atrocities.

Thanks to you and your team, there are a few hardliners absent from the scene, and we can now be more magnanimous in helping both sides reach a lasting agreement."

"Yes sir," Devon agreed half-heartedly, "but don't forget we paid a heavy price. We lost Taffy Thomas, Tony Betts, Mark Webber, and John Tully. And Alan Doyle has had to leave the Service; the surgeons couldn't save his arm."

Sandford showed genuine sympathy. "Yes, I regret the casualties on our side. Did you ever find out who killed Tully?"

"We found him behind an oil tank outside the siege house. We can only assume he stumbled across McSweeney."

"And who was that little man who was found by the Garda Siochana wandering across the fields near Nolan's house?"

"I heard later that he was Joe Coyle, once a pretty big wheel in the IRA's war machine. Not much use to anyone now. He's in a mental institution just outside Dublin. Apparently, he's lost all touch with reality."

Sandford made to reply, but Devon cut him off. "I'm sorry to interrupt sir, but I need to know how you got everyone out of Bishopscourt before the RUC swooped? I haven't been able to talk to anyone. It's as though they've vanished."

The General let a smile run across his face. "In a sense they have, dear boy. We posted them all around the world. We'll give them a few years away from the spotlight before we bring them back to Blighty. I believe in keeping things neat and tidy. As far as clearing out Bishopscourt is concerned, it was no big deal. We knew the RUC had pushed the politicians into letting them see what was going on. I simply whistled up a few transport carriers, sent over a team of engineers, and had everything stowed and in the air within five hours."

"It must have been quite a team to clear the base in such a short space of time."

The General smiled. "We have access to all kinds of resources. Let's just say there were enough bodies to shift the mountain of gear you chaps had accumulated. We even had room to spare after we drove all your vehicles into the belly of those flying beasts."

Devon stared at him with more than a hint of admiration. "And what happened to the two IRA men we were keeping there?"

"Mr Perry and Mr O'Brien? We scooped them up with everything else. Gave them new identities and parcelled them off to Canada. They've enough to get them started, but they'll have to work for a living if they want to keep their heads down. I think we've heard the last from those two."

"What forced the RUC's hand?"

"It seems that policeman Vennison, who was with you in Dublin, made a few calls to his headquarters. To be fair, he seemed to have put together the picture rather well. Seems to be a good man."

Devon was happy to put the record straight. "He is, sir. I doubt we'd have gotten as far without his help."

Sandford seemed to ignore the statement. "Anyway, that's why we got the message to you in Dublin, telling you to make your way back to Holyhead rather than go to Bishopscourt."

Sandford looked longingly at the plate of fresh-cream delicacies in the centre of the table but appeared to decide he had had enough. "The reason I asked you here Devon is to discuss another little project I'm involved in. The PM has just asked me to head up a new office to look after the kind of things we'd rather not leave to our existing agencies."

"What kind of things?" Devon interrupted, knowing that the term "office" was Whitehall-speak for an undercover agency.

"Let's just say we'll be working directly to the PM only, and we'll be liaising with a similar outfit, which is being put together in Washington under Presidential executive powers. There's a lot going on in the world. Things are changing fast, Mr Devon, and we need to change with them. The Middle East is ready to explode, and despite what many analysts would have you believe, the Russians haven't gone away."

"Where do I come in?"

"I want you to head up our end, and I want you on the next flight Stateside. Are you up for it?"

Devon thought of his life over the past few years. The almost claustrophobic pursuit of McSweeney was all-consuming, but now that it was over, what was he going to do?

He thought too of the last time he had worked in America, and of the small brunette-framed face he would always carry inside his deepest memories. He turned towards the General: "Count me in."

A small well-kept graveyard is tucked away behind a Presbyterian church on the Antrim Road in Belfast. It has more than its fair share of garish tombs and moss-covered domed vaults. In one corner a simple marble stone stands sentry over a well-kept plot, regularly tended by a devoted sister. She was not there today, but a tall man was placing a bunch of fresh chrysanthemums on the base of the headstone.

Martin Vennison looked at the name of John Turnbull etched in gold lettering against the black background. He remembered fondly the shock of white hair that bobbled from side to side as Turnbull walked.

He remembered seeing that same hair matted in blood and lying on a cold drawing room floor. It was that stark image that had made him pull the trigger on Liam Nolan.

He had reconciled himself with the killing, even though it went against all the principles of policing that Turnbull drilled into him. He didn't regret his actions, but he knew they had made his position untenable as a policeman.

He reached into his jacket pocket and withdrew a badge that had been sheathed in a brown leather wallet. He pushed aside the soil on the grave, burrowing down more than six inches. He stuffed the badge into the hole and covered it with soil. Then he stood up.

He spoke down to the headstone. "I told you I would make someone pay."

Martin Vennison threw a quick salute, turned on his heel, and marched out of the cemetery.

He whistled happily all the way down the path.

# Author's Note

I visited the Bishopscourt base on several occasions whilst the RAF was still in residence. I even played on its small golf course fashioned between runways (yes, it actually existed!) and drank gratefully cheap beer in the Mess. On those occasions, as a working journalist, I had no reason to believe Bishopscourt was used for other than its stated purpose as an RAF base. I still have no reason to believe otherwise.

However, in the murky world of counter-terrorism, a base such as that described in *Someone Has To Pay* would be a Godsend to the Intelligence authorities. If such a base was used at any time during the so-called "Troubles" of Northern Ireland, then I can think of no better, no more versatile location, than Bishopscourt. Hence the literary conjecture.

Throughout the seventies and eighties, the base was shared between the RAF and the civilian Air Traffic Control Centre based at Prestwick in Scotland. When the site could serve no further purpose for Air Traffic Control, the civilian staff left. The base ostensibly remained manned by RAF personnel until its final closure in 1995.

Today, what's left of the base is now in the hands of the private sector. What you'll find there is a thriving, friendly community, living in former base accommodation homes, and newer housing developments overlooking the disused runways. Well, they're not quite disused. They are home to regular car and motorcycle racing events. I'm told you won't find better circuits anywhere.